THE WOODEN SHEPHERDESS

RICHARD HUGHES wrote poems and plays as well as novels. It is for his novels that he is best remembered and not least for his first, *A High Wind in Jamaica*, which received great critical acclaim when it was published in 1929 and which was made into a film in 1965. *The Wooden Shepherdess*, the sequel to *The Fox in the Attic*, is the second part of the trilogy he called *The Human Predicament* which was unfinished at his death in 1976. This edition includes the opening chapters of the final, untitled volume, which hitherto have not been published. Richard Hughes was born in 1900. He was married to the painter Frances Bazley and lived most of his life in Wales.

Richard Hughes

THE WOODEN
SHEPHERDESS

With the unfinished fragment of
the final volume of the trilogy
The Human Predicament

THE HARVILL PRESS
LONDON

First published in 1973 by Chatto & Windus

This paperback edition first published in 1995 by
The Harvill Press
84 Thornhill Road
London N1 1RD

1 3 5 7 9 8 6 4 2

A CIP catalogue record for this title is
available from the British Library

ISBN 1 86046 013 5

Printed and bound in Great Britain by
Selwood Printing Ltd, Burgess Hill

CONTENTS

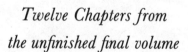

Some Characters First Introduced in Volume One

IN ENGLAND

AUGUSTINE PENRY-HERBERT: aged 24. Was 'hero' of
   The Fox in the Attic.
MARY: his sister. Married to a Dorset landowner and
   Liberal M.P.
GILBERT WADAMY: her husband.
POLLY: their only child, aged nearly six. She and her uncle
   Augustine are devoted to each other.
NANCY HALLORAN: her nurse.
MINTA: the under-nurse.
WANTAGE: the Wadamys' butler.
MRS. WINTER: the Wadamys' housekeeper.
NELLIE: Mrs. Winter's sister.
[GWILYM: her husband (recently dead).]
SYLVANUS: a baby, their 3rd and only surviving child.
JEREMY DIBDEN: Augustine's closest Oxford friend and a
   neighbour of the Wadamys in Dorset.

IN GERMANY

BARON WALTHER VON KESSEN: a distant relative of Augustine's
   living at Schloss Lorienburg in Bavaria.
ADÈLE: his wife.
FRANZ: their eldest son.
MITZI: their eldest daughter, aged 17, with whom Augustine
   fell madly in love, but before he could tell her so she
   went blind and vanished into a convent.
OTTO: Walther von Kessen's half-brother and general facto-
   tum: a retired Colonel who lost a leg in World War I.
PUTZI HANFSTÄNGL: An ardent Nazi in whose cottage at
      Uffing Hitler was hiding when arrested
      after the Munich 'putsch'.
REINHOLD STEUCKEL: a distinguished Munich lawyer.
LOTHAR: a starry-eyed young patriot, who took part in the
   'putsch'.
[WOLFF: Lothar's brother. A young guerilla and political
   assassin, who hanged himself in the attics at
   Lorienburg.]

A*

BOOK ONE

The Wooden Shepherdess

Chapter 1

Aʙᴏᴠᴇ, in the dried aromatic scrub, an early cicada churred.

A watersnake flashed in the dwindled summer cascade scarcely tinkling into the one pool deep enough to swim in—yet high up these hollow banks wrack dangled from washed-out roots, spring's melting snows must send a torrent down this wide gully of hot white stones. . . . Out of the quivering overhead heat a big butterfly flopped on the rock beside them, and opened its wings to the sun.

"What a mean scar! How come?" the girl asked curiously, feeling the back of his head none-too-gently with her fingers.

You couldn't quite call her a child—but certainly not a grown-up. . . . Like him, she was stretched on the rock chin-on-knuckles: wide blue eyes gazed out of sunburn and freckles straight into his, so close he could feel her breath on his cheek. You couldn't *quite* call her a child . . . and he stirred on the hard stone, withdrawing a little—but then settled back on the same spot exactly, for anywhere else was too hot to touch.

Her sun-bleached hair was cropped like a boy's. She was dressed in a boy's blue denim overalls bought at the village store, faded and softened almost to rottenness by much sun and much washing; a blue canvas work-shirt (ditto, and some of the buttons undone). When she had caught him there swimming stark naked, no wonder at first he had thought it was only a boy and hadn't bothered! When it wasn't a boy he had pulled on shirt and trousers without stopping to dry himself: she, though, had simply stood there and watched him and when he sat down to pull on his shoes had simply sat down beside him and started to talk. For this young English stranger arrived in New Blandford from

3

nowhere, his six-foot frame adorned in such threadbare and clumsily-mended incongruous clothes . . . "We" wanted to know every last thing about him, it seemed!

She had proved full of questions. Indeed she had asked much too much that she mustn't be told (or allowed to find out, if he wanted to keep out of trouble). However, he liked her. . . . If not any longer entirely a child it was clear she didn't yet know it: she seemed still as open and friendly and— unadolescent as one. "That, on the back of my head? Where somebody slugged me", he told her, and smiled.

She felt it again (having nothing finer to sew with had left a raised seam on his scalp, like a sail). "It's scary!" she said: then hitched herself on her elbows an inch or two even nearer and lay like a lizard, smelling sweetly of sun. Out of his damp iridescent wet mop (each hair a miniature prism to split this intense white light) she saw droplets of water still trickle to dry on the golden tan of his broad intelligent forehead, his peeling nose. . . .

The water glittered. The glassy air warped in the heat: heat struck up at them both from the rock as well as down from the sky. Their faces touched, almost. A tiny sweat-bead had formed on one of her freckles, and crept down the nose one inch from his own. She screwed up her eyes, and puckered her lips like someone beginning to whistle. . . . Then—with her eyelids still shut so tight that they quivered—her hand fumbled open the front of his shirt and slid right inside, warm against skin still froggy a bit from the creek: "Sakes!" she exclaimed, "What makes your heart hammer *so?*"

Firmly he felt for those fingers and gently withdrew them: let go the moment he got them outside, and asked in a voice as flat as he could what her name was. . . .

Blinking incredulous eyes wide open and suddenly sitting bolt-upright, "Ree" she said absently. Then for no obvious reason she shot away six feet from him, skiddering over the rock on her pointed behind the way little apes do. "Anne-*Marie*" was volunteered huffily, over her shoulder. Then she relented a little, and told him: "Was named for a Louisiana grandmother. .... Yeah, and your name too's.... 'Augusteen': that sure is French!"

She'd pronounced it almost as French; but before he had time to protest (or even to wonder how she'd discovered it) back she was, close: "Lookee!" she urged, and was making him look at her shirt's breast-pocket under the bib of her overalls. 'REE' was clumsily chain-stitched across it in coloured wools, below a coloured-wool turtle: "You feel my turtle—it's sure s-soft!" she invited, and tugged at his hand (but he wouldn't).

The next thing she said was: "Loan me your shirt, so I embroider your name like all ours," and 'T, I, N, O'—she was spelling it out on his chest with her finger, glancing sideways up at him: "'Tino': is that what folks call you, back home?"

He told her firmly that *none* of his friends called him Tino. Whereon she relapsed at last into silence: yawned, stood up, and began to undress.

"All the same, I don't smoke cigarettes!" she shouted, apropos of nothing, her shirt over her head and her jeans round her ankles: "Do you smoke cigarettes for Chrissake— or what *do* you do?" She wriggled her feet out of trousers and sneakers together. "*And* I don't drink liquor, I hate it!"

Expecting just tomboy bare skin as she peeled off her tomboy attire, it came as a shock to see all the modish crêpe- de-chine she wore under it.

"Well? My hair fell out with the fever—so what?"

Then—peach-coloured crêpe-de-chine nonsense and all— she dived straight in off the rock; and Augustine's thoughts reverted to Mitzi with rather a bump.

*

Mitzi . . . Unseeing grey eyes, spread fingers among the breakfast things finding her coffee-cup for her like feelers. . . .

The passage of months and oceans had shrunk her image to something small and bright and picture-like: something seen as if looking back through a tunnel, or down the wrong end of a telescope. Something that danced in the air like a kind of medallion above this alien Connecticut pool, and yet was enough to convince him he'd never love anyone quite like Mitzi again for the whole of his life. If only he'd had a fair chance before she went in her convent to teach her there isn't a God to go in to. . . . Sorrow rose stale in his throat.

For a while he stood there transfixed, unconsciously probing his scar with nails that were stubby and broken and traces of tar in the quick—till a hair got caught in a cracked one. Roused at last by the twinge he turned his back on the river: abandoned the child to her swimming, and started off home through the woods with his feet slip-slopping along in the span-deep sand of the overgrown buggy-road, mind still heavy with Mitzi. *Her frost-pink face, half hidden in furs.* . . .

And again last winter's bitter taste of despair, in a throat too dry to quite hawk it up.

Chapter 2

'BUT surely the time has arrived to put Mitzi right out of my mind altogether!' Augustine told himself, deep in the heart of these woods right across the Atlantic.

The sun shone dappled through trees overhead, lighting up the odd leaf like a bit of stained glass: by the time the light reached the ground it was green, like being under the sea. . . . They were lovely, these lonely Connecticut woods; and yet not a bit like Mary's Dorset woods around Mellton, not only because of the conifers here and there but because of this wholly impervious undergrowth everywhere, making you stick to the tracks. Bushes, each one like a myriad green eyes. . . . Trees so thick with leaves that you hardly saw branches, let alone trunks. . . .

Moreover these trees were hardly any the same as in England: not even the ones which used English names, for this 'oak' was never a real English oak nor these 'elms' real elms.

As he absently slapped something biting his wrist Augustine considered how different the woodland creatures were too, here. Chipmunks: brown furry ground-hogs—and skunks, he'd been warned about skunks (if you scared them, their smell could drive you out of your house and your senses). Porcupines . . . Squirrels even were mostly grey ones and black ones, seldom the squirrel-colour . . . Birds of strange plumage and voices . . . Only the deer coming down to the creek at dusk seemed anything like the same (but now he nearly fell over while trying without stopping walking to slap at his ankle).

Woods that were paradise—almost: that is, apart from plants which brought you out in a rash and these bites (for now the brutes were biting him right through his shirt, and he twisted an arm back trying to scratch exactly between his

7

shoulder-blades). Funny that nobody here would admit they were bad even here, in hilly Connecticut: 'Ah, down in Jersey they're *real* mean!' they said.

But unlike as these were to English woods, in spite of the pines they seemed even less like the serried echoing boles of those man-made Bavarian forests like endless insides-of-cathedrals. . . .

Here he reined in his wandering thoughts with a jerk: for hadn't he made up his mind to put Bavarian Mitzi right out of his mind altogether?

A rustle of leaves in a rare breath of breeze. . . . Did these woods hold other small dryads like Ree? For they don't have children in France, and he'd missed them: those German children were really the last he'd made friends with for ages —till Ree. . . .

This set him once more wondering just how old little Ree really was (for 'growing girls' one doesn't go near with a barge-pole!). That ominous crêpe-de-chine . . . And 'I don't drink liquor' did seem a funny remark for a child (a funny thing children should even bother to say so, he meant). However she must be a child still, Augustine decided: for only an absolute child could have gone on touching a man in that innocent way little Ree had kept touching him.

'I don't drink liquor. . . .' But all Americans seemed to be funny that way about drink: Prohibition had made it a kind of obsession, they talked about drink all the time like the English talk about weather! New York (so they told you, with relish) was fuller of speakeasies now than ever there'd been saloons; and many were pleasanter places, which meant that any restaurant not serving liquor (in teapots or something) soon had to put up its shutters. All over the city the little stills bubbled, and 'London Gin' which had cost ten cents the quart to distil (they printed their own English labels) retailed at twenty-five cents the shot. Why, even out here there was hardly a farmer who didn't distil his own rye or corn. . . .

Prohibition had split America—split her as nothing had split her since slavery! This was democracy's ultimate nightmare, a nation attempting to tyrannise over itself with The People's Will plumb-opposed to the people's wishes. . . . No wonder 'a-law-is-a-law-is-a-law' had completely ceased to apply over here where drink was concerned, and the whole Enforcement Machine was corrupt right up to the White House. But poor little Ree—what a country to bring up a child in!

*

With the Canada border a mere dotted line on a map, imported liquor still trickled through by the truckful. Enforcement Patrols were unpredictably venal or violent: times cash passed and the convoy passed, times both sides shot it out to a finish—but either way, plenty got through.

Then those other road-convoys, which also were armed with machine guns—the ones which came thundering in from the thousands of miles of beaches where fast 'contact-boats' outstripping the revenue-cutters had landed the 'Rum Row' stuff. . . . Three weeks ago, that travelling salesman who gave Augustine a lift out of Hartford had downright insisted the stranger must sample the 'genuine Scotch' in his flask: for it came, so he proudly declared, "from Rum Row" (in fact it was palpable bath-tub, tasting not very much worse than the worst they sold in Montmartre). Trundling along those leafy Connecticut lanes in his ancient Buick, the man had gone on to instruct the ignorant Englishman newly arrived that 'Rum Row' was the fleet of liquor-ships come from all over the Globe and lying at anchor just outside territorial waters, since there they couldn't be touched. This vast Armada, he said, was not only the Longest Bar in the World but the Largest-Ever Assemblage of Shipping in History. . . .

Up till that moment Augustine had sat very still and said nothing; but now had decided to get out and walk.

Chapter 3

For somebody reared like Augustine, the life he'd been leading these last few months seemed compacted of stuff so strange it already felt almost a dream; and indeed even now he still felt half in a dream—even here in these alien woods, on his way from the pool he had swum in and met that American child. He felt any moment he'd wake up at home: back in Wales, up above all those empty enormous rooms which he never used in his little white attic under the roof with the moon staring straight in his eyes.

To Augustine it might seem a dream; and yet he'd been certainly changed by it. Coarsened—or made just a little more 'realistic', if that is the word you prefer. It was much as happens in war: for just as a boy when his voice breaks now sings bass but loses his top-notes, so must the need for adjustment to action and danger—the downward shift of his whole emotional gamut to take it—leave him calloused a bit at the finer, more sensitive end of his thinking and feeling. So now as Augustine ducked his height to bob under a bough overhanging the trail, or leapt a log with the litheness of somebody young who had spent half his youth on a marsh after wildfowl and now had the added litheness the sea gives, his thoughts were no longer concerned at all with the abstract riddles the Universe holds. 'Significant Form': all those wonderful pictures he'd bought and left behind him in Paris—what crap!

But 'My poor little Ree, *what* a country to bring up a child in . . .' It suddenly struck him he'd failed to ask where she lived, or even her surname: so now he had probably lost her again, this nearest approach to a friend he had made since he landed.

She'd seemed so disposed from the first to be friends: not a

bit like Trudl and fierce little Irma had been to begin with,
or Rudi and Heinz (for those German children had certainly
taken some taming, although in the end one couldn't help
getting fond of them).

Schloss Lorienburg, though. . . . At the time it had all
seemed real enough; but once over here in the New World
he found it incredible anywhere quite like that feudal
German castle existed these days, or dug-outs like Walther
and Otto its lords! As for her brother that double-dyed
lunatic Franz, if he weren't so absurd with his dreams of
another Great War it would almost be frightening. . . . Somehow it seemed so unnatural finding young Germans, chaps
one's own age, still wrapped in Laocoon-knots with such
antique neuroses as Franz and indeed more alien, more
incomprehensible even than old ones. . . . 'Well', said a
Voice: 'then what would you say of a girl who even last
winter—the winter of 1923—could choose to go for a nun?'
And Augustine startled a lizard no end by swearing out loud:
for why must each train of thought he embarked on end up
back with *her*?

Augustine had tried so hard for so long to forget her. July
this was now and all this sun-baked American boscage was
dried-up and dusty, with leathery leaves that began to look
tired: yet right back in France. . . . Yes, back in the spring
when from Paris right down to the coast all the trees had
been only in bud—and even that night he'd arrived at
St. Malo, wasn't it 'putting Mitzi right out of his mind altogether' (like now) which had kept him mooning around the
ill-lit quays so late that even the bistros were closing, the
night last spring he got slugged?

Trees, he noticed, grew wild over here that were prized in
parks and gardens at home; and now he heard in his mind's
ear Nanny's voice raised in alarm and a Mary who called to
her child reassuringly (this was when five-year-old Polly had
climbed 'that American tree' in the Mellton arboretum, and
couldn't get down).

Dear Mary, *dear* Polly! He hadn't seen sister or niece for ages—why, not since October last year!

October; and this was July, with each day still getting hotter and hotter. He wasn't half-way to his shack, yet already as sticky and hot as before he'd been swimming at all. The very ground gave out heat: even here in the ovenish shade it was burning him right through the soles of his shoes. The trees smelled of heat. His head rang too with all this incessant trilling (some sort of cricket, perhaps— or were they cicadas?) and all this bronchial twanging of frogs like catarrhal guitars. Katydids . . . Insect-noise more than made up here in din for the rareness of bird-song: not like those tiny British insect-sounds you must listen for, rather an earsplitting clamour of insects and frogs you could hardly shout down. No wonder Americans just didn't notice the shattering row in their towns when their very woods were as noisy as this was! 'Americans never hear absolute silence' Augustine opined from his just-three-weeks' experience of America, scuffing the sweaty deposit of mosquitoes off his neck with the side of his hand.

Then once more he thought about home, and how quite the best thing about those Dorset downs was their silence— except for the larks. . . . For almost more than anything else Augustine loved riding alone with his sister up there on the silent downs where the thymy turf was a spring-board— though purely for pastime and Mary's society, not sharing Mary's inordinate passion for hunting (but Mary had had to forgo her hunting for almost the whole of last winter with starting a second baby, she'd told him in one of her letters to France).

Over here they *shot* foxes, and 'hunting' turned out to be walking-up birds with a gun! Yet surely Americans weren't proper foreigners: more some kind of near-Englishman, like in the Colonies? That's why such strange aberrations as shooting foxes and using words wrong here struck you at once: though of course when genuine foreigners shot them—

or kept them for pets, like that queer little beast at the Schloss which Mitzi. . . .

But surely the passage of time and his lately—well, call it discreetly 'more extrovert' life should have cured him by now completely of calf-love, and . . . blind Carmelite nuns?

*

It was two long miles from the pool to his shack, through that normal New England ninetyish summer warmth which a Briton just wasn't used to. He got there dripping with sweat and covered in bites.

By now it was mostly his own misty sea-marsh in Wales that he found himself thinking about: the cool of his huge stone empty ancestral house, with its hundred unlit chimneys to count; and the gunroom, its centre and focus. Or otherwise, Mary and Polly in Dorset—at any rate *Home*! For he suddenly felt he had had quite enough of America. . . . What was the use, though, of pining for home when how to get out of this blasted country at all without telling them how he got in was the crux?

Meanwhile Mary would soon be having that baby. . . . Indeed as Augustine stood on the porch and pulled back the screen-door to enter, it suddenly struck him that 'June' was what Mary had said in that long-ago letter to France—and this was July! So by now that baby'd have come. . . .

As he let the screen-door swing-to behind him Augustine reflected that he and Mary had never been quite so apart before in the whole of their lives: indeed it seemed plumb against Nature for her to go having a baby, and he not even to know had it come yet or not come.

Augustine himself had written home once (from Sag Harbor, awaiting the ferry across the Sound his first day on shore). But he'd told her nothing apart from the fact he was still in the land of the living, and given no kind of address to write back to. He didn't dare: for Gilbert and Mary were man and wife—and Lord, if Gilbert ferreted out the least

inkling of what he'd been up to and how to get on his tracks
there'd be trouble!

In spite of feeling so homesick, Augustine was hungry: so
lit his oil-stove (they called it 'kerosene' here just to fool you),
and put on a pan. But this baby of Mary's. . . . Alas, what on
earth sort of present could anyone find in a place like
America fit for Mary's new baby—supposing it really had
come?

For his new little nephew or niece. . . . "Well, which is it
this time I wonder?" he asked his eggs out loud while they
boiled (but the eggs only bubbled). The thought of a new
little 'Polly' was lovely. . . . But that would make Gilbert
livid: they'd have to keep on till they turned up a boy for
Mellton, but quite the last thing Gilbert would want was a
quiverful.

As for it being a boy . . . Augustine hoped not: for the
thought of an Infant Gilbert was just a bit much.

Chapter 4

A<small>N</small> 'infant Gilbert'? Had Augustine been in Mellton Church that day he'd have quickly been reassured. There was hardly a blaze of flowers in here, just a discreet vase or two round the font; and the christening plainly a quiet one.

This was a Dorset and not a New England July: yet even here, in the cool of his ancient church, the vicar was hot in his cassock. And getting impatient: they really were shockingly late!

There was no one in church yet at all, bar himself at his post by the west door. Like Gilbert, the Village were much disappointed this wasn't an heir. They weren't the cap-touching kind, as the vicar well knew; but an heir would have meant such a different class of festivity—large marquees on the lawn, and a Silver Band in attendance: tea and champagne for the gentry, whisky for all the big tenants, beer for the poor . . . and at least a thirty-pound cake. As it was, what villagers had assembled (mostly ones in arrears with their rents) were waiting outside in the sun, and absorbed in admiring their graves.

The vicar loathed waiting this end of his church, because from here he couldn't help seeing his special bête-noire. This was a half-ton Victorian limpet stuck to the Norman chancel-arch where most churches carry no more than a hymn-board—a huge Open Book (the Recording Angel's, no doubt) that was bound in polished red granite with pages of Parian marble. The heavenly ledger's Parian pages displayed the virtues of PHILIP WADAMY ESQ^{re} (Paxton's disciple who'd glass-roofed the whole central quad at the Chase); and although the curves of the pages were carved in perspective, the black-letter writing they carried was not.

A double-size pair of pink marble hands stuck out from the
ancient masonry, clad in frilly white marble cuffs, pretending to hold up the weight—which was really upheld by
acanthus-leaf corbels of cast-iron covered in low-carat gold.
Always he tried not to look; but his eyes just couldn't keep
off it. . . .

How late were they now?—Well, where was his watch?
In vain he patted his stomach and chest in the hope of
locating it.

The old man was feeling a bit on edge anyhow, always
finding this kind of occasion his chiefest thorn-in-the-flesh as
a country incumbent. The effrontery of these infidels in high
places, blandly expecting the Church to embellish their social
occasions of 'hatches, matches and despatches' with frills
of religion—something they just found pretty or quaint!
Marriage-vows made at the altar not knowing the difference
between a vow and a contract, nor even suspecting there was
one: promises made at the font to bring up a child in the
faith they themselves had forsaken—and godparents chosen
more for the help they could give in the ways of the world
than of heaven. . . . Often such godparents didn't bother to
come; and supposing they did turn up might be Jews, Turks
or Hereticks for all one dared to enquire.

Why hadn't he gone to the Wadamys straight and made a
clean breast of it? "You who parade your open unfaith, you
yet have the nerve to bring your own child to the font—and
even then you couldn't be punctual. . . ." Ah, but a queer sort
of Christian priest that would be for the parents' sins denying
baptismal grace to the child! For this was a Sacrament:
Water and Word would as certainly graft this unpromising
Wadamy bud in the very Body of Christ as . . . as even an
Archdeacon's son.

It was Jeremy Dibden of course that the vicar meant, that
unsatisfactory friend of Augustine's. 'Poor old Dibden!' he
thought: 'There can't be much sweetness even in brand-new
Archidiaconal gaiters when finding your only boy, whom

you'd always meant for the Church, mixed up with this Wadamy lot and already a self-declared atheist.'

Sadly the old man sighed. 'No, I must play my priestly part—and trust His Omnipotent Power to find the way, in the end, to His Own.' So he said to himself, still absently patting his cassock in search of the missing watch (he had only been waiting ten minutes although it felt like an hour).

But then he remembered: the watch was right underneath, in his trousers.

Trouser-pockets are sometimes awkward to get at, in cassocks. He had in the end to hitch cassock and surplice right up to his armpits, and hold them there with one hand while he fumbled it out with the other. A brace-button broke; and that very moment a sound behind him made him turn round—to find that the folk from the Chase had arrived, with that papist Nanny bearing the infant in front and a rag-bag of sponsors apparently rigged out for Ascot!

They stood there watching in silent amusement, while (like the first-act curtain in Farce) cassock and surplice came down with a run.

*

But at last exhortations and dissertations were over, the babe through the mouths of others had promised her promises.

Now the vicar was taking her into his arms. Nanny Halloran pursed her lips, for that clumsy old man was crushing the christening-robe which was Honiton lace and more than a hundred years old (Father Murphy had said she could come if she tried not to listen too much).

The vicar said "Name this child", and the godfather mumbled.

"Susan Amanda" Mary prompted, rather too loud.

The vicar looked down at the baby: the baby stirred and looked up at him, wide-eyed as a kitten. "Susan Amanda, I baptise thee in the Name of the Father . . ." (his voice was utterly prayerful, and trembled indeed with love for what lay on his arm) "And of the Son . . ." (as the water touched her again she screwed up her face) "And of the Holy Ghost. Amen."

The third time the water touched her, she wailed. The villagers stirred, for they knew what that wail meant—that was the Devil come out. . . . Some of them even instinctively glanced at the north door, being the way he must go; but Catholic Nanny Halloran pursed her lips yet again as the baby was handed back and she smoothed out the lace. For this hadn't been real baptising. . . . However, it might be better than nothing: "One just has to hope for the best," Father Murphy had told her.

Meanwhile Mary stood twisting her handkerchief round her fingers. She had found it even worse than what she remembered of Polly's. How *could* Gilbert have wanted it? "Just for the sake of the Village," he'd told her; and "Why needlessly hurt the old fool's feelings? Anyway haven't we had all this out before over Polly, and didn't you end by letting Polly be done? So why stir up hornet-nests now over nothing?"

So atheist Mary had swallowed her principles. Still, didn't Gilbert care how obscenely disgusting so much of this was? "Delivered from Thy Wrath" harked back to the vengeful gods of the jungle! My *poor* little sweet! (she was longing to kiss her baby but too many people were watching). "Conceived and born in sin"? What a horrible lie—and indeed how absurd, when the marriage service itself said. . . .

How Mary wished she had gone to the vicar in spite of Gilbert and made a clean breast! But what would have been the use? That silly old man could never have understood.

Gilbert, in formal trousers and spats with his tall silk hat on the pew in front (but wearing only a *short* black coat for a girl-child), stood by a pillar smoothing his gloves. Gilbert himself had heard everything, listened to nothing. 'That went very nicely,' he thought: 'But thank goodness it's over, and now we can get back to serious matters. . . . But bother, here comes the vicar!' Gilbert was well aware that vicars expected a kind word or two on occasions like this: "Ah, my dear Vicar! I hope . . ."

'I *must* trust in Him to find His own way . . .' thought the vicar, escaping from Gilbert as soon as he decently could. Once out of sight in his vestry he fell on his knees to pray for the child (but he had to be quick: they had asked him over to tea, and it wouldn't do to be late).

*

These were crucial times—this summer of 1924—for a rising Liberal statesman whose voice was at last beginning to make itself heard in the Party's councils; and Gilbert had much on his mind. Labour in Office had scarcely attempted to check Unemployment: MacDonald was much too occupied dangling Dawes in front of Herriot trying to winkle him out of the Ruhr, and Ponsonby at it ding-dong with Rakovsky (wits said the Bolshevik emblem ought to be Hammer-and-Tongs). Hitherto the Liberal watchdogs had felt themselves blissfully free to bite both sides (and each other); but now the time had arrived to decide the issue on which to withdraw their Party's lobby support and to let this minority Labour Government fall. That would mean yet another election (the third in a couple of years); and our chance—if we choose the issue correctly—to win back the erring working-class vote. . . .

So, with all his legitimate hopes, this hardly a time for Gilbert to welcome Augustine's vagaries as well to worry about. Still, duties are not to be shirked. . . . One's own wife's brother (it's in *Who's Who*): if he gets in a mess one can't just stand on the touchline.

Gilbert rehearsed the truant's misdeeds. Offending his German hosts by decamping like that: consorting all winter with arty riff-raff in Paris, and then disappearing and giving us all such a fright. Now, breaking silence at last with a quite inexcusably uninformative letter which gave no hint of his whereabouts—that is, apart from the Sag Harbor postmark and something about a ferry. . . . He said not a word about where he'd been all these last four months, about why he had gone to America, what were his plans; and who could fail to read into such studied mystification involvement with something—or somebody—*most* undesirable?

There in the States, where his social standing. . . . The States, where so many laws lay about to be broken a stranger could hardly help breaking one (buying a lady's inter-State railway ticket—or teaching Latin in Texas): a place where the boy was only too likely to fall into really bad hands, out there on his own. . . .

The *Gazetteer* said Sag Harbor was down the far end of Long Island: the 'ferry' he spoke of must cross to New London. So now on the way home he'd have to put it squarely to Mary—and surely she wouldn't be difficult? Surely it stood out a mile: *in the boy's own interests* something had got to be done?

Chapter 5

THE godparents' shoes were unsuited to grass: so Trivett trundled them round by road in the Daimler, while Gilbert and Mary walked home alone through the park. Gilbert, his tall silk hat enhancing the set of his jaw while tending to hide the uneasy look in his eyes as he nerved himself to his task: Mary, her flowery hat in her hand and her red-gold curls exposed to the sun—and a stubborn set to her lips.

"That brother of yours," said Gilbert at last (it was rather unnerving how like at times she looked to that brother): "I think I'll get the F.O. to contact our Embassy, quietly."

"Do be careful!" said Mary, alarmed.

"Esme Howard's our new man in Washington: Howard's the soul . . ."

"Suppose you start something? You'd better look out."

"I very much fear lest the boy's in some serious scrape: more so perhaps than he knows. Your *brother*—I'd never forgive myself," countered her husband with simple sincerity.

"He's twenty-four now: he isn't a child."

Gilbert shrugged. "I'd go over in person to help him, if only . . ."

"But why not let him alone, as he obviously wants?"

In the heavy summer shade of a huge oak Polly's small piebald pony (the one that Augustine had given her) stood on three legs and swished at flies with his tail. He nickered as they approached, and Mary stopped to examine him. Meanwhile Gilbert resumed: "I'd go over myself like a shot, but I can't be possibly spared at this crucial moment; you see that, dear, don't you? And Jeremy's too—far too lightweight, too inexperienced." (Jeremy having been unsuccessfully sent to look for his friend when Augustine vanished in France.) "So what I propose . . ."

"Just look at his feet!" interrupted Mary indignantly: "Really you'll have to get rid of that blacksmith, he's hopeless!"

In park turf otherwise perfect stood one errant thistle; and no one was looking when Gilbert took a quick run—spats and all—and neatly kicked off its head.

After that they talked of indifferent matters (but both on their guard), till they reached the cool and the dark of the Yew Walk where even the scent of the blazing roses outside hardly penetrated. There Gilbert tried a new tack. Augustine's letter said nothing about coming home: what about his estates? His agent in Wales seemed decent enough, but was old; and wasn't this just how estates got into a mess? "But Augustine shouldn't be too hard to trace, with that postmark to go on. The ferry he spoke of must cross to New London: that means he'll have gone to Bar Harbor, or Newport—or possibly Marblehead: this time of year there aren't many places that anyone goes. And that sort of upperten summer resort will be stiff just now with Embassy chaps. . . ." For surely Mary must see for the boy's own sake the Embassy'd better get their hooks in him pretty damn quick?

But this time Mary said nothing. 'Gilbert's on tenterhooks', Mary thought, 'over his post in the next Liberal Ministry—deadly afraid lest his brother-in-law does something embarrassing. . . .' Mary had guessed a lot more clearly than Gilbert himself what lay behind his sudden solicitude: for Gilbert never allowed unworthy motives to rise to the surface of even a private mind 'so schooled' as the unkind Jeremy said of it once, 'only to see the best in everyone, starting of course with himself!'

Thus husband and wife arrived at the house feeling sadly at odds ('Mary is being difficult . . .' 'Gilbert is being absurd . . .'). But the garden door was overhung by Mellton's famous late-flowering yellowish-white wisteria, dripping with bees; and a bee stung Gilbert's neck, which took their minds off the rift for a while.

*

Once tea was over, Mary went up to her room. There the baby was brought for its six o'clock feed, and although it was really her bedtime Polly came too (it was good for Polly to take an interest).

"My birfday tomorrow!" said Polly.

"Bir*th*day, dear," Nanny corrected, and crackled her starch. "You're old enough now to talk properly: tomorrow you'll be . . ."

"I saw you!" Polly interrupted, triumphant: "There was six!"

"'Little-Miss-Sharpeyes'," said Nanny (Polly had caught her getting out the coloured cake-candles for Minta to take down to Cook).

Once Mary had lifted her breast and fitted the strong little mouth to her nipple it instantly started to suck; and "Who've you invited to come to your birthday, darling?" she asked.

"Only dogs," said Polly with finality.

"What—no Mrs. Winter?" said Nanny: "No Mr. Wantage?"

"Yes of course them! But, *and* only dogs."

"Not even your Father and Mother, Miss Polly?"

Polly looked up in surprise at so silly a question, and didn't bother to answer. But after a long pause she added: "I do wish Gusting would come!" and sighed from the depths of her heart. Augustine—the key performer erstwhile at all Polly's birthdays. . . .

With Susan's prehensile little sucker dragging her nipple the mother lapsed into a daze; but in spite of her mind's increasing milkiness all her thoughts (like Polly's) went back to the distant Augustine.

Indeed what on earth was he up to? For even this latest letter said nothing; and ever since going abroad his letters

B

were all of them like that, they never said what you wanted to know. His letters from Paris had talked about nothing but Art—not a word about even why he'd left Germany!

Art indeed seemed to have suddenly gone to his head: Modern Art, 'Significant Form' and all that from Clive Bell. A Cézanne, a late Van Gogh and a little Renoir: Picabia— he seemed to be buying the lot! And as for the really aberr- ant eccentrics, the ones even he called the Wild-cats—the Cubists and so on: while frankly admitting he couldn't make head-or-tail of their painting he still flopped about near the flame, like a moth! Cock-a-hoop at even seeing Derain afar in some café, let alone really meeting Matisse. . . .

Augustine was hoping to meet a certain 'Miss Stein' whose salon these fanatics all frequented; but that apparently never came off, for his last Paris letter of all had said he was leaving post-haste for St. Malo (it seemed some young French poet who lived there might take him to visit that eminent Cubist across the water at Dinard). He must have dashed off to St. Malo without even stopping to ask if Picasso this year was at Dinard at all (which he wasn't, as Jeremy later dis- covered); and there—from St. Malo—he'd just disappeared!

She shifted Susan across.

Her husband, her brother. . . . So much poor Mary did love and admire them both; but she'd long ago given up hoping to cope with the way those two underrated each other. Probably Gilbert expected Augustine would end up in gaol—an American gaol, and in all the American papers! Dear Gilbert, on this sort of issue he could be his own worst caricature. . . .

All the same, whatever Augustine was up to was very certainly Hush—and *Gilbert had got to be stopped*!

The conviction struck Mary so forcibly she almost cried it aloud: her milk ceased coming, and Susan set up a howl.

Chapter 6

I N the ovenish midnight dark the ominous sound of a rogue mosquito grew higher and shriller the closer it drew to the sleeping head on the pillow. Augustine stirred at the sound, and woke just before the brute could alight to feed on his ear.

He woke from a nightmare in which he was pushed on a public stage with an unknown play going on, and had had to learn his part while he played it. Lying awake, he reflected that this was indeed a pretty fair picture of how he had spent those lost four months between St. Malo and here: for he'd never intended becoming a desperado and hadn't a clue as to how to conduct himself. . . .

Pacing the late-night quays at St. Malo, a lawful and lovesick traveller. . . . Then he remembered nothing until the sound of that rhythmical watery gurgle-and-plop, gurgle-and-plop in the pitch dark and feeling of rearing and reeling each time he came-to (and went under and came-to again). A genuine dizzy swaying and reeling of everywhere, fused and confused in the dark with the swaying and reeling and pain inside his own stomach and head. Noise, and the cold; and the smell of tar, and of bilge water slopping up at him reeking of dead rat and well-oiled machine guns and burst pots of paint and the vomit all over his clothes. Overhead, fearful impacts of metal on wood. Pain—and the perishing cold; and an absolute blank in his mind about whether he'd ever left Paris, and where he was now. And nobody with him down there in the darkness and noise, apart from a cat having kittens. . . .

In short, the English Milord had been slugged for his bulging wallet and flung down any old hatchway alongside the quay—down one just about to be closed as it happened, the ship being ready to sail; and there had lain sprawled,

without money or passport, in the battened-down hold of a
schooner bound for Rum Row. By the time Augustine came-
to they'd been out in the pobble surrounding the Île de
Cézembre—and already off Ushant before he was found.

Alice May's thirsty cargo was stowed in the main-hold,
amidships: this was the forehold, which only housed the
spare gear (including the guns they would need when they
got there as well as the fenders and ropes which had broken
his fall when that dockside thug slung him down). If they'd
not had to look for the cat they adored they might never have
found him—not even off Ushant.

*

The Master was Cockney, the Mate was from Hull: a fond
pair of old friends who played the giddy-goat all day with
each other, and kept the crew in a roar with their practical
jokes and music-hall backchat but handled their ship as a
maestro handles a fiddle, and blew on their men as a flautist
blows on a flute.

Faced with a wholly unwanted concussed Augustine and
nowhere to land him they'd had to make use of him, turning
him into a rum-running Able Seaman as best they could.
They mightn't have had to cope with Augustines before, but
their touch with this one was faultless. Once back on his feet
and fit for light duty (with sail-thread still in his scalp and
still inclined to see double), they started to tease and play
tricks on him just like each other. From moment to moment
he never knew if those two were fooling or serious: this made
his sea-apprenticeship none too easy—but left him with no
time to think (which was really the point, as he realised now).

They had made no bones at all about being rum-runners,
looking on Prohibition as just a low-comedy villain whom
every right-minded person must want to help foil; and you
weren't even breaking the law (so they told him) provided
you stopped outside territorial waters and sold your stuff for
the contact-boats to run in. On the Row, moreover, the
prices were golden. . . .

Liners can chug more-or-less straight across; but west-bound sail finds it pays to make a big detour, adding a thousand miles to the distance but dodging those northern waters where headwinds prevail and working down south to pick up the Trades. So the schooner's course for the Long Island coast she was bound for had taken Augustine to seas that were streaked with more greens and blues, and more bluey-greens and greeny-blues, than even Pisarro in Paris had painted with: amethyst rollers veined with turquoise and shot with emerald, flecked with gold and swallowing snow. Week after week those nights when the stars slowly swayed right-to-left, left-to-right past the fingering topmast and, deep in her shadow, the flattish curve of her hull streamed sparks in the inky darkness below. Dawns with the sun leaping suddenly out of the sea astern like a searchlight: days with one blazing sun overhead and the waves tossing back a myriad sparkling suns of their own—but with rainbows of spray sweeping over the deck, and a cooling breeze. . . . All the same, life at sea wasn't all beer-and-skittles; and once they'd ensured he would dance to their tune like the others they made him pull ropes like a seaman, shoot stars like a mate, tally accounts like a supercargo—and cook, when the cook got D.T.s.

His first time out on a topsail yard had been absolute hell, for you climbed the ratlines and then you sidled away from the mast with your feet on a fly-away swinging footrope—and balanced waist-level against the heaving yard, with your hands full of gear so only your quaking belly left to hold on with knowing if once you let your feet swing forward from under you're going to be bucked straight backwards into the air; and eighty feet up you smash like an egg if you tumble. It's merely a matter of balance of course, and pie as a ground-level ploy for any well-found nursery-governess: still, up aloft there and giddy with height, that first time of all he had nearly fallen to death for no reason other than fear.

Off the Jersey coast that weather had blown itself out. It

had then turned southerly, bringing them drifts of summer
fog which meant that they had to feel their way blind with
the lead all along that submarine gorge where the Hudson
River continues under the ocean. They carried no lights now
at night and sounded no foghorn or bell as they nosed in-and-
out all the blazing and blaring legitimate traffic converged
on New York.

One night a four-pipe Naval destroyer lately transferred
to the coastguard had loomed on them suddenly out of the
midnight mist, herself blacked-out and showing only her
chimney-sparks. Then all at once they'd arrived in waters
which teemed with shipping which all—like themselves, and
the harrying coastguards—was blacked-out and silent, whatever the darkness and fog. Yet these had been only the
fringes of Rum Row's fleet, that seemingly endless and almost
motionless belt of shipping which wallowed twelve miles off-
shore—blind-eyed and silent year-in and year-out and in
parts nearly nose-to-tail from Florida right up to Maine—
either anchored, or barely idling along, or adrift with their
ground-gear gone and crew paralytic (when on look-out,
you had to guess which). There was shipping here of every
flag under the sun except the American: all ages and classes
of sail, steam and diesel: some ripe as pears and wholly un-
seaworthy, others as smart as a dream—and all of them
loaded down to the scuppers with drink.

Apart from the constant risk of collision, danger out here
came less from the Law than from hijacking pirates in
speed-boats armed with quick-firing guns. For, unlike the
Law, these couldn't be bribed; they wanted your cash entire
or your whole consignment, and killed you first to save
argument. Contact-boats suffered worst, being small and
perforce having thousands and thousands of dollars with
them in currency: sometimes, however, small rum-ships
themselves were attacked, unless alert and well armed. So
(with a shrouded gun on her foredeck now and a shrouded
gun on her poop and her lifeboat kept at the ready) *Alice May*
had stayed just as clear as she could of all comers while nosing

along the low-lying Long Island coast to her final berth off
Montauk.

*

As Augustine tossed on his sweat-soaked bed, with a
sudden qualm his stomach recalled being shot at: skedadd-
ling into the dunes and crab-grass caught in the beam of
a searchlight, guns pop-popping behind in the dark and
bullets that horribly *pinged* and *plopped* in the darkness
around, while he wished himself safe back on board till he
nearly burst with the wish.

The Gilberts of this world only cross oceans in liners, with
visas and all the right introductions: they pass through
Customs, and never neglect to sign Embassy books. They
would surely take it amiss if they learned of one of the family
landing as he had one pitch-black night on a lonely Long
Island beach from a sinking launch with a gunwhale-high
load of the stuff under gunfire, and knocking a coastguard
for six.

Chapter 7

THE effect of fear his first time out on a topsail yard had been near-paralysis, causing the strength to run out of Augustine's muscles like water out of a bath. But the night that unlucky beach-landing fell straight in the arms of ambush, fear caused catalysis rather: it lent him the strength of ten, and his muscles themselves took charge. His fist had shot out of its own accord, and before that unfortunate coastguard surfman could up with his carbine, had caught him precisely on point in the dark—the smiter was gone twenty feet ere ever the smitten had slumped to the ground.

Then had come searchlights and shouting and shooting; but self-propelled legs which jinked like a hare's in-and-out the leaping shadows of seven men after him carried him into dead ground in a two-three seconds, and dropped him flat on his face well below the beam of the light. Thus pursuit had blundered right over him. . . .

Only then did his brain wake up and begin to enquire what all this was about. It had plenty of time to wonder: for dawn was a long way off, and his trousers were soaking.

All night he had lain in a berry-bush, longing for *Alice May*. Then morning came, and he crept out at last. Since the contact-boat he had come in was sunk and its skipper in clink, he'd got to find other means somehow to get back on board; but the gunfire and general brouhaha had so scared the locals that no one would run him back to his ship. This guy who alleged he belonged on the Row. . . . He wasn't a Rum Row type—and these men were born suspicious. Clearly that Coastguard Patrol knew more than they ought; and word started getting around that maybe this was the unknown stooge of the coastguards. . . . On which Augustine had had to make himself scarce pretty slippy.

Amagansett was hopeless; and even the quiet East
Hampton (where last night's fleeing trucks had rattled the
birds from the sleeping elms as they streaked through the
streets) had proved too hot for him. More by chance than
anything else he had legged-it across to Sag Harbor, and
there had written that only letter to Mary (no wonder it
hadn't said much!) while waiting the plush old *Shinnecock*'s
pleasure to ferry him over the Sound to New London.

Reaching New London, at first he had still had hopes that
he might get back to his ship; but he soon abandoned all
such, for the place was full up then for the boat-race and
lousy with coastguards. Indeed it had seemed too risky to
linger about near the sea any longer, and so he had taken the
inland road with nowhere to go in particular—just thumbing
lifts. This had brought him in turn to Hartford, Torrington,
Litchfield and lastly the New Blandford fork, where a rustic sawbones bound for some kitchen-table appendix had
finally dropped him. So here he was now at New Blandford—
and much good it did him! For even here lying low in the
woods he reckoned the Law must sooner or later catch up
with him. Even taking the commonsense view that the police
had so much else on their minds they were hardly likely to
bother with him, he was in effect an outlaw: he hadn't a
passport, nor without telling his tale any hope of getting
one—therefore no hope at all of escaping out of the
country.

As for money. . . . Thank heaven the Captain insisted he
took some earnings with him 'in case'! But now, with his rent
paid up for three months, there were only very few (ill-
gotten) yellowbacks left in his wad with the (equally ill-
gotten) greenbacks; and no one would give you a job—he'd
rightly or wrongly been told—if you couldn't show papers
and looked such an obvious alien.

In short there seemed nothing else to be done but to sit
here and wait for the end. Of course, when the blow did
fall. . . . Well, Gilbert would certainly go up in smoke. Even
Mary: how would *she* take it? And all his civilised friends. . . .

B*

Just imagine Douglas's moue when he heard of Augustine
in gaol for resisting arrest with violence! Even young
Jeremy's wry "Old Augustine to think he's a he-man and
start knocking coastguards about: can't he *ever* grow up?"

But that wasn't all, for now he'd a friend over here to consider as well—that innocent child. . . .

Soon after parting with Ree at the pool, Augustine had
feared he might never again see this 'nearest approach to a
friend he had made since he landed'. However, he needn't
have worried: the very next morning he'd come on her
mooching around on her own (and quite near to his shack,
as it chanced). Since then, he and Ree had become fast
cronies: her company solaced the lonely present although it
couldn't expunge the past, and they spent nearly all their
time in each other's company. Ree at least seemed quite
unaware of their difference in age. Age-groups are largely
conventional placings in terms of society, scarcely apparent
(it can be) between two people alone by themselves; and
these two only met tête-à-tête. Like a closed 'binary system'—
a star-couple floating in space—they would flit in and out of
each other's lives as if neither had other attachments, and
never saw each other against a background of company.

Each for their separate reasons, meeting with nobody
suited them both. So they seldom went near the village, and
even then they were careful to keep out of sight like a couple
of redskin spies. Indeed they seldom came out into open
country at all, but stuck to the woods where the going being
so slow disguised the fact that Ree had never been used like
him to regular pounding mile after mile—for even exploring
the woods they tried to avoid frequented buggy-roads. Ree
indeed showed such a marked predilection for lonely and
hidden places to take him that mostly they probed the
deepest and darkest thickets they could, worming their way
by overgrown paths where the trees in some inaccessible
gully had never been cut or cleared since the Dawn of Time:
primeval haunts where the foot didn't even touch ground,

but sunk thigh-deep through leaves and rotting or rotted wood. . . .

Ree seemed to adore to creep into caves and cracks in the outcrops of rock, where together they'd squeeze in some secret hole like a couple of badgers setting up home. Although she was nimble most times as a monkey, at others she seemed to go strangely helpless and asked to be lifted over or out of things—not that Augustine minded those times, for it gave him a kind of 'motherly' feeling towards her. . . . And as for talking—nineteen-to-the-dozen they talked! So what about Ree, when she found that the hand she'd so trustingly held belonged to a wanted criminal? *Not* very nice if she happened to see him arrested. . . .

Next morning, to drive so sorry a picture out of his mind as well as to ease his nostalgia, Augustine started at last on a cautiously-worded new letter home:

"*Dear Mary,*" he wrote: "*This village stands at a cross-roads. . . .*"

Chapter 8

THE 'cross-roads' Augustine wrote of were really only cross-buggy-roads, woodland trails that had never been metalled or oiled. Hardly anything used them today, apart from some local flivver or summer-girl on a saddle-horse—or sometimes, even, still a horse-buggy or two. You were five good miles from the State road where through-traffic went and the all-night liquor trucks roared with their lights out down to New York. Moreover apart from the church (and a few scattered shacks in the woods), Augustine's 'village' had very few buildings to boast: just the Big Warren Place, the Little Warren Place, and a smithy.

He wrote of the church—which was tiny and old, looked nearly disused and stood half buried in trees. Its proportions were naïve and lovely (Ree said "somebody British called Wren" had sent over the plans, but if so it was Wren in unwontedly simple 'Shepherdess' mood). All wooden she was, that little deserted shepherdess; and barring her shingles, her green copper vane and her bell which nowadays couldn't be tolled, all white—apart from peeps where the weathered white paint had peeled and showed her shell-pink undercoat. Alongside the church stood abandoned an ancient and gaunt Tin Lizzie (a T-model Ford) without any engine: it looked (he wrote) "like a giant black daddy-long-legs in widow's weeds" with its height and its tatters of canopy. Standing so long it had sunk in the earthen road right down to its hubs.

Next he described the empty 'Big Warren Place'. Behind nearly impassable bushes, buried in trees and against a solid background of trees, it reared the top of a lofty Doric façade with most of the architrave missing. This too was all wooden of course, and once painted white like the church. It was huge

34

(by New England standards), and haunted, and half fallen down.

The 'Little Warren Place' had doubtless been built as its dowerhouse. Now it lodged the Neighborhood Store, selling everything: boots and canned-beef and hairnets and axes and cough-cure, as well as those 95-cent blue canvas work-shirts which everyone wore—even girls. There were staybones and lamp-wicks, and whisky-stills (leastwise the parts for one, listing each separate item merely as 'Useful for Various Purposes'). Old Ali Baba slept up above his cave in all that was left of a handsome Colonial bedroom: "I went up with him once to look for the right size of nails, and three legs of the big brass bedstead had gone through the floor". The neighborhood stock of kerosene stood in a powder-closet. Home-made Infallible Cattle Cure too was dispensed from a one-legged object that once was a Sheffield-plate urn; and, this village store served also as Club, where everyone met whether wanting to buy things or not. . . .

All this seemed to be perfectly safe to write home (though the letter would have to be mailed in New York, for Augustine knew all about postmarks). And yet he paused. To Augustine himself it was just the place's forgotten and tumble-down look which seemed so attractive, compared with the cared-for and handsome 'Colonial' villages all-dolled-up-to-the-nines which he'd seen on his way here; but what of the Mary he wrote for? The English in general only cross oceans with all the right introductions and go to the usual places: it wouldn't be easy to make her believe such a scene could exist over here, for this *New* England corner was certainly fifty years more out of date than anything left in the Olde one. The Wadamy circle's American travels were all so strictly confined to skyscraping towns and exclusive resorts, and the oh-so-hospitable gilded chain of the friends of their friends. . . .

The smithy, alas, was in an even worse state and provided one nothing at all picturesque to write home because it had burned down too often (Ree said of the smith that fires were

the principal source of his livelihood). This year's edition
had merely been thrown together from second-hand galvanised sheets already lacy with rust or gone into actual
holes. The smith mended farm machines—when he could
(which was seldom); and jobs which defeated him just
stayed standing around "Which at least," said Ree, "gives
the vines and poison-ivy something to grow on" (all those
long, sticky, tendrilly things that Augustine so much disliked; and the burrs big as rats). He also sold gasoline—
canned, for he hadn't a pump—which "helped no end with
his fires". Also this smith, Ree alleged, had a terrible crush
on someone called Sadie who wouldn't look at him "spita
she's kinda his niece . . .".

No, perhaps the smithy *and* smith were both of them better
left out. So he took a fresh sheet, and started instead to draw
for Polly a mother skunk with her little ones—queer little
black-and-white creatures all feathery tail and no head, as
he'd watched them once with bated breath on his porch. As
he did so, he wondered what sweet-hope-in-hell he'd got
that he'd ever see Mary and Polly again—quite apart from
the new one. . . .

If only he'd had the sense to give himself up straight off
when he landed, and tried to explain! For Augustine well
knew what a fool he had been: it was no use pretending he
hadn't, and any day soon he was likely to pay for it dearly.
But yet . . . Even now, as he feathered the tails of his skunks
with elaborate flourishes—plumed them indeed like Victorian hearses, so black seemed his future—something from
under his mind was struggling up towards daylight but
couldn't quite make it, like bubbles in mud. For the fact was
that though he hadn't one bit enjoyed being shot at, now it
had happened he wouldn't have had it unhappen again for
all the gold in the world. That unbridgeable chasm at Oxford
between the men who had fought in the War and the
boys too young for it. . . . Now he too had been shot at and
might have been killed; and for-crying-out-loud, what a
load of guilt that took off one's shoulders—even admit-

ting one's 'War' had lasted for only six seconds (or seven at
most)!

When at last Augustine looked up from his drawing he
saw that excited face at his window. . . . He dropped his pen,
and jumped to his feet with a sense of relief so intense it took
even himself by surprise that a grown-up man (one who had
fought and been shot at and might have been killed!) should
have come to depend on a child to quite the extent he had
come to depend on this Ree. For he had to admit it: time
spent in her company sang with a whole new octave of notes.
Yet who was this Ree? It had puzzled Augustine the way
she had never once mentioned her parents, or said where she
lived—let alone shown signs of wanting to carry him home
and exhibit her prize, as most children would. Was she
native? Or was she a summer migrant, one of that youthful
holiday crowd from the country outside, which sometimes
invaded the store like a flock of starlings then vanished again
in a flock—like starlings?
As well as its woods the 'township' included some four or
five miles of small stony hills with scrub on their tops, and
stone-walled fields lower down where grass fought a losing
battle with sumac and rocks. Here there were small scattered
farms built of timber and weather-board: long left unpainted
and grindingly poor, there was hardly a building apart from
the house—just an outside privy, a rusty old pump in the
yard, the fag-end of last winter's woodpile and mostly not
even an ice-house. The old Yankee stock which had built
them and farmed them had long been dwindling: for genera-
tions, Yankees go-getting enough had all gone West leaving
only the rather more feckless and pleasanter characters—
men not over-given to work, so that one little struggling
farmstead after another had given up struggling. Empty,
some of these tumble-down houses had tumbled right down
or caught fire; but others had lately begun to be bought up
cheap on mortgage as family holiday-places by painters and
writers not quite arrived enough yet to make Provincetown,

followed by other adventurous small-income city-folk. . . .
That seemed the likeliest background for Ree. Down in the
valleys the much more prosperous farms had thriving fields
of tobacco and slatted tobacco-barns, herds of black-and-
white Holsteins in huge metal byres, towering tubular silos
and clanking wind-pumps raised on legs taller even than
silos; but most of these nowadays seemed to be owned by
Swedes—and she certainly wasn't a Swede!

But anyway here the mysterious creature was, dancing
about on his porch and agog with a plan she had formed. . . .

Chapter 9

REE hadn't been consciously secret about her home: it was just that with so much else to be talked about 'home' seemed a waste of her precious time with Augustine. For nowadays parents and even sibs had shrivelled away in her eyes to the veriest 'things', like the dull old tables and chairs. Even her father, to whom she had once been so close, was now little more than a weekly lingering smell of five-cent cigars.

Poor Bramber! For Bramber Woodcock adored his children, and yet all summer he hardly saw them at all. He worked the whole week in New York, arrived each Saturday worn to a frazzle, slept half Sunday, woke to face bills and overdue handyman jobs—and late that night worn anew to a frazzle was back in the steam of New York: while even those precious weekends his darling Ree, the daughter he mostest adored—all day and half the night too the girl would be out.

Jess Woodcock also got little good from her daughter. Stuck at the farm from June till Labor Day, driven half-crazy by ants (let alone by children and chores, for none of these summer folk had the money to modernise), Ree was her great disappointment: the eldest, yet nowadays no help at all.

The Woodcocks of course were by no means alone in their woes. In these last few years (whether due to the War or the I.C. Engine or Freud) from ocean to ocean thousands of half-grown young had suddenly all like that burst out of their families, cut themselves loose and advanced on this dangerous rudderless post-war world in packs of their own: self-sufficient as eagles, unarmoured as lambs—like some latter-day Children's Crusade, though without any Cross on their banners or very much else and indeed little thought in their heads but their youth and themselves. You'd have

39

thought they'd been found *and* reared under gooseberry bushes for all it apparently meant nowadays having mothers.

The holiday teenage young from all over the township had formed their own pack and lived in it wholly all summer, ignoring their homes except when hungry or sleepy or needing money. Their oldest ultimate Nestor (and only local among them) was Sadie: the pack had allowed that 'kinda his niece' of the blacksmith to keep her place in their ranks however long-in-the-tooth, because of the glamour attached to a girl believed to have paid her way through Law School driving occasional liquor-trucks only to get a machine-gun burst through her shoulder just before sitting her finals. And down at the younger end little Anne-Marie Woodcock had just scraped in before quite reaching her teens by acting hard-boiled. She was game for adventure as any and every-one liked her; but what had undoubtedly turned the scales was the name she had earned as a bit of a biscuit already if given the chance—and young as she was, the males in the pack gave her plenty. . . . Maybe she simply reckoned this intimate fingering part of her price of admission, or maybe she found herself missing her father's erstwhile fondling: in earlier happier times he had fondled her more than a lot, and his loving fingers had left very little untouched.

For Ree, it was only this new-found life-in-the-pack which had meant very much before she took up with Augustine; and granted the essence of life in a pack is forty-feeling-like-one this wasn't so very much changed even now, for she felt 'like one' with Augustine. His company kept her blissfully happy—provided she didn't begin to wonder. . . . But wondering left her sorely puzzled. He seemed to like her, and yet. . . . Indeed you'd have thought he liked her a *lot*, but. . . . Well, what boy had ever behaved a bit like Augustine provided he liked you at all?

For Ree's was a culture-pattern where no boy out of his diapers failed to get all the manual fun they allowed from the bodies of girls he liked once out of their diapers too: yet

Augustine's fingers had never shown even the faintest desire to molest her, however lonely the places she took him. True, she was well aware that as boys grow big themselves they lose their taste for a 'child' in the skinny, physical sense; but the thought that Augustine's culture-pattern was one so deranged as to class *her* a child even now that her 'turtle was soft' (as she'd told him the first time they met) never entered her head. It is quite on the cards that the burning desire she had lately begun to feel for his lips and his fingers was partly at least no more than her need for their bare reassurance he liked her.

*

As for Augustine, where Ree was concerned his head was still in the clouds—or the sand, you can take your choice which; and here she was, dancing around on his porch agog with a plan that had come to her in a dream—which surely augured success!

Last night she had dreamed of a golden, sleeping, fairy palace with rows of beautiful marble pillars to stroke, where she found herself changed to a dazzling fairy princess with a prince on his knees at her feet. As she woke, her plan was already half-formed. This sleeping palace must mean the Big Warren Place (since to her that ruinous derelict breathed of romance): so today they two must battle their way through the bushes and climb in together where no one had entered for years, whereupon her dream would come true. . . . Therefore she routed Augustine out of his shack, and told him with dancing eyes she was tired of dreary old woods but this would be something new.

When a rather reluctant Augustine (aware that he couldn't afford to get caught on a prank of this sort) enquired what on earth she expected to find when she got there, she waxed mysterious: told him, the place being haunted she hoped for a ghost—and ghosts were the Cat's Pajamas, apparently. . . . Anguish so suddenly clouded her eyes at his hesitation he finally had to say Yes.

Chapter 10

As Augustine lifted her over the boundary ditch her breath on his cheek felt cool, which proved what a scorcher the day was. Alas, here on land there was nowhere at all to get out of the heat: even here in the depths of the trees they were both of them soaked in sweat. It was better by far at sea, where even down in the tropics was cooler than this: in the belly perhaps of a close-hauled mainsail, half-standing and half-reclining, cooled by the steady downflow of air with your back in the curve of the canvas and feet on the boom. . . . Once, though, for a lark the skipper had put her about and he'd only just woken in time not to get catapulted into the ocean!

At this recollection he burst out laughing; but Ree squeezed his fingers to stop him (and Ree was quite right, for there might be someone in earshot across the road at the store and they simply *mustn't* be heard).

When at last they had fought their way to the house Ree just couldn't wait to get in: so Augustine tore off a sagging shutter, and heaved her light weight up and over the sill— but he did it with so much strength that she tumbled inside on her nose. Her jeans were too tight and too tender: they split, and a pale efflorescence of all that incongrous crêpe-de-chine escaped through the rent on her rump. Then she stood up; and the fingers she'd used to wipe the sweat from her eyes had streaked her features with dirt, for the floor where she'd fallen was thick. . . . But before he could even begin to tease her she pressed her grimy self to his side and "*Just you and me!*" she began, in a tense little voice which sounded rehearsed.

Then she stopped abruptly—appalled: for were these those golden and faery halls she'd expected to find? The room where they stood was dark except where some broken

42

shutter admitted a pallid influx of ivy with glimmers of daylight among it: dazzled eyes from outside only started to see
again slowly, but now her sight was returning and never in
all her life had she seen or imagined such dirt! The cobwebs
hung in swags and festoons from the ceiling. Felted dust had
shrouded the shelves and walls, leaving never an edge nor
sharp carved cornice anywhere—only everywhere curves
with a surface like heavy sheenless silk (till you touched it);
and faint but horrible smells. Though the furniture mostly
was gone, some pieces had proved too massive and ugly for
moving. . . . The springs of a cosy-corner had burst through
the covers, displaying the grinning and mummified corpse
of a rat in the spirals of one of them.

Dust on the floor was so soft and deep it accepted their
footprints like snow. So Ree (like the page in the carol)
imprinted her small ones inside his big ones; and thus they
moved off, a procession of two—but only to find that the
whole ground floor was shuttered and dark and silted like
this with dust, while in places the smells were far worse.

They came to the staircase. The elegant spidery handrail
felt sticky under its dirt like toffee partially sucked; but it had
to be clutched if you wanted to get up at all, for most of the
stairs were rotten or missing.

Above there was rather more daylight; but little to see by
it, other than drifts of dirty dead flies as if someone had
started to sweep them in heaps; and flies' wings stuck to
their sweat, like feathers to tar. It was not till high in an
attic, at last, that they came on a relic of even the smallest
romantic interest: a closet, stacked with Civil-War-Period
journals (the Last of the Warrens was killed in that war
Augustine was told, and the house shut up ever since). But
even those newspapers crumbled to bits when you touched
them.

Almost in silence, and more depressed every moment, they
wandered from garret to garret where giant fungi throve
under shingles gone missing and hundreds of birds had
flown in to add their droppings to those of the bats. Then all

of a sudden they burst a door which was jammed, and . . .
found themselves high on the rickety brink of a wing which
had burned: so below them, the whole way down to the
ground, there wasn't a floor.

Dead-sick at her stomach and almost too giddy to stand,
Ree cringed from the gulf in fear; but Augustine stood right
on the edge, looking down. Ree reached out a wavering hand
to grab him but couldn't force herself near enough: hating
herself for her cowardice, knowing she'd *die* if he fell, yet . . .
almost wanting to give him a shove. Augustine's topsail yards
had cured him for good of vertigo: now when he saw how she
in her turn was green with the fear of heights the fool began
showing-off on a charred and teetering beam—he balanced
along on his sea-legs with nothing below him for three
storeys down. . . . Ree crammed her grimy fist in her mouth
like a baby, and screamed.

When Augustine got back safe-and-sound, he was laughing; and that was The End! It made her so mad that she
kicked him—hard, on the shins—with her eyes full of tears:
while her firm resolve not to cry in front of him gave her the
hiccups. They started down. In silence except for her hiccups
they both climbed out of the window they'd used to climb
in—and now she wouldn't be helped. In silence (except for
the hiccups) they parted. But once he was well out of sight
she let the tears flood.

How horrible everything was, and how horrible he was!

Chapter 11

THERE were times when Augustine was downright home-sick for *Alice May*. In this limboish mark-time life he was leading, past recollection was often so strong that even here—cooped up in his inland shack—he would hear the slatting of sails. The morning after that fairy-palace fiasco, while waiting for Ree to appear (for he took re-appearance for granted in spite of yesterday's tantrum), he sat on his only chair with nothing to read but a Sears-Roebuck catalogue someone had left—for use—in the jakes. Thumbing the leaves, he came on a page of sou'-westers and oilskins. . . . The air smelled suddenly salt in his nose, the floor began to heave and he found himself seized with a terrible longing for ships and for adult masculine company. Clank of the pawl as you heaved on the winch: the smell of Stockholm tar as you worked it into the dead-eyes, of linseed oil as you rubbed it into the mast: monkeying up the ratlines to spend a misty hour aloft on watch at the masthead. . . .

Suppose he up-anchored from here, went down to the coast and hung about waterfronts? So many seamen these days jumped ship in American ports that there might be a chance of a berth and no questions asked, in spite of no seaman's card! Other men did it. . . . Arthur Golightly, that ox-like American found at a café table in Paris reading Macpherson's *Ossian*: when Arthur wanted to cross the Atlantic he always worked his passage—if 'working' was ever the word to apply to Arthur, who boasted he'd lost on merit alone more jobs than anyone else in Montmartre (he had just succeeded in losing a night-watchman's job in a graveyard: or else, as he grandly invited, Augustine was welcome to doss in his canvas booth any time). At sea, said Arthur, once out of port you could only be 'sacked' in the literal sense (i.e. with a weight in the bottom and string drawn tight round the neck). But it never quite came to that, even if once the pilot was dropped you did no work whatever as usual. Signing of course for the whole round voyage, once the ship docked on the other side if Arthur wandered ashore and never came back the skipper was only too glad.

Monumental American Arthur, the son of a Great War General, only taking to this way of life as a means of avoiding West Point himself! But his rough-hewn face was the face of the norm-busting proletarian worker on Bolshevik posters (apart from his pimples): the muscles he never used were those of an elephant. . . . There of course was the rub: for if Arthur put in for a job as a stoker he looked it, whereas Augustine's all-too-obvious Oxford-and-upper-class skin was something he wasn't yet snake-like enough to know how to slough. Who would ever believe he could work with his hands? And once they began asking questions the risk of arrest was appalling. Still, if things went on much longer this way he would bloody well have a try: it was better than sitting around like a mesmerised rabbit, awaiting the coup-de-grâce. . . .

But where on earth was Ree? She had never before been as late as this in arriving to claim him.

Even a job in the galley'd be better than nothing, if all else failed.

Alice May's galley was built on the deck, amidships: once, he'd been put on to cook while the schooner was bowling along with half-a-gale on the beam (somewhere off Chesapeake Bay, but a long way out to keep the Gulf Stream under her). Somehow the cowl on the chimney which ought to swivel was jammed so the wind blew down it, and sulphurous almost invisible smoke blew out of the ash-pit. In order to breathe at all the galley door had to be open, so every wave which swept the deck as she rolled had flooded him up to the knees and hissed into clouds of scalding steam on the stove—but he'd had to stop in there with his eyes tight shut and coughing his lungs out in order to hold the

great iron stewpot on to the top of the stove whenever it tried
to dance. . . .

How he wished he was back there now!

From earliest childhood, most of Augustine's happiest
memories seemed to be *men*. His mother had babied him
terribly. Right till the age of four he'd been made to ride in
a pram while Nanny pushed sedately behind with the Under-
nurse in attendance, and lucky Mary capered in front. He
remembered that shameful vehicle now: it was white with
Oxford-blue wheels, and when he got big his carroty curls
were squashed between his skull and the canopy. . . . Therefore no wonder his favourite sport was always escaping from
Nanny! Nanny herself of course couldn't run, but Mabel the
young Under-nurse had been picked for her legs—and
clocked pretty good on a fifty-yard sprint. So Augustine in
turn had grown adept at going to ground the moment he got
out of sight. Thus, the very first time he'd been taken to
Newton Llanthony to visit his uncles in state, the child had
been bolting like this with the whole open length of the
terrace ahead but had slipped inside through a door left ajar
while Mabel was rounding the Orangery. This was the door
of the sacred gunroom; and there was Great-Uncle William,
surrounded by guns one of which he was taking apart!

Great-Uncle William those days had smelled of black gun-
powder even more than cigars, for right to the end of his
shooting career the General stuck to an old muzzle-loader
for wildfowl as lighter to handle (a connoisseur's choice which
nearly cost him an eye, reloading too quickly on top of a
smouldering spark so the old clay pipe he used to pour in the
powder blew up in his face). Uncle William had greeted the
fugitive 'baby' gravely, as man to man; and most of the rest
of the morning was spent discussing the whole art of shooting
as well as the cleaning and care of a gun. Meanwhile Mabel
had raced all over the garden, hollering: "Come out of that
bush this moment Master Augustine—I see you as plain as
plain!" Or again: "If you don't come down from that tree I

go straight to y'Runcle." But uncle and nephew were equally deaf to her hollers.

Thenceforth, whenever he had to ride in that beastly pram he insisted that Nanny must pile his snowy quilt with fir-cones: these he threw in the air one by one, and sat in his pram-harness blazing away with his popgun and crying "Hi lost!" while Mabel earned her pay in the brambles retrieving his birds. . . .

"*Hello, there!*"

Startled clean out of his skin by a stranger's voice in the silence Augustine looked up; and gaped at an unknown girl's silhouette framed in his doorway against the light—and fuzzed by the fine wire mesh of the screen.

"Well. . . . Do I walk right in, or are you saying your prayers or sum'p'n?"

Without waiting an answer she strode straight past Augustine across to the window, remarking: "Believe me, I sure would hate to intrude!" There she paused to curse (with affection) the horse outside she had hitched to a tree, then flopped on his bed in her oil-stained ill-fitting two-dollar ex-army cotton-drill breeches, flipped out a Lucky and struck a match on her teeth.

"C'm on! Let us get us acquainted. You're Augusteen. I'm Sadie." He looked a bit blank, so she added; "Your durned little two-timing woodchick's kid-buddy". A con-tinuing pause. . . . "Wood*cock*, bonehead!" And when it was clear that Ree's surname really meant nothing at all to him, "Darrrrrling Anne-Marie—do you get me?"

He'd got her at last. . . . So this of course was the black-smith's ambiguous niece! All the same 'kid-buddy' my foot, for the girl was all of twenty and could be no younger than he was. . . . She reeked of powder and scent, and he studied her now with a growing distaste. In the 'Pack' an especial glamour attached to Bootlegger Sadie: to him however this slab-faced wench seemed far from attractive. All he saw was a stocky brunette in unbecoming attire, with heavy eyebrows, greasy white skin, yellow-stained fingers and hair coiled over her ears in snails with the pins falling out.

She stopped the best part of an hour. She pumped him with personal questions and said she thought Limeys were cute; and only left in the end when he couldn't give her a drink. Even then her scent hung around; and he stripped off the bedding she'd sat on to air it outside in the sun.

*

Of course it couldn't have gone on for ever, Ree keeping Augustine her private discovery hidden from all the others—not with her absence so frequent and friends so inquisitive. Yesterday, blundering tearfully home from the Big Warren Place she'd been caught by inquisitors right off-balance and far too upset to fence.

So now the news of her find was finally out, and the Pack were poised for the pounce.

Chapter 12

SADIE was only advance-guard. Late that night, long after
Augustine's bedtime, the Pack arrived in a bunch: he
was wakened by Ree reluctantly yodelling "Whoopee!"
right in his ear (but soft, like the note of a song-bird), and
opened his eyes to find his room was full of electric torches
and shadows. They'd come (Ree explained rather glumly,
avoiding his eye) to throw a surprise party for him here on
his roof, and he'd got to get up.

Augustine looked round him indeed in surprise: boys and
girls of school age out together—at night, with no one in
charge! He was more than a little dumbfounded. The British
upper-class culture Augustine himself had been reared in
had tended to 'sex its pubescents in half' as Douglas had put
it at Oxford. They kept the two halves apart and taboo to—
indeed, repelled by each other by means of hideous protective
disguises and ritual masks: "Les jeunes-filles-en-herbe all
covered in gym-tunics down to their calves," said Douglas;
"And boys right down to their heels in repressions and acne,
until. . . ."

"Till all of a sudden the girls 'come out'—like sweet-peas!"
put in Jeremy (whereupon someone had said something
coarse about pods).

But Augustine had got to admit this lot looked gay and as
pretty as pictures! The party ought to be fun. . . .

The night was dark, so they climbed the ladder they'd
brought and hung their lantern high on his chimney, the
only light otherwise coming from fireflies and fitful glimmers
of lightning. The night was sultry as well as dark, so the
whole lot stripped to their underwear: boys in their white
cotton B.V.D.s and girls in their crêpe-de-chine cami-knicks.
Up the ladder they went in the dark, and perched astride the

ridge of his roof in a row. Soon they were singing and joking pretty inanely, eating huge slices of melon they dribbled all down them and drinking red wine from the neck of a carboy they heaved hand to hand. The wine was heady, so presently each now-and-then one lost his or her balance: rolled down the shingles and fell from the ten-foot eaves with a plonk.

Augustine had lost touch with Ree from the start and his first next-neighbour up there was a girl called Janis, a charmer who claimed to be gone eighteen (which wasn't quite true) and also claimed to be Scottish. Augustine liked her a lot.... But Janis fell off; and this left him now next Ree's cousin Russell, a beautiful lad with contortionist's double-joints in his shoulders who wrapped his own arms round his own neck from behind like a scarf, and could also talk if he liked in blank verse. Augustine and he got on fine . . . until he too fell off in the very act of contorting, and dropped with his hands clasped under his chin.

Bella beyond in the draggled next-to-nothing she wore had had too many swigs at the carboy by now for a fifteen-year-old to talk very clearly; and yet she was all too keen to converse. But it didn't last long; and instead of astride the ridge she was sitting side-saddle, which meant when Bella finally went that instead of rolling she slid and tore what little she'd got. They all fell off like that in the end—or else fell asleep and fell off.

As dawn broke Augustine and Sadie were left to the last: so Augustine fell off on purpose, leaving Sadie up there alone. Silhouetted against the pale green sky in exiguous pink crêpe-de-chine and stockingless garters (and scented this time with Citronella, to ward off the bugs) Sadie the lone survivor had started to sing, in a powerful deep operatic contralto. Augustine kept under the eaves to be out of her sight on his way back to bed in the waxing daylight, picking his way through the light-coloured sleeping heaps—for, feeling the cold, they had mostly crept together in heaps in their flimsies (he found Bella's puppy-fat arm right across Russell's face obstructing the breathing, so moved it).

But Ree was sleeping alone, and shivering. Made slightly reckless by wine, this way and that he divided the swift mind as to whether to carry her in under cover; but thought in the end 'better not', and brought out a blanket instead. Just as he tucked it round her she sat up straight and was sick out loud (since she 'didn't drink liquor' it must be the melon had done it?). Then, without noticing who he was, she wound herself tight in the rug and was instantly back asleep.

That morning Augustine slept late. When at last he went out to retrieve his blanket he found his green purlieus battered and trampled, but everyone vanished. The blanket however still lay exactly as Ree had crawled out, like an empty cocoon. The carboy was gone. But when he looked up he saw they'd forgotten their lantern: there it still hung from his chimney, the tiny flame still orange through smoke-blackened glass in the face of the noonday sun.

Augustine's letter to Mary (in which he'd already described the wooden church as "a little deserted shepherdess, scorned by her faithless swain the derelict Ford": "Ali Baba's Cave" with its stills and its staybones and so on) remained to be finished. But last night's party was surely a bit altogether *too* Malinowski. . . . Those fabulous Trobriand Islanders, this with a vengeance was Whites keeping up with the Browns! He'd never seen, never *dreamed* of anything like it. . . . He felt most loth to write home about it because it had left him far too disturbed, as if something was cracking inside— and excited. The fact is he didn't know yet what to think: was this Progress or Decadence? Augustine didn't feel ready as yet to commit himself—quite. It was shocking, girls getting drunk—even anyone not quite grown-up. . . . Yet one thing at least was fully apparent: life here could be mighty enjoyable—Sadie apart.

The better to think he sat down, and at once fell asleep in the sun. Sleeping, he dreamed of that fateful day back in Wales, the day he came home from the Marsh to his empty echoing house with a drowned child doubled over his shoulder, and found to his horror on lifting it down it had stiffened bent double. But there things changed: for he knew in this dream (without knowing the reason) that this time he couldn't just leave the tiny waterlogged body all night as it was in its sopping clothes on the sofa—he'd got to undress it, like putting a live child to bed. Yet as soon as he started to do so, he found that instead of bare skin underneath this child was downy all over with delicate fur; and a fur attractively soft to the touch, like a mole's. . . . When he pulled her last vest over her head—leaving all the downy body uncovered except for the socks—he saw that the wide-open eyes in the small dead face were alive and were eagerly watching him take off her clothes: nor were these even the pair of eyes which belonged, they were Ree's. . . .

He woke on his back in the sun with his larynx cramped in the soundless act of a scream, and his body-pores squirting sweat.

Chapter 13

IN theory some vague kind of Freudist, in practice Augustine tended to treat all lids as something to sit on: he found his repressions the one thing he couldn't repress with impunity. This was something built-in, which only an earthquake could shift. His shattering dream (what on earth was he up to with Ree?) had hauled him half up by the roots; but he hadn't a clue as to why.

As for that party, he still couldn't make up his mind: therefore the less said to Mary about it just yet, he decided, the better. He finished his letter without it. The letter was then wrapped up with the present he'd bought for the baby (a treasure from Ali Baba's Cave); and the package finally mailed, he arranged, in New York.

*

'If only Augustine were home!' thought Mary. 'There's something so solid about him, as well as intelligent. . . .'

Mary this morning was feeling badly in need of Augustine's help. The problem was Nellie, a problem which couldn't be solved yet couldn't be any more shelved—poor tragical Nellie! First. . . . No, first came that hydrocephalous baby, and only then little Rachel drowned untimely—and now her tuberculous husband was out of his pain at last.

Now that Gwilym was dead she couldn't stay on in that lonely hovel they'd lent him to die in: for Gwilym's sect was a poor one, whose maximum pension for Indigent Ministers' Widows was ten pounds a year. But what possible job could the widow find with a baby hung round her neck and millions of others already hopelessly looking for work? What was she fit for?—Some sort of nursery-governess?—Quite; but not with a baby! For who among all Mary's friends would take on a growing working-class child who must presently go

to the village school and bring nits, impetigo, bad habits
and even bad accents into the house? It sounded callous, but
mothers had to be tough about this sort of thing and put their
own children first. For Polly's and Susan's sake she wouldn't
do it herself, so she couldn't ask anyone else to. . . .

If only Augustine were home! There was nobody else to
advise her. She couldn't ask Gilbert: right from the start
(when Rachel was drowned so soon before Nellie's new baby
was born and her husband sent home as incurable) Gilbert
had warned against getting involved. To his way of thinking,
a Liberal Humanist's proper concern was with social
measures in general only: private do-gooding only deflects—
is unfair to the rest, and therefore morally wrong. He was
scathing as hell on the 'conscience' which boggles at one
Nellie starving in close-up but swallows a million in long-
shot. . . . Who else? Jeremy's clergyman father, she'd heard,
was now Arch-something which sounded terribly powerful:
Jeremy though had just gone abroad for three or four months
before being put in some government office or other, and
atheist Mary hadn't the nerve for approaching prelates
direct. . . .

Thus Mary was thinking about Augustine already the
morning his letter arrived (with Gilbert away up North on
the moors, she could read it in peace). Inside the package,
addressed 'For the Very New Baby—in case,' was a crude
glass pickle-dish: moulded in deep intaglio into the bottom,
the bust of a woman in Ninetyish corsage had round it the
legend in Ninetyish script: 'Love's Request is Pickles'. The sight
warmed Mary at once: for here was a christening-present
which none but the old Augustine she loved could have
possibly sent! Next came some drawings inscribed 'For
Polly, with love': one was of deer with floppy white tails, and
another called 'Mother-skunk with her Little Ones'. Not
that Augustine drew very well, but Polly she knew would
adore them. . . .

Unfolding the letter, she saw at once there was still no
address to write back to (and yet so much she was longing to

c

tell him, with Susan and all and those snapshots of Polly the day she was six). And as for the letter itself, reading it made her heart sink: it was all about places, with next-to-no people—and as for Augustine, it gave her no news at all. It mentioned—barely—'a child I met bathing last week'; but said nothing at all about anyone else he had met, not even its parents! Just only one child, and otherwise buildings and woods. . . . Laying it down, she thought of that Moslem painting of bows firing arrows without any archers and battering-rams knocking walls down with no one to wield them. . . . What could excuse him for writing this Baedeker-stuff to his sister, his nearest friend in the world? It saddened her, seeing how far he and she had somehow drifted apart. . . .

But then came Wantage, bearing a fresh lot of toast with a message from Mrs. Winter who asked, Could the Mistress spare time to see Nellie a minute before Miss Polly's lessons? And Mary had to say Yes, she would ring.

Just as a stop-gap arrangement, Nellie was giving Polly 'first lessons': she bicycled down every day with her ten-months child in a basket strapped to her handlebars. Three weeks only remained, however, before Miss Penrose the proper governess came—bespoken since soon after Polly was born, as one must if one wanted a good one (and that re-minded Mary: she'd best take a look, Mrs. Winter had said that as well as repainting the schoolroom needed repaper-ing). Three more weeks—if it even lasted that long, with Nanny so jealous that things were already well-nigh im-possible! Nannies were like that, apparently: really Augus-tine was right, it was utterly mad having servants.

And now she had got to see Nellie. She dreaded the interview: dear little Syl was all poor Nellie had left in the world, and half last night—till three o'clock struck, and her stiffening brain was longing for sleep—Susan Amanda's loving mother had pictured against the darkness horrible pictures of babies torn from the breast. . . . No one had *said* it of course; but what was the need? For it stood out a mile that with Nellie's living to earn little Syl must be put in a Home.

*

That pickle-dish was a 'treasure', so Mary stowed it away
in the treasure-drawer up in her private retreat before even
ringing the bell. But the parcel's wrappings already had
found their way to the Housekeeper's Room, where Wantage
had gone to borrow some scissors to cut out the stamps. "The
blunt ones," Mrs. Winter said firmly (her best embroidery
pair might never be used for paper). "So George still collects
stamps, do 'e?"

George was brother Ted's eldest boy back in Coventry.
"George?" Mr. Wantage said absently: "George . . ." Then,
after a long pause: "Yes 'e do."

He snipped, but without sitting down: for gone were the
days when he used to spend half his off-duty hours slumped
in the big basket-chair over there by the window! Indeed he
seldom nowadays came here at all except (as iron custom
dictated for butlers) to meals. The Room just wasn't the
same place it used to, since Nell. Not that he'd got any
grouch against Nellie herself the poor thing, and one must
make allowances: still, her sitting silent for hours on end
staring into the ferns in the fireless grate, or loving her babe
like an octopus loving its only fish of the week—it gave you
the creeps! But even that wasn't the lot(and he quivered his
nose).

Mrs. Winter looked at him, troubled. A shame that his
habits should have to be upset by Nell! Poor old Fred, there
wasn't much comfort for middle-aged bones in his pantry;
but what could she do, when her sister just couldn't bear to
go home to that lonely old place till she had to? She must sit
somewhere. . . . The Schoolroom was being repainted against
that governess came—and as for the Nursery, Nanny would
never let Nellie sit there!

Meanwhile Mr. Wantage sniffed as he snipped, convinced
that his sensitive nose told him 'baby'. It lingered; and that
was what most got his goat—that baby, in here!—Laid out
to kick half the time on the old horsehair sofa: he'd hardly
dared even sit down since the day when he'd sat on a sopping

napkin. I ask you! In what other Housekeeper's Room in the country had babies ever been changed?

"Seven!" said Wantage aloud: "Poor old Ted!"

"It's a packet," agreed Mrs. Winter.

"Bought his own three-up-and-two-down out at Canley. Detached. And Select. But not much fun with that lot of nippers—not any three-up-and-two-down."

"Twins twice over you told me," she said; and thought in her own mind: 'Poor *Mrs*. Ted!'

"Mind you, I feel right sorry for Nellie: I hope she finds somewhere to go!"—and he certainly meant it.

"She's up with the Mistress this moment, talking things over."

He put back the scissors with care. "Now if Mr. Augustine was home and they asked him, I bet you he'd send her to Wales to caretake that big empty house—with her baby and all, and perhaps the old woman as well."

Mrs. Winter eyed him aghast: for her mind's eye saw old water-stains marking a drawing-room carpet and by them the caretaker, wondering. . . .

"I know!" said Wantage, a higher note in his voice: "But finer feelings is something as some of us can't afford when Belly's the Master. And mark my words, Maggie: your Nell would rather go down below and stoke for Old Nick than ever let go little Syl." Then he paused in the doorway, and added: "But anyway, that horse isn't a starter: for nobody knows where His Lordship has got to, to ask him."

Poor little brat . . . and poor young Nellie! He hadn't meant to be harsh but a thing he couldn't get out of his mind was the look he had caught in the mother's eyes, more than once, as she watched her baby crawling away from her over the floor: the look you see in a cat's eyes watching a bird.

Chapter 14

I N years Augustine was far too old for the pack, like Sadie; but after that party they seemed to be only too keen to adopt him, at least as some kind of elderly mascot. So now the lonely Augustine had no more need to be lonely, nor focus it all on to Ree: for they carted him everywhere with them—if willing.

'If willing. . . .' Because at times he still had his doubts. These girls weren't quite—not quite Miss Porter's Farmington kind of American Girl, if you know what that means— the charming innocent cultured sort with orgies on Cokes and candy bought at the Gundy, their meetings with males confined to those two-a-term decorous Sunday Callers received after worship at Congo or Pisco (that is, if you don't count 'Speech Correction' with Mr. King in the Gym). These were a kind Augustine was rather less used to: they drank even more than they smoked (mostly whisky from half-gallon jars, it was easier come-by than wine and knocked you out quicker) and frequently passed right out, if they didn't throw up. Nor did they—putting it mildly—show many traces of shyness with boys. Of Sadie, Augustine was downright afraid: she would eat him alive for two-bits by her looks, and once when she caught him alone she had slipped her shirt off her shoulder to show him her scars. She told him she had one hole he could sink his finger right in, and had laughed like a drain when he bolted. Among those nearer his age than Ree it was Janis, the Scottish charmer he'd sat next first on the roof, that he cottoned to most: for Janis never made passes.

Nor were these boys exactly coon-coated Yale boys: these weren't Fitzgerald types with prestigious rides to offer in dashing Oaklands, Pierce-Arrows or Stutzes. These were a kind more likely possessed of down-at-heels knock-kneed flivvers of various ages (though Tony'd a ten-year-old Buick, and Ree's cousin Russell a seven-year Dodge): "Cars going from time to time," Augustine had said of them once, "rather than place to place." Still, there seemed to be always just enough cars off the sick-list whenever the pack did want to go places for the whole pack to pile in together, in heaps.

In Augustine's old world you didn't kiss any girl till you and she were engaged; and with such ideas he was bound to assume (at first) that these boys and girls must nearly all be engaged, from the kissing, in spite of their youth and in spite of it proving a bit confusing at times sorting out which was and with which (especially piled in the back of a car with one rug over the lot of them). Not that Augustine was likely to guess one-tenth of what happened under that rug: for when-ever he piled in among them himself it was Ree he took on his lap, being proud to have Infant Innocence lying intact in his arms (even if knowing no better it sometimes nibbled his ear); and by common consent, the rest of them left their elderly mascot almost untouched. No doubt they sensed that six-or-so half-ripe females and males cleaving together all one whacking great flesh in a communal fumbling act would be more than Augustine could take at his somewhat later, more two-and-two stage of development. Also—a thing to be glad of with innocence such as his to be guarded—be-lieving in deeds not words they never *talked* smut.

As for Ree.... Well, it made her pretty despairing at times with the others around all the while nowadays and Augustine anyone's prey—and Janis she couldn't abide! But the fact that whenever she sat on Augustine's lap he still kept his hands from exploring her sensitive parts (and never-never-never had kissed her) was something by now she accepted completely: indeed she had come to love him so much it was even part of his charm.

Apart from sometimes drinking themselves unconscious (Ree 'never touched liquor' because she found just wine quite potent enough), and petting, and charging around in cars, their other amusements were plenty and various. Horseback-riding was one. Janis herself owned a saddle-horse—weedy, a hollow-backed broomtail bought for twenty-five bucks—which never got corn (she swore it only ate rocks): Sadie could boast of a genuine mustang (the creature was ancient and only half-broken and bit), and farmers would rent them for next-to-nothing provided you didn't mind saddlery falling to pieces. Augustine and Janis were two who often went riding together for miles; and on these occasions Ree most often went with them, though horseback-riding made her so sore that she limped and had to sleep face-down in bed—even if she didn't fall off.

But another amusement was swimming—and Ree could swim like a fish. They most of them could, and with far better style than the self-taught Augustine. Even Sadie in spite of her gammy shoulder could dive like a gannet. It also was pretty spectacular watching young Russell's dislocate limbs come right out-of-joint in the crawl, like a panic-struck octopus. Janis-the-Scot however, because of some phobia Augustine failed to uncover—she *said* she'd had a great-aunt in Orkney betrayed in innocent youth by a seal—wouldn't go within miles of the water: she even would shut her eyes driving cars over bridges, just aiming herself across like an arrow.

As time went by Augustine almost forgot his danger and need to lie low: he rode about with them openly everywhere just like everyone else. He even entered the store nowadays without peeping first to see if strangers were there. But one day Janis and he had just arrived in sight of the store when out came a man in some sort of uniform, pistol in holster: flung his leg over a huge red 'Indian' motor-bike leaning against the porch and stood there shading his eyes. Everyone froze, and for several seconds he studied the hate in their faces. But then the engine roared at his kick: he turned in a hair-pin bend with his heel in the dirt and was gone (as

Russell, the Poet and Student of English, remarked) "like a
fart out of Hell".

"Old rubbering meanie!" said Janis disgustedly.

"Peeking around New Blandford the whole fugging week!"
said Sadie.

Augustine's spine felt crawled by a covey of ice-cold
spiders. He timidly asked if anyone knew who the Trooper
was looking for.

"Keeps his goddam trap shut!" Ali Baba said, and spat
like a field-gun.

Chapter 15

H IS stomach well down on its way to his boots, Augustine's
first idea was to run for it—get himself right out of here
while the going was good. For once arrested he hadn't a hope:
it wouldn't cut very much ice with the Judge to tell him he'd
never intended becoming a rum-runner, all this was no-wise
his fault—it was Fate's, it was merely the way that things had
worked out since the night he got slugged. That was all very
true, but would hardly explain to the Court how come he'd
been caught red-handed landing the hooch and had knocked
out an innocent coastguard and bolted.

But where should he run to? The sensible answer was
surely New York, if he couldn't get back to sea straightaway:
in a country place a stranger sticks out, and it's always said
to be easier fading out of sight in a city. He'd give it some
serious thought. . . . But his countryman's every instinct
revolted: he hated and feared all cities, and anyway how
could he possibly live in New York? His wad—the money the
skipper had thrust in his hands at the very last moment—
well, even out here it was dwindling fast and would be gone
in the city in no time. He'd plenty of money in England, but
couldn't get any sent over with nothing to prove who he was
when he wanted to draw it: while as for working—if even to
ask for a job meant filling in forms and producing identity
papers. . . . That really left only crime: perhaps he could get
in touch with some bootlegging gang in the city, so hope
to get back to Rum Row in the end? But even he had the
sense to know that becoming a gangster was only a pica-
resque pipe-dream for someone like him: he was such a hopeless amateur, life would indeed prove 'nasty, brutish, and
short'.

No, for the moment at least there was only one thing to be
done: he must really go into hiding, right here in the woods—

he must leave his shack and live for a bit à-la-Fennimore-Cooper in one of those badger-like holes in the rocks he'd discovered with Ree. From there he could still keep an eye on his shack (if mosquitoes left him an eye that would open) and know if they searched it; and if they didn't—because after all his alarm might be just a lot of fuss about nothing, it could be the Trooper was really looking for somebody totally else. . . .

But someone was trying to catch his attention: he turned, and there at his elbow was Ree. She was quite unaware of his panic and wanted to take him across to the church, where she said she'd discovered a brand-new species of Giant Church Mouse. He warmed to the poppet at once. He might as well go, for it wouldn't take long and the Trooper was anyhow gone for the nonce. It would anyway give him a minute or two to think. . . .

Inside, the building smelled of old pinewood and spiders. And there indeed was her giant 'mouse'. . . . But it looked, said Augustine, "more like an Anglican vicar in cassock and surplice collapsed in the heat of his service". In fact the recumbent incumbent was only a black-and-white cow which lay there chewing the cud, and together they put her outside. But Ree still wanted to linger apparently. Perching herself on the back of a seat she asked if Augustine believed in ghosts.—Well, not so much ghosts exactly, as sperrits. . . . In short: did he think he'd a soul?

Something stifled Augustine's instinctive 'No': he was curious what she was getting at. Gently he probed her. . . . Yes, sure-mike she herself had a soul and she'd lately wondered if he had, since other folk too had some of them souls she believed. For instance her Pop—he had one for sure! She didn't of course mean quite this kind of soul (and she waved a hand at their whitewashed Christian surroundings): a gen-u-ine soul all the same.

He questioned her further. It happened just before falling asleep, she explained. You felt like your body was sinking

from under you (this of course was relative, i.e. the 'you'
—your 'soul'—rising out of it). Not that you ever seemed able
to get very far from your body, in fact all she'd ever achieved
was to hold her soul lying prone right on top of her body a
minute or two—it would then snap back, like elastic. But
Pop was an adept: not only could Pop stay out of his body a
full five minutes but even constrain his soul to sit up while
his body lay flat! But not even her Pop could get his soul right
off the bed and make it step down on the floor—let alone
leave the room where his body was laid. . . .

Where on earth had she got the idea? It was Pop who had
taught her a long time ago, when sometimes she slept in his
bed. She struggled for words, and Augustine guessed rightly
how much this tremendous mystic experience meant to her—
guessed too she hadn't told anyone else in the world but
himself (and the Pop who connived). He must watch his
step, or he'd hurt her. . . . And so "As for getting your soul
right off the bed and across to the door", in a serious voice
he advised her not even to try. For suppose it should wander
right off? Yes, suppose 'she' got lost and never got back to her
body at all? She would then be a ghost without having died!
This terrible thought made her shiver: she jumped down on
to her feet, and (bodies and all) they both went out in the
sun. But his ghostly advice had impressed her:

"It makes me so happy you're spirichool too," she whispered, and slipped her hand into his: "I sure was sure that
you must be. It maybe accounts. . . ."

"Accounts for what?" asked Augustine, and added "For
something about me which puzzles you?"

"U-huh."

Augustine had learned by now that this aspirate grunting
meant 'Yes'; but just what it was this accounted for, that he
couldn't get out of her.

Him, to be told he was 'spirichool'! Even the dear little
goose herself, who'd ever have guessed. . . . He would have
to be careful not to give pain, but some day he'd try to get
into her noddle that all these feelings are purely subjective

and something to do with pressure of blood in the brain: that
there's no such thing as 'spirit' or 'soul', like there being no
God. . . . But then he remembered his dismal failure the time
when he tried to tell her there isn't a God: how she'd blushed,
and shied off the subject. . . . Indeed Ree had found it
acutely embarrassing—almost as bad as when her science
teacher in school had suddenly blurted out to his class that
he as a scientist had to believe in God, just as the page in the
Wenceslas carol believed in the king whose footsteps he trod
in. Everyone then had opened their mouths in acute dis-
comfort: of course they 'believed' in God, but He wasn't a
thing to be mentioned except in church—like the things you
never mention except in doctors' offices.

Why are girls so prone to these strange superstitions?
Good Lord, she was almost as bad as—and just for a moment
Augustine saw Mitzi again as he'd seen her first in Cousin
Adèle's overheated and overcrowded hexagonal drawing-
room standing behind her mother. That cold and serious
white face with its large grey thoughtful eyes: the carefully-
brushed fair hair, reaching nearly to her waist and tied back
with a big black bow: the long straight skirt with its black
belt, the white blouse with its high starched collar; and
curled on the sofa in an attitude of sleep but bright eyes wide
open lay that fox. . . . But just for a moment only; and how
many weeks was it now since Mitzi had even entered his
head?

Chapter 16

THERE came a day when Ree had the grippe, so Augustine and Janis for once went riding alone. They were both of them secretly glad though nobody said so. Their horses seemed glad as well—Augustine's hireling and Janis's darling broomtail—without that lumbering third on their heels; and they cantered or walked side-by-side all morning with never an inch of nose out in front.

They stopped for a picnic lunch in the cool of a ruined, roofless mill a long way from home. Outside the gaping door with its curtain of vines two hobbled horses nibbled the same bush; and within, on the earthen floor two riders munched their salami together, feeling more friendly towards each other than ever before—so wholly in tune indeed that they started telling each other about their childhoods. They found they had both been afraid of the dark: Augustine because of the tiger he knew lived under his cot, while in Janis's case the lurking beast was a bear. Then Augustine described his fear that if he didn't jump out of the bath the instant Nanny pulled up the plug he'd be sucked down the waste: his sister Mary though older was just as scared, and he spoke of his awful panic one time when Mary had jumped out first and toppled him back in the water right on the gurgle itself. So Janis confessed to the time when under her frock her pants fell down in the middle of running a race on Parents' Day, and she'd wanted to die. . . .

After that they were silent awhile. But at last Augustine embarked on a story which never till now had he tried to tell to anyone else in the world: the nightmare story of what he had suffered the first time he visited Aunt Berenice at Halton.

He started off lightly enough just describing this Aunt: "The kind of intelligent woman that nobody knows how to live with. My Uncle had loved his ancestral home, but he

67

took more and more to exploring in countries unfit for a woman to go to and left my Aunt Berenice at Halton alone." This Halton, Augustine explained, was a beautiful sixteenth-century manor house right in the heart of the Black Country. There (in the halcyon days of Augustine's earliest childhood soon after the turn of the century) almost as fast as Gilbert Murray translated the plays of Euripedes, Aunt Berenice performed them. The setting was perfect. A sunken court-yard served as an outdoor stage; and the L-shaped house behind, with its grey walls clothed in magnolias, offered a ground-floor door for mortals to go in and out and a balcony overhead where gods could appear.

"Aunt Berenice didn't lack talent, and people would come from miles around—a few already in cars, but more in carriages still and older children from schools arriving in horse-drawn brakes. They sat on some long stone courtyard steps which served them as benches, and listened to Death-less Verse—and were purged by pity and terror, provided the rain held off."

The pit-head hooters could hardly be heard for the cooing of pigeons and singing of all kinds of birds, for the house was still surrounded by fifty acres of ancient woodland effectively hiding the tips; but its walls were already beginning to crack on account of the mines running under, "And last time I went, just after the War, the house was said to be so unsafe it would have to be all pulled down."

"What a sin!" said Janis: "That darling old place!"

Augustine continued: "I must have been barely four, and Mary seven, the summer our mother took Mary and me to Halton—although she knew her sister couldn't stand tinies about her, like people who can't stand cats. The play was *Medea*, and the part suited Aunt Berenice down to the ground. Jason was somebody good from London and so was Medea's Old Nurse, but the rest of the cast were locals. The schoolmistress led the Chorus: the butler was Creon, con-demning his mistress to exile with verve. Medea's two children were meant to be two little miners' brats from the village, but right on the morning the two little brats got mumps."

There was only one thing to be done: Augustine and Mary must wear the clothes (albeit Augustine's tunic reached to his ankles) and act, though totally unrehearsed. The 'Children' have anyhow little to do in *Medea*—they don't even open their mouths till near the end, when their mother begins to kill them. "They die off-stage of course: the audience hears a childish scream from the palace, followed by two little voices protesting—but very briefly—in Deathless Verse. And presently two little bodies are seen up aloft in the dragon-car on the roof as Medea sets off (by air) for Athens. Mary's curls did well for a boy and she'd acted before: I was much too young to understand 'acting', but Mary they thought could push me around and the butchery done off-stage allowed for plenty of prompting." Indeed it permitted Mary to speak for both, if reciting even a couple of lines of Deathless Verse should prove a bit too much like finishing up all the fat on his plate for four-year-old lips.

Since Nanny and Mabel-the-nursemaid were out there watching, Mary had taken charge of Augustine entirely. Each time before leading her garrulous brother on to the stage she gagged him with one of the monster peppermints Mabel had furnished, and told him he wasn't to utter on any account 'like being in church'.

"And in fact it all seemed just like being in church only more so, with all those dressed-up people intoning meaningless words in meaningless voices—except that in church you're safe in a pew where the clergymen can't get at you but here you were right in among them, and dressed in sort of surplices almost everyone seemed to be clergymen."

Still, with Mary there to protect him he surely ought to be safe; and in fact his first time down in the courtyard among them wasn't too bad, in spite of he mustn't speak. While those two old people intoned their responses the child had plenty of time to search with his eyes for Nanny—or anyone 'normal'.... And look—there was Mabel sitting right up at the back! He waved, and took out his giant bull's-eye to show her; but Mary yanked at his arm all too soon and hauled him off to the house. . . .

Janis listened, but only because she wanted to listen. She had never read the *Medea*, and wondered more than a bit what on earth all this was in aid of.

Chapter 17

O UTSIDE the roofless mill, Janis's animal squealed with delight as Augustine's playfully nipped its neck. Inside, Augustine moved a little closer to Janis to dodge the creeping sun. She widened her eyes; but he seemed now scarcely aware of his audience, blurting his story out in jerks as if every separate word were a separate fossilised lump on his chest.

"But then it got worse and worse. Each time they took me out in the open there was Aunt Berenice—gaudy as hell in her Colchian robes, and getting madder and madder. The way it appeared to me, in real church they notice a clergyman getting like that: they hustle him off to stand up high in a special cage to shout, and don't let him down till the fit is over. But no one did that with my Aunt, and now she was mad she wouldn't let Mary and me alone: that's what was most alarming of all, the way she pretended she loved us!" For little Augustine was well aware how extremely this wasn't true and normally just kept out of her way on the rare occasions he saw her, but now whenever he tried to bolt someone had always got hold of him. Thus when the time came to follow the stage-direction '*she gathers them passionately into her arms*' and he felt himself gathered, he lost all control—gave way to panic, and bit her. 'Oh, darling mouth . . .' she snarled, going on with her hugging just as if nothing had happened. She finished her speech with her finger bleeding on to her batik and '*followed them into the house*'.

Augustine's story was growing more and more incoherent, but what happened next in fact was this. Once inside, he retreated behind his sister expecting the worst: yet that terrible Aunt ignored him. She stopped by the door, mumbling witchily under her breath (really rehearsing her

71

speech while waiting her cue): then all of a sudden was gone.
Mary and he were alone. The curtains were drawn, and
outside a big black cloud had covered the sun: indoors it was
almost dark—till there came a flicker of lightning, followed
by thumpings of thunder that drowned the droning voices.
Then a long pause, dismal with certainty something frightful
was coming without knowing what (for biting is always
punished).

'I want to go somewhere,' Augustine told Mary loudly
(the lightning had made it seem darker than ever in here:
they could hardly see one another).

'S-sh!' said Mary, 'You'll have to wait. First, you've got
to be killed.'

'*Killed*. . . .' So that's what mad aunts did when little boys
bit! "Same as a farmer I'd seen grab one sheep out of the
fifty penned in a fold, sit it upright on a bucket and cut its
throat while the others just watched. And a picture hung on
this Halton nursery wall: the boy tied up while a man dressed
very like Aunt stood over him waving a knife. . . . It was Isaac
of course, and Nanny had told me the boy didn't get killed
after all; but now I knew that she must have been wrong!
And Mary I knew would really just watch, for the way she
said 'killed' had sounded she didn't care two pins I was going
to be sat on a bucket and have my throat slit."

Meanwhile the remembered blood gushed down, the
remembered sheep went suddenly limp with its tongue
hanging out. But Augustine had stood there impatiently
rocking from foot to foot, because there are needs which
won't wait even for murder. . . . Suddenly Aunt Berenice was
with them again, and 'Now!' thought Augustine. But no:
for instead of taking a knife and sitting him up on a bucket at
once, "*Oh abhorréd* . . ." she whispered to Mary: and then
when Mary looked blank, "Go on! *What shall I do? What is it?*"
she prompted.

"*What-shall-I-do-what-is-it-keep-me-fast-from-Mother,*" his
sister whispered, like learning your prayers after Nanny.

"'*I know nothing. Brother! Oh. . . .*'"

"*I-know-nothing Brother-o, I-think-she-means-to-kill-us . . .*"

Out in the courtyard the Chorus voices ended in a dying fall. All of a sudden Aunt Berenice turned on Augustine, her glittering eyes half starting out of her head: "Now scream, you little beast!" she hissed, and shook him. But Augustine was far too terrified to scream. "You, then!" she said, turning in disgust to Mary; and out of a face still perfectly placid Mary let out a yell that had nearly burst his ear-drums—just as he felt the warm flood coursing down his leg.

This had been one of those nightmares where people 'change'; and after that scream even Mary—his only protector, his last anchor in the world of sanity—went mad as Aunt: she started gabbling meaningless words in two loud singsong voices! Yet those words weren't quite meaningless enough, for again he caught something about 'Mother' and 'Means to kill us', and 'Has a sword'.—But this wasn't Mother, though . . . or, was it (for the worst thing about a nightmare is never to be quite sure who people are)? And she hadn't got a sword—or had she? For now to his suggestible eye a blade indeed seemed to materialise out of nowhere into that terrible bleeding hand.

"I was so petrified I still didn't scream: for if even Mary was one of them after all there was no help in the whole world left to scream for."

As he struggled out the unwilling words Augustine relived his fear, waves of it prickled all over his scalp as he spoke. Scarcely intelligible though he was, something of what he was feeling got over to Janis; and Janis was deeply moved: "Why, you puir wee thing!" she exclaimed, and kissed him.

Astonished—but strangely released—Augustine returned the kiss. Thereupon with a happy shiver she melted into his arms and they lay on the ground together, all infant terrors forgotten, the whole length of her body pressed against his, bone to his bone. After a moment or two their mouths met again, and she opened his lips with her tongue.

Chapter 18

WHEN Augustine and Janis got back they were riding a
long way apart. Augustine was flushed, and Janis was
white to the lips. But then, thought Janis, what Englishman
ever had morals? Let all American maidens beware, for that
famous English coldness is sheer hypocrisy: inside they're
just as much lechers as any Latin—and more of a menace
because at least with a Latin you know where you are!

You'd suppose she'd want to keep quiet about it; but no,
she'd a duty. Like wildfire the news ran around that Augustine was not to be trusted: he didn't know where to stop!
For these were all 'good' girls, be it understood: which
merely meant not taking the ultimate step which made you
a bad one, finding it simple—with practice, and help from
the boy—to get complete satisfaction without.

That Augustine was equally shocked and looked on
Janis's morals as worse than a whore's entered none of their
heads: for they hadn't a notion how widely the code he
conformed to differed from theirs. His English Gentleman's
one started off from the premiss that girls are 'cold' and
'pure', which means that Nature has left them without any
carnal urgings at all unless and until engendered by love.
Perhaps his knowledge of girls was small, even granted his
country and class; but Augustine had always been led to
suppose that a girl, on the rare and almost incredible times
that she starts, most certainly wouldn't have started a thing
that she didn't intend to go through with; and then for the
man to draw back is the grossest of insults (could even lead
to her suicide, bearing in mind that she wouldn't have
possibly done it unless knocked clean off her perch by a
deeply passionate love she thought was returned). So once
this girl had begun and Augustine had let her begin he felt
deeply committed: not that he'd had any wish to draw back,

74

for few young men are lucky enough to start with anyone half so attractive as Janis; and Janis indeed had seemed consumed by a passionate love compared with which Cleopatra was almost an icicle.

Janis moreover had done her best to inflame him as well: right up to the very last moment of all when, just in time, she had hit him across the face (for how could she know he wouldn't abide by the rules of the game like a wholesome American boy?).

It was telling Janis that story about his childhood had crumbled his last reserve—like a Chow when at last it consents to uncurl its tail; and if only he hadn't, this mightn't have happened. But then he might never have known what a sink she was, and have fallen really in love! For Augustine had liked her so much, till now: indeed only now he was finished with Janis and hated her guts did Augustine discover he must have been more than half in love with the girl before this horrible thing occurred: while Janis discovered herself to be half in love with this terrible guy right now, even since . . . could it even be really *because* of the way he'd behaved?

But how could those two make it up, when each of them felt so grossly ill-used and insulted by someone without any morals at all? Janis could never forgive his brash assumption that she was the stuff unmarried mothers are made of: Augustine could never accept the idea of a man being used as merely a 'thing', without any nerves or needs of his own— as just an impersonal post for a girl to rub herself on. . . .

But the Pack had plenty to think about other than sex. The problem of getting their drink, for example. That Trooper whose ominous call at the store had scared Augustine so much: it wasn't Augustine at all he was after. Normally Troopers were not concerned with enforcement (Troopers were State police, Prohibition was Federal law and Connecticut one of the only states where the Eighteenth Amendment had never been ratified): this was a nosey fellow however, and hand-in-glove with the Federal agents—as soon appeared when a number of farmers' stills were discovered and seized, farmers whose names he had found in the ledger as billed for those sundries 'useful for various purposes'.

Troopers should never know more than is good for their health. One night this Trooper crashed a trip-wire suddenly tautened across the road: his machine was wrecked, he broke two ribs and his nose and the fat was properly in the fire. It was proved to the hilt that none of those raided farmers had done it; and yet it seemed odd if they really knew nothing that every last one of them had such a cast-iron alibi just for the night it occurred.

Thus for a time the Pack went thirsty. Their usual sources had suddenly dried and it took them a while to discover the Dew Drop Inn, that road-house ten miles out on the New Milford Road.

Prohibition was commonly blamed on the late war in 'Yurrup': American Mothers (they said) had wangled it through while their sons were fighting in France. Ree's cousin Russell agreed in blaming the War, but argued more subtly: "Your darned War packed in too soon", he complained to Augustine, "with hardly a shot fired" (he meant, an American shot). With an army of four million men— nearly twice the whole population of Wales—there were probably fewer American soldiers killed in total than Welsh ones. . . . General Pershing had done his best but he hadn't had time: thus America found herself left with a wealth of hatred minted for war still nowhere near spent, yet suddenly robbed of its object. "To cap it," said Russell, "the country was acting just like a turtle with bellyache (Boy, you could hear her gut rumble right through the horn!) blaming the world outside for her pains and drawing back into her shell, poor nut, to escape them!" In short the country had gone Isolationist, putting herself out of arm's-reach of any out-sider to work off hostility on: thus America *had* to divide against herself, to work off all this excess war-emotion (and surely safer this random way Prohibition provided, than any more rational fission of class-against-class or Black-against-White). "Just like a lonesome old monkey reduced to fighting front legs against back, his hind feet doing their best to scratch out his eyes and his teeth sunk deep in his own private parts. . . ."

If Russell was right, thought Augustine, the pundits would call this whole Prohibition behaviour-pattern 'Play Therapy'.

Hardly indeed was 'peace' declared before left-wingers began letting bombs off: all over the country a million men at once were on strike—and in Boston even the City Police struck. What Russell called a 'Kilkenny-concatenation' of squalls of hurricane force and from every point of the compass soon had the Washington law-makers tossing around like corks. "Those days, if a statesman wasn't a lightweight he sank—like President Wilson was sunk. So under Pussyfoot pressure it isn't surprising those corks in Congress and Senate all voted like corks!—However", said Russell, that wise young man: "These lightweight guys on Capitol Hill weren't born yesterday—No, Sir! They'd voted Dry because they were pressured; but all the Enforcement Laws they cooked up don't work—couldn't ever have worked—and why? Because it's my truly-belief they were never intended to work."

So the whole Enforcement set-up, Augustine thought, was meant to be crazy as well as it was so? Intended or not, the legal provisions seemed certainly odd to Augustine, with selling liquor a crime yet you couldn't be faulted for buying it—only for toting it home, and that was a breach of the Constitution itself! Yet once you were home you were safe. You'd think that the one thing you do with a drink that really mattered a cent was you drink it; and yet they hadn't made even a misdemeanour of drinking the stuff once you'd got it to drink.... These anomalies mightn't have mattered so much if everyone wanted to make the thing work; but when most of you didn't.... Well, such were the rules of the game.

Chapter 19

ONCE big money has got involved, popular national games that attract professionals soon turn ugly and bloody. Nor had professional bootlegging teams got far to look for bloody-minded recruits: for among those four million 'Veterans' trained and conditioned to kill there was hardly a tithe of a tithe who had fired one shot in anger in France: all too many had found their lives as Enlisted Men just months and months spent training, followed by even more months spent waiting discharge—with virgin trigger-fingers still itching.

However the pulsing heart of the game lay more in its nationwide amateur wing, for it filled a long-felt want by releasing the lawless frontiersman buttoned in every American business-suit. Year after year the Amendment remained unrepealed for a simple reason: not even the Wettest of Wets really wished it repealed since, under its aegis, the young (and the not-quite-so-young) could unload their anarchical he-man instincts, and flout the Law with the bulk of the nation's approval. To such, the liquor itself was not much more than a symbol. At dances, whenever a stag stepped out of the stag-line and Janis (or some other girl who was getting a rush) by-passed the Brooks-Brothers cut of his clothes to look for the bulge of a flask before saying 'Love to', teenage addiction to liquor was seldom the cause so much as a likely result: that illicit bulge was simply the badge of his manhood—a scalp.

But now this manner of scalp was harder to win than it had been, down New Blandford way. Those raids had forced you to go ten miles further afield for your rye. This greatly increased the risk to your skin: for the Eighteenth Amendment had made 'Transportation' of liquor a breach of the Constitution, which meant that even the auto itself which

was caught with liquor aboard it was forfeit and Honour
required you—if chased and you knew you couldn't escape—
to tread on the gas and drive for a pile-up. You ditched the
other guy too, if you could; but if not, straight into a tree or
a wall so that all the Federals got was a write-off wreck (only
last year, up in Maine, it was doing just this that Russell's
big brother got killed).

If they chased you they shot-up your tyres; and the cars
which belonged to the Pack were none of them speedy, they
hadn't the hope of a snow-flake in hell of escaping if chased.
So you just had to trust your supplier to know if an ambush
was set and to send you away empty-handed for once—
provided his spies didn't fail him.

Much of this lore Augustine extracted from Russ before
anyone thought to warn him about that brother. The rest
came mostly from Sadie: for lately his early reactions to Sadie
had changed. That reputed Student of Law, who reputedly
once drove trucks for a mob and everyone said had been laid
by the Big Shot himself—since Sadie made no parade of being
a 'good' girl, aiming rather to have you suppose her worse
than she was.... Of course she was terribly unattractive, but
really not such a bad old thing after all in a way....

Ever since his famous 'insult' to Janis, Sadie had grudgingly showed a new-found respect for Augustine: in spite of
his accent this wasn't no vaudeville Clarence or Claude and
she didn't mean Maybe! This started her figuring over again
what had landed him here—right out in the sticks, in a no-
account place like New Blandford, and bumming around
with a bunch of no-account kids. Who was the guy, anyway?
Some sort of British Lord? For this wasn't no brush-ape—
No, Sir! Spita look like he trim his own hair with a handsaw,
and spita his threads let in daylight and sorta smell ocean like
someone he maybe jump ship on the sea-board, she'd tell
the world he had background—and how! The guy was high-
class, in any crowd he'd be high-class.... Sister, your slip
is showing....

Indeed (but without getting goofy about him like Ree) it had dawned on Sadie that making burlesque-show passes— Kee-rist, with that old routine she had loused things up good and proper! She better had mend her manners. . . . Little-Miss-Dirtymouth, go fetch the soap. . . .

Anyway, Sadie had turned off the heat and Augustine responded. Regarding the tricks of the trade and ways of outwitting the Law this Sadie certainly knew her onions; and ever since Janis he'd felt more and more like attempting a getaway. Therefore he made great efforts to stomach the scent she was always drenched in and started attending her antinomian seminars, drinking in all the expert instruction he could. This Sadie had guts, as well as she knew all the ropes: she might even prove useful support if ever it came to the push. . . .

Hold hard, though! For passing the time of day in a friendlier way with a Sadie was one thing—perhaps even picking her brains; but accepting actual help from a creature so common was altogether. . . . However it had to be faced that there wasn't much practical help to be hoped from the rest of the crowd! Lord, he was fed to the teeth with the place: not one of them here would he really miss when he left, apart from Russell (and when he remembered it, Ree . . .).

How he longed to be home!

Chapter 20

'Home. . . .' At Mellton, the topic still was Nellie's living to earn.

"Well," said Wantage to Mrs. Winter, "How about teaching Ted's for a start?" Coventry Ted, with his seven. . . . For nowadays Ted hadn't only that shed out back for assembling the racing machines and 'specials' he thought up himself: he'd a man for repairs, and a lock-up shop with Swifts, Rudge-Whitworths and pumps—and a cash-down house (Detached. And Select) of his own. A cut above sending his kids to the Board School. . . . But anywhere else cost the earth, with all those brats: some private schools had the nerve to charge eight guineas a term! So be doing a favour to both. . . .

Mrs. Winter and Wantage had finished their midday meal (Head Housemaids come to the 'Room' for the pudding-course only, so now again the two old friends were alone).

"Face it," said Wantage, "It's all she knows how."

"She's only done infants. How old's his George?" Mrs. Winter enquired.

"Fourteen, he's out of it. Works with his Dad. And last lot of twins is the only other two boys."

"Age what?"

He thought for a moment. "Just after the War." (Five-year-olds: otherwise, only girls. . . . Mrs. Winter sighed with relief.) "Mind you," said Wantage, "She can't live off Ted's. Food and lodging alone could be close on a quid—or more, with a child: prices is chronic."

"The Mistress is paying her two bob an hour."

Wantage snorted. "She better not ask Ted for that! He'd tell her to go chase herself. What—twice his mechanic?" He paused. "See? Ted's is a start, like: she got to work up a connection—three lots at the least."

"That won't leave very much time for her baby."

"What of it? Sixpence will pay for a minder. The point is she got to earn something to put in his belly, that's what. A couple of years and he'll eat like a hawk."

Mrs. Winter thought for a moment; and then: "You better write Ted and see what he says", was her verdict.

Wantage still had the wines for dinner tonight to see to, but turned in the doorway: "Pi-anner?" he asked; and when Mrs. Winter said No she can't play a note, "Ted'll expect the pi-anner. Get her do one of them postal courses: it won't take her long."

And then he was gone.

Ted, come to think of it (Wantage's steady hand was decanting a vintage claret), Ted hadn't done too bad for himself after all, hadn't Ted; and All his Troubles were Little Ones.

Ted. . . . They'd been born out Binley way, Fred and Ted Wantage. There weren't any pits at Binley, those days: they'd been born on a Gentleman's Farm, where their father was a cowman before he got horned in the groin at a serving, and died. By then both boys had seen enough cows for a lifetime (even today Fred couldn't stand milk in his tea): so when Fred was given a chance of Service at Stumfort Castle he'd jumped at it—chances like that one don't grow on trees! But then, Fred was blessed with the proper physique and demeanour for indoors. . . . But Ted was a spindle-shanked runt, with neither the height nor the calves for a footman—and worse, couldn't wipe that eternal grin off his face: so Dad's old employer had paid his indentures and Ted had been sent into Coventry city itself to learn with an uncle.

Ted's uncle was one of the last of those old Master Weavers who once had made Coventry ribbon so famous, with even elaborate portraits woven in silk. This intricate art was performed on rings of cottage looms grouped round one single communal source of power; but factory looms were driving them all off the market—by now on a cottage loom you could hardly earn your steam (and you durstn't use kids on the treadle for power these days, however much money it saved). Ted had seen the red light, and once his indentures were worked instead of proceeding to journeyman gave up his art altogether for bikes. He had gone in the Humber Works, to learn all over again.

Then came the year when the Old Queen died, and black ribbon had sold by the mile: black sateen for little girls' hair-bows, black silk for hats, black velvet for bonnets—and crape, you just couldn't turn out enough of it. . . . Fred had thought his brother was crazy: he oughter at least gone in Cash's and pulled in a tradesman's wage setting up the looms for it wasn't all unskilled girls, there were jobs for a weaver. 'Crazy'. . . . But was he? For now Brother Ted had a loving wife and bulging quiver of 'Troubles': that handsome three-up-and-two-down, and a bicycle shop of his own. While Fred. . . .

Fred sighed. But his mood of self-pity didn't last long: after all, what he'd got was security. Service was no bed of roses, but still. . . . 'Old Servants': savings or none, they don't leave you starve—not the genuine Gentry. In Coventry, plenty were starving—or near it—or had been till lately, though things were looking up now. And Ted had lost most of his nose from a splinter of glass when Dunn's shop was smashed in those Broadgate riots on Peace Day, five years ago (the mob had gone mad with rage at the sight of a Lady Godiva parading *in all her clothes*).

He wrote to his brother that night, and three days later he got the reply.

*

That last talk of Mary's with Nellie-the-three-times-bereaved had ended, as always before, with the fatal words left unsaid. Adoption, or put in a Home: what else could be done with Syl if Nellie must go out to work? But Mary had found herself quite unable to say it, the clearer it got that the mother herself wasn't thinking on those lines at all. And now,

thank heavens it hadn't been said: for only today Mrs.
Winter had come in to tell her the problem was solved and
the whole thing was settled, that Wantage had heard from
his Coventry brother and Nellie could live there in lodgings
he'd found (*with* her baby) and go out to teach by the hour—
respectable shopkeepers' children and so on. . . .

Mary's relief was intense—tinged by only a tiny chagrin
that she hadn't been even consulted, and once they'd got
the idea they'd settled it all by themselves with no help from
her after all she had done. . . . Still, relief was what she'd felt
most; and the Housekeeper's face as she told her had beamed
like the moon. In two more weeks Miss Penrose (the
Governess proper) was due to arrive: the solution had come
just in time—and Lord, what a load off her mind!

The first half of August was wet, but today the sun had
returned. The peonies blazed; and as Mary leaned from her
window above it the sweep of her August garden bathed in
the August sun reminded her somehow of Rubens, both as
to colours and curves (and even the smells). Below on the
terrace a thrush was tapping a drunken snail he had found
asleep in the poppies: everywhere birds were singing their
thanksgiving after rain, and somewhere unseen in the garden
Polly was singing too.

Out on the velvet lawn a blackbird fought with a worm.
Beyond in the shade of a spreading cedar—a Renoir sight
to be never forgotten—Susan Amanda slept in her canopied
pram, while Minta sat on a canvas stool beside with her
straw hat forward over her eyes: one hand gently jigging the
pram, as she read the sixpenny love-romance which she held
in the other.

Then Mary saw Polly as well, slowly crossing the grass—
slowly, because of the robin she hoped would alight on her
shoulder (Polly was clever with robins). The sky was like
angel's milk. . . . With a swelling heart so large that it nearly
reached to her mouth, every inch from the crown of Mary's
head to the tips of Mary's toes rejoiced at being alive.

When her long meandering song was all unwound, Polly had climbed from her singing-post in the fork of the podded laburnum just where its trunk emerged from the mock-orange thicket (which still smelled sweet even now the flowers were over); and once she despaired of the robin, had made her tiptoe way to a formal place between high hedges of box. Here was a formal circular goldfish pool, starred with lilies and edged with a coping of stone, surrounding a tiny fountain; and here, looking down on the pool, was seated one of her closest and quietest friends: a life-size figure in bronze. He wore a hat that was flat like a clergyman's: still, since he wore nothing else apart from the wings on his feet he probably wasn't a clergyman. Much more likely (she thought) an Indian, being also so brown.

Polly climbed on his lap and started to whisper, cooled by occasional wafts of spray: for he it was who listened to all her secrets now she had no Augustine.

Chapter 21

IN America Coué was really last year, but the young are so seldom right up to date that each morning Ree still rolled out of bed in her tousled pyjama-trousers (all summer she slept without tops) and stood in front of her mirror repeating the magic words: "Every day, and in every way, I get better and better". By this, all she probably meant was cuter and cuter. A fist next rubbed the sleep from her eyes, enough to allow them to see if her breasts had grown any more in the night and that tiny mouse-back of hair down in front. Then she wrapped her rather innocuous bust in a towel and thumped downstairs to wash in the kitchen.

But Ree today was sick at heart as she brushed her teeth in the sink; and later when dressed she could hardly face her breakfast cereal. Clumsy Junior kicked her chair as he passed, and she nearly burst into tears: life was devoid of meaning, she wanted to die. Baba was squealing over her prunes, Earl had an ocarina, her mother's voice clacked on and on like the wheels of a train. . . . Ree was longing to be alone: so she went outside in the yard and sat in the earthy gloom of the privy for nearly an hour, watching the dancing motes in the sunbeam that slanted down from the heart-shaped hole all 'specialists' cut high up in the door for seeing if anyone's there.

It couldn't be, couldn't be true! When Janis had first come back with the story of how he'd insulted her, Ree was completely incredulous: Janis was lying, the wicked old Potiphar's Wife! For he wasn't that sort of a boy, as who knew better than Ree? But he must have been fully aware of what Janis alleged, yet made no public or even private denial: so doubt had begun to creep in, and every day and in every way got worser and worser. . . .

86

"*Ree!* Darn the girl, where you got to? Here's Russ!" The high-pitched voice was her mother's, so Ree came out of the darkness at last. All her dazzled eyes saw at first was her mother batting away at the flies as she emptied slops in the soakaway: then out in front she saw Russell's Dodge. He had called to tell her the Pack were off to the lake for a swim: so she ran upstairs to put on her swimsuit, hoping with luck she might drown.

Russell's brother had died a hero's death, fleeing from dry-law cops: so whoever it was might drive to that roadhouse out on the New Milford road to fetch the communal liquor they all agreed that it mustn't be Russell, for one in the family's surely enough. But the rest of the older boys had a rota. Augustine at first had been out of all this as a guest and a stranger; but once he'd discovered about it he told them this just wouldn't do, and after his insult to Janis they'd weakened. To start with he'd gone as a passenger only, showing his face to Micky Muldoon at the Dew Drop Inn and learning the routes: for they rang the changes, and seldom returned by exactly the way they had come. But tomorrow, Sunday (it was to have been today, but today all the cars were wanted because of this trip to the lake), he'd be making the trip on his own in Russell's old Dodge.

He wasn't much worried by thoughts of chases and federal agents, since Micky Muldoon must surely pay through the nose for immunity: no, what worried him most was the risk that the car broke down for his knowledge of wholly reliable Bentleys wouldn't help much with a broken-back Dodge. Or a casual Trooper might ask for the driving licence he just hadn't got; and enquiries would start. . . .

But now these worries were all put off till tomorrow: today as he piled into somebody's car already wearing the swimsuit he'd bought at the store they were only off to the lake for a swim. . . . Russell and Ree and the rest of them—even himself, in all this heavy knitwear and serge! In England that sort of nonsense went out with the War: nowadays

D

upper-class youthful fashion in Britain even decreed both sexes kept their embarrassment under control and swam together in nothing at all when they could, like the Swedes. But here the Law and practice alike forbade you even to swim in cotton, which clings: it had to be wool, full-length and with sleeves, and even the men wore a minimal skirt. As for the girls, they were never seen so completely upholstered as times like these when dressed for a swim.

Chapter 22

THE lake was a winding reservoir high in the hills, with a wonderful view from the top of the dam (where sometimes they dived) right over the country below. You drove off the New Milford road at a weatherworn board which read: 'NO *automobiles* NO *gunning* NO *fishing* NO *swimming* THIS MEANS YOU'—but seemingly nobody minded, and everyone used it. From there the approach was a difficult track through the pines. This presently forked: one prong slid down a steep incline to the dam, while the other meandered along through the trees to the shallower end of the lake a mile further on. Today the car in front turned off for the dam; but the next ones honked so loud on their horns that they stopped, and an argument started from which it emerged the majority wanted to go to 'our island'. . . .

This faery island they'd found and adopted lay half-way along the lake in a bend of the winding shore. It was tucked in a cove and right out of sight till you got there, and couldn't be reached at all direct from the dam. Since the Pack could never divide the divers gave in, and bumped back along a vestigial cross-trail on to the shallow-end track to rejoin their fellows—though arguing still.

Reaching the end of the lake at last, they stopped their engines and all spilled noisily out on a tiny beach. There they found a family bivouacked: father asleep in the sun with his hat pulled over his eyes, mother busy with cutlery cans and cardboard cups, infants shrieking in inches of water, and twenty yards out the grandmother floating about on a truck-tire. These the Pack—including the family's own boy and girl as completely as everyone else—all ignored, and trod over or through.

The cove with the tiny islet they sought could only be reached from here; and you got there by threading your way

for twenty minutes at least from boulder to boulder between
the impassable woods and the mere itself. A secret island,
with birch trees bowing over the water: an island, they all
believed, which nobody knew.

At first they waked the echoes, and splashed through the
shallows; but once escaped from the world of men and well
out of sight of the family camped on the beach, the Waldenish
mood of the place began to take hold and even these boisterous creatures all fell silent. Indeed henceforth they were
almost as quiet themselves as the trees: nobody spoke as they
crept along, nobody splashed any more: they moved without
sound at one with the water, the stones, the woods, the
August day, and each other—and almost believing in God.
Smelling of pines themselves, they advanced on silent feet
that clung to the rocks much more like roots on the move than
feet: with leafy fingers, and eyes brimming over with sky
(except for Ree, whose eyes were full to the lids with Augustine).

Above them the woods were dense as a wall. Below them
the lake was clear and still, with waterlogged boughs on the
bottom that laced the vivid reflections like ghosts. . . . Like
—like that something white underneath in a pool, on the
Marsh back in Wales; and with almost its earlier pang
Augustine's heart mourned again for the ill-starred child he
had found.

There was one more jutting of tree-clad rock still to round.
In the silence, Augustine's thoughts still dwelt on the loss to
the world of the poor little drowned one: he quite forgot
where he was. The rest of them too were so quiet that no one
could possibly hear them coming, and far too intent on their
mood and each other to notice voices themselves. Then at
last they turned the corner and reached the cove and looked
across to their private island; and saw on it under the birches,
under those feathery leaves. . . .

For Ree (and indeed for most of these boys and girls) this
was the first time they had seen it although they'd imagined
it hundreds of times: the two-backed monster performing.

*

All the way home Russell's old Dodge seemed hardly able to stagger. The valves were sticking, and causing cardiac trouble; and doctor's-orders clearly were that it mustn't hurry up hills. Thus Russell and Ree arrived long after the others. The journey seemed endless, and Ree felt sick all the way. When Russell asked her just to run round to Augustine's shack and tell him the Dodge wasn't fit to drive to the Dew Drop Inn next day, she refused: so, late that night, Russell was forced to go round and tell Augustine himself.

In bed that night Ree couldn't sleep. It was bad by daylight, but worse in the dark: for against the darkness her eyes shut or open couldn't help seeing those coupling bodies. So this was what 'lovers' did—though it looked more like murder than loving. But where was that blissful and magical melting-into-each-other she'd always imagined? Instead all this panting, and moans. . . . In fact it must hurt like hell; and she thrust both hands in between her legs as if to protect herself, taut as a bow-string.

So Janis had hit him! It seemed past belief that Augustine should secretly want to do this to us girls, her kind and gentle Augustine. True, he'd tried it on Janis not her; but suppose one day those hundreds of times when he'd had her alone in the woods, he'd begun. . . . As the night wore on her nipples started to ache, and a burning began in the pit of her stomach: she tossed on her bed till the sheet was twisted like rope. If he had, could she conceivably even have let him and not minded how much he hurt her, because this was something he wanted so much and which she had to give?

It was nearly dawn when at last she slept—to dream about windows with red lace curtains, and birds.

Chapter 23

Next morning Augustine was lucky. Soon after breakfast that Sunday Bella's big brother Erroll had come on a visit: he drove his Second-Vice-President (Sales)'s shining 'Bearcat' Stutz, with a whopping great polished copper exhaust all along one yellow cheek like somebody playing a flute (whether with or without his Second-Vice-President (Sales)'s permission, no one enquired). Erroll had driven all night and ought to be left to sleep in peace; and anyway everyone felt that the less he knew of the errand it went on the better for Erroll, if something went wrong. . . . Out of sheer niceness of feeling moreover they didn't tell Bella either: one hates to occasion a brotherly-sisterly rift. As for Augustine, they told him no more than that here after all was a car for his use.

Augustine rejoiced: this wasn't his Bentley, but still. . . . And once ensconced at the wheel of that big yellow Stutz on yesterday's road past the way to the lake he rejoiced even more. The local lanes had been grim with their 'thank-you-marms' and outward banking at blind right-angle bends and general absence of surface, but now he was out on the State Road at last he felt with a steed like this his errand should soon be over. That was what everyone thought: he'd be back in a brace of shakes, and long before Erroll could wake.

Micky Muldoon looked always half asleep: his single wandering bloodshot eye was heavily lidded, his paunch was the conical kind which carried a belt like an architect's 'swag'—depending below it and purely for ornament. But Micky never forgot a face. The Stutz out front was a stranger, and yet when Augustine came through to the back demanding a gallon of rye it was served—after one quick glance— like a packet of peas. There wasn't a soul in sight as Sadie disposed the couple of half-gallon jars behind in the rumble-seat under a rug (Sadie'd insisted on coming: "Just" she had said "for the buggy-ride").

Turning the car in the driveway, he started for home at an easy cruising seventy—all this part of the route being free of serious bends and fairly empty. Indeed the Stutz was the fastest thing on the road: there wasn't much, but whatever there was he passed it as if it were standing: even a Jordan Playboy—that open Bearcat went like a bird! Only a Mercer Raceabout gave him a moment of trouble; and that had a driver as young as himself behind its monocle screen who seemed just about to let go of the wheel altogether to have both arms for his girl.

Sadie had started to sing in tune with the engine, as some women always do from the moment the engine starts; and even her adult and rather throaty contralto recalled that time his Bentley and he had driven Polly to Dorset, and Polly's treble throughout had accompanied the Bentley's sonorous bass. Polly was deemed to have caught a cold, so her Nanny had wrapped her in rugs and scarves like a pea in a pod; but her voice was clear as a lark's. . . . Augustine glanced a little askance at the Sadie singing beside him now, in breeches and open shirt—so open her grimy underwear showed. The painted cupid's-bow on her mouth was at odds with the natural line of her lips: the hairpins were popping out of her greasy hair as the wind of their speed took control and the nearer coil was uncoiling down to her shoulder.

From her he glanced in the mirror. The Mercer had dropped out of sight, but a quarter mile back he descried a car that they certainly hadn't passed: "What's that behind us?" he asked.

Sadie knelt up on the seat to look backwards over the folded top. "Gee!" said Sadie, "That's no market model: a custom-built 'special', I guess!" Then she added with bated breath: "It could be a supercharged Dusy. . . ." and almost bowed at the name.

A Duesenberg! Worthier metal—and something which

even his Bearcat apparently hadn't the legs of: still, he'd give them a race. What fun! He would set himself to hold them at bay till his New Blandford turning. . . . Elated, Augustine trod on the gas and started a Christmas carol. The needle crept up the seventies, speed foreshortened the curves in the road and it took all his skill to hold her on bends. Ecstasy sang in his blood: it was nearly a year since he'd sat at the wheel of anything fast. . . . But the Mystery came on apace. Sadie still knelt on the seat, looking back. As the distance between them lessened, its couple of yards of nose grew larger and clearer: Dusy 'special' or not, this wasn't no private citizen's job—its windows were more like embrasures built for machine guns, and only a big-shot gangster would possibly use such a car—or else, if it fell in their hands. . . . She was sweating right to the roots of her eyebrows even before the siren started and "Christ!" she exclaimed, "*C-c-cops!*"

Like a prick of a pin, her voice and the eerie wail of the siren together punctured Augustine's ballooning elation: the singing blood in his veins turned to lead. Something out of his childhood raised a forgotten head and he even started to pray, but of course unconscious he did so. He glanced at the dashboard again: the needle had grudgingly flickered its way up to nearly eighty and stuck, for this was an uphill road: yet in spite of the extra weight it carried of bullet-proof plating that hotted-up Dusy behind came dreaming along at nearer ninety—and as for reaching the New Blandford turning, he hadn't a hope!

He counted they wouldn't start shooting his wheels until they got close, with the end of the chase so certain; but only a minute at most was left to get off the high-road somehow.... Moreover they mightn't be hunting alone, and suppose he rounded a curve and found they had blocked the road with a truck? With a sudden pang in his heart he thought about Russell's brother and losing the only life he'd got for a nonsense and nearly gave in and drew up.... Indeed perhaps he'd have done so except that there, right ahead, was the

back of Tony's old Buick—snailing along with Tony and
Russell himself.

Swerving out to avoid them, he saw on the opposite side
that old 'NO *automobiles*' board on the edge of the woods
which marked the track to the lake—to the lake alone. . . .
Sadie by now couldn't bear to look back: she was crouched in
her seat facing forwards, expecting the shooting to start.
Augustine braked so hard as he broadsided into the track
that she banged her face on the screen and her nose began to
bleed: "You're dog-gone crazy!" she gasped through her
rattling teeth, as the Bearcat bumped about on the washed-
out trail: "*There's no road out!*"

Then they heard the scream of the Enemy's tyres as it
skidded round Tony's Buick that tried to get in its way and
followed them into the woods.

D*

Chapter 24

THE chase was now a slow-motion one down a zig-zag slot between two walls of trees, with the going so rough that anything over fifteen miles an hour would buck you out of your seat and no earthly springs or axle could take it. It wasn't a question of speed, it was simply up to your driving; and underslung Bearcats weren't designed for this sort of thing. But the track snaked about through pinewoods and spruce so dense that at least you were now out of sight, however close the pursuers (who'd silenced their siren now, so you just couldn't tell).

Everywhere, hot smell of spruce with an overhead sun.... Augustine clung to the wheel like an organ-grinder's monkey clings to the neck of his master; and Sadie hung on to the dashboard. Augustine's mind worked fast, with a kind of frozen awareness that seemed not wholly his own and yet dictated the answers. If only the springs would hold, and the sump didn't catch on a rock. . . . True, ahead there was no way out; but ahead at least lay that fork, with a fifty-fifty chance that the cops would follow the wrong one. . . . And yesterday's cross-trail ought to be passable even for Stutzes: by lurking hidden in that while the cops—whichever the track they took—overshot, he could cross and then double back to the high road, greatly increasing his lead by the time they'd discovered and turned—if indeed they ever found somewhere to turn on a track so narrow and hemmed in by trees. So Augustine pressed on, and the pungent boughs lashed his cheeks as he swerved to avoid the worst of the potholes and rocks (as with less than ten inches clearance he had to). He passed the fork, drove along the shallow-end track, drove into that cross-trail and half-way along it, and stopped.

The cops overshot him all right, but somehow they saw him and fired a revolver-burst as they passed. The shots went

wild, yet nearer to heads than to tyres and neither Augustine
nor Sadie enjoyed it. Both of them ducked down almost too
low to see out, while Augustine let in the clutch and they
managed to lumber forward—moving as fast as they dared
on alternate bare rock and cord-road, and thrashed both
sides by the lurching trees. Their hearts were still in their
mouths: for the cops hadn't wasted time attempting to turn
—they had gone in reverse and pursued them like that, tail
first (though bucking about too wildly, now, for even a
copper to shoot . . . for the moment).

Augustine was just about to debouch on the further track
(in triumph, for now the Dusy *must* stop to turn) when they
saw their way to the high-road blocked by Tony's lumbering
Buick: the cretin had followed that Duesenberg in. Thus they
were properly cornered, with only one way to go: down the
track which led to the dam and to only the dam. . . .

Already Augustine's nerves were strained, and maybe this
second stroke of ill-luck could have sent him a little light-
headed: he thought of the dam right ahead, and there came
a flash of vision so vivid it hurt in which his mind's eye saw—
like watching an epic scene in a film—that knife-edge top of
the dam with his yellow Bearcat driving across it. The top
of the dam would be hardly as wide as his wheels, if indeed it
was that wide: on one side the deepest part of the lake, on the
other a sixty-foot drop to a horrid ravine so the slightest error
or even a stone out of place. . . . If he screwed himself up to
drive over that dam, would the Duesenberg dare to follow?
His vision said no: it showed the intrepid Bearcat crossing
alone, while everyone held their breath. . . . But he mustn't
take Sadie with him, this desperate crossing was much too
dangerous: "Jump, girl!" he grunted through grinding teeth
as they bumped and slithered downhill, half the time crab-
wise, scree flying right and left: "Jump out—I'm driving
across it!"

Yet Sadie showed no sign of jumping: instead she crouched
in her seat struck dumb, with incredulous face. 'Drive across'
that dam: had the guy gone crazy?

Augustine had need of his eyes close-range not to run into trees or slide off the track altogether: moreover his mental picture was still so intense he'd have anyhow scarcely seen the actual dam as it came into view. Just as they reached the shore he jabbed her ribs with his elbow, "Wake up and jump, you bloody loon: I'm not taking you!"

But still she sat tight, now surer than ever Augustine was out of his mind: for the guy had been there often before—he must know you couldn't ride even a bicycle over this dam because of the overflow chute in the middle which cut right across it—a detail his 'vision' had somehow left out; and even a Bearcat can't take a water-jump. . . .

Twenty yards on to the concrete she suddenly came alive, yanked the wheel from his hands as the lesser evil and toppled them into the lake.

As the car hit the surface a wall of water reared like a tidal wave and fell on the pair of them, forcing them down in their seats. So they sank with the car. But twelve-foot under the water the Bearcat gently lit on the slope of the dam and slowly began to roll; and somehow they floated clear.

Both heads were well under cover among a tangle of boughs at the edge of the lake when the Dusy appeared at the top of the scree. It didn't come down. Two rather grim-looking, under-sized types jumped out. Their pistols were in their hands. They ran down on to the dam, and scanned the water for swimmers. None were in sight. . . .

They stared at a floating map. They stared at the eddies and patches of oil and bubbles that hid the Bearcat resting below on its side; and one of them crossed himself with his pistol.

Chapter 25

O N their way back with Tony and Russell, while Tony's Buick lolloped along and the two drowned rats in the back seat dried in the sun they held a council of war. Like as not (was the gist of what Sadie said) that this was the end of the whole affair: that no one would bother to drag the lake—and be damned to whoever's water-supply this was—or even to raise the wreck: for this sort of minor incident happened each day of the week. But Tony and Russell were not so sure this had happened by chance: it looked like somebody got their knife in the New Blandford crowd. That Trooper. . . .

"But what about Bella's brother?" Augustine asked: for Augustine couldn't take quite so lightly the loss of that Second-Vice-President (Sales)'s beautiful Stutz, and the rod in pickle for Erroll.

"Shucks!" said Sadie: "You don't imagine he told his boss when he swiped his Stutz? No, Sir! They'll figure on thieves: Erroll won't even be fired, if he keeps his trap shut and Monday at eight in the morning he's back on the job by rail." When Augustine still looked unconvinced, she added: "Boy! The folks we have to worry about ain't Erroll, it's us."

For Sadie admitted to just one fly in the ointment: their faces were known to that couple of cops who at present thought they were dead, but suppose that later they saw them around? "Then you better grow new faces," said Russell over his shoulder: "And don't be seen in the county until you done it, for everyone's sake."

"Yeah, take a powder!" said Tony, and sounded his horn at an ancient Chevvy that shimmied all over the road.

"For the public good," said Russell, "as well as your own."

"But where can we go?" asked Augustine.

99

"Plenty of places," said Russell. "The country's big. Massachusetts. Vermont—or why not Quebec? It's a chance to see the world."

"Yeah, Quebec—cross over the border for Chrissake!" said Tony. "A darned sight safer. . . . Jeeze!"—and he nearly shied into the ditch as a truck overtook, for his steering-gear was apt to do more than you asked it.

" 'Oh God, Oh Montreal!' " Russell quoted. "French Canada. . . . Doubtless you're fully conversant with eighteenth-century French?" he enquired of Augustine: "The unspoiled tongue of Voltaire?"

"Yeah, 'Potates frites'!" said Sadie: " 'Chiens chauds'—Bill-of-fares I seen it."

Tony chuckled. "Better take along your own steaks. Boy, what those Frenchmen up there use for eats isn't nobody's business."

"Frogs," said Russell. "And probably snakes. Squirrels. They're all half-Indian."

But suddenly Tony waxed nostalgic. It seemed that he'd spent the whole of one summer up there in the north, on the Saguenay River. . . . "Logging. Oh boy, that's the life!—*Jee-ee-eeze*. . . ." For now his steering-wheel had started a wobble so frantic he had to let go altogether until it had righted itself. "Russ! What say me and you string along?"

"Ride up all four of us?"

"That's it. Just a two-three days, me and you. Maybe tomorrow?"

"O.K. by me," said Russell.

"But . . ." said Augustine, for now the time had arrived when he'd got to come (partially) clean. In a tragedy-voice he told them all crossing of frontiers was out where he was concerned: for his passport was lost.

Russell guffawed. "Say, that's rich!"

Once again Tony let go of the wheel altogether, but this time to slap it: "Boy! Get a load of that! Guy can't go Canada. . . . Why? 'Lost me passport!' " he mimicked. "Bonehead, where do you think you are at, now?—Yurrup?"

"You mean it won't have to be shown at the frontier?" Augustine asked, incredulous.

"Frontier's an ugly word," said Russell: "We call it the border."

But Sadie looked serious. "Guy's got a point: Immigrant Quotas and all that boloney. Without his American visa they could act mean when it come to letting him back."

"But going I won't need to show one?"

"Listen, kid!" counselled the prudent Sadie: "No: better you stop the right side of the border or else you might get stuck up there on the wrong side."

"But they won't ask for anything driving *up* there?" Augustine persisted.

Now it was Russell's turn to look incredulous: "Visiting Canada? Riding with free-born American citizens willing to swear you're British, and Canada British soil?"

"Cripes!" said Tony: "The guys up at Rouses Point aren't so crazy as have me halt this old jalopy, so she could die in her tracks and block the whole road."

Lord! All the weeks that Augustine had taken for granted he couldn't escape from the country without that passport stolen in France, when all he'd apparently got to do was to drive to the border and cross it to British soil! It couldn't be true. . . . As for coming back, he nearly told them that once he got out of their sacred United States they wouldn't see him for dust; but refrained, as it sounded rude.

Instead, when the other suggested starting tomorrow at dawn he merely agreed without comment.

That morning Ree slept on and on. When she didn't appear at breakfast her mother suggested a touch of the sun, and dosed her.

Today being Sunday her father was home, but she didn't get up till noon and refused her dinner and wandered off to the store for a comforting Coca-cola just as Tony's Buick arrived with Augustine and Sadie inside it behind—looking rather the worse for wear.

When the story was told, Augustine and Sadie were heroes
(Augustine at least enjoyed it: he'd never had reason to feel
like a hero before): and only Erroll looked glum. For Erroll
would have to leave for the Depot at once to be back on time
by rail.

Chapter 26

No one might bother maybe to raise the Stutz, but the whisky was far too precious to waste. So just before midnight a diving party set out. They were all of them boys, and it had to be done at once to be first in the field. They doused their lights at the 'NO *automobiles* . . .' board for fear they'd be seen and followed and drove to the fork by the light of the moon, then prudently hid their Fords in the cross-trail, scrambling down the rest of the way to the dam on foot.

The moon was full, and its glare so bright that it even showed colour—at least, a few strong colours glowed like the runes on the underwing of a moth in all this general murk-and-silver. The woods were black, but the lake with its scatter of stars was almost blue; and the dam was a bar of the palest brass. They undressed; and their naked bodies were white where their clothes or swimsuits had been, but mahogany-dark where these ended at faces and legs and arms.

The distant hills looked hardly solid at all: a bank of cloud in the west looked solider far than the hills.

Augustine and Russell and Tony were with them in spite of intending so early a start: Augustine, to show them the place where the Stutz had drowned. This he thought he knew; but he didn't it seemed, for by night all distances looked so different. Finally everyone stood in a line all together, ten feet apart, and dived as a team; and Russell it was who surfaced at last with a whoop.

Finding the wreck was one thing, but salvage another. The wreck lay fully twenty feet down; and even the classiest divers didn't seem used to depths. Only Augustine himself in the end, whose diving was far from classy, was able enough at holding his breath (he'd practised it long before learning to swim, as a child in his bath). Under the water, the Stutz had rolled on its side; and by luck the lid of the rumble had opened. But twenty or more feet down the pressure hurt his ears and he worked in a panicky frenzy: his head as well as his lungs seemed bursting, the water that forced itself up his nose felt more like a knife—like having one's adenoids out without anaesthetic. Sadie however had stowed the jars so snug that neither was broken; and finally one by one he managed to surface with both.

Meanwhile that bank of cloud had risen a bit: it was brownish black below, though its top still glittered with moon like those turbulent floes of Danube ice he remembered, and glimmered with distant lightning.

Clearly Augustine needed as well as had earned a drink: on that they were all agreed—and as well, could do with a drink themselves. But the spot was a trifle exposed, if anyone came (for rumour travels like fire, and soon every son-of-a-gun for miles around would be diving): therefore they put on only their shoes, and trooped back into the edge of the woods with their clothes tucked under their arms. Thank God by now the mosquito season was over! They found a clearing, and squatting round in a naked ring on the carpet of needles and leaves they uncorked a jar and passed it from hand to hand. Gurgling, smacking of lips. . . . Nothing so formal of course as toasting Augustine's achievement, and yet their esteem came through. . . . They were far too engrossed for chatter, and looked with their almost invisible blacked-out (sun-burnt) faces and limbs—thought Augustine —some savage tribe with a bizarre tribal design of tattooing nearly as odd as the mandril's. Absurd as they looked, Augustine was moved by a quite unexpected wave of affection: he found himself really minding the fact that after tonight whatever his future held it wouldn't be them.

But now that mounting bank of cloud had reached the westering moon; and his darling savages all disappeared, as the sultry night went suddenly dark with a little moaning wind.

A flash of lightning—and out of the nearby trees above them a dreadful scream. . . . Feeling his way downhill inch by inch (for he hadn't a torch), it was Sadie's 'uncle' who'd screamed and dropped his grappling-iron when the lightning showed him, under the trees, a coven of seemingly headless leprous trunks with only the stumps of legs and arms. . . . But the almost instantaneous crash of the thunder drowned his yammering flight.

The lightning—the scream—the crash of thunder; but then came the rain, and even the scream was forgotten. It fell not in drops but in pailfuls: you felt its weight as it fell, and it wiped the leaves off the trees like wiping a slate. At first the falling water was warm and they felt no chill, but soon the deluge had turned so cold that it chilled them right to the bone; and seconds later it started to hail. Stung by the hail, and bewildered, they jumped to their feet; and as flash followed flash, by that awesome light they began to scramble back to the place where they'd parked the cars. They were still stark naked, and very afraid: for the lightning was all around them, violet and blue and yellow—you smelled the discharge as it leaped from tree to tree, and even below them it skiddered across the hissing rain-furred lake like ducks-and-drakes. And the thunder! The noise didn't really matter of course, but it had its effect for their ears were beaten and battered by noise like blows. Then a luminous ball came floating over the trees, and one tree burst into flame.

At last they found the cars. These were both of them flivvers: one of them hadn't a top, and they didn't attempt to put up the other one. Neither did anyone try to dress: it was hopeless, for some of their clothes were lost and the rest impossibly wet. But they cranked the handles and somehow the engines were made to fire, and they started for home. The track was a torrent, but long-legged flivvers don't seem to mind and at last they were out on the highway—too thankful at being alive to think about anything else.

By now it was two in the morning. The worst of the storm had passed, though the rain still fell.

They dropped Augustine as close to his home as they could without using an axe (for year by year that trail had narrowed to little more than a footpath). Nearing the shack with his prize jar under his arm and his bundle of clothes, Augustine was more than astonished to see a light: had he really forgotten to blow out the lamp when he left? But then he opened the door, and—dripping all over the floor, and shivering nearly enough to shake out his teeth—he smelled such a welcoming smell and saw such a warm, domestic sight: there was Ree at his lighted oil-stove, tending a steaming enamel jug. . . .

"Coffee," she said "You need it, I guess!" and this time turned her back as he towelled himself and dressed.

Chapter 27

WHILE the coffee was being drunk Augustine cooked
bacon and eggs, and the shack was filled with an even
more savoury smell. They ate in a leisurely way with their
plates on their knees: when finished, they wiped their plates
with their bread and ate that too. After this, instead of him
taking her home at once (for the rain had stopped) they sat
a while in the lamplight talking, entranced—these two alone
together again at last, right back where they used to be before
the Pack had found out about him and spoiled it. Whatever
is was they said doesn't matter much, except that nothing
was said about parting tomorrow (although of course she
knew). What mattered was rather the feeling of being two
voices almost turned into one, with once more nobody else
in the world but them; and nothing to break the spell. Like
those times such ages ago when together they used to creep
into holes in the rocks 'like a couple of badgers setting up
home'.

Late as it was, what both of them really needed was sleep.
But she showed no signs of going; and Augustine was equally
loth to tell her she must (though he knew he ought). They
sat very still, and at times hardly even talked. Once Ree
tried to save a moth that was blindly burning itself to death
on the lamp, yet the more she tried the wilder its dashes
against the heated glass till antennae and even wings were
spoiled. But she made no other move. Once or twice
Augustine looked at his watch; but he kept on putting it off,
and dozed.

Then all of a sudden the circling storm had returned, and
thunder jerked them awake. Augustine went to the door.
The darkness, the sheets of rain and the lightning. . . . Going
was out of the question now: she'd have to sleep on his bed

for what was left of the night he told her, and he would lie on
the floor. She made no answer, but merely narrowed her
eyes as people do with a headache; and didn't move for a
moment. But then she finally crushed with her eggy fork
what was left of the charred and suffering moth to put it out
of its pain: stood up, and kicked off her shoes.

A yawning Augustine was spreading rugs for himself in a
corner when something made him turn. From the bed an
almost inaudible voice had said "I'm *not* ashamed, so you
needn't put out the lamp when you come". He looked: she
lay on her back stark naked, lit by a flicker of lightning
brighter than any lamp; and his loins were seared by a pang
that seemed the lightning itself. "I don't *want* you put out
the lamp," she repeated: then cupped her half-apple breasts
in her hands for her elbows to take her weight, and playfully
ran her two little feet up the wall like mice till her hips were
lifted clear.

His heart was beginning to thump so hard that it hurt his
chest. But when she heard him crossing the floor and rolled
on her side towards him, the arms she outstretched as he
loomed above her were truly the match-stick arms of a
child. . . . She couldn't know what she was doing! And what
was he doing himself? He suddenly bundled together her
scattered clothes, and dropped them almost on top of the
face that was lifted to kiss: "Get up!" he said in so brutal a
voice it surprised him, "And cover yourself".

She snatched a blanket right to her chin where she lay.
Her face went smaller and smaller, her eyes went larger and
larger, her mouth fell open and started to shake. He turned
away; but he couldn't go back and lie down, so paced the
floor with his mind in a turmoil. He didn't speak again,
for he didn't dare—as well as feeling ashamed in such
strangely conflicting ways. Again and again he saw those
feet running up the wall . . . and after, the pain in that small,
terrible face. There wasn't a sound from the bed; but nothing
would make him look.

Then daylight came, and Tony honked his horn from the road.

*

Augustine was gone. . . . As soon as her misery let her think, Ree dwelt for a while on making him care by hanging herself from a beam. She imagined the scene when they found her. . . . She hoped that God wouldn't mind too much —if there was a God, who could let things happen like this! But whether there was one or not there anyhow wasn't a rope, so instead she had to get into her clothes and go home to face the music.

A God? Till now she had never bothered her head about it. Everyone took Him for granted without a thought: like the air, which you never bother to *think* that you breathe. Even now her 'doubt' was only the fleetingest notion, in at one lobe-of-the-brain and out at the other, because quite simply it wasn't a question which ever really mattered a cent —and even less at a time when you suffered as much as this.

Chapter 28

SINCE Augustine had had no sleep and Russell so little
Tony and Sadie took turns at the wheel all day, leaving
those two to sleep in the back of the Buick in peace—if 'peace'
you could call it, or 'sleep', for Augustine! A-child-is-a-child-
is-a-*child*. . . . And again and again those feet running up the
wall, and the face that was lifted to kiss. . . . And the shaking
mouth in that face as he'd seen it last, with the blanket pulled
to her chin. . . . The journey passed like the kind of half-
waking, half-sleeping dream a delirious patient endures.
Augustine noticed almost nothing outside—barely the hot-
dog stand where they stopped for lunch, and a glimpse of
Lake Champlain one later time that he opened his eyes. The
insistent Goodyear hoardings mile after mile were more like
voices shouting than anything seen. However all day the
Buick excelled herself: more than two hundred and fifty
miles in eleven hours without any serious trouble. So just
before reaching the border they stopped for Tony to cross
the leads to a couple of plugs: that started her coughing her
head off, and made her seem all-too-ready to die in her
tracks if flagged, and hold up the traffic. Thus Tony proved
right: at Rouses Point they weren't even stopped, nor stopped
at Lacolle on the other side by the Mounties.

As soon as the border was crossed into Canada, Tony
began to wax lyrical over his 'logging' days: though he had
to admit it wasn't big timber for lumber, just second-growth
trash for the paper-mills in Chicoutimi (mills where the mill-
girls paddled about in tepid water, and all the machines were
hidden in steam). But Augustine heard only snatches. That,
and a bit about horses trained to haul out the stumps with a
single gigantic jerk; and a bit about building the stuff into
rafts. . . .

That face, as he'd seen it last. . . .

The next thing he heard, the logging seemed to be over
and Tony'd arrived where the Assuapmoussoin River runs
into Lake St. John. There he seemed to have joined the
canoes of the Pointe Bleue Indians just setting off for a
season's trapping up towards Hudson Bay (up there you
everywhere went by canoe, said Tony: there weren't any
trails in those northern forests apart from the 'portage' tracks
round the worst of the rapids and river-to-river at water-
sheds). Tony had still got plenty to tell when a back-tyre burst
within yards of a run-down roadhouse. This, on that ancient
model of Buick, meant changing a rim (not the whole of the
wooden wheel); and with bolts rusted in it called for a
hammer and chisel at least. So this seemed an omen to stop
for the night; and the place looked cheap.

While they sat round a table waiting to eat, Tony's story
went on. Mostly canoes weren't paddled *up*-stream (he explained) on turbulent rivers like this one: the Indians stood
up and punted, although they could none of them swim and
believed even pulling somebody out of the water to save his
life would bring you bad luck. . . .

But Augustine hardly listened: a-child-is-a-child-is. . . .

The banks of the river, said Tony, were lined with eerie
skeleton camps: for they never took down their tent-poles,
cutting them fresh each night (*is-a-child-is-a* . . .). Even these
days they still wrote letters and wrapped things in birch-
bark. They smelled. . . .

While Tony talked on and on and Augustine's mind went
round like a mill the roadhouse family ran in and out
arguing hotly in patois. Papa was a beady-eyed forty, and
thin: Maman a bleary-eyed thirty, and fat; and the number
of children ran into double-figures at least. They had caught
a wretched bullfrog and kicked it about like a ball, while the
Holy Virgin smiled from her lamp-lit niche and a red-haired
baby tobogganed around the room on his pot. They were
lively children all right—apart that was from the eldest, a
teenage girl (she looked Ree's age, or hardly older at all)
who sat in a corner alone. She was pretty, and rather sweet;

but the vacant look in her eyes as well as the cold contempt
the little ones showed her told you at once that she wasn't
all there. At first Augustine's gaze had wandered her way as
he thought about Ree; but she turned her skirt right back
on her lap as if no one was here to see, and carefully measured
the girth of a naked thigh at various points with a length of
string. Then she dipped the lemon a teasing brother gave her
in salt, and munched it with evident relish. In dumb-show one
of the children explained the red-haired baby was hers: while
everyone laughed, and seemed to expect the Yankee four to
join in. In spite of all which the oniony supper itself when it
came was remarkably good; and they went to bed replete.

Augustine's room was an attic whose door wouldn't shut,
and which smelt of citronella and ponds. The window was
set so low that even lying in bed you still couldn't see the sky:
you lay looking down through the dirty mosquito-screen at
a lake on the opposite side of the road. An old man was out
in a leaky boat in the path of the rising moon—singing, and
hauling in traps of eels. Augustine must have slept for a
moment and dreamed, for now he too was slipping about
in a boatload of squirming eels: yet he somehow wasn't
'Augustine' at all, he seemed to be Ree (or was it the eels
which were Ree? It was hard to make out). Then he woke,
and the eels disappeared. Instead, inside the lids of his eyes
lay Ree stark naked stretched on her back and cupping her
breasts in her hands as she ran her feet up the wall till her
loins were lifted clear. . . .

How many hundreds of times had Augustine been over
and over it all in his head! Someone under the Age of
Consent . . . *A-child-is-a-child—or*, IS *it?* Suppose. . . . But
what else could a person have done? No wonder this rent
him, and flung him about on his bed like people in Bible
times got flung about by a devil!

The door was open of course, and she must have been
barefoot: he heard no sound till he felt a tug at the sheet and
opened his eyes on somebody shadowy standing over his bed.

In panic he thought of the daft girl. . . . "Move," said Sadie, "and give a poor wench some room."

He moved. It was Fate, he had no more fight . . . but because of her onion-and-patchouli breath he kept his face as far as he could from hers.

With the cold-porridge parody over, he slept like a log. Then daylight came, and he woke to the sound beside him of stifled sobs.

"What's the matter?" he asked.

"I guess you was virgin?"

Augustine made no reply.

Then another sob, and "You're not very kind, not even to kiss me before it!" the girl complained.

Tony had told them his Indians smelled half-way between gipsy and fish: though he said that camping with them you hardly noticed it, sleeping on pungent spruce-boughs. . . .

Tony's shooting the rapids in Indian canoes had sounded exciting. Suppose . . . but no, he must get to the Governor-General's office in Ottawa quick as he could to apply for another passport. He'd cable Mary at once. . . . But first he had got to get everything clear: just bleating 'A-child-is-a-child-is-a-child' and 'What else could a decent fellow have done?' didn't do any good, the pain in that small terrible face as he'd seen it last was something that never could be undone —a weight that he couldn't crawl out from under. For he was the one who had clumsily done it to someone he loved, and who loved him. . . . Thus it was no good asking how else could a person with decent instincts behave: somehow he'd some-where got out of step . . . and this load on his heart, this leaden lump at the very core of his being seemed mighty close to what people like Mitzi must mean by 'sin'!

But there couldn't be 'sin' if there wasn't a God to offend— which there wasn't, of course. . . . And so, was it Freud whom Augustine in fact had offended against? Or the God Who Didn't Exist? Or would some wholly impartial observer, perhaps, have deemed him in Dutch with both?

A God 'like the air' (Ree would say) 'which everything breathes . . .'. 'Like the air' (as Mitzi might add) 'which certain creatures can also fly in—though even they have to learn. . . .'

Augustine turned his eyes to the low-set window and there, on the lake below, he saw reflected the rising sun. It seemed to be hung from the tips of a line of pines which bordered the very top of the picture upside-down.

BOOK TWO

The Meistersingers

Chapter 1

'GOD, like the air, is something which everything breathes —and certain creatures can fly in. . . .'

Think back now to the previous winter, when Mitzi's second retina slipped and she lost the last vestige of sight. She was always a rather detached and withdrawn sort of girl; and the shock of this total blindness at seventeen was bound to turn her in even more on herself, or on God—and that prime distinction no longer was easy to draw, now the strain of bearing what couldn't be borne had snapped like an overtaut wire. For now, when she probed to her own very innermost pinpoint 'I am', it was like looking into a tiny familiar room through a window and finding herself instead looking out—upon landscapes of infinite width: no longer her little 'I am' inside there at all, but only His great 'I AM'.

The times when a separate 'Mitzi' still seemed to exist were no more than a lingering nightmare she hoped to be rid of for ever as soon as she woke up after His likeness, a nun: no longer her little 'I will' there ever again, but only His WORD.

Her father regarded convents as more-or-less human litter-bins, meant for the tidy disposal of girls of good family Fate had unsuited for life in the world (as their 'natural refuge', to put it a little less crudely). The family too were agreed that now she was blind there was nothing else to be done with her. . . . Still, he hadn't been finding it easy to broach: so when she told him herself that she wished to become a nun, he was so relieved at her common sense that he kissed her.

Augustine (we know) looked on convents as dangerous webs like a spider's where any girl buzzing anywhere near one was doomed—in a trice she'd be whisked inside and wound hand-and-foot in a habit, sucked dry and the mummy

hung up out of sight before you said knife; and even Walther
had no more idea than Augustine—or Mitzi herself—that
convents were nowadays harder by far to get into than out
of. Her choice of that neighbouring Carmelite House at
Kammstadt where one of her aunts was Prioress seemed a
choice so obvious, surely he'd only to write to Adèle's holy
sister and tell her the girl would be coming. . . . So when the
Prioress wrote by return flatly refusing to even consider
taking a blind girl, it set him right back on his hunkers.

The Reverend Mother's refusal was firm. To her way of
thinking Carmelite Convents were no easy havens for mis-
fits but front-line posts of continual ghostly danger and
struggle, and nobody blind could possibly live to the difficult
Carmelite Rule. They were places of wonderful happiness,
given a true vocation; but, knowing her Walther, she felt
pretty sure that the whole crazy idea came from him: that
the girl had merely consented—no doubt in a state of
hysteria. Still, she had couched her letter in terms such as
Christian Charity coupled with upper-class manners and
family ties permitted. She stressed the Carmelites' Rule of
Silence: for surely even a Walther must understand the
unbearable strain of silence on someone already cut off by
her blindness! But then (not to seem too abrupt) she went
on to describe all the reading a nun has to do, both alone
and aloud: the Office, with all its intricate daily changes. . . .

At that, 'Hold hard!' thought Walther, beginning to get
back his wits: 'But what about Braille?' For there must be
missals and so on in Braille. Anyway, Carmelites weren't
some teaching or nursing Order whose need for their eyes
was obvious: these were Contemplatives merely, just kneel-
ing around all day and waiting for beautiful thoughts. So
perhaps the woman had got in the habit of being dis-
couraging: all she needed was just a little persuading—or
pressure. . . . And 'pressure' started him reckoning high-up
connections in Rome, where if need-be appeal could be made
to the Holy Father himself—since one wasn't the Freiherr
von Kessen for nothing!

So Baron Walther wrote off to Rome in that tiny feminine hand which belied his gigantic bulk and almost needed a microscope, confident all would come right if the right strings were pulled. As for Mitzi herself, she was quite unperturbed from the first. She was one who'd her Marching Orders from God; and even a Prioress cannot thwart Him.

Meanwhile, re-reading the Carmelite Mother's letter, Walther had noticed a postscript that 'Mitzi had better come to be talked-to'. All the Prioress meant was that somehow the girl must be shown how her true vocation lay *in* the world, but not *of* it—with possibly comforting talk about Lourdes; and she knew that she ought to see the poor girl and explain things herself, not let the parents or even the Parish Priest perhaps make a hash of it. Still, given Mitzi's frame of mind, it is hardly surprising if when she did 'go to be talked-to' the the interview passed not quite as the Reverend Mother expected.

That morning the children had gobbled their breakfasts, had filled their pockets with sausage and slung their toboggans and carried Augustine off for an all-day jaunt in the snow, which kept him far from the scene (and suspecting nothing) when presently Father and Mother and Mitzi and coachman set off on that fateful visit to Kammstadt. Their heavy old two-horse family sleigh was terribly slow, and they lunched on the way; but at last the horses came to a halt— and the sound of the sleigh-bells.

No one expects of a simple Carmelite House, with its score of Sisters, the grandeur of some mediaeval great abbey with hundreds: still, Walther was pained at finding this place didn't even look specially built. It was just a commonplace middle-class house, set back from a quiet middle-class road in a Kammstadt suburb behind a high garden wall; and this hardly seemed proper retreat for a nobleman's daughter, which made their pretended rejection of one even more outrageous. However, he pulled a bell in the garden wall and a smiling apple-cheeked Extern admitted them, one by

E

one, through a narrow wicket beneath a leafless acacia. They found it doubly dank in the frost-bitten yard inside, since the wintry afternoon sun was already too low to slant over that wall; and even the life-size St. Joseph with snow on his shoulders could hardly solace Walther's sense of fitness, guarding an all-too obvious former *back*-door.

They were taken first to a cubby-hole ten feet square where in secular days some drudge would have polished the boots and knives. Refreshments were brought them (the daintiest cakes, and a kind of tisane); and a wispy paraffin stove was lit, but it tempted no one to take off their furs. Then at last the Portress returned. She led them up back-stairs crusted with varnish and ushered them into the parlour.

This was a bare room, seemingly colder than even the yard outside: a room moreover with only three walls, for the fourth was mostly that fixed portcullis (or 'grille') of stout iron bars with spikes that you have to talk through to nuns. 'Like bloody bears in a zoo!' thought Walther, now more than ever disgruntled (that very morning his answers from Rome had arrived, and hadn't been helpful at all). But Mitzi—in tailor-made grey coat-and-skirt of thick winter cloth, with a neat felt hat and her long yellow hair looped up—sat down on the chair by the grille she was led to as gay as a cricket, and trying her best not to show it.

Chapter 2

THAT unusual, joyful calm; and indeed the rock-like look of that will. . . .

As soon as the Prioress drew back her curtain she saw that this was no docile creature dumbly obeying her father's orders; and no hysterical creature either—no desperate eel on a hook. She realised almost with shock that those big grey useless eyes were brimming with *joy*; and behind, from the shadows, she heard the Sub-prioress only too audibly gasp her astonishment. All she'd intended to say was better forgotten—leastwise the comfort, and talk about Lourdes: yet nothing could alter the fact that admission was out of the question, today's exaltation was something unlikely to last and a nun was a nun for a lifetime. . . . Silence on top of her blindness must sooner or later drive anyone 'odd' (the bugbear of every enclosed community): nowhere on earth would the girl find a convent imprudent enough to take her.

But better than simple refusal would be to convince this unusual child that she must have mistaken God's will—even then not by openly saying so, rather by helping her figure it out for herself how impossible blindness rendered the Carmelite Rule. . . . So the Prioress plunged, without any preamble, straight into details of Carmel's day: a day of eighteen hours in winter and nineteen in summer, "because our fatigue itself prays better than we could". The deafening clapper which woke them at half-past five (in summer at half-past four): the hours of said or silent worship in Choir: the solitude in their cells, the menial labour, the study and intricate reading-aloud: the strict enclosure, which meant that from now for the rest of her earthly life she would never once leave these walls. And throughout, like a kind of refrain, she stressed that almost perpetual silence "so dear to us who have eyes".

If the creature wasn't quite beyond measure pig-headed or even a trifle deranged, surely her own common sense must show her this just was not humanly possible. . . .

Nothing, however, seemed able to shake the girl's conviction that God had called her to live to this Rule, this Rule and none other. She barely pretended to listen, for given that premiss her logic was simple: to Him who required this of her all things were possible, therefore the means and conditions were up to Him to work out and in due course He would. 'Means' weren't Mitzi's concern: she was one who had Marching Orders from God, and was therefore no longer open to argument.

Thus time passed. As the darkening room grew darker and darker, the shining of Mitzi's eyes grew apparently even brighter. Faced with this yellow-haired, shining-eyed, shadowy object erect in the gloaming beyond those double-banked bars, the Prioress started all over again—determined this time to speak plainer. This time she would cross every *t* and dot every *i*. . . .

What was it, then, which so suddenly brought to the Reverend Mother's mind the late Pope Leo's words to the 'Little White Flower' (the fourteen-year-old Thérèse), when she too had made her exceptional plea for admission to Carmel? "All's well," the Holy Father had said: "All's well, if God wants you to enter you will." That child was now 'St. Thérèse of Lisieux': a bare generation ago, yet already a canonised Saint! And what was it made her ask herself— rather, what was it asked her almost like Peter dreaming at Joppa: 'Dare you call "blind" these eyes which the Lord's own Finger has touched, and *opened* for purposes of His own?'

Thus, even while she continued speaking, she found herself knowing she mustn't handle this case alone any longer in spite of the special grace of her office: those doubts which had entered her mind had seemed less thoughts of her own than like some alien signal, repealing the whole of her argument. . . . Could they be heavenly guidance? That very question meant that she needed advice: for a Carmelite knows too well the ways of the private schizoid mind to accept as authentic a 'voice' or a 'guidance' unless confirmed in the common mind of the Sisterhood. Putative guidance must always be laid before Council. . . .

Meanwhile Walther stirred on the chair he was much too large for. His bottom ached, and the woman seemed to be wandering. Parting with Mitzi was anyhow trying enough, and all this argle-bargle was taking too long. . . . He was taken quite by surprise when the Prioress all of a sudden dismissed them, a trifle abruptly.

Chapter 3

By now it was much too late to start home through the forest. But only the coachman was sent to sleep at a Gasthaus, for no one of consequence stays in public hotels and Walther's custom (whenever he had to stop in town overnight) was to billet himself on his man-of-business in Kammstadt, the lawyer Krebelmann.

Krebelmann was a Kammstadter born and bred: a man with obsequious mouth and contemptuous eyes and a nervous trick of shifting his papers about for emphasis when he spoke, and another ridiculous one of leaning back when he walked as though he carried a tray. But no one denied he was shrewd. The Krebelmann house was roomy and old and over-ornate, having once belonged to an infant heir whose affairs Herr Krebelmann managed, and then changed owners nobody quite knew how. It stood on Kammstadt's principal street; and was gloomy, as though it felt come-down-in-the-world nowadays with only a small-town lawyer's family in it.

Walther had found himself more and more seeking the lawyer's advice these days; and tonight the two had plenty of pressing things to discuss, while Frau Emma took Adèle and Mitzi away to talk women's-talk and to coo at the latest baby—or rather, to coo at the tiny upturned nose which was all that emerged to breathe from a sea of wool, like a miniature schnorkel.

*

Back in the Convent too there was anxious discussion. The Reverend Mother had spent a whole hour in private prayer, then summoned her Council and laid the problem before them. At first they took the common-sense view: they agreed

124

that blindness would handicap far too severely the strenuous life of a nun, and the applicant must be refused. But the other Council Sisters had never seen Mitzi, and when they asked the Sub-prioress what she had thought of the girl she said "That you just can't argue with Grace!" That loosened the Reverend Mother's tongue, and she spoke the name already so much on her mind: Thérèse Martin, the child who in spite of refusals had gained admission to Carmel when still under age—to become a Canonised Saint. Then, sorely perplexed, all four of them jointly offered the problem in prayer.

Mother Agnes of the Holy Face, the oldest Religious among them, eased the tension a bit when she asked the Prioress why she considered the question was one which need be finally settled now? This blind girl offered herself to God as a Postulant only. Postulants wear no habit: they're not even Novices yet, let alone Nuns—and may never become so, for not every tadpole grows to a frog. That rests in the hands of the Lord. Since only a 'No' at the present time need be final, why *not* allow her to come—thus leaving the Lord to reveal His will in His own good time?

Postulants take their place in the convent life, but only like guests who can leave any moment they want to. Surely this girl would presently leave of her own accord when she found it impossible? Also, said Mother Agnes, Advent was only a few days off (in the penitential season of Advent the silent seclusion of Carmelite life grows even more rigorous): "No normal time for a normal admission, I grant you; but coming in Advent surely this girl whom words can't convince will see for herself all the sooner that blind girls cannot go on . . .".

"Unless," the Sub-prioress added in a little more than a whisper: "Unless the Lord's will really *is* otherwise. . . ."

What Mother Agnes said turned the scales: the Council agreed, and presently so did the Chapter. Formally asked by Chapter, the Bishop gave his consent. Thus was that Wednesday the Twelfth of December settled for Mitzi's

admission as Postulant, albeit few of the Sisters imagined
she'd stop very long (perhaps barely the end of the year).

*

Mitzi of course was fully convinced this was final; and
Schmidtchen got down at once to preparing her darling's
(flannel and calico) trousseau.

Walther gave all the credit to Rome: for there *must* have
been high-up pressure to cause such a sudden surrender. Indeed, in his eyes, this all went to show that even if ancient
nobility nowadays cut little ice in the secular world in the
Church it still counted for something—at any rate, ancient
nobility backed up like his with a couple of Curial cousins (in
short, things always did come right in the end if the right
strings were pulled).

Returning at last from Munich to seek his bride, Augustine's
first intimation of what was afoot was the children's thunder-
bolt words as they flocked to the station to meet him: for no
one had thought to tell him before, since no one supposed
him concerned. A second Persephone's Rape! In his calendar
'Wednesday December the Twelfth 1923' would remain ever
after his unforgettable date of historic despair.

Those desolate hours he spent alone in the snowy forest
kept him again off-stage when Mitzi set off on her second
and final journey; and long before Walther and Adèle got
back he had fled from their castle and even their country. All
they found on return was a cryptic note saying nothing of
why he was going, or where. . . . He had humped his own
bags to the train and forgotten his guns: Otto said he seemed
half off his head.

Only ten-year-old Trudl, loving Augustine herself, had
spotted his trouble was love; and Trudl of course wasn't
telling.

Chapter 4

WEDNESDAY, December the Twelfth. . . . That heavy old two-horse sleigh had plenty of room for all four of them, Father and Mother and Mitzi and coachman—and luggage.

Soon after ten in the morning it passed from the comforting homely smell of cows through the hollowly-echoing castle gate, and crossed the causeway; but since there were drifts that day in the forest it didn't arrive at the convent gate till dusk. There they were once again left to wait in that tiny carbolicky room for an hour or more before the Portress, candle in hand, returned to lead the way to the parlour.

Mitzi could hear hushed voices behind the curtains; and even before she was called to the grille, and the curtains were drawn aside, she guessed that the struggle wasn't yet over. . . .

The time then was half-past six. At six, the Sisters had walked in procession to supper chanting the *De Profundis*: then eaten their meal in absolute silence without sitting down and in front of a skull on the table—for such was their custom. In other than seasons of penance, they'd then have adjourned for that pleasant hour of recreation together which, being one of the rare occasions they talked, was the hour most often ordained for receiving a Postulant. But this was Advent, with no such hour of recreation allowed them; and so tonight they'd assemble only briefly, and break their silence for only so long as was strictly needful for Mitzi's formal reception among them.

For Mitzi's reception, that is, if Mitzi was still unconvinced. . . . For now (as everyone knew) she was still barred out behind that grille in the parlour, and hearing one last attempt by all four Sisters-in-Council in concert: one final attempt to dissuade her from risking her own neck (and theirs) on the perilous cliff-face of Carmel. . . . "Elijah's unscalable mountain," she heard them describe it, "Where one weak climber imperils herself and impedes all the others."

But Mitzi, in spite of the strain of this one-against-all resistance, was not to be moved; and indeed how could she be moved when she knew herself driven on by Something— oh, greater by far than her reasoning self? So at last the useless reasoning ceased; and the sound of a key in a lock came to tell her the door of Enclosure at last stood open in front of her.

Hands reached over the threshold to guide her. A gentle pressure told her to kneel, and something was held to her lips which must be a crucifix. Rising again, she felt them turning her round to face the door she had come by and bow her farewell to the world. Then she heard that door on the world being locked, and her father blowing his nose.

*

Schacht (the financial dictator) had lately trebled a land-owner's troubles by stopping inflation so suddenly: cash was instantly scarce, and with bank-rate at 15 per cent credit impossible. Forests are largely capital work; but now all capital work on the land had to cease and men be laid off, or stretches of forest be sold—and who, these days, had the money to buy them? Mitzi's problem at least was settled, while all these other things weren't: so as soon as they reached the Krebelmanns' house tonight the Baron retired with his Man of Business, and started discussing his thorniest prob-lems at once. Walther might feel heavy-hearted at parting with Mitzi, but had to put Mitzi right out of his mind and get down to it—heavy-hearted or not.

It was well after midnight before the two men finally left their papers and sat down to supper. The women had long ago gone up to bed. The Krebelmanns' peasant slavey always breathed through her mouth, but now her eyes were gummy with sleep as well as she served hot consommé, sipped from cups while munching a wealth of steaming sausage and so on—and afterwards, beer.

When Walther at last went up to bed, his wife never stirred. Her face was hidden; but Walther concluded she must be uncommonly deeply asleep by the way she gave no sign even when he none-too-quietly kicked off his boots: and although it wouldn't be fair to call that a downright attempt to wake her, he found his wife's continued coma no small annoyance because, in spite of the beer, he didn't feel ready for sleep himself and wanted to talk. For now he had come to bed not even financial worries could keep his thoughts any longer from Mitzi: recalling the long-ago days when his little darling would climb on his lap to play with his watch-chain, and used to squeal with delight if he chucked her high in the air and pretended to let her fall. . . .

When finally Walther heaved his huge bulk on to the bed, it swayed and creaked: but still his helpmeet lay with her back towards him, as if he didn't exist. Above the head of the bed a pious picture oozed with unction. Facing its foot, a photograph hung of a furious Tanganyikan elephant rather too much enlarged. There was nothing to read. . . . He blew out the candle, and lay 'full of tossings to and fro till the break of day'—like Job. For it always tended to happen like this to Walther, that what had seemed so certain by day seemed much less certain by night. Now it was altogether too late he'd begun to have qualms: had their final solution of Mitzi been really the right one? His poor little Mitzi . . . as if her blindness wasn't burden enough! And now for the very first time he allowed himself to imagine what life must be like for a girl of her age, in that holy hen-coop. . . .

If only his wife would respond He reached out an arm towards her for comfort, and touched her. At that his senses began to stir: they were sluggish enough, but surely the marital act at least might serve to distract his thoughts. . . . He rolled against her; but Adèle jerked away, and left him only a pillow wet with her tears.

Chapter 5

MITZI had heard that door on the world being locked, then felt them lead her along with a guiding hand on each arm. They were taking her first to the Choir for her Consecration. From there she was brought in silence (already alert, in spite of her exaltation, to notice each landmark of turning or staircase or stumble) to what by its echoquality sounded a largish room that was filled with a gentle and happy twitter of voices, like birds. Here she heard herself being presented to each of the Sisters in turn (though with all those sacred names and identical-feeling clothes, how hopeless it seemed attempting to know them apart!) and felt her face being kissed all over by welcoming nuns.

But then the Sisters returned to the Choir, and Mitzi found herself left with a single strong young hand on her arm and a single strong young voice in her ear: for each new arrival in Carmel was given some senior novice as 'Guardian Angel', to help her and guide her and show her the ropes. This strong young voice (which had some sort of foreign accent, she noticed) was hers. Her 'Angel' conducted her first to the novices' own Recreation Room, and then to their own place of prayer (for except at Mass they weren't allowed in the Choir). Then they returned from the Novices' Wing to the Nuns' own, equally freezing, part of the house.

In Carmelite convents, even at times when speech is allowed, nobody speaks in passages or on the stairs any more than one ever speaks in the cells themselves: so Mitzi kept being drawn into specially-licensed cubby-holes, called 'speech-corners'. There she'd be given Angelic advice rapidfire: for example, that underclothes folded and slept on in bed aren't quite so icily cold to the skin in the morning. At last, however, they entered the vacant cell where a Postulant always spent her first few days as the Sisters' guest, in their

special care. Here her Angel silently helped her unpack
and presently left her, in cold and darkness and strangeness,
alone—with her face still covered in kisses that smelled of
beeswax and incense and soap.

That Angel's accent . . . it sounded a bit like the German
our visiting English cousin had spoken. 'Augustin' . . . Mitzi
smiled, recalling his gentle voice and his strangely silent
shoes; and his clothes, with their faint smell of peat-smoke. . . .
But also that terrible time when he'd tried to read Schiller
aloud (though he'd meant it kindly enough). All the same,
her Angel was anyhow probably Swiss not English; and
surely this wasn't the moment—with Home and the World
so newly behind her—to think about anyone out of the past?
Instead she had better get down at once to discovering all
she could of this cell she was housed in. She stretched out her
arms to measure its length and width, and found it so small
she could certainly never get lost in here! Her hands then
found the hairy blanket, spread over a mattress of straw so
round, being newly stuffed, that she feared rolling off in her
sleep. Laid across it. . . . Of course, all this cold cardboard-
like cloth was tomorrow's black Postulant's dress, with its
cape. Then she knelt to explore the plain plank bed underneath, on its trestles. Below that bed, her hands found a basin
with something rough folded over it—something which must
be her towel. . . . Where then was the water to put in it?
Turning too quickly on hands and knees, she nearly knocked
over the tall crock of water with ice in its neck which stood
by the wall.

Still down on all-fours, and with hands that were quickly
growing too numb with cold for the task, she explored this
wall till they came on an empty shelf, and above it a sill;
and above that again her fingers stuck to window-glass
coated with frost.

*

Meanwhile, downstairs—and crouched on folded pads of

their habits, because they never used chairs—the Reverend
Mother and Novice Mistress discussed this problem-daughter
of theirs: this girl who had verily taken Carmel by storm.
For whether or not she stayed they had to make plans 'as if'.
So what about daily tasks? This being winter, all work in the
garden must be ruled out (though even in summer, how
could she ever be trusted to weed without pulling up plants?).
And as for most normal indoor tasks. . . . At least, the il-
luminating of texts and work on vestments and altar-linen
were certainly out.

"She could . . . could she count altar-breads?"

"Surely—and even be taught to pack them, by feel. It's
wonderful what they can learn: she might even be taught to
feed the chickens, in time." The Prioress covered her own
eyes to see what blindness felt like, using her free hand to
grope.

Then what about lessons? Before her profession a nun must
have studied Theology, Dogma, Canon Law and Church
History, also getting the Carmelite Rule and the Con-
stitutions almost by heart: with someone who couldn't read
for herself this would mean much reading aloud by her
fellow-students, and much individual teaching—if scholarly
standards weren't to be lowered. . . .

"Of course they mustn't be lowered!" The Reverend
Mother uncovered her eyes: "Her Instruction ought to be
even stricter and drier than most: for our Daughter's
principal danger lies in too much emphasis on the Sublime,
on anything tending to introspection." She paused, and her
hand went back to her eyes. This blindness already had
raised the girl to a more than natural pitch of nervous
intensity, something quite out-of-key with the fruitful hum-
drum of daily monastic life as every Religious knows it. That
had to be watched. . . . "So far as the Rule allows, she
mustn't be too much alone—especially now at the start."
She paused again. "She's going to find our sense of community terribly hard to acquire, in all this silence and
solitude."

"True, Mother." Even Carmel's Enclosure itself (thought the other) is separate not from but deeply within the created world, like a beating heart.

"Think how many girls anyhow come here supposing the only souls they have to bother about are their own! I believe I was like that myself; and for one like our little Maria upstairs, cut off from her sisters by blindness as well. . . ."

As the Novice Mistress rose to tend the guttering candle, she tried to think back to her own novitiate. Yes, she too had been slow to discover that those whom God has joined together in Carmel are never truly asunder: not even when 'there is neither speech nor language among them', like David's nights and days, and his stars. But one thing was more important still; and the two nuns fell in a troubled silence, aware without needing words that the same thought occupied both their minds. The first thing of all to be learned in the life of Religion is Humble Obedience, for that is the source of all other graces; but how could they ever teach this to one so certain she knew God's will and everyone else was wrong? Richly endowed as her spirit was, this girl had a terrible lot to learn before she could even begin to understand what it meant becoming a nun. . . . As the Prioress prayed for the requisite help and strength (for this daughter's calls on her wisdom and love would be boundless) she heard the other one say: "It is no easy cross that is laid on us, Mother".

The Carmelite's cross: that empty cross awaiting its human lodger.

Then the two nuns took their candle and climbed to the newcomer's cell. They moved, on their rope-soled shoes, with that wholly inaudible glide which Contemplatives always adopt to avoid disturbing each other on carpetless floors, and in empty echoing rooms; and they opened the door without knocking. Mitzi, absorbed, was quite unaware of them. Just as their candle's beam shone into her pitch-dark cell her wandering hands had encountered the cross hanging over the bed; and there they had stopped their wandering, feeling it over and over with longing and awe. The two women stood there in silence, and watched her feeling and feeling that plain wooden cross as if storing its feel so deep in her fingers that fingers alone ever after would call up its substance and shape of their own accord.

Loth after all to disturb her, the older women withdrew still unheard. But with troubled minds: for in Mitzi's candle-lit face there was something which only increased their foreboding. Last thing tonight, at the end of their hour of meditation in Choir, they would say a silent Ave of special intention for Mitzi because of that look in her face.

Downstairs again, "Perhaps she had better be put in the laundry to work?" the Novice Mistress suggested.

The Prioress nodded. For there, with the hot smell of God steaming up in her nose from wet wool and wet cotton and bubbling suds and His touch in the silent correcting hands that were laid on her own when she made a mistake. . . . Where else could she better learn that a Carmelite's God is not only the God of the Choir and the lonely cell—*if* He gave her the grace to learn?

Chapter 6

H ER fingers numbed by exploring, Mitzi alternately rubbed her hands for warmth and nursed them between her knees.

As the Nuns had foreseen, shut up in her private darkness inside the general darkness she tended to find this Carmel where God had sent her essentially solitude: somewhere meant for the lonely perfecting of separate souls. A community of Solitaries. . . . Down in the Choir the nuns were singing the Antiphon after Complin and distant snatches reached her, even up here, of a thin unaccompanied wailing monotone seemingly better attuned to some desert anchorite's cell than a church. As if only their bodies assembled (she thought), their souls still climbed alone each one her separate Jacob's-ladder to God.

A solitude—and a silence. At eight the big bell tolled its nightly reminder that now 'Great Silence' began, when no one would speak to another till after Prime in the morning. All outside sound was muffled by snow. In the Choir the Miserere was heard, as the Sisters punished themselves in the dark on behalf of a suffering sinning world and the holy souls of the dead; but everywhere else there was absolute quiet, with nowhere the tiniest sound. Not the drip of a tap, not a mouse.

Time passed, with Mitzi still blessing her blindness for making her even more wholly alone in the presence of God than the others. But then, through this outer unending silence, she started to hear from inside herself as it were a gnawing: faintly, a drip . . . drip . . . drip . . . like a leaking out through a hole. Now that the struggle was ended, the strength she had borrowed to win it was draining out of her, going. . . .

Then even that 'air' which everything breathed and Mitzi
had thought she could fly in—her wings found suddenly
nothing to beat on, no God any longer there to support them.
She called on her fingers to summon that sacred resource
which their tips had stored up; but her fingers disowned her,
and sending them groping across the wall revealed her cross
itself as now no more than two joined-up pieces of wood. She
wasn't in Carmel's 'solitude' any longer but truly alone—in
the felt absence of God.

Mitzi had learned from one earlier time like this to trust in
God just as much when He wasn't there. But why must she
bear yet again this unbearable separation? The time before
she had still been down in the easy foothills; but now she had
climbed to the point of no return with a lifelong ascent of
Carmel lying in front of her, looking (as everyone said it
would) too hopelessly steep and rough and dark to climb
by herself alone. Yet this lost climber-in-spirit had learned
already it wasn't the slightest use looking over her shoulder,
back at the fading glimmer behind where He'd left her: lost
sight of, He reappears only in front. Those comforting left-
behind lights below in the valley . . . though long ago
shining above her as guiding stars they were now but the
empty shells of God, which God one-by-one had discarded
unfolding before her.

A God for ever unfolding: His presence a journey—and
endless. Abandoned on quick-rock shifting under her feet
where she couldn't even stand still, she must choose the
darkest part of the darkness ahead to climb into until it might
please the Eternal Becoming to show Himself *new*. . . .

'Abandoned'? But how could He ever absent Himself for
a moment from Carmel, His Holy-of-Holies? Rather it must
be she who had somehow absented herself from Him. She,
who had felt so certain the will she obeyed had been none of
her own, but His. . . . She, who had gone on insisting when
Reverend Mother and all those holy Sisters had said in their

wisdom 'No' . . . Had God all along been speaking through
them, had she made a dreadful mistake in persisting?

She knelt by the bed determined to pray, for she must
have an answer at all costs—straining in prayer every
muscle her soul possessed. 'Peradventure He sleepeth, and
must be awaked. . . .' Yet how could anyone pray with God
not there to be prayed to? Her prayers with nowhere to go to
could only echo inside the empty walls of her head; and that
strength wherever it came from was now so utterly gone and
she felt an exhaustion so total she dropped off to sleep where
she knelt, and did it without even noticing.

*

Nine! Now a whole hour of Silence had passed. It was time
for Matins and Lauds; and the bell woke Mitzi, still on her
knees. She was stiff with cold, and her underneath cheek on
the blanket was numbed and creased.

She undressed and crawled into bed. But the blanket was
cold; and by now she hadn't the warmth in her body to
warm it. Her teeth were wanting to chatter: she clenched
them, and lay as still as she could. But her neck felt especially
cold and bereft: for she'd loved the hair that was shorn,
treating it often like some warm pet animal when she was
lonely. Moreover her head was beginning to spin with things
and places and people, whirling in any order of time. The
day when total blindness had finally struck her. . . . She saw
once again that black cloud under her eyelids curtaining
more and more—to the sound of sleigh-bells buffeted back
by close-packed trees, and a brotherly pressure against her
side like an ignorant Siamese Twin. . . . Then her father's
droning bulk the evening before; and across the table, behind the rainbow of candles, a blur with an English voice so
slurred with wine that he dropped some frightful clanger. . . .

Then came Schmidtchen's lullaby voice—for darling
Schmidtchen always came in the dark when called:

> Der Mops kam in die Küche
> Und stahl dem Koch ein Ei . . .

Bells, and peculiar kisses: identical-feeling clothes, and in-
cense-and-cleanliness smells. . . . Bells and chants, double-
counterpointing Schmidtchen's incessant circular ditty,

Der Mops kam in die Küche . . .

But now behind the Leitmotiv of that comforting voice the
slow giant tick of the clock in the castle roof grew louder,
the smell of fox and of human urine stronger: a cold quivering
nose was thrust in her hand, while something ammoniac
hung from a rope which creaked—then turned to the
creaking stays of Emma Krebelmann, crooning into a smell
of baby. . . .

But bit by bit the kaleidoscopic phantasmagoria slowed,
till little was left except the sensation of ghastly increasing
bodily cold.

Da kamen all Möpse
Und gruben ihm ein Grab . . .

She was plunging up to her waist in the courtyard snow (in
spite of the queer idea of a 'presence' felt so close that she only
need stretch out a hand for help—but couldn't).

Der Mops kam in die Küche . . .

Tremendous, the caged-in kitchen heat at home when anyone opened the kitchen door! But instead a shiver shook her
shoulders, and soon from head to foot she was shivering.

Da nahm der Koch ein Löffel
Und schlug den Mops entzwei,

She could see it coming—the cook's enormous ladle of ice—
as a single paroxysmal shiver shook her. She jumped out of
bed in her flannel nightgown, swinging her arms like a cabby:
she pummelled her body and worked her limbs, she bounced
up and down on the floor of her cell (but barefoot, and trying
to make as little noise as she could) till her heart was bumping about in her ribs like a flustered hen in a basket: pumping
the sluggish blood in her arteries back into pricking hands
and feet, and even her dithering brain.

As she danced from foot to foot, she found herself looking calmly at something she never had really looked at before: at herself, from outside. Or rather (panting a bit as she bent and stretched) at God-and-herself, from outside—this minuscule Mitzi, an infinitesimal grain of sand which because it had once been lifted and swirled in the tide had come to think of the tide as her own to command.

That sensible 'guardian angel' whose practical talk she realised now she had dared to despise, this girl (she thought as she got back in bed) was the one to be copied—and humbly, if ever she hoped to become remotely a Sister pleasing to God.

She gave a prodigious yawn, and settled herself for sleep. ... Then was bounced out of bed by a clapper that went off outside like a ton of knights in armour falling downstairs. It was half-past five, and her first Carmelite day had begun.

Chapter 7

Emma Krebelmann too must rise before it was light, with all those children to wake and be given their breakfasts: with ten-year-old Sigismund laid up in bed with a broken rib, and Liese and Lotte and little Ernst to be muffled in scarves and packed off to school—and likely as not Ernst's breeches to mend before he'd be fit to be seen. This morning, moreover, she'd meant to make some special coffee herself for the Baron and Baroness, ready for Gretl to take to their room when they woke.

Gretl of course was down much earlier still; and the Mistress had found the wood already blazing and roaring away in the kitchen stove, where now she stood with the whole of her mind in that savoury simmering jug—till startled out of her wits by the stertorous snort (so close that it sounded inside the kitchen itself) of an old horse clearing the sleep from its nose, and a tiny jingle of bells. She turned to the window. Close outside in the courtyard the sleigh was standing, its candle-lamps paled by the growing daylight and clouds of steam hanging over the horses' heads in the frosty air.

Emma hadn't bargained for Baron and Baroness making so early a start, and a splash of coffee nervously spilled on the stove-top filled the kitchen with instant aroma. "Gretl!" she called, "Dear God be quicker can't you with heating that milk, and take the rolls out of the oven, and—*Gretl!*" she screamed, with both hands plucking the curlers out of her hair: "Where on earth have you put that English marmalade specially kept for the Baron?"

By now she could hear the guests descending, and rushed to the stairs just in time to snatch out of their sight little sleepy Ernst without any breeches at all. But it wasn't till Baron and Baroness finally left that she got back sufficient

poise to send Liese and Lotte back up to their room like
scalded cats, for Liese to properly brush her hair this time
and Lotte to put on stockings which matched.

"How many days till Christmas?" Liese and Lotte argued
it hotly, dawdling along to school with their arms round
each other's necks—each one saying the other one ought to
go back to infant school if she didn't know how to count.
Then they heard the town-hall bell, let go of each other and
started to run leaving Ernst behind to be late for his different
school alone.

'Little' Ernst. . . . In fact he was rather large for a six-year-
old, slightly running to fat; but with big brown eyes which
looked at you straight. At school he was one who suffered
more often than most from what the children called 'head-
nuts': a rap on the skull with bony knuckles in passing, which
Lehrer Faber used as a cure for little boys dreaming. For
Ernst was given to dreaming in school, and to filling his
slate with dragons instead of sums.

*

Still, Christmas came to the Krebelmanns' house in the
end whoever was right; and what Ernst had asked from the
Christus Kind was a violin of his own. But his father couldn't
stand noise, and the boy was anyhow much too young: so
the Christus Kind had made a mistake on purpose and what
he got was a clockwork train. He was so disappointed he
secretly hammered it flat (if he couldn't get strings, at least
he could get percussion).

Christmas came to the Castle; and there the table was
spread with silver and china and beautiful tulip-shaped
glasses, white ones for drinking beer and dark blue ones that
were filled with berries and flowers; and everyone laughed
and joked till the meal was over.

Then came the time for the presents. Behind closed doors
Walther was playing 'Stille Nacht, Heilige Nacht' on the

Steinway, and all the others stood in a line outside singing the melody—Trudl's treble voice and Adèle's contralto and Franz's tenor and Uncle Otto's bass, while Irma managed a thin clear descant (the tears running down her face, as they always did when she sang). Even the twins stopped turning somersaults over the sofa; and only Mitzi was absent.

At last the doors were opened. The children held their breath and gasped at the tree with its star on top, and the tinsel 'angels'-hair' wound in-and-out of candles that glittered on all the presents in shiny wrappings; and nobody wanted to move.

Christmas came to the Convent, too; and Mitzi found that nuns knew how to be gayer than ever anyone was at home— the air seemed humming with happiness.

Chapter 8

Now it was 1924 at last: New Year's Day, and then the Feast of Epiphany. One more week, and Mitzi might have a visit. . . . But Adèle was torn in two about whether or not to go, for now both twins had mumps and Irma seemed to be sickening. Still (thought the mother, divided), Mitzi was bound to be homesick and counting the days: it seemed too cruel to disappoint her by stopping at home.

But Walther refused point-blank to come: he said he had "too much business to do". Neither could Franz, for he'd gone off skiing to Innsbruck; and Otto had had to take his leg to Munich, to have its chafing socket adjusted. So Adèle would have to spend a night at the Krebelmanns' house alone; and Emma Krebelmann frankly bored her. . . . Of course, she *might* take Schmidtchen. . . . Indeed with a Hospital Sister installed in the house, and the two already at daggers-drawn, it might be as well to keep old Schmidtchen out of the sick-room awhile.

When the Krebelmanns learned that Freifrau von Kessen would once again honour their house with her presence (but this time without the Freiherr, and only Fräulein Schmidt in attendance), Emma began to grumble. It seemed to her once too often. But Gustav insisted. Indeed he was shocked: such un-Christian thoughts were unheard-of (it isn't the rich that a Christian ever leaves out in the cold). So Liese and Lotte were bidden to share a bed to allow this funny old Fräulein Schmidt to share their room (there were plenty of rooms, but it saved a stove); and once the convent visit was over, Adèle retired again to that creaking bed— but this time facing the charging elephant all alone. Yet she couldn't sleep; and indeed she wished she had never come, for the child had seemed so remote when she saw her mother—had made so little pretence that the visit gave her pleasure, but seemed to be counting the minutes till time was up and her visitor had to go.

Behind her remotemess the child had looked so happy. . . . Yes; but how could one ever have guessed that darling Mitzi would truly be happier there in that gloomy place than at home? Or was that bluff, and in fact she couldn't forgive the mother who'd let them put her in there? No, for her happiness looked so serene it could never have been assumed. . . .

Still, it was hard to believe that once-on-a-time one ever had been her Mother.

*

Mitzi lay awake too. Her Mother had told her that Uncle Otto was gone to Munich because of his leg. . . . She recalled his parade-ground bark as he'd read her aloud that bit out of Thomas-à-Kempis—as if 'passing out of one's self' were an order as simple as 'Halt! Form fours!'

But that air, which *everything* breathed. . . . Who was she, to have ever supposed it was meant for a Mitzi to fly in? Her Uncle Otto was just a typical breather who never attempted to soar: yet surely a better Religious than she was, because his religion was humbler and simpler—made fewer demands on the Lord. . . . For the Universe wasn't a two-some of Mitzi and Mitzi's Maker, He'd millions of other Christians to care for. His infinite kindness and goodness had seen her through one particular difficult patch, that was all.

She was now quite resigned to facing the darkness ahead with the confidence born of no longer expecting to see *any* dazzling light.

Chapter 9

WALTHER said 'business' kept him from visiting Mitzi, when really he couldn't face seeing his daughter behind those bars. Yet 'business' was partly true, as 'bars' reminded him: Toni Arco's letter from Landsberg Fortress had lain on his desk for a week. Toni wanted his help, and something had got to be done. . . .

Set on its little hill in its charming bower of trees, Landsberg hardly looked like a fortress: more like a very select sanatorium. 'Fortress-confinement' was strictly intended for Gentlemen, ones who had merely burned their political fingers somehow and lived as guests of the garrison rather than prisoners. "Landsberg was never meant as a common clink", wrote Toni, "for dumping the criminal rabble they've started sending here now."

Sharing his sylvan retreat with this gutter-mob gave him a pain in the neck. Even walking alone in the frosty garden the young Count couldn't avoid them: bare knees lobster-red from the cold in the shortest of leather shorts, bull-throats bulging from open shirts with floral braces or Tyrolese jackets and bursting with raucous song. . . . Of course he'd complained to the Governor: still, couldn't Walther perhaps do something about it? Pull some string, and get this riff-raff removed to where they really belonged?

Walther sighed. He would pull what strings he could. . . . But Mr. Justice-Minister Gürtner was no friend of Walther's, and partial to this particular rabble. Poor dear Toni, his nose must be right out of joint. Just four years ago, when Toni had burned *his* political fingers (though all he had done was shooting the Communist tyrant Eisner dead), Landsberg had felt so proud of him, made him their guest-of honour. . . . However, today they had Hitler and all his

pards from the Munich Putsch in the place and no doubt
they made it abundantly clear to Toni who was the White-
headed Boy of Landsberg now.

When Franz gets back we must send him to comfort
Toni. Meanwhile one could only counsel patience: these
clowns were merely there on remand, next month they'd be
sent to Munich and tried for their part in that clownish
Ludendorff Putsch. Then Hitler himself would be almost
certainly run out of town and deported to Austria, being an
alien. Once he was over the frontier, Hitler'd be Austria's
trouble; and gossip said the Vienna police had a warrant out
for him—cheating his sister out of their father's pension, as
well as dodging the call-up. . . .

Walther had got thus far when Otto rang up from Munich.
The doctors had found that it wasn't merely his artificial leg
which needed attention: the pain and ulcers he suffered were
due to his shattered hip-joint shedding fragments of bone,
and called for the surgeon's knife. They said it had better be
done at once—that same afternoon. . . .

It seemed the very last straw to Walther, thus to be left on
his own in such difficult times. For it meant he would now
have to do all the paper-work normally left to his brother;
and as for finding the papers, among those mountains of
stuff all over Otto's office how could he hope to discover
where anything was?

But worse was to come. Three days later a call came
through from the eminent surgeon himself. He wasn't too
happy about his patient: the operation had been successful,
but Colonel von Kessen's temperature raged and he might
be threatened with septicaemia. Walther of course was
aghast: did this mean (he asked) that his brother's con-
valescence was likely to prove a prolonged one? On that the
Professor hummed and hawed, but the upshot was that he
wanted Walther or one of the family there on the spot.

Walther himself couldn't possibly go. But Franz had got
back just then from the mountains; and so, instead of visiting

Toni in prison, he found himself sent post-haste to visit his uncle in hospital.

*

There Franz learned from the nurses the secret reason behind the surgeon's alarm, which couldn't be put in a telephone call. Delirious half the time, the Colonel-Baron was talking—or rather, shouting; and shouting all sorts of things which shouldn't be overheard about caches of Great War weapons the Allied Commission had failed to unearth, about people who called themselves 'Sondergruppe Something' and German officers training somewhere abroad. . . . They had shut the babbling Colonel away in a room by himself; but his voice was awfully strong—and just suppose some informer went to the French!

So Franz sat down by his uncle's bed to listen with care; and his blood ran cold. To begin with, 'Special-group R' was clearly no wildcat private affair as the nurses supposed, but a highly secret Bendlerstrasse Department—concerned not only with cadres of German officers secretly sent to the Bolshevik Army for training but German armament factories building on Russian soil: with a Junkers factory somewhere near Moscow secretly turning out German army aircraft (which, under the Treaty, Germany wasn't allowed to build herself); and all over Russia German factories turning out German poison-gas, German shells. One even caught whiffs of a pigeon-hole plan for a joint Russo-German pincer-movement on Poland, to wipe their common enemy right off the map and restore their old common frontier. As well as von Seeckt (the Commander-in-Chief), such names as General Schleicher came in; and Radek, and Trotsky. . . .

Von Seeckt in league with Trotsky—the Archangel Michael in league with Satan himself? Yet that (thought Franz) was these simple soldiers all over: too keen on repairing Germany's body to spare one thought for Germany's soul. Franz had long been aware of the kind of thing his uncle was

up to but not its extent; and his hair stood on end at all this
high-level stuff. . . . Uncle Otto had got to be silenced. He
asked the Sister point-blank how soon the Colonel was
going to die; but she shrugged her shoulders. He went to the
surgeon next, telling him bluntly his patient's ravings en-
dangered the Reich and demanding some sedative drug. But
the surgeon shook his head. He said he was well aware of the
tenor of Colonel von Kessen's febrile delusions but waved
that aside, since a doctor could only prescribe on purely
medical grounds. After which he conceded the case was
indeed a proper one for sedation and mentioned that this
had already been tried; but he said that the Colonel's resistance to sedative drugs was abnormal.

"Then what about something stronger—Good Lord!"
asked Franz, enraged by this Hippocratic hypocrisy:
"Knock-out drops, to keep him under for good?"

The surgeon looked at the angry young fellow in silence:
nor was it easy to tell what the Great Man was thinking,
because of his hooded eyes and a face criss-crossed with
duelling scars. But then he went on to explain that the latest
treatment for sepsis was something he called 'ozone', a
variant kind of oxygen formed by electric discharges. You
bubbled it through the wound; and he'd heard of numerous
cases where obstinate festering wounds had improved. The
machine was a bit too noisy for use in a public ward, but the
sterilising effect of this extra unstable oxygen atom released
from what was in fact no more than an oversize oxygen
molecule. . . .

Weeping tears of rage, Franz hurried back to the patient's
room. There he found an electric cable already plugged into
the wall and pink rubber tubes running under the bedclothes. Then they switched the contraption on; and the
normal hospital smell of carbolic and ether was drowned in
the smell of electric sparks. But surely the coil must be
wrongly adjusted to make such a clatter? The noise was
frightful, preventing you hearing one single sentence the
patient uttered. . . .

Franz wasn't an absolute fool, though always a little slow in the uptake.

When the mercury dropped, the delirium ceased and the patient began to get better, the surgeon hid his surprise that the novel treatment had worked. Soon Otto began to complain that the ozone tickled him bubbling through his flesh. There were outraged tears in his voice, for the German Officer fully prepared for pain or death still can't endure being tickled—it's not in the Code, nor catered for in his training. So Otto was moved to the 'bath-ward' (another latest idea) where he sat in a bath of running hot water without any surgical dressings at all, drinking down gallons of beer and eating enormous steaks with the sweat pouring off his face.

Three days later, after a huge discharge of pus and bone, the patient returned to his bed now well on the road to recovery. Franz might perhaps be able at last to find himself comforting Toni in Landsberg after all.

Chapter 10

WITH Hitler locked up in Landsberg the Nazi Movement had come to a sorry pass. At the moment of Hitler's arrest he had scribbled a note appointing as Caretaker-Leader—*Rosenberg*: hardly the livest of wires, and one whom most of the others disliked and despised. But 'Caretaker-Leader' of what? For the Party was banned, its printing offices closed and all the people who really mattered arrested or fled abroad.

Göring was now in Vienna, and still laid low by the wound he got in the Putsch. A Jewish doctor had patched him as best he could, then his friends had smuggled him over the frontier to Innsbruck; and there he had lain in hospital, wracked with pain from the gash in his groin and heavily drugged, till his wealthy wife arrived in Vienna and moved him into a decent hotel.

Another who'd managed to make Vienna was 'Putzi' Hanfstängl, Hitler's patron among the Intelligentsia. There, at first, he had filled in time with Esser and Rossbach plotting a raid under arms to rescue Hitler from Landsberg—till Hitler himself put a stop to it. Left thereafter with nothing to do, Putzi conceived the plan of seeking out Hitler's widowed sister here in Vienna. This was the sister (according to Walther) whom Adolf Hitler had bilked; but Putzi'd a hazy idea that she might have her brother's ear, and he wanted her on his side.

However, when Putzi found her at last in a rotting tenement, living in squalid poverty, quite such an abject couple as she and her teenage daughter Geli hardly seemed likely to have much influence: still, he had taken them out for a drink. Geli was brassily pretty, and afterwards Putzi carried her off to a music-hall. Pretty—but sentimental and commonplace: Putzi was soon convinced he was wasting his time, in spite of her bubs—and to think that this little piece was the Führer's only niece!

Moreover he longed to be home for Christmas, so presently took the risk. This time he crossed the frontier on foot, through a railway-tunnel, wearing dark glasses and hiding his famous jaw in mutton-chop whiskers (his height he couldn't disguise). But once he got home nobody seemed very keen to arrest him, and soon he moved about Munich openly. Thus when the Landsberg Nazis were moved to the former Infantry School on the Blutenbergstrasse for trial, Putzi was one of the first to visit his friend in prison.

Putzi had brought his little boy with him to see 'Onkel Dolf' as a birthday treat; and had struggled, in spite of the noise of the tram, to impress on the child what a Great *Good* Man this was. For the nonce the Baddies had locked him up in their dungeons; but one day 'Uncle' would burst his chains, and triumph. . . .

'Dungeons, and chains. . . .' What a sorry let-down for the child it was when instead of all that a kindly blue-coat—blessed with a wonder-moustache like bicycle-handlebars—led them along to a bright, well-furnished and almost cheerful room overlooking the Marsplatz and filled with the lovely sound of trains! For there stood Uncle Dolf—and there wasn't a chain in sight. . . . But the child soon forgot his first disappointment, entranced once more by his darling 'Uncle's' lively affection ate eyes and the man-to-manway he spoke to you, using his hands when he spoke and rocking heel-and-toe with his head on one side when he listened. But most of all was the child enslaved by that magical voice: there were notes which set the table itself vibrating, and tingled the tiny fingers which touched the wood. Then Uncle climbed on a chair to fish about on the wardrobe-top for his secret box of sugar-cakes, afterwards setting the child on his knee to share them and talking to Putzi over the little boy's head. As for his coming trial, he simply pooh-poohed it: he'd only to tell from the dock just a few of the truths he

F

knew about General Lossow and all *his* plots to blow the
whole prosecution sky-high.

This Putzi passed over in silence but inwardly didn't
believe it. Whatever he'd said in the tram his political hopes
were shattered: High Treason was hardly a charge you could
just laugh off! Let this optimist cut all the capers he liked in
court, conviction was certain; and long before Hitler came
out of gaol they'd all be forgotten. This was their own fault of
course for banking too much on any one man: without him,
it all falls to pieces. . . . The future looked irredeemably black.
It was nice to find his friend so cheerful, but even euphoria
can't do away with facts.

*

Meanwhile the date of the trial was drawing near.

Visiting Otto in hospital, one day Franz brought with him
Reinhold Steuckel (his friend the Eminent Jurist), laden with
fruit and copies of *Simplicissimus*. Reinhold indeed had insisted on coming. Franz had brought him with some re-
luctance, for surely the ultra-intellectual Reinhold and Otto
the simple soldier couldn't have much in common—but only
to find them hitting it off together at once. For during the
War they had served in the same part of the line; and Franz
was amazed to discover how much his illustrious elder
civilian acquaintance seemed to know about up-to-date
Army politics, Army gossip.

Presently Reinhold spoke of the coming trial. Otto would
only be fit for discharge two days before it began, and certainly couldn't endure long hours in court; but Reinhold
insisted that Franz at least stopped on for the fireworks, and
promised to get him a seat. Ludendorff: after Hindenburg,
surely the greatest name that the War had produced, though
admittedly somewhat blown-upon since. . . . Half the
journalists in the world, said Reinhold, were coming to
Munich to see the great General Ludendorff tried for High
Treason. "But don't you bother your head about Generals!
No, the fellow to watch is the late Lance-Corporal: how will

he play *his* cards? Will he shift all the blame on to Ludendorff
—shoulders broad enough surely to bear it—in which case
the worst he faces is deportation? Ah, but that means taking a very back-seat—and back-seats, somehow, aren't in
character. Even suppose it meant facing a firing squad he's
the sort who couldn't help sticking his neck out. . . ." "But
surely, Justice-Minister Gürtner. . . ." Franz struggled to
interrupt, while Reinhold raised a hand to show him he
wasn't allowed: ". . . which it couldn't of course, for he
isn't that dangerous.—Yes: you were going to say, my
friend: 'An Ajax defying the lightning, but knowing that
Mr. Jupiter-Gürtner won't let Ajax really get hurt'."

"*I* wouldn't go, even if I were fit," said the practical Otto:
"For what can his antics matter? Whatever he says or does
at the trial, Hitler has now no political future: he's finished—
and Gott sei Dank!" Otto had scant respect for his former
despatch-rider, knowing a little too much about him (things
he kept locked in his breast, since other names were involved); and little as Otto liked Ludendorff either, it didn't
seem decent to witness the General's shame.

But Franz was persuaded: since everyone seemed so sure
that Hitler would be deported, it seemed a bit silly to miss a
German's very last chance of hearing him speak. He would
stop on at least for the first few days, to see how the trial
went. . . .

Even then he might never have stayed if he hadn't run
into some friends his own age who could talk about nothing
else: for one of these friends was Lothar Scheidemann,
Wolff's younger brother—that Wolff who had gone off his
head and hanged himself in the Lorienburg attics, the Wolff
who had been Franz's hero. . . .

Not since their schooldays had Franz seen Lothar until the
day when they buried Wolff; but ever since then he had tried
to keep up with him. Lothar was all he had left of the glorious
Wolff.

Chapter 11

So Otto went home alone that Sunday. On Tuesday the trial began, and it lasted a whole five weeks; but Franz and his friends didn't miss a single public hearing, and even the Eminent Jurist looked in whenever he could.

Reinhold of course was among the glittering throng on that final gala occasion of Tuesday, April the First 1924, that All Fools Day when the sentences were pronounced. Men in the court were in full-dress uniform: ladies wore red-black-and-white cockades of the old Imperial Colours, and loaded the nine convicted men in the dock with flowers as if they were prima-donnas (for only nine were convicted though ten were accused: the angry Ludendorff had to endure the shameful eclipse of the only acquittal).

Hitler's performance at least had deserved the bouquets. Reinhold had hardly guessed a quarter of Hitler's audacity, not only not taking shelter behind the Old War-Lord but stealing the limelight from Ludendorff right at the start; and once he was in it, he never let anyone shoulder him out of it. Journalists come from the whole wide world to see the great Ludendorff tried stayed on to listen entranced to this unknown man who was putting the whole Prosecution itself on trial. He spoke to the Press direct with hardly a glance at his judges, and made the headlines every day all over Germany. As for the Foreign Press. . . . You had got to admit this was honest and forthright stuff, these days, from the hypocritical Boche; and the foreign papers duly admitted it.

Even in England Gilbert had glanced at brief reports before March was out; and even the English papers by now had learned to spell 'Hitler' properly.

Hitler made no pretence that he hadn't intended to topple the Weimar Republic, and boasted he'd do it yet. But was

that 'Treason'? For who were these traitors of 1918 to prate
about Treason? His only regret was his failure—so far. . . .
His scathing indictment against the chief Prosecution wit-
nesses (Kahr and Seisser and General Lossow) was first and
foremost that they'd been the cause of his failure; and
second, that they—with their Monarchist plots for a
Wittelsbach restoration and taking Bavaria out of the Reich
—were fully as guilty of treason against the Reich as he
was. . . . On which Prosecution Counsel rose to object, and
the wooden-faced judges looked even more wooden—for
more than one had been present himself on Kahr's invitation
that night in the Bürgerbäukeller, and knew very well what
he'd come for. . . .

"The place for all three," said Hitler, "is here in the dock!"

But Hitler reserved his bitterest taunts for General Lossow,
the turncoat whose 'officer's honour' allowed him to turn his
coat not once but twice in a single night: the scabrous Army
Commander who'd called out the Army against the Holy
Cause of raising Germany out of the mire. . . . One day the
Army would recognise their mistake of November the Ninth:
one day, the Army and he would march shoulder-to-shoulder
—and Heaven help anyone then who tried to stand in their
way! Thank God that the bullets which felled the Residenzstrasse Martyrs were fired by mere civilian police, and the
Army's honour was clean of that infamous massacre. . . .

Oh, the fire and the force of the man—as if all Germany
spoke with his voice. . . . And oh, that ferocious magnificent
voice! Deep and sonorous: harsh, or strong, and resonant:
sometimes it sounded soft and warm, but only the better a
moment later to freeze your spine. Franz was carried away
by it clean off his feet, like almost everyone there.

Out of the miscreant three, it was only Lossow himself who
even attempted to put in his place this jumped-up Corporal
daring to criticise Generals: "When I first heard that famous
tongue I was quite impressed; but then each time I heard it
again it impressed me less and less." For he soon discovered,
said General Lossow, that this was merely an ignorant

dreamer: someone whose golden tongue outstripped a less-than-average brain, with scarcely a single idea he could call his own and no practical judgement at all. No wonder in Army days he had never risen above Lance-Corporal's rank —it was all he was fit for. "And yet," said General Lossow with withering scorn, "this nincompoop now has the nerve to imagine himself a Gambetta—or even as Germany's Mussolini!"

But then the tables were turned: for the General had to submit to a cross-examination by Hitler, and Hitler contrived to pierce even Lossow's patrician hide till—turning a vivid purple—the General thumped the floor with his scabbard and stumped from the court for fear a blood-vessel broke.

Last Thursday had been the day of Hitler's final peroration. So! People accused him of taking too much on himself. . . . Must the man whose conscience drives him to save his country modestly wait to be asked to? Or is the Worker 'taking too much on himself' when he puts every ounce of his strength in his task? Does the Thinker 'wait to be asked' before burning the midnight oil to achieve some discovery? Never! And neither must someone whose Destiny calls him to lead a nation. He too must wait for the call of no other will than his own: he must flog himself up the lonely peaks of power, not 'wait to be asked'. "For make no mistake!" he thundered: "I want no mere 'Mr. Minister Hitler' carved on my tomb, but 'Here lies the Final Destroyer of Marxism'!"

Lothar was nearly turned out for applauding; and so were dozens of others.

"As for this Court," said Hitler, turning his eyes full on to his judges for once: "I don't give a fig for its verdict! The only acquittal I care for will come from the smiling Goddess of History: come when I and the German Army finally reconciled stand side-by-side before that eternal Last Court of Judgement, the High Court of God."

Then Hitler sat down.

*

Once you cooled off, it was all just a little absurd; and General Lossow was probably right that the man had no practical sense, no sense of proportion. But still, it did seem a pity the Government had to deport such an ace-entertainer: Politics hadn't got many his like.

Deportation of course would have spelled the end (thought Reinhold), as well the prisoner knew; but by proving his own guilt up to the hilt he had played his cards in a way which had made deporting him just what his enemies couldn't do. Or at any rate, couldn't do yet: for the mildest sentence the Code provided for proven Treason was five years' fortress-confinement.

But *five years'* total eclipse for Hitler, like Toni rotting forgotten? The Code did also provide that the prisoner could be released on parole after serving a bare six months; and with Justice-Minister Gürtner tipping the scales of Justice, a little bird said. . . .

Chapter 12

So Hitler returned to Landsberg, shattering finally Toni's peace: for instead of the former handful of Nazis with him, the fruits of this main and one or two minor trials had now brought their numbers to forty—including Willi, still limping a bit from the wound he got in the Putsch. With Hitler allowed all the visits he cared to receive, this formerly quiet retreat was a bedlam indeed in Toni's eyes.

Few of these visitors came empty-handed. On Hitler's thirty-fifth birthday (bedazzled warders informed the Count) the flowers and parcels had filled some three or four rooms; and for Willi, like all the rest of the starveling rank and file, life had never before been so easy. They'd all the fine food they could eat, sent in by those outside admirers; and when they had eaten too much, a private gymnasium where they could work it off afterwards.

Hitler himself could never take part in their sports, for a Leader must never risk his charisma by being defeated—not even at dominoes. Thus he began to show signs of putting on weight on his prison diet of prime Westphalia hams and the like washed down with occasional brandies. His cheeks began to fill out, and he seemed more relaxed: his mind still ran like a mill-race, but nervously more relaxed. At first his harangues to the Inner Circle had never ceased; but no one on holiday wants to hear nothing but shop, so presently some bright lad remarked to the Führer that all this ought to go in a book—and it worked. Thereafter Hitler spent most of his time in his private study, writing *Mein Kampf*. The rays of the midsummer sun shone in on the rosy cheeks of an almost contented Hitler, dictating to Hess by the hour what Hess took down on a battered old Remington. That left everyone else pretty free to enjoy his own form of fun: which in Willi's case mostly was reading Westerns, and practising on the flute.

158

In short, they had nothing to fear but release.

*

It was not till July (that July of 1924 which had seen
Augustine already ensconced in the New England woods)
that Franz paid at last his belated visit to Toni. They talked
about anything rather than Hitler. The passing effect on
Franz of those trial speeches had long worn off—and anyway,
wasn't the man in gaol for the next five years and his bolt in-
contestably shot? For Franz (like most other folk) took 'finish'
for granted.

But two days after this Landsberg visit Franz and
Reinhold met by chance in the Marienplatz and Reinhold
carried his young friend off for a drink. The Eminent Jurist
didn't seem nearly so sure: " 'Five years', say you? But that
prison sentence was only a farce, for Berlin's benefit. Redwitz
thinks he'll be out by August; and once he rids himself of
Rosenberg's crazy racist ideas the man could go far. . . . But
look! That's Carl over there, with his tongue hanging out:
he's a bird-witted scamp but one of the intimates. Let's call
him over, and hear the latest." Reinhold cupped his hands
to his mouth: "Carl, my treasure!" he called like hailing a
cab: then he whispered to Franz as the man approached, "I
can't ever help teasing Carl: if I go too far you must kick me
under the table".

Franz recognised 'Carl' at once. Two days ago they had
found themselves sharing the pleasant walk from Landsberg
Fortress back to the railway station. Both had remarked on
the singular baroque charm of that little town set on the
wooded banks of the Lech; and both had joined in deploring
Sir Hubert Herkomer's infamous 'Mutter-Turm'. But once
in the train this fellow had talked about nothing but Hitler:
how he and Hitler were close as two peas on a pod, and how
Hitler prized his advice. By Kaufering Junction Franz had
had more than enough, and had got in a separate carriage.

But Carl at first was a bit hard to draw. "There is no Nazi
F*

Party: you know very well that the Courts have dissolved it,"
he said morosely, and sat there biting his nails.

"True. But this new 'Nazionalsozialistische Deutsche
Freiheits-Bewegung' which did so well at the spring elections:
don't we see all the same names? The old Nazi nucleus,
bound man to man by the bonds which Adversity forges?"

This touched Carl on the raw: " 'Bound together' my
foot!" he exclaimed: "They're fighting like cats." Then he
added, defensively: "That's betraying no secrets: they do it
in public, worse luck!"

"I did hear that Rosenberg threatens to prosecute
Streicher and Esser for Defamation," said Reinhold. "In all
this fun-and-games, whose side are you on?"

Carl drew in his chin a bit primly: "It isn't so much any
question of sides as of levels. Rosenberg ranks as a lofty
Thinker: with Strasser and Röhm he stands for our highest
Nazi ideals. But Streicher and Esser are Calibans: sub-
human brutes, who must both be kicked out of our Movement—and kicked so hard that it hurts, it's the only language
they understand."

Carl drained his glass with a flourish, while Reinhold
murmured to Franz: "But Streicher and Esser. . . . Observe
that they too wear metal-toed boots." Then Reinhold continued aloud, to Carl: "It must be horrid for decent chaps
like yourself and Rosenberg, both of you intellectuals, forced
to consort with such Canaille as Streicher and Esser. . . . But
by the way," he added off-hand: "They tell me that poor old
Göring's been kicked out already? Why's that—except that
Göring's knocked out by his martyr's wound, and recovering
somewhere abroad?" ('Unlike Esser and Streicher,' he left
unsaid, 'so very much here on the spot'). "But what has
Glamour-Boy done?"

"I know, I know. . . . But you see, Röhm needs a completely
free hand rebuilding the Militant Arm and Göring might
try to take over again if he could."

Reinhold's knowing look was downright embarrassing:
catching his eye the poor Carl wriggled, and looked con-

fused. . . . "But what has *he* got to say of all this—the Leader himself, God bless him?" asked Reinhold, erecting his finger as if in a miniature Fascist salute. "Doubtless you visit him often?"

"Of course—I am closeted with him weekly." Carl's raddled face broke into satisfied smiles: he was never the man to stay solemn too long, and his smile was the key to his charm. "I must put him wise, or—shut up in Landsberg with idiots like Hess—how else could he know what went on?"

"So you are his eyes and ears? Dear boy that must help him no end, with your balanced searching intelligence." Much as Reinhold enjoyed this teasing, he let that fact not appear at all in his flattering voice. "And doubtless the Leader opens his mind to you too, so there's much you can tell us. For instance: I take it his noble soul is wholly delighted at Röhm's astounding success resurrecting the Storm Troops?—Although some less altruistic spirit, perhaps, might fear that the stronger they grow the more Prime Minister Held gets alarmed and postpones his release. . . ."

Carl shook his head: "Why on earth should that organisation's success affect Hitler's release? As Held must know, the Frontbann is nothing to do with Hitler: Röhm insists on the Militant Arm's complete independence of civil Party control."

"Oho! So all Hitler rules nowadays is the purely political arm?" Carl nodded. "And yet, a little bird tells me that even here some folk in the Party would like to see Hitler brought down a peg."

"The terriers yap while the mastiff is chained." Carl laughed, but a little uncertainly.

"So, then: at least Political-Generalissimo Hitler would have to approve such purely political changes of stance as this new competing for seats in Reichstag?" (No answer; but maybe Carl was too busy ordering drinks.) "And Rosenberg, Strasser and Ludendorff hand-in-glove with that 'Patriot' group in the North?"

Carl's face was a deeper red. "But that's only tactics . . .

and tactics should surely be left to the man on the spot. . . ."

"By whom you must mean Rosenberg—Leader 'pro tem'," said Reinhold; and something in Reinhold's voice made Carl glance up at him warily, scenting further danger. Then came the crucial question: "But all these public insults to Thinker Rosenberg, insults to Hitler's own Deputy-Designate: doubtless the Führer always comes down on his Deputy's side—and with every ounce of his weight?"

Carl seemed so unwilling to answer that finally Franz chipped in: "But my friend Lothar says that Rosenberg's just a louse they want to help Hitler get out of his hair!"

Thus it was Reinhold who kicked Franz under the table; but just too late. Carl looked at the interrupter with shocked distaste, then rose and began to make his excuses. But Franz ignored the kick for the sake of a parting shot: " 'The Louse' they all of them call him, and 'Pie-faced Highbrow'! While Esser and Streicher they think the world of. . . ."

"Now you've torn it!" said Reinhold, as soon as the two were alone.

But Franz only frowned. "Lothar says it's all in a terrible mess: he is near despair. If Hitler but knew what goes on. . . ."

"If he 'knew'? Do you think he depends for news on that vain little fool? He's as many eyes as a fly—and I bet you they don't miss much."

"Then why, if he knows that what's left of the Nazi Movement is tearing itself in pieces, does Hitler just sit there in Landsberg and dream?"

"Come-come! Would you have him clamp down on dissensions and reappear later to find the Party united . . . behind someone else?" (Franz was struck dumb.) "He can well afford to sit dreaming in Landsberg: the only job on his hands at the moment is setting his friends by the ears—and that he could do on his head."

"You mean . . . he's deliberately pulling down all he's given his life hitherto to constructing?"

"Exactly. For isn't it better to burn empty shoes yourself

than leave them for somebody else to step in? And once he comes out of gaol what he's built up before he can build up again. So let me make a confession: I used to underrate Hitler, but now for one single decision of downright genius off comes my hat to him. *Rosenberg*—picking the one man to take his place who couldn't conceivably! Just imagine the fugitive Hitler, crazed with pain from his broken shoulder: there's five bare seconds to think in before his arrest and in which to scribble 'Herr Rosenberg, YOU lead the Party from now'. If that wasn't genius, tell me what is."

"Then you purport to find," said Franz heavily, "depths in this fellow of cunning which I, though a student of politics, had not discerned?" (Reinhold concealed his amusement.) "We've no mad charlatan here, you suggest, but a Machiavelli?" Franz paused for a term of frowning thought, but finally shook his head. "No. For that doesn't tie up at all with the Hitler who launched that imbecile Putsch."

"Mind you, I think he's changing," conceded Reinhold: "I think the run of Wagner's 'Rienzi' is over. We'll see no more of the martyred 'People's Tribune'. His next production is much more likely 'The Meistersingers'—of course with appropriate changes of casting: the gifted amateur learning the rules of the silly professionals' game and beating them at it hands down. . . ."

He signed to the waiter to bring him the bill; for much as he liked young men he couldn't help tiring of Franz.

*

That 'imbecile' Putsch. . . . Reinhold, alone on his way to the Courts for a boring case, gave rein to his new conception of Hitler's political genius: of Hitler, that is, as someone whose 'imbecility' lay in thinking five jumps ahead of everyone else.

That fore-doomed Putsch. . . . Well, suppose it had never been launched: what then?—And this seemed the right approach: for indeed if Hitler had failed to stage his mammoth diversion the very same night might have seen Prince

Rupprecht made King—and would likely have seen Bavaria leaving the Reich, the signal for similar fragmentation all over Germany. . . . Germany back to the days before Bismarck, in fact: the one thing Hitler had got to prevent, if he aimed at one day ruling a whole German Reich—prevent it at even the risk of his life.

His Daemon would stick at nothing to get to the top! Down Reinhold's spine ran a shiver, in spite of the summer weather.

And yet (thought Reinhold) were genius and utter determination enough for an ignoramus whose incomprehension of anything more than the here-and-now of hand-to-hand politics seemed abysmal, for one who could place his ideological trust in that worthless Rosenberg rubbish? What could this untaught guttersnipe know of the world-situation, of all the multitudinous issues he'd find on his plate if he ever did get to the top?

Surely a mind as untutored as his was like one of those maps in the Middle Ages which only showed the cartographer's own stamping-ground in accurate detail, surrounded by fabulous beasts and Terra Ignota and Ocean. Supposing he did 'flog himself up the peaks' to the ultimate summit of power, how could a man like that survive for a day when he got there? This kerbside and beer-hall stuff, till now, had been mere snakes-and-ladders: you picked yourself up none-the-worse and made a fresh start if you put a foot wrong. But the higher he got the harder he'd fall; and he'd find those 'peaks' he aspired to were one continuous butter-slide. . . .

Reaching the court, Reinhold the Eminent Jurist startled an usher by spanking his own behind like someone scolding a horse: "Reinhold Steuckel," he murmured: "You eminent goose! You were getting as silly as he is, you'd lost all sense of proportion!"

So Reinhold took his seat in the court reassured. . . . Or, was he?

Chapter 13

ONCE that Mammoth-Spectacular Trial was over other
sensations followed it, other headlines; and ninety-nine
people out of a hundred forgot it—even the politicians
themselves, so busy (like Gilbert) keeping their eyes on the
ball. As for Tom-Dick-and-Harry (or Gustav and Emma
Krebelmann), politics after all was just a Cloud-Cuckoo-
Land lived in by Cloud-Cuckoo-Landers, and hardly im-
pinging on real people at all. If only historians knew that
what matters to real folk has to be something real! Something
like getting one's claws into Walther von Kessen's forests, or
Gretl scalding her hand too badly to sweep. . . . Or our own
little Ernst still catching trouble at school (for how could the
Goddess of History smile on a boy who couldn't remember
her dates?).

'Eleven-five-*six*' was the date of the Founding of Kammstadt, that most important of all historical dates! Lehrer
Faber had boxed his ears, and tried to rub in the digits with
One, One, Five, and *Six* 'head-nuts'. For Kammstadt was
two years older than upstart Munich, founded Eleven-five-
eight—a fact no Kammstadter ever ought to forget. Moreover the founder of both, the great Duke Henry the Lion
("No NOT his father Duke Henry the Proud, you block-
head!") had honoured our founding by combing a beard
which had never been combed for years ("So you see how
we came by our name of Kammstadt"): and two of the
broken teeth of that overtaxed comb were the proudest relics
the town possessed.

Still, nobody really minded head-nuts; and after all, with
fifty boys in the class what else could the boys expect?

Learning here was all of it learning by rote, and lost was
the child who altered a single word (as you tended to do, if

165

weakly you let yourself think of the sense). But even para-phrase was a peccadillo compared with writing left-handed. Each time that Ernst did this the crime was promoted: from head-nuts, through ruler-cuts on chilblainy knuckles, to lay-ing him bare-bum over the table and switching with hazel-rods. When even that failed (little Ernst's young friends having nicked the rods with their knives in advance so they broke), the Teacher even tried Reason: for surely it stands to Reason that nobody writes with his left?

Lehrer Faber, with bristling red moustache and a look of thwarted ambition in piercingly bright blue eyes: this was the Fountain of Knowledge. . . . When lessons were done and the school exploded there always remained a quorum of small boys jostling round him, bombarding him with their questions six-at-a-time. There was nothing the Lehrer didn't know, from astronomy down to sexing lady and gentleman worms and how an aeroplane flies.

Little Ernst was often one of the jostlers—not that he always had something to ask, but because he liked to be part of a lump (any lump, whatever its object). One day he found he had somehow jostled himself right up in front, but a question luckily came: "Herr Lehrer, I know you can't fly just by hanging on to the string of a big enormous kite; but suppose you tied your kite to an eagle, couldn't you?"

When he got home, his mother was anxious to know what Ernst had learned that day in school. For answer, he silently took his old toy rabbit and made it zoom through the air with its long flannel ears outstretched, pretending he'd got an eagle. . . .

But what was the use of even a real eagle to someone who hadn't a kite to tie to it?

*

Meanwhile, for Hitler in Landsberg August passed and September too without his expected release; and as Reinhold hinted he might, he gave the whole discredit for this to

Röhm. He suspected Röhm and his growing 'militant arm' of malice prepense, of intending to keep the Munich authorities too much alarmed to want Hitler at large while behaving just well enough not to get banned themselves. In October his six months were up: yet October passed, and November . . . and Hitler chalked up a very bad mark against Röhm.

The December Elections however at last did the trick. For now the tide had apparently turned, and even that right-wing electoral coalition the Nazi remnant had joined lost more than half of their seats: so the 'Nazi Menace'—if ever there really was one—no longer existed. . . .

The Munich authorities heaved a sigh of relief and turned him loose just before Christmas.

Counting back to the day of Hitler's arrest, he had been 'out of action' for thirteen months. No one was wearing his shoes, he had seen to that—though Röhm had apparently cobbled-up some sort of pair of his own. Now he must make a fresh start; but not entirely from scratch, for this time (thanks to the Trial) everyone knew his name—and nobody knew his plans.

Chapter 14

IN an elegant house in an elegant quarter of Munich, at
half-past six, an impatiently-waiting child hears a visitor
kicking the snow off his boots in the hall: then a hop-skip-
and-jump, and he's riding high in the visitor's arms while he
breathes "Dass D'nur wieder da bist, Onkel Dolf!" down
the mothbally neck of the visitor's blue party-suit. And how
that fine little four-year old hero had grown since the day
when they shared those cakes in the Blutenbergstrasse cell!
"But where have you hidden your new baby sister, you
rascal?"

However, before the four-year-old hero could answer his
long-lost Uncle was pleading with Father to play him the
'Liebestod'. . . .

Hanfstängl glanced at his guest in surprise. Why, he
looked so well; and they'd hardly yet said How-d'you-do!
Could a fit of the old nervous tension be on him again so
soon? Well, Wagner's music was always the cure—like Saul.
So he sat himself down then and there and thundered the
'Liebestod' out on his big concert grand, while the bust of
Benjamin Franklin danced all over the lid.

The listener seemed to have grown quite plump: as he
stood with his feet apart and his head on one side, his serge
suit strained at its buttons so much that the little boy eyed
it in wonder. But just as the last of those healing Lisztian
fireworks died on the air, in came Mother with little Herta—
and Uncle was kissing her hand and gone into ecstasies over
our baby, and saying again and again how sorry he was for
all the trouble he'd caused her at Uffing. . . .

What 'trouble' at Uffing? The boy could remember
nothing, apart from some baying of dogs in the dark; and
surely those hadn't been Uncle's dogs which had made all
that noise?

As a matter of fact he found there was little he could remember at all about Uncle Dolf—apart from the all-important fact that he loved him, and always had.

Then the sliding doors slid, and they moved in to dinner. This Coming-out Dinner was served in style, by candlelight. Turkey and small-talk. . . . Hitler professed himself greatly impressed by this highly artistic use of candles instead of electric lamps: it showed superior taste. He seemed altogether impressed by this cultured, upper-class home which his hosts had acquired; and the 'feine Gegend', the upper-class neighbourhood. "Hanfstängl," Hitler declared: "You are quite the most upper-class person I know!"

Suspecting no irony Putzi was pleased, and preened. For his friend was clearly doing his best (minding his *P*s and *Q*s, and careful to use the right knives and forks), but could do with a lot more taming and teaching yet; and Putzi fancied himself in the role of instructor to genius.

Pastries and small-talk. . . . The child was abysmally bored. Uncle Dolf was the only person at dinner who spoke to him even once; and that was merely recalling some infantile joke he insisted they used to share, though the boy had forgotten it. Spanking, forsooth, those 'naughty' carved wooden lions on Father's chair. . . . Couldn't Uncle see how this three-year-old's babyish stuff embarrassed a four-year-old hero? So then he turned his thoughts to the tree, and the presents to come. He had asked for a sabre, first; and he hoped there'd be no hanky-panky, the Christkind would bring him a proper cavalry one. But next on his list of requests was that cooking-stove everyone teased him about. . . . Would the Christkind think him a cissy like everyone else did—a boy who wanted to cook? Would Uncle Dolf think him cissy? That terrible thought made him blush to the roots of his hair, and he couldn't swallow his tart.

Wine, and a deal more small-talk. . . . Herr Hitler drank

almost nothing, yet seemed to be warming up. He told one cruel satirical prison anecdote after another, making them laugh as he brought Count Toni to mimic life—and then his warders, even producing their tread in the passage outside, and the turn of a key in the lock, all done with that magical voice.

In his pictures of prison life he was palpably playing for sympathy. Putzi however decided that prison had done him the world of good, for a rest and a regular life had been just what he needed. No doubt he was now a saner and wiser man; and perhaps the future was not so black after all. . . . He thought of Frederick the Great, and reminded Hitler that after the Battle of Hochkirch even 'der alte Fritz' sat biting his nails on a drum and had thought he was done for.

But Hitler brushed aside all serious talk of the future: tonight was a festive night. Instead he started in bubbling spirits to tell them stories of life on the Western Front. Mostly these were good-humoured enough—though he seemed to have got it in for some Colonel von Kessen, a stuck-up Bavarian Baron whom Hitler mimicked while everyone laughed till the tears ran down their faces (even the little boy managed a loud guffaw, though he'd no idea what his parents were laughing about). Hitler contrasted this toff with his earthier Sergeant-Major Amman, of whom he spoke warmly; and also the sterling Lieutenant Hess. . . .

Next he started a parody howling and whistling through his teeth till there wasn't the battle-sound of a German or French or an English gun that his mimicry didn't include; and they gasped with surprise at his skill when he even attempted the composite roar of a Western Front artillery barrage, complete with Howitzers, Seventy-fives and machine-guns. The windows rattled, the furniture shook; and a rueful Putzi thought of his upper-class neighbours startled pop-eyed out of their Christmas peace. Whizz-bangs, and rumbling tanks: the screams of the wounded. . . . They laughed more uncertainly now, no longer sure it was quite so funny—this mimicking voice of the plump little man in a

blue serge suit who never forgot a sound: the retching cough
of the gassed, the glug of somebody shot through the lungs.

'Stille Nacht, Heilige Nacht' on the concert grand. . . . It
was time for the longed-for Bescherung, the Tree and the
presents at last; and they all put on holy faces. But 'Stille
Nacht' was for only so long as they stood in a pious line and
sang: once Uncle had started showing the little soldier the
way to hold the sabre which Baby-Jesus had brought him
the music changed to a stirring Nazi March. Moreover this
was the 'Schlageter March' which Father himself had composed in the martyr's honour (shot by the French, in the
Ruhr). In its sad-sombre parts the bass notes imitate drums,
and then comes the wild ferocious 'Pfui!' refrain:

Zwanzig Millionen—die sind euch wohl zuviel,
Frankreich! das sollst Du bereu'n!
Pfui!

'*Pfui!*' Stirred to ancestral depths, you crammed all your
hate and contempt for the dastardly French in that single
yell *Pfui*. . . . Catching the mood from elders themselves too
moved to notice, the little boy waved his wooden sabre and
slashed at the heavy furniture ('Pfui! Pfui!'), trying to make
it bleed. But now a sudden torrent of words from Hitler
howled down the grand piano and even the 'Pfui' refrain
itself: how the War must be fought all over again in France,
but now against France alone so that France could be
brought to her knees and Paris shattered to rubble, the
French crushed under its ruins like cesspool rats. . . .
    The pianist snatched his hands from the keys as from red-
hot coals, aghast at the screaming devil his music had raised
in his guest. Was this any 'saner and wiser man', who still
could suppose we would ever be left alone in the ring with
France? But penned for a year with only ignorant blockheads
like Rudolf Hess with his Clausewitz-Haushofer-Rosenberg
nonsense. . . . Indeed, half in love—so far as he *could* fall in
love—with 'mein Rudi, mein Hesserl'. . . .

Meanwhile the little boy dived head-first in a sofa and lay there blindly slashing—berserk, completely cuckoo. From the tree a tilting candle dripped hot wax on the face of the china doll in the crib.

*

When at last he was sent up to bed the boy was bursting with sleep like a bud but still beside himself with excitement. He dreamed of the Christus Kind and his Uncle Dolf in identical old blue bath-robes riding away on a truck together in triumph, while Benjamin Franklin waved a sabre and danced on the top of that tiny stove you could really-and-truly cook on (the stove which he prudently hadn't unwrapped till he got it upstairs).

But then, in his dream, that cooking-stove grew and grew till its chimneys hid the whole horizon in smoke; and Benjamin Franklin vanished like everything else.

Chapter 15

Tʜᴀᴛ same Christmas Eve Mellton Chase held another
impatiently-waiting child: for Augustine had lingered
in Canada right through the fall into winter, and only
today was the truant expected home at last.

The delay had begun with some Oxford friends Augustine
had found at Government House: they had shown him a deal
of kindness in Ottawa, pressing Augustine to wait for at
least a few days before booking his passage home—and to
tell the truth, he hadn't felt wholly averse to enjoying their
flesh-pots awhile after living so rough. Then at one of their
parties he met a wandering South Carolinan called Anthony
Fairfax. This was a young man of just his own age, but with
manners so old-world and courtly they made him feel in
comparison ill-bred and boorish—and yet this hidalgo had
built his own automobile himself at home by hand. . . .
Moreover by now the fall had begun, the crimson Canadian
fall when the maples light up like lamps and the pumpkins
flame on the porches: when peaks are revealed overnight
crystal-sharp through the suddenly clarified air—the tops of
far-off mountains hull-down behind the horizon, of ranges
you couldn't have guessed all summer were even there.
At this wonderful time of year, and attracted as well as
intrigued by each other, it didn't take much to send the two
of them off together in Anthony's home-made car exploring.
They started towards the North. Soon they found themselves driving on trails intended for horsemen at most,
through virgin forest by compass: up ridges and down
ravines, with an axe kept ready for chopping down trees and
a pick for dislodging rocks and a hand on the door-handle
always ready to jump.
By day they were far too busy to talk; but rolled in their

rugs at night they talked till they fell asleep. Apparently
Anthony's old-world charm included a firm belief that
duelling, courts-of-honour, and being a three-bottle-man
were still today the *sine qua nons* of *noblesse oblige*; and that
Negroes ranked at most as one of the higher primates. . . .
Augustine assumed that any Don Quixote with such a
sensible feat to his credit as building his own mechanical
Rosinante was bound to be joking; but Anthony also
assumed that Augustine was joking—no gentleman really
could doubt such obvious truths as these; and this mutual
notion that neither meant what he said had enabled the pair
to argue with endless good humour.

Once nights had begun to grow chilly they slept as close
to the fire as they could; and Augustine would never forget
that night when he woke by the dying embers, in darkness
smelling of spruce and with stars big as glittering eggs up
above in between the tree-tops, roused by the plain-song of
timber wolves seeking their meat from God—what men call
howling. . . . Yet neither night nor day was there ever a
wolf to be seen: not a shadow slinking between the daylight
trunks, nor even at night the greenish glint of a pair of eyes
in the light of a firebrand.

Presently even the midday sun was losing its strength
and they met the earliest warning wisps of a powdery snow
so light that they waved in the wind like smoke. This was the
season when even the bears move south and begin to think
about sleep: so the young men made what city-wards haste
they could before getting caught out there by the white
Canadian winter.

Once they were back in the city, Augustine had barely
had time to think any more about 'home' before there came
thicker falls of a heavier snow which patted the face like
fingers, and froze to eyebrows and lashes, and curtained from
sight the opposite side of the street—even hid the friend you
could reach to touch with your hand. Then the weather
turned fine again, with horse-drawn sleighs on the streets
and the air so cold that breathing it felt like taking in needles

of ice. But it wasn't so much this phenomenal cold out of doors as the heating inside the houses which sent him hurrying round to the shipping-office at last: for Augustine had stood the heat of a North American summer—just, but the ovenish indoor heat of a North American winter defeated him. Either he had to get back to an English country-house winter so imperceptibly warmer indoors than out, or die.

It pleased as well as surprised him when Anthony said that he thought of visiting Europe too: they could share a cabin.

*

Augustine had cabled to have his Bentley sent to the docks: so at Mellton tea-time the pair arrived together hot-foot (or rather, hot-tyre) from Southampton.

While Anthony gazed at the fine Jacobean front of the largest private house he had ever seen, a welcoming Wantage opened the door; and Augustine was shocked to see how much his old friend had aged in so little more than a year. He was thinner than ever, and balder: the lump on his throat was bigger, his eyes stuck out even further. . . .

And there was Polly, and—Lord, how Polly had grown! He would hardly have known her. . . . But Polly had turned unaccountably shy: she hid her face in her mother and wouldn't look at him, let alone speak. So the meeting they both had been longing for ended in merely the mousy smell in his nose of little-girl's hair as he stooped to the back of her head, being all he could get at to kiss. For the truth was that out of the two of them not only Polly had 'grown'; and poor conservative Polly had no need of looking to tell her the changes which time and absence had wrought in her cherished Augustine. That voice from the hall might still over there have seemed laughably British; but here it had sounded distinctly American. . . .

Chapter 16

So Augustine was back at Mellton at last; and (after those first few minutes) surprised to find how little had anything changed. This woke him up to the fact of how much he had changed himself: he found himself looking at Mellton with more of a critical eye, and wondered how Mary could stick it—this dead-alive life spent running a great big house that was perfectly able to run itself while Gilbert footled around with his politics. Mary had got in a groove: it was time for Augustine to wake her up. . . .

As for Mary—delighted as Mary was at having him back —she noticed how much more sure of himself he seemed; but she only thought how often that merely betokened a 'self' no longer so worth being sure of, for Mary as well as her child was convinced any change in the old Augustine must be for the worse. Meanwhile Wantage was telling Cook how Mr. Augustine's frame had thickened: he moved his limbs in a different way, perhaps just a little abrupt and clumsy for one of the gentry. . . . Indeed it was only Gilbert who (grudgingly) thought him even a trifle improved—apart from his accent of course, but that would soon wear off in civilised company.

Because of this Great Occasion Polly had come down to tea; but she sat all the time with her eyes glued to her plate.

Indeed they were fortunate having a stranger like Anthony there as a lightning-conductor: he charmed both his hosts, and his polished manners put everyone else on their mettle.

So much, then, for growth and the passage of time: except that after Augustine had gone up to change, and observed laid out on his bed his evening clothes which so long had hung in a Mellton cupboard, he sadly reminded himself that those cute little moccasins made by a genuine Indian squaw and intended for Polly would also be much too small: at best they might one day do for Susan Amanda. . . .

But then his long-unaccustomed efforts to fight his way into an overstarched evening shirt cut short all further reflection, and caused him to shout across the passage to Anthony: "Say, how in heck does a tortoise get into its shell?"

*

Augustine was right: Wantage had certainly aged. The pains in his back were worse, and his palpitations were something chronic. His thyroid was bigger; the Mistress had said that the next time the doctor came to the house she would get him to take a look. Meanwhile he suffered a lot from his temper nowadays too: he would bite off poor Maggie Winter's head over nothing, and all the younger maids were properly scared of him. 'Nervy'?—Well, yes; but how could he help his nerves being edgy a bit when nowadays nothing went right?

The latest disaster was Jimmy—that Jimmy he'd loved as a son, and so often chastened like one. For when Jimmy was just about ready at last for a Second Footman he'd got himself caught in the shrubbery fooling around with that little chit of a kitchen-maid, Lily. When Lily had started to swell —the pair of them barely sixteen—they'd *both* of them had to be sacked. . . . That was the end of Jimmy in Service of course. But Ted had helped over Maggie's Nellie, and Wantage had hoped if he wrote to his brother Ted in Coventry, Ted might have took Jimmy on and taught him bicycles. Now Ted had wrote there were too many Coventry boys themselves out of work for that: apprentices served their time on a pittance, but due for a skilled man's tenpence-halfpenny an hour were sacked and a new boy took.

Ted had said to tell Mrs. Winter her sister was well and the baby coming on fine. . . . Yet now it was gone nine o'clock, and he'd let the whole day slip by without passing the good news on—so took up with Jimmy he'd been, on top of his work.

Once Wantage had left the gentlemen over their port (the Master and Mr. Augustine and Mr. Augustine's American), having no Jimmy to help any longer he'd ought to be making a start on those silvers to wash and the glasses; but likely as not would have barely got into his apron before the coffee was rung for. . . . And then he'd got to fetch up the near-champagne for the Servants' Ball: for tonight there was mistletoe hung in the Servants' Hall, there'd be dancing from ten till midnight (and half the Gardens and Stables bamboozled away from the straight-and-narrow by giggling hussies, you bet your bottom!). As Wantage pushed through the green baize door from beyond it came startled squeaks and a scurry of feet—them females, stark staring crazy the lot of them! Maggie had offered him one till the new boy came. . . . No fear! Sure as eggs if feather-head girls like them gave a hand with his silvers they'd wash the spoons in with the forks—or something equally daft, so he'd have to wear his palms sore rubbing out the scratches. . . .

But then came the sound of the bell. "All right, I heard you!" he muttered, and paused at the drawing-room door to make quite sure he was wearing his proper benevolent butler's face.

Wantage was stumbling up the cellar steps with the champagne-type when he called to mind that letter from Ted with its news about Nellie: he'd better deliver the message now before he forgot it again.

Wantage was panting a bit as he pulled back his favourite basket-chair well away from the fire—and flopped. For crumbs! he could do with a few minutes' rest. . . . These days the dear old Room was its own self again, now Nellie was gone. In the brass Benares vase there was holly instead of flowers, the same as on every Christmas Eve for time out of mind. . . . No changes ever in here—unless that was new, that scratch on the 'Cherry-ripe' frame?

Relaxing, he stretched his legs till his hip-joints cracked like a couple of pistol-shots; and "Letter from Ted", he

began. But when he had told her the good news at last, all
Maggie vouchsafed was something about him neglecting his
Herbal Balm for those joints. . . . The ungrateful bitch! His
loose plate chittered against his few sound teeth like the
castanets and he barely managed to swallow the sudden bile
in his throat. . . . But 'Hold hard, Fred!' he admonished himself: 'Get a grip, before you say something you know you'll
be sorry for. . . .'

Meanwhile Maggie was thinking: 'So Nellie is well, says
he! *And* the baby coming on fine! Then he doesn't know
much. . . .' For what of the letter she'd had from Nellie
herself which said little Syl had come out with the measles—
bad, but that Nellie durstn't let on because of her pupils
with Christmas coming which anyhow meant no teaching
and so no pay? That Brother Ted was a broken reed: he'd
encouraged Nellie to come there and teach, but almost as
soon as she'd got to Coventry Nellie had written that pupils
were harder to find than what Mr. Wantage had said and
she'd have to move into cheaper lodgings. That meant
moving to somewhere right in the warren-like middle of
town and travelling out to her pupils in Earlsdon or Hearsall
Common by tram or bus—or walking, to save the fare.

'By a stroke of luck' (she wrote) she had found an upstairs
room at one-and-fivepence a week in one of the courts
off Godsell Street; and Maggie could picture her now, in
her garret 'above the Balloon-woman' (dropsy: the only
'balloons' downstairs were the woman's bedridden legs).

*

Maggie had never seen it of course, that entry off Godsell
Street. It was under the room where a watchmaker worked,
and so dark you instinctively ducked. The entry was flanked
by a butcher's shop, and down one side of the cobbled yard
ran the ramshackle lean-to shed where he killed his beasts
(the City Surveyor called this 'Seventeen Court' but to
everyone else it was 'Slaughterhouse Yard').

The whole row of dwellings were just one-up-and-one-down, with a single outside tap in the yard for the lot and the sanitation all down at the end. They were centuries old, their woodwork rotten and riddled by mice. The doors from the yard opened straight on the downstairs rooms; and Nellie's stairs led up from behind the Balloon-woman's bed —in a room that was nearly all bed.

Chapter 17

I N Coventry, Christmas Eve had begun with the scraping of spades. A fall of snow overnight had muffled all sound in the city till just before dawn, when this scraping of spades on the paving-stones had begun.

Dawn had revealed these huddled buildings' usual sordid grime exchanged for a silver beauty; and Nellie had gazed in amazement, for even the narrow yard which her window faced had its share of glistening change. As if by Merlin-magic (all yesterday having been spent re-reading Tennyson's 'Morte d'Arthur') the rusty old lean-to-shed where the beasts were killed was turned to a pure white knightly tournament-tent; and above this mournfully-lowing pavilion the backs of the next-door court were a magical castle wall— each window-sill plumped with its silken cushion of white, where sparrows fluffed into little brown balls dug deep for yesterday's crumbs. Dog-tooth fringes of icicles graced the leaking gutter above; and beside the pavilion door that bundle of poles and the wheel-less pram were turned to a jewelled trophy of arms. . . .

'White Samite, mystic, wonderful!' Even the cobbled yard was a carpet of virgin white till an aged wizard shuffled out in his tattered and ancient Army greatcoat, turned his face to the wall where he stood and stained a patch of the snow with yellow.

Nellie had gone out early to fetch the feverish baby's morning penn'orth of milk (though mostly he sicked it up); but even as early as this the snow in the streets outside was rutted and fanned by skidding lorries and drays as they swerved to avoid a fallen costermonger's horse. There the animal lay spread-eagled, an angry policeman perched on its head while the carter did nothing to get it back on its feet but busied himself collecting the rolling cabbages spilled from his cart, and swore. The three pawnbroker's balls on the corner were turned to a triad of guelder roses.

But even by noon the thaw had begun; and now, when dusk prevented her reading her small-print Tennyson any longer, everything dripped.

'The Lily Maid of Astolat' . . . but Nellie's window faced to a biting wind so had to be kept shut as tight as its sagging frame allowed, with the aid of a paper wedge. It was clouded over with steam. The fire in the grate was a tiny glow at the heart of a carefully-husbanded shovel of slack and dust; and the drying napkins strung from wall to wall had filled the air with a pungent chill. In the darkening room the nearly-invisible baby cried and grizzled without intermission, and pawed at his ears with his woollen gloves. But with less than a penn'orth of paraffin left in the bottle it seemed too early to light the lamp, so she wiped a patch of steam from the window and tried to look out.

During the all-day thaw great clods of snow had slipped from the faery tent, revealing the holes in the rusty roof below; and gone was that carpet of virgin white—round the communal tap the melting snow was trodden down to a grey and horrible porridge, which even the kids no longer tried to make into balls. The streets would be ankle-deep in slush, and Nellie's galoshes had holes; but she hadn't eaten all day and the cramp in her stomach told her she'd got to eat something to keep up her strength: so she pinned the throat of her jacket as high as she could with her old jet brooch, abandoned the crying baby and sallied forth in the gloaming.

The court was lit by a single gaslamp over the entry. Just as she closed the outside door the flickering light came on, the lamp-lighter lowered his rod and shuffled away on his round. But Godsell Street was already ablaze with light from the lighted windows of shops and pubs; and Broadgate was even brighter. Here there were dazzling plateglass windows filled with Christmas fare: with holly, and gentlemen's

elegant double-breasted suits: with ivy and tinsel, and
ladies' dresses with ostrich-feather stoles: or with yew and
holly and paper-chains garlanding oak-coloured Jacobean
suites, the tables set with dozens of festal glasses and china
and knives and forks. In short, there was food and gifts and
decorations galore; and in spite of the weather and slush
underfoot the pavements were packed. But most of the
crowd only stood and gaped, or made up with joking and
chaffing each other for having no money to spend any more
than Nellie herself.

In Smi'ford Street the crowd poured back and forth to-
and-from the shouting hucksters and naphtha flares of the
market stalls beyond, in a throng so dense that the trams
despairingly clanged their bells and slowed to a snail's-pace
—shouldering people out of their way like a steamer shouldering waves. In that market, food that wouldn't keep over the
holidays sold tonight for next-to-nothing; but Nellie hadn't
the courage to face those boisterous crowds. . . . From the
narrow alley of Ironmonger Row came the smell of frying at
Fishy Moore's, but the queue reached out to the Bull Ring.
. . . So Nellie turned into darker and even narrower streets
where the crowd was a little less dense, though even here
she steered well clear of the doors of the raucous pubs not to
risk colliding with someone propelled from within.

Here too there were tempting smells: the frying of faggots
and fish, and along the kerb potatoes were baking and
chestnuts roasting on buckets of glowing coke. But Nellie
contented herself in the end with a penn'orth of groats for
Syl, a paper of chips and a screw of tea for herself. Since
tomorrow was Christmas Day, she did half think of joining a
queue for two-penn'orth of bacon-ends; but the fifteen bob
in her purse had to last for at least another couple of weeks.
Already she owed the doctor five bob, and he still had to
keep an eye on the baby's infected ears.

The chips were nearly all gone by the time that Nellie got
home. The house was dark; but she paused on the doorstep,

and strained her ears for the click of needles (the invalid
earned her living by knitting, yet never used lamps being
much too afraid of a fire). But silence, tonight. . . . So she
must be asleep—thank God, for her tongue only ceased with
her needles and Nellie was longing for bed!

She tiptoed round the bed to her stairs, and found that
someone had left a jam-jar on one of them. Striking a match,
she saw it contained a tiny portion of tongue with a sprig of
holly on top; and she burst into tears.

For Nellie's new neighbours were like that, in Slaughterhouse Yard. The butcher pitched tongues and trotters and
hocks in the brine-tub just inside his slaughterhouse door:
somebody called him away by ringing his shop-bell, somebody else kept watch. They never took much, for fear Old
Skinflint found out—which made even less when you came
to share it all round.

Chapter 18

COVENTRY's Christmas morning, and everyone woken by bells who hadn't been woken already by children....

The bed-ridden woman downstairs told Nellie that Norah it was who'd reminded the cutters-up of the newcomer (Norah, the ten-year-old red-head who more or less ruled the Yard). Norah had downright insisted the widow be given a portion too, since fair is fair—and besides, her baby was ill. Then Norah had brought Nellie's round last night with the dropsical woman's own portion, while Nellie was out; and stuffing the mouth of the jar with a sprig of Christmas holly had also been Norah's idea, to save it from cats.

Norah was always the one with ideas. . . . Didn't Nellie agree that at Christmas whoever goes short little children *got* to get toys? But toys cost money; and few of their Dads just now had regular jobs, which had left it up to their older brothers and sisters somehow to raise the money themselves. None of those scatter-wit boys could think of anything better than barkin' (carols); and even the girls thought only of buying those twopenny bundles of snippings the dressmakers sold, to make into clothes for dolls. But Norah'd had teams out roaming the country for holly, and other teams raiding the graves for withered floral crosses and wreaths: then even the youngest had helped strip the frames, and Norah's father (who'd used to work for a florist's) had shown the bigger ones how to wire on the holly and turn out proper professional Christmas crosses and wreaths they could sell to the shops.

This morning from end to end of the Yard there'd be plenty of bleeding thumbs, but never an empty stocking. . . .

The speaker was propped on an old brass bed that was cock-eyed because of a broken castor, with both her balloons in their hangar (the blankets were raised on a cage). She

wore her sparse grey locks in permanent curlers to keep them
away from her bloodshot eyes, for fear these missed some
happening outside her window. The drooling lips had still
got plenty to say about Norah—the duckie who carried her
weekly parcel of knitting round to the pawnshop and did her
shopping, the little sweetheart who emptied her slops (but
none too often, to judge by the smell).

The needles clicked in time with the tongue, and Nellie for
once was willing to listen: for Syl had screamed all night and
now he was sleeping.

Although she was undisputed leader of all twenty-seven
walking kids who belonged in the court, it was strange (the
Balloon Woman said) that even Norah couldn't do nothing
with Brian—the poor little scrannel! For Brian came from
elsewhere, in spite of he spent all day in our Yard if he could
(and if somebody left a latrine unlocked might doss on the
seat all night), since he loved dumb beasts so much he could
never tear himself away from the slaughterhouse. . . .

Brian must have a home and family somewhere; and
Nellie asked where he came from. But nobody knew: he had
just appeared in the Yard as if from thin air, that day when a
mad bull chased the butcher up into the rafters. There in the
roof was the roosting butcher yelling for help; and when
everyone ran, there on the ground was this unknown six-
year-old dragging a bucket of water across to the bull—and
standing stroking its nose while it drank. Brian had haunted
that gloomy shed ever since, loving the beasts and giving the
butcher what help a little boy could with the killing and
flaying and carving the carcasses.

Caked as he always was in blood and dung (for no power
on earth could induce him to wash), you'd hardly have been
surprised if the other children had shunned him—especially
Norah, who made such a thing about cleanliness! Watching
the Yard from your window however you saw it was just
the other way round: it was Brian himself who wouldn't have
any truck with the others. He never ventured far from the

slaughterhouse door, and bolted inside it if Norah so much
as looked at him. . . .

Nellie had noticed this too: it was almost as if that Temple
of Death with its blood and darkness and stink was the only
place in the world where a boy felt safe. . . . But the sight of
that lone little ghoul caressing the beasts he meant to help
kill fair gave Nellie the creeps: thank heavens at least on
Christmas morning he couldn't be there, with the whole crib
empty and closed—neither oxen, nor child.

Now Nellie couldn't escape if she would, for she'd lent her
hands for winding a new skein of wool and the winder was
taking her time. But the latter had turned from the subject
of Norah and Brian to talk about Norah and Rita's Dad. . . .

For Rita Maxwell's Dad was one of the Yard's (and therefore of Norah's) knottiest problems: feeding his whippets on
raw eggs whipped up with port—as of course he had to, to
win—apparently left him unable to feed the Maxwell family
too. Even the weeks when he won he never told anyone just
how much—and mostly wouldn't come home till the money
was gone.

The pawnshop of course was the Poor Man's Bank, where
chattels acquired in prosperous times could support their
owners when times grew worse (till when, those chairs could
be sat on and tables be eaten off: something you couldn't
have done with a savings-account). You'd expect the
Maxwells in-and-out of the pawnshop? But no, the Balloon-
woman said—and added that Norah surprisingly sided with
Rita's Mum, when Mum chose hunger for all of them rather
than part with her overstuffed sofa or Rita's christening-mug.
For more money passed through the old bugger's pockets,
urged Norah, than anyone else's down Yard: he got to be
brought to his senses, and merely putting that off by stripping
their home to the bare walls and floors would be rotten weak-
minded. . . .

Now things had come to a head. Last Saturday everyone
knew the old bugger had won: yet he'd once again left them

with not one penny-piece in the house when he vanished. With Christmas coming and all, Rita'd run sobbing to Norah to try and persuade her Mum just this once. . . . But Norah'd a better idea, and she told her friend: "You leave that sofa and mug where they are! What you and your Mum got to do is to rub his nose in it proper by pledging his Sunday suit."

Finally Norah had won; the suit had been pawned, and now the whole Yard was agog because last night late the old bugger come home after all. . . .

A sudden wail from above told Nellie the baby had woken. She dropped the rest of the skein on the bed and slipped from the room; but she'd barely got back upstairs when a row broke out in the Maxwells' house so prodigious it brought the whole Yard to their windows. Nellie had just reached hers when the Maxwells' door flew open and out shot Rita, narrowly missed by a flying boot as she fled into Norah's house in floods of tears. . . .

In no time the story was all round the Yard. This morning that unpredictable Dad had got out of bed in a proper Christmassy mood; and after his bacon-and-eggs in a kitchen filled with the smell of that prime bit of beef in the oven, "Dad send me upstairs . . ." gulps Rita, still barely able to speak. And then it comes out with a rush: "I'm to look in his Sunday suit and fetch him a Five Pound Note for me Mum, as a Present!"

The way of a leader is hard. Once the news got around, those Christmas stockings were all forgotten and Norah's name in the Yard was mud. She ought to have guessed Our Rita was such a gormless sap she'd never have gone through the pockets.

Chapter 19

B UT back to Christmas at Mellton. For Polly, this turned
out a heavenly Christmas after all: she had woken at five
with her shyness all gone in the night so had crept into
bed with Augustine to share her stocking, and found herself
loving the new Augustine as much as the old one. But
Gilbert could hardly be finding it heavenly—Gilbert, that
little Jack Horner gloomily chewing his thumbful of Dead
Sea fruit.

For Gilbert had pinned all his Liberal hopes on the coming
election; and then when it came it had ended in three-out-of-
four of last time's Liberal seats in Parliament lost. With
Asquith their leader himself gone down to a Labour opponent at Paisley, and Gilbert's own 'safe' Liberal seat only
saved by thirty-two votes, a fat lot of hope he had now of
a place on the Treasury Bench in any foreseeable Liberal
ministry!

How had this disaster occurred? This Christmas morning
he started racking his brains as soon as he woke. Since we
had put Labour in office and only we could eject them, we'd
held the Joker—the choice of a Dissolution issue entirely to suit
ourselves; and what better choice—what rottener wicket for
Labour to bat on and better for Liberal bowlers—than
choosing MacDonald's Russian Loan, which was stealing the
Tories' anti-Bolshevik thunder as well? We had only to ram
home the criminal folly of putting in Russian pockets the gold
we would put in the pocket of Britain's own workless at home,
and. . . . Why, even without that last-minute-kick-in-the-
crutch of the Red Letter Scare this should have seen Labour
down for the count, and the Liberal Cause triumphant.

Instead we were now outnumbered three to one even by
Labour—and *ten* to one by the Tories. . . . For Fate had

snatched our Joker out of our hands, on its very way to the table: that was the dire effect of Labour's premature fall in the tea-cup storm over Communist Campbell's arrest and release.... The premature Dissolution this caused had meant that the crucial Russian Debate never even took place, and had left us lugging the Loan stone-cold to the hustings instead of fiery-hot from the parliamentary anvil.

As Gilbert crept out of bed he couldn't help harking back to MacDonald's strangely asinine moves throughout the whole Campbell Affair: first charging the man with incitement to mutiny, then withdrawing the charge in a way which stank to high heaven and really had left the Tories no choice but proposing a vote of No Confidence. . . . But then a new idea came to Gilbert, so bizarre it made him cut himself shaving: *if Campbell hadn't existed, would Ramsay have had to invent him?* In short, had all this just been a diabolical trick to duck the Russian Debate? To cheat the gallows by cutting his own throat himself the night before in the death-cell, by means of that Censure Motion the Tories had never intended to press? Then.... Why, even that typical Ramsay-ish huff which had forced a last-minute vote. . . . Then even that huff was a fake.

Dabbing his cheek with styptic, Gilbert hurried to get to breakfast before the young men arrived: for he wanted to try out his novel idea of Ramsay-the-Machiavel on Mary in private, because if true (so he pointed out as he cracked his egg) it unmasked a wholly unethical cowardly cunning which must put Ramsay for ever beyond the pale in the eyes of a man of principle. Mary shrugged her shoulders. She had certainly thought the House's proceedings on Campbell Night a trifle Alice-in-Wonderland, even by Mother-of-Parliaments standards—and that's saying something! For in with the 'Ayes' for the Vote of Censure had trooped the Government's own supporters, while both other Parties in panic revoked and had voted solid against it—indeed they'd have foiled the Government's suicide-bid by sheer weight of

numbers, had Simon's amendment not given the death-wish
a second chance. . . . But *had* the whole Campbell Affair, she
wondered, really been cooked up by Ramsay right from the
start as Gilbert supposed? Probably Ramsay himself didn't
know the answer, because (as Jeremy said so often they called
it 'Jeremy's Law') the 'Idealist Statesman's essential gift is a
righteous right hand blissfully unaware what his crooked
subliminal left is up to'. In short, political life is as full of
unconscious meanings and motivations as poetry. . . .

Meanwhile Gilbert had moved on to other election
themes: the festering state of the Party's 'Reunion', with both
sides worn to gangrenous sores wherever Lloyd George and
the Party Machine came in contact: 'No Trespassing' boards
signed 'D.L.G.' all over Liberal Wales, and a tourniquet
clapped on the vital flow from the little man's moneybags.

Mary said something. . . . True (agreed Gilbert), what
mattered was less the hopeless seats we'd allowed to go by
default than the possible seats we had fought and so dismally
lost; but how could Party morale survive when Lloyd
George's refusal to cough up the cost of a candidate left so
many with no one to work for and vote for?

"Are you listening, dear?" said Gilbert; and Mary said
Yes, she was. . . . But can't Gilbert see (she was thinking)
what locking his moneybags means is that Lloyd George is
running no risk of winning elections so long as Asquith
survives? That brought to her mind John Simon's story: how,
after the previous election, Gilbert Murray had wanted
Asquith himself to take office with Labour support, instead of
the other way round. . . . Ah, but that would mean "finding a
niche for Our Little Friend," which was something which
Asquith refused to even discuss. . . . So Asquith too would
be taking good care no risk of winning was run so long as
that meant high office for D.L.G.; and two such leaders,
only agreed in their common desire for defeat, were only
too likely to get their way!

"Are you listening, dear?" Gilbert asked her again; and
Mary again said she was. . . . So the Liberal Party was

G*

doomed, she decided: when one of them died in the end it would be too late. She studied her husband's face. What would Gilbert do, when he found that his leaders themselves had condemned him to forty years in the wilderness? Oust them for somebody new—but for *whom*?

Or else . . . But no, for surely Gilbert would never abandon his Party! After all Gilbert was Liberal born and bred. Three centuries back an earlier Roundhead Gilbert had bought the Mellton estates from their bankrupt Cavalier owners, and ever since then the Chase had sent to the House its Whig and later its Liberal squires. . . . All the same, she couldn't quite get out of her mind another of Jeremy's nastier dicta (said apropos Winston Churchill lately leaving the Liberal Party —ostensibly rather than have to support the Socialist Party in office): 'No, the Man of Principle never deserts his Party: he brands the Party itself for deserting him and his principles'.

Then the door opened and in came Augustine's charming friend, an American young Mr. Fairfax intrigued by kippers but thankful to find that this elegant British home had coffee to offer at breakfast as well as tea.

A young Mr. Fairfax, too, who felt it a privilege being the Christmas guest of an eminent British Statesman. He'd always been taught to hold the British House of Commons in high regard, all American politics being so crooked.

Chapter 20

Paris called him, and Anthony wasn't intending to stop on in England long; but above all else in England he wanted to hunt.

From a card pinned up in the hall he learned that a Boxing Day Meet would be held at Tottersdown Abbey, and privately hoped that Mary would offer to lend him a mount. But Mary advised him to wait, since Boxing Day Meets were never for serious hunting but more for working off Christmas dinners and half the county followed on foot (privately Mary preferred to keep him under her eye if she took him out, which could hardly be done in a Boxing Day scrum).

So Mary hacked to the Meet alone with a groom. But Anthony wanted to witness it all the same, and persuaded Augustine to tramp there with him over the downs (while Polly most unwillingly stopped at home).

On the way, Augustine described the Abbey—the house they were going to see—as "a fake-Victorian mansion, though really built in the Middle Ages". After the Dissolution, he said, a motley succession of secular owners had kept on trying to fake the Abbey to look up to date; and because of its elephantine size, each spent so much that the next generation had had to sell it—which started the tale of an Abbot's Curse. One of the earliest hid its barbaric old Gothic front behind a Renaissance colonnade: then a Georgian lowered the pitch of the roofs, and a Regency owner clad acres of stonework in stucco he painted to *look* like stone. But no one had total success till the late-Victorian Henry Struthers who covered the stucco in ivy, added a vast Gothic-revival porch with arrow-slits, hid the Georgian roofs behind gargoyles and battlements, stained-glassed a number of windows—and lo, today from top to toe it looked a completely Victorian edifice!

"All the genuine monkish stonework and carving appears convincingly imitation, seen in the context of Struthers; and even the ruined Chantry looks utterly bogus, apparently built round a vaguely Florentine fountain and planted with Wellingtonias."

Anthony asked who lived there now; and that special note of constraint which protests that you're neither snobbish nor anti-Semitic infected Augustine's voice as he named "Nathaniel Corcos, First Lord Tottersdown". Very much richer than any previous owner, this one alone had made no attempt to alter the Abbey's appearance: "The old boy feels it exactly suits his style—as a pure Sephardic Jew with a pedigree long as your arm and a fortune centuries-old whom everyone takes for a nouveau-riche".

On arrival they found a crowd of hundreds milling around on the four or five acres of gravel, or fighting its way to a long white table where flunkies in gorgeous flunkery served hot punch: a tiny handful of horsemen surrounded by people with no idea what it meant, getting kicked. Younger hounds were barging their way through the throng like professional footballers: Whips and Huntsmen struggled vainly to get them under control, and cursed the silly women who tried to pat them and fed them on sausage-rolls. No wonder that Polly was left at home in a mob like this!

They caught one distant glimpse of Mary, on foot. Wisely she'd left her mount for the groom to hold till the final moment when hounds moved off; and now she was chaffing a tiny farmer who sat a Gargantuan beast which probably pulled the plough. . . .

Then Augustine gave a sudden cry of delight, and darted away through the crowd towards the house. Hurrying post-haste after Augustine and blocked by a glowering Polly's-age child on a Shetland pony so low he nearly fell over it, Anthony only acknowledged her "Damn you, look where you're going you oaf!" by politely raising his hat without looking round. Then he found Augustine engaged with another

young man, and clearly both overjoyed at the meeting—
although this only showed in their twinkling eyes, and at first
they hardly spoke (but when they did speak, both spoke at
once).

For Augustine was not the only truant lately returned to
Dorset. Archdeacon Dibden was Rector of Tottersdown
Monachorum and this was Jeremy, just got back from a four-
months spent in Russia and Central Europe. That was
to be his last fling of freedom before getting swallowed up
in the Civil Service, a fledgling Assistant Principal. . . .
"Call me a 'Postulant' rather," he'd just been insisting before Augustine joined them: "For what more strictly enclosed Contemplative Order exists than the English Civil
Service?"

With him were Ludovic Corcos (the son of the house), who
was one of his oldest friends; and an even more dazzling
Gentile lady. Augustine's attention was fully engaged, but
she quite took Anthony's breath: she couldn't be more than
her twenties, and visibly winced when Jeremy called her
"My Aunt".

When hounds had at last moved off, half of the crowd
went home. The rest of them tried to 'follow', but didn't
know where to go: for the Hunt had instantly disappeared in
a mist which made the occasional horn or the hound giving-
tongue seem to come from anywhere, back or front. In twos
and threes they slowly zig-zagged about, plodding in twenty
acres of heavy plough until they succeeded in reaching the
nearest fence—to find that beyond it lay thirty acres of heavy
plough, where they finally stuck.

Watching the last of these plodders fade in the mist, "La
nostalgie de la boue . . ." murmured Jeremy: "Strange, that
this British liking for playing in mud has only a name in
French."

"There's probably something about it in Freud," said
Ludovic.

"Indeed there is!" cried Jeremy's Aunt.

'Then his grandfather *must* have been married twice', thought Augustine.

*

It still was too early for lunch, so Ludovic led them up to his den. He closed the stained-glass window, swept a scimitar off the sofa to let them sit and opened his limed-oak cocktail-cabinet.

"Mud and Blood—the English sportsman's gods, his Heavenly Twins", mused Jeremy: "Little wonder that under *their* aegis he won the War!" He paused while his good hand lifted the paralysed one to clamp its fingers convincingly round his glass, then added, "At least in sports like sailing or mountaineering the life at risk is your own."

"Chaps do get killed," said Augustine.

"Not actively killed by the fox—more's the pity."

"Then what about pig-sticking?" Ludovic interposed. "There, if you take a tumble the boar himself disembowels you."

"Ugh!" said Jeremy's Aunt (by now they were all of them calling her 'Joan').

"The man with only his spear, the charging boar with his tushes—and hard, like stubbing your spear in the trunk of an oak."

"Ludo!" Jeremy cried: "You little savage, don't tell me you really enjoyed it!"

Inwardly Anthony boiled. Sure, he'd got wise in the end to Augustine's corny notions of fun; but this Jeremy guy with his polio arm.... You'd take that Yid for the only White Man out of the bunch by the way the other two talked!

Meanwhile in Ludovic's mind was revived that intoxicant, loose-reined leaping out of the dark of the Moorish cork-woods: out over boulders and sunlit palmetto, and galloping blind with eyes for only the jinking quarry in front where a fox-hunter wouldn't have risked his horse at a walk. Boars have killed lions.... He silently smiled at his manicured nails as he dreamed of his twelve-and-a-half hand Barb and a

Tangier boar standing ten-and-a-half with its back to the
Rocks. . . . But then some sixth sense took him across to the
window. At what he saw, looking down through the coloured
glass, he stiffened: that enigmatical huddled group on the
gravel, which suddenly changed its hue as it crossed from the
amber pane to the red. . . . He turned to his guests: "Forgive
me a moment, Father may need my help. I'll be back, but
meanwhile fill up your glasses."

He slipped from the room.

'Fill up your glasses. . . .'

The Bedouin say that a man's soul travels only as fast as a
camel: the man whose body moves any faster must wait for
his soul to catch up. Jeremy'd come home much too quickly,
by train—and had left his soul far behind where the singing
Danube giddies through the Visegrad Narrows. Spotting a
Sliwowitz bottle he poured a man's-size tot for himself, then
poured out one for Augustine.

Augustine accepted it, lost in dreams of his chase by the
cops in the Dusy: the Bearcat's plunge from the dam—and
who says the fox can't enjoy it, at least in retrospect?

Anthony's homesick eyes were searching the labels in vain
for Bourbon. . . .

Joan had only eyes for Augustine. He looked so uncannily
like his cousin Henry, killed in the War only five days after
they'd secretly got engaged.

Chapter 21

At Mellton Gilbert was glad to be spending the day alone, with so much to think out. But first he'd some tiresome letters to answer; and then he remembered he'd got to consider his figure these days, so made his reluctant way to the ex-Mausoleum which housed his squash-court. There he changed into shorts and for twenty minutes or so woke the cavernous echoes, practising shots. After that he took a shower (thank God the water for once was really hot!).

With Asquith losing his seat (thought Gilbert, starting towards the house), things were tricky indeed. That business of choosing a Party Sessional Chairman. . . . When some of them tried for Collins (the new Chief Whip) the Little Welsh Goat had turned very nasty; and when it was put to the vote got elected (Gilbert himself had abstained: he profoundly distrusted Lloyd George, but when hitching wagons to stars it is fatal to hitch to the wrong one).

He crossed the lawn, where Polly in scarlet leggings and gloves was exercising her latest puppy as well as her governess. Vaguely he waved his racket, but Polly was too taken up with her puppy at first to respond until Miss Penrose sharply reminded her: then she shouted something he didn't bother to hear. . . .

On the loggia Susan Amanda was braving the raw December air in her pram; but he passed his encapsulated baby without a glance, for Gilbert by now was hungry for luncheon as well as so busy distrusting Lloyd George—and Lloyd George's latest Land Reform ideas in particular. *Any* meddlesome mucking-about with the age-old, delicate structures enshrining the tenure of land was something which Gilbert regarded with righteous horror; and who could know more about that than Gilbert, a model land-owner himself? But this latest scheme would be virtual Nationalisa-

198

tion: something disastrous for farmers—they'd all be hamstrung by County Committees and town-bred officials who
couldn't tell late-sown barley from quitch; and disastrous for
landlords, since all they would get for their land would be
Lloyd George 'Bonds'—not even hard cash. As for any young
man who wanted to break into farming, he hadn't a hope:
for this hare-brained 'hereditable tenure' idea accrued to
some sitting tenant's unmerited profit and penalised everyone else.

Gilbert lunched alone, then shut himself in his study and
lit a rare cigarette to help him think. . . . That little Welsh
crook had somehow smuggled a hint of this into the Party
Manifesto, which Strachie declared had cost us a lot of votes
in the agricultural West. This blatantly Socialist measure
would have to be fought tooth-and-nail at the coming Party
Convention, or else the 'Liberal' Party must lose any rag of
pretence to the name. He'd better join forces with some of
those sensible chaps from the North: such men as Runciman
. . . Geoffrey Howard, of Castle Howard . . . Charles Roberts,
involved through his wife with the Carlisle Estates. These
were sound Liberals all; and thoroughly sound about land,
as well as hating Lloyd George.

Nobody really liked or trusted Churchill; but what a pity
our arch-antisocialist should have left us just when we
needed him most!

Pettier men might sneer at Winston, and call him a turncoat—indeed, a twice-over turncoat, because he had only
crossed to the Liberal side in the first place just in time for the
Liberal Landslide of 1906. But Gilbert was quite fair-minded
enough to respect an integrity careless of cries of 'Turncoat!' incurred on behalf of a Higher Loyalty. . . . Still, for
himself he hoped that final sacrifice wouldn't be called for—
yet.

Gilbert had got thus far when a white-faced Wantage
asked him to come to the telephone. Testily Gilbert told him
to take a message; but Wantage insisted, the Master must

speak himself. The call was from Tottersdown—something
had happened, there'd been an accident.

Then a voice on the phone told Gilbert that Mary had had
a fall. They wouldn't know till the doctors had seen her of
course, but she might have broken her back.

Chapter 22

MARY hadn't broken her back, she had broken her neck.

The cause of her fall was that glowering Polly's-age child so low on her Shetland pony that Mary couldn't see her before she began the jump, and had had to swing her horse half-round in the air as she landed. She fell on her head, and at first they had thought she was only stunned as she lay awry with her bowler-hat crammed down over her face; but then they noticed she didn't seem to be breathing, and crowded round her telling each other to "Stand right back and give the lady some air!"

"Don't be a fool!" said the child (who hadn't even been touched): "Can't you see she's dead?"

"No I'm not!" (So Mary supposed she was saying, though only groaning hollowly into her hat.)

She even supposed she was struggling on to her feet, and was much surprised when she found that she hadn't moved. Her head was dizzy, she didn't know where she was but she felt no pain, and didn't even feel bruised except for her face. She was quite unaware that she barely breathed: it was just she apparently couldn't move, or feel—that neither pain nor volition could enter or leave her head, since the rest of her *wasn't there*. . . . 'I must be a cherub!' she thought; and passed right out just as somebody felt her heart and sent for a stretcher.

*

In Tottersdown Cottage Hospital, X-rays showed the seventh cervical vertebra cracked: she was 'gravely ill'.

For hours Augustine and Gilbert sat in the medical smell of the Superintendent's Office, each walled up in his own suspense and barely aware of the other; but then the doctor decided he'd have to allow them to see her now, or risk that they never saw her again alive.

When they reached the bed they found that pleasant, intelligent boyish face a swollen, unrecognisable black-and-blue with eyes too puffy to open. However she seemed to be conscious, and even endeavoured to speak though quite unable to make herself understood and dribbling over the sheet. When Gilbert tried to take her hand, he found her paralysis passed from the limp to a rigid stage like rigor mortis—as if her body already were really dead.

Yet the spark of life in her lingered on, and on. A few days later that rigor began to pass, the swelling and bruising began to subside: though even after her eyes could open again she still couldn't properly see as they wouldn't focus yet.

*

When a couple of weeks had passed and Mary was still alive (and had even begun to speak comprehensibly—just), the doctor began to call her a 'hopeful' case. To Mary, he cheerfully talked about rest; but he told her husband and brother bluntly that though she now seemed likely to live the damage was done for good: the rest of her life would be spent in a chair.

He brought out charts. When that vertebra cracked, he explained, the dura mater (the sheath of the spinal cord) had got twisted and torn. Since the lesion was lower down than most of the brachial plexus she might recover the use of her arms: but certainly little more. Sensation as well as control was destroyed—except in time (perhaps) for her arms, and even some of her breast. . . . Meanwhile, however, she seemed to be making wonderful progress: her bladder already showed signs of working again unaided, which meant that the common danger of fatal kidney infection was almost past. In short, the autonomic system didn't seem badly affected: she shouldn't get gangrene or fail to digest her food, as the severed body was learning to work on its own.

When Gilbert asked how soon he could have her home, the doctor pointed out she would need a nurse for the rest of her life of course; and said that he knew of one he could specially recommend, who was used to spinal cases. . . .

Frankly, Gilbert was marvellous: even Augustine was forced to admit he'd misjudged him when Gilbert—the arrant careerist—told the doctor he'd never resign the intimate care of his wife into other hands: for the rest of her life he would nurse her night and day, and sacrifice everything else. True he had little nursing knowledge as yet but surely could learn; and what a paralysed wife would have need of most was love.

*

So Runciman, Howard and Roberts were left after all to fight Lloyd George on their own; and Gilbert informed the Whips they must write him off as a Liberal vote in the House. They could but respect his decision, but begged him at any rate not to resign his seat—it was much too precarious.

Meanwhile he studied medical books and badgered the Matron to teach him that kind of jiu-jitsu which nurses call 'lifting'. However, the doctor insisted still that there must be a proper professional nurse in charge in case complications arose; but when Mary was moved to Mellton at last and the nurse arrived, that only served to show how right Gilbert was. There was little she didn't know about nursing, but almost nothing she knew about anything else—and if Gilbert had not been constantly there as well, her talk would have driven intelligent Mary mad.

Indeed as it was Mary had 'glooms' which were next thing to madness, spells of a nightmare confusion which couldn't tell life and death apart. In these 'glooms' her protective belief in total extinction at death should surely have saved her; but now that collapsed in the face of a bodiless conscious state so like the traditional soul-after-death. Perhaps its roots had never been more than emotional, deep in forgotten childhood terrors of hell: for now these ancient terrors raised their forgotten heads. Again and again they caused her to 'dream' wide-awake she was dead, and helplessly being sucked into hell like a child in her bath down the plug-hole.

Augustine had rescued his pictures from Paris to hang in her room. The Renoir and even Cézanne were all right; but in Mary's 'glooms' the late Van Gogh made her worse, and it had to be moved. In her glooms there was one thing only could bring her back to reality: Susan Amanda's weight, the first thing her arms had faintly begun to discern; and the baby's warmth on a partially-sensitive breast.

Gilbert was blissfully happy: it seemed like a second honeymoon having Mary entirely dependent upon him at last. And at night it gave him a strangely elated feeling I can't describe to be handling Mary's body while Mary slept without it possibly waking her. Added to which, that awkward question of whether the errant Liberal Party deserved his support any longer was decently shelved: this couldn't have come at any more opportune time.

Nowadays Joan was settled at Tottersdown running her widowed half-brother's house, and in general keeping him company now that Whitehall was just about to swallow up Jeremy. Ludovic, Joan and Jeremy called at the Chase to enquire; and Gilbert was struck by the beauty of Joan just as everyone else was.

*

Before he landed, Augustine had meant to indulge his nostalgia for Wales as soon as Christmas at Mellton was over; but Mary's accident stopped him. Meanwhile his agent was urging him: dry-rot had started in part of the Newton roof and it ought to be seen to at once, so now that Mary seemed out of danger he made up his mind to go there at least on a fleeting visit. But little time could be spared there enjoying the salty fresh air: for the first few hours at least must be spent with the expert he'd sent for, crawling about in the Newton rafters.

There they found dry-rot fungus far more extensive than first supposed. It was going to cost the earth to get rid of, for after such long neglect it would mean re-roofing at least one wing—of a house that size! The only alternative seemed to be pulling the whole wing down; but that would leave him with only a measly twenty-nine bedrooms as well as new kitchens to build, and the cost might be even larger. Augustine had never spent more than a tenth of his income, yet even so. . . .

The land at Newton was strictly entailed and none, he knew, could be sold: he was lucky indeed in possessing another perhaps more viable property. This had once been a minor country estate on the fringes of ancient Swansea, which Swansea had swallowed and built-on and now was a thriving part of the town. The ground-rents brought him in little; but soon the earliest leases must start falling in (which would one day make him a very rich man indeed by the standards of West Wales gentry); and meanwhile, money could surely be raised. . . .

Augustine was anxious to get back to Dorset as soon as he could, but perforce must stop overnight in Swansea to call on the lawyer who held all the deeds and collected the ground-rents and so on. Bright as that lawyer turned out to be, legal business can seldom be done in a hurry: as well as the builders to keep an eye on, Augustine's first visit to Swansea was hardly likely to prove his last one. . . .

Henceforth though he spent all the time he could in Dorset with Mary he'd have to keep dashing to Wales with so much to attend to there, being born with this silver millstone hung round his neck. . . .

Chapter 23

Yes, the ways of the rich man are known to be full of trouble; but even the poor have their cares. As the Coventry winter slowly gave way to spring Syl showed no signs of beginning to talk; and when his mother tried with a ticking watch it appeared that perhaps his measles had left him deaf. However, young as he was (he wouldn't be two till October), the doctor assured her the drums should heal now the discharge had dried provided she took good care that he didn't get chills.

So long as the March winds lasted all she could do about that was keeping him in, though the room was damp and it hadn't a door (only a makeshift barrier stopped him falling downstairs); but once the weather was really warmer and less conducive to chills she wrapped him up and wheeled him out in the open whenever she had the time. Often, too, Norah would borrow him, cramming her brother's football-stocking over his head so it thoroughly covered his ears: for Norah agreed that fresh air must do the ailing baby good—always provided it couldn't get near his ears.

This was the season when Coventry families worked their allotments from dawn till dusk, pausing only to stir their bonfires into a blaze for cooking their midday stew with leeks and parsnips straight from the ground. Norah's Dad's allotment was one of the ones out Quinton way (down Little Park Street, and out on the Quinton road): it was well within reach with a pram, and so this is where Norah mostly took little Syl. Part of the time he slept while everyone dug: part of the time she lifted him out to crawl in the sun: part of the time she tried to teach him to walk. As well as a careful succession of things to eat (and Mum's little patch of medicinal herbs, such as comfrey for poulticing sprains), Dad grew daffs for the market. Often Syl would arrive back home still smelling of bonfire smoke, with a single wilting daffodil clutched in a muddy fist—'as a present for Mum'.

Of course these crowded strips of allotments weren't like the open country, only the next best thing; but soon the real picnicking season would come, when droves of Coventry children out of the slums—some of them barely able to toddle, and nobody older than Norah in charge of twenty or thirty or more—would fill their pockets with bread-and-jam and spend all day in the Warwickshire meadows whenever there wasn't school. A century back, the moribund city was shrunken away from the line of its ancient walls like a shrivelled kernel inside a nut: since then the population had grown ten times but the bounds of the area built-on had hardly extended again at all, so green fields weren't too far from these crowded tenements even for tinies. Often these (piperless) Pied-Piper parties wouldn't get home till dusk: for what harm could they come to, in lanes and woods and fields—if they kept a good look-out for bulls? It was better than having them run under horses' hooves in the trafficky streets, or moitherin' Mum.

On these occasions all babies had to be left behind, for you can't push prams through hedges or drag them across ploughed fields. But next year perhaps, once Syl was able to walk. . . .

*

And next year perhaps, once the Nazi Party had been rebuilt. . . . But meanwhile the first thing Hitler had to do was to get the legal ban on his Party lifted by promising good behaviour. This was conceded less out of trust in his word than contempt for so sorry a rump as the Nazis had now become: for his tactic of setting his friends by the ears, till nowadays few of them loved him any more than they loved one another, had paid: as a menace Hitler no longer existed.

He chose, for dramatic reasons, the Bürgerbräukeller to

hold his first Reconstruction Meeting. But almost none of the Nazi big-wigs showed their faces: Ludendorff, Strasser, Röhm and Rosenberg all stayed away, and Göring was still abroad (he was also struck off the rolls).

Lothar was there, in a modest corner, and saw how Hitler's eloquence swayed the faithful: the women sobbed, and disruptive elements stumbled tearfully on to the platform to pump each other's hands. But after all, who were these 'faithfuls' apart from second-rate scamps like that Carl whom Reinhold delighted to tease, and a handful of dewy-eyed youths like Lothar himself? The only Nazis present of any importance were Frick and Esser and Streicher—pretty small beer when compared with those others who stopped away.

Those four absentees: Ludendorff, Rosenberg, Strasser and Röhm. . . .

To begin with, Hitler decided he'd no further use for the former war-lord: Ludendorff's pagan nonsense was proving a needless provocation to all respectable Christians (including the Munich government). But in that case the corpse of his great reputation had better be finally buried, for fear his support was lent to some rival party; and President Ebert's death gave Hitler his cue. He egged silly Ludendorff on to run for President, knowing this bound to end in fiasco; and when the candidate didn't score one per cent of the votes it was 'Exit LUDENDORFF, laughed off the stage'.

Rosenberg. . . . Hitler knew he would lick the hand which laid on the lash, if he laid it on good and hard; and so it proved. But Röhm and Strasser were rather more difficult nuts to crack.

Gregor Strasser, the ablest leader of those who still believed in the 'Socialist' half of the National-Socialist Programme: a big young man who dressed in home-made breeches and black wool stockings, and looked like a block of oak in spite of the rather absurd little Tyrolese hat he perched on his head. Somebody much too important and useful to do without, yet much too honest to want around. . . . But his Leftist ideas might go down well in the North, where the Movement had hitherto scarcely been heard of—and Strasser was one of the few with a Reichstag seat. . . . So Hitler dazzled his eyes with a new and almost autonomous job, and this was not the first (or last) time Hitler managed to lull his suspicions. Thus '*Exit* STRASSER', transferred to Berlin to preach the gospel among the benighted Prussians; and Hitler was free of his somewhat embarrassing eye.

The fourth absentee had been Captain Röhm: a dyed-in-the-wool professional soldier with battle-scarred head and broken nose, and a purely soldierly way of seeing the world. He trained his Storm Troops on Army lines, like a kind of Irregular Territorial Force: whereas all Hitler wanted were street-thugs, trained not in warfare but merely to break up his rivals' meetings and guard his own. Moreover the Army were likely to look askance at a private force that was too like themselves—and winning the Army's favour had now become Hitler's lodestar, never again must he find himself facing the Army's guns.

Röhm addressed Hitler as 'Du' and could never forget he had once been Hitler's discoverer, almost treating the Party as merely a 'Civil Arm' of his Storm Troops run by his protégé Hitler the mere politico. . . . That was the final straw: if Röhm wouldn't come to heel he would have to go. So in April 'go' Röhm went—at the end of a most almighty row. He resigned his command of the Storm Troops, severed all ties with the Party and vanished abroad to serve the Bolivian Army as soldier of fortune. Thus it was '*Exit* RÖHM'—at least for the next five years.

Ludendorff, Rosenberg, Strasser and Röhm. . . . Hitler was left undisputed cock-of-the-dunghill.

Chapter 24

ARCHDEACON DIBDEN was out so much at committees and visitations that Joan had plenty of time on her hands. Thus she was often over at Mellton: for Gilbert was showing signs of shortage of sleep—he had rings round his eyes and a nervous twitch in his cheek, and was only too glad of an afternoon nap while she read to Mary aloud.

Gilbert showed no signs of jealousy over Mary with Joan, the way he undoubtedly did with Mary's beloved brother. Indeed he pressed her to come there whenever she could: perhaps not least because Joan was indeed such an exquisite creature to have in one's house ('Like a rare work of art,' as he told himself, 'or some virginal flower'). Moreover she made no attempt to conceal her admiration of Gilbert's heroic self-abnegation; and this too was something about her he greatly liked.

As for Augustine, apart from the time he spent at his sister's bedside he came to rely more and more upon Joan for congenial company, taking her long walks over the downs or talking tête-à-tête by the Rectory fire. But they seldom talked of themselves: for now Augustine had fallen in love— and alas, it was more with the South Wales miners than Joan. Rather as Byron adopted the Greeks, and other romantic Englishmen tend to adopt their own alternative alien group (Albanian bandits for instance, Somali tribesmen, or Esquimaux), so had Augustine discovered and fallen in love with his miners and talked about little else. The blood of Welsh Princes ran in his veins (or at least he quartered their Arms), but his blood in fact was thoroughly mixed and his education and outlook exclusively upper-class English: thus he could feel these miners as kin on the one hand who made him feel proud he was Welsh—and yet at the same time creatures remote enough from himself for the alien charm to work.

It may seem strange that Augustine had only discovered the miners so lately. The Valleys had always been close in the topographical sense: yet Augustine had barely seen even a pit-top before, since his usual route to-and-fro was the beautiful rural one by Llandilo and Brecon which by-passed the whole Industrial South—you wouldn't have known it was there. But that Swansea lawyer of his was leading a double life, conveyancing only by day and by night conducting a male-voice choir which won prize after prize; and on one of his visits to Swansea, Augustine got taken with him to one of these singing marathons up in the anthracite country. After the concert he spent the night in a miner's cottage, watching a ninety-year-old with a miner's blue tattoos on his face who danced on his hearthstone half through the night after everyone else was in bed. This little old man liked his pint but he never went into a pub nowadays, he said—not since the dancing in pubs had been stopped by the bloody police. . . .

Next morning Augustine promised a prize for their next Cymanfa Ganu. That, and his likeable manner, earned him a trip down a pit; and to him this whole way of life was a revelation. It bowled him over, and ever since then he took every chance he could get of exploring the Valleys—even so far afield as the Rhondda. As for the miners, strange as he was they seemed to adopt him much as that teenage American pack had done.

The miners' talk, and the way they sang, and the plays they acted—oh no, it wasn't by any means only their physical prowess which singled them out as the Chosen People if ever there was one! They certainly didn't lack brains, and many who'd worked underground all their lives had somehow acquired an education as good as his own—or perhaps even better than his was. Their pride. . . . It made him feel proud in his turn that he too could claim to be Welsh (even though he belonged to that much-despised Class, the 'Uchelwyr'). Indeed he admired them so much that even their little weaknesses only endeared them the more to him. . . . Wasn't it strange (so Augustine told Joan) how useless the skilfullest miner was with his hands at anything else? An out-of-work miner could lie on his face and burrow into the hillside a couple of hundred yards like a mole till he reached the seam, then inch himself back feet-first dragging his bag of coal to the open air with his teeth (thus leaving the hillside a dangerous honeycomb): yet if the same man tried to nail together two pieces of wood, the result would disgrace a child. . . .

In this way week was added to week till Augustine and Joan knew every Dorset ramble for ten miles round, and Augustine and Joan between them (no single voice could have possibly lasted out) had read to Mary the whole of Proust.

Chapter 25

So Strasser had moved to the North, and was hard at work for the Cause. . . .

That Presidential Election which ridded Hitler of Ludendorff proved quite a close-run thing between the more serious candidates. Finally, seventy-seven-year-old Field Marshal Hindenburg just scraped in; and Reinhold used the excuse of a legal case in Berlin to sniff the changed political air of the capital now we'd a Junker instead of a working-class President.

One of his oldest and ablest political friends in the North was that veteran 'Patriot', Arno Lepowski. The previous year, while Hitler was still in gaol and his Party proscribed, this Count Lepowski had worked with Ludendorff, Strasser and Rosenberg rigging a 'Völkisch Coalition'—the one which had netted the Nazi anonymous remnant a handful of Reichstag seats, including a seat for Strasser; and then the Count had formed a high opinion of Strasser—the only Nazi with any future, according to him. For the Count brushed Hitler aside as a featherweight, lacking the stuff of a leader: "A febrile weathercock, useful perhaps down South; but the solider Protestant North distrusts his sort. If the Nazis want to cut any ice up here they had better forget about Hitler and hitch their wagon to Strasser."

"I beg to differ," said Reinhold.

"I happened to run into Captain Röhm just before he sailed, and he made my hair stand on end with his tales of what Hitler is like to work with. Poor old Röhm, he got so excited his scars lit up like the comb of a cock! Each twopenny problem has to be solved by Hitler himself—though half the time it has only become one because of his own vacillation. Again: if you offer advice he throws it back in your face, then three days later announces that very decision as if it was his idea from the first. Indeed Röhm doubts if Hitler has ever produced one single idea of his own: he filches the lot, he's a peacock naked apart from borrowed plumes—an ideological scarecrow."

"With great respect," said Reinhold mildly, "isn't that always the stuff that leaders are made of? Of course I mean the Caesars who get to the very top, not the high-minded Strassers who merely win our esteem."

The aged and deeply furrowed face of the Count took on an ironical look, with cool grey eyes more ready to be amused than convinced: "Then what becomes of the typical charismatic leader's obsessional Grand Idea that he's ready to die for? His superhuman will, which forces unwilling disciples to follow his Great Ideal like sheep?"

"Thus Spake Zarathustra—not the revered Lepowski, who knows no leader has ever forced men to do things against their will. We only imagine he has."

"Proceed," said the Count, no longer smiling.

"The world-shaking 'Leader' is just what Röhm described: a tabula rasa without any will or ideas of his own at all, but a superhumanly sensitive nose for what potential followers think and want. He must find that out before the bulk of them know it themselves, then announce it as *his* unchangeable will—when of course they will follow his lead like sheep, because that's the way they're already unconsciously wanting to go."

"So that's your idea of the famous 'Führerprinzip'?" mused the Count: "No need for Democracy's ballot-boxes because the Leader himself is a walking box, with sensitive ears where everyone posts his vote? But come! That's merely a human weathercock, not what we mean by a 'Leader'."

"Aren't you forgetting your Leader's implacable will?"

"But you've just denied him a will of his own at all!" cried the Count, amazed.

"I only denied him the choice of his will's direction: I never denied him its strength. It's the strength of will they so signally lack themselves which makes the herd so dependent on him. Themselves they pursue their ends so feebly; but he lets no obstacle stand in the way of their faintest unspoken and even unrealised wishes. . . ."

But now Lepowski had had quite enough. "What a pair of old wind-bags we are!" he grumbled. "We've lost ourselves in the clouds. . . . Let me see, where did all this start?"

"You thought the Nazis ought to ditch Hitler for Strasser. But if you ask me, Hitler won't give them the chance."

"These Nazis—a so-called 'national' party almost unknown in the North, with only a few thousand members and those at each other's throats. . . . If *you* ask *me*, it is Strasser who ought to ditch the Nazis and join some party which counts. They can only thrive on despair, and will disappear altogether now our Seven Lean Years seem over."

"Yes, I agree that by all the rules they should now fade away—and doubtless they would, if it wasn't for Hitler."

The old man made an impatient gesture: "Your *Hitler, Hitler*—I'm sick to death of the name!"

"Very likely—but don't think you've heard the last of it!" Reinhold's Cassandra-like tones confronted the frank disbelief in Lepowski's face. "He is powerless now; but can't I get you to see he's the very archetype of a Leader—the pure Platonic Idea of 'Leader' with everything normally human left out?" Lepowski tried to break in, but Reinhold was not to be stopped: "Consider how far he has come already, though starting from nothing—an ignorant workhouse tramp. And remember I've watched the diabolical skill of his every move: his technique leaves Machiavelli's '*Prince*' at the post, for he sees at least five moves ahead of everyone else. But the nub of the matter is this: he is bound in the long run to come to the top because—in the long run—no one will try to stop this uncanny clairvoyant who *knows what Germany wants.* That's more than she knows herself—but all the same it's what she is doomed to receive at his hands some day, however little she likes what she gets when she gets it."

"If what you mean is the German rabble. . . ."

But Reinhold brushed this aside. "The rabble's a bogy we

H

make too much of: they only want bread. But think of
Germany's middle classes, the class from which Hitler himself once sank to the gutter—and therefore knows what it's
like, that fate which all of them fear like hell. Imagine the
secret desires and hates of our solid Bürgerlich little shopmen
and civil servants, our teachers and Lutheran pastors, our
skilled artisans and our farmers—imagine that Freudian
nightmare released into waking life! Imagine the coming to
power of everyone terrified out of his Spiessbürger wits by
inflation, and everything else which has hit him these Seven
Lean Years: who longs for a chance to hit back at something
or someone, he doesn't care who or what!"

The Count curled his lip in derision: "So that's what you
think your Hitler can bring to fruition! But how on earth,
with so tiny a following?"

"Listen: you've got to look on Hitler's 'tiny following' more
like the first few cases of plague than as any normal minority."

Reinhold had done his damnedest to carry his case but had
failed to convince the more experienced Count. For the
Count was older, and steeped in national politics all his life:
he was bound to look on his witty young friend as a bit of an
amateur—coming from Munich moreover, and seeing his
every Bavarian goose as a swan. A Prussian himself, at the
back of Lepowski's mind remained the undeniable fact that
the master-folk were the Prussians. The Reich was a 'Federal'
State, but Prussia was twice the size of all these former petty
kingdoms and princedoms and duchies rolled into one; and
national politics flourished in Prussian Berlin alone. A would-
be national leader who spent half his life-span frigging about
in some potty city like Munich was wasting his time: once he
got to Berlin he would have to start again from the bottom.

The politician who didn't know that fact didn't know
much; and Bavarian Strasser had done the only sensible
thing in removing himself to Berlin as soon as he could,
leaving addlepate Hitler to crow in his own backyard (said
the Count).

Chapter 26

Bᴜᴛ Hitler, Strasser—how could these distant rivalries ever matter to Coventry?

Here the picnicking season had really come at last. If you passed those allotments and followed the Quinton Road for a mile or two you came to the line of poplars which guarded Quinton Pool; and there began those seven Elysian Fields collectively called 'The Chesils': a tinkling stream, and a sheep-dip—and wonder of wonders, a donkey with cloven hooves! A spring where watercress grew for the picking; and even cowslips (rare in the arable county of Warwick, because they need permanent pasture and cannot survive the plough). Where it was dry there were harebells and lady's-slipper and scabious: where it was damp forget-me-not grew. There were trees to climb, and bushes for hide-and-seek: later on there'd be hazel-nuts—even walnuts, and prickly Spanish chestnuts.

The Chesils of course were a favourite haunt of Norah's horde; but even here there was just one field where none of them ever went, though there too sheets of pale pink lady's-smock painted the meadow (as Warwickshire Shakespeare says) 'with delight'. This was that seventh field down Baginton way where Quinton Stream runs into the Sowe; and they shunned it for fear of a certain and horrible death. For where all those tempting king-cups and bullrushes grew it was bottomless bog, and each generation of children had scared the pants off the next with tales how that bog could catch you and swallow you down if you even peeped at it through the hedge.

By now it was tulip-time at Mellton: moreover Mary's chair had arrived (a metal contraption which moved on pneumatic wheels, with hidden padded supports for her body

217

and inconspicuous straps), so Mary too could be taken out in the open air. Twice the great occasion had been postponed because of a fill-dyke deluge of rain which seemed more winter than spring; but then at last came a day when the sun was shining into her downstairs room and everything sparkled. The chair was brought to her bedside, and Nurse and Gilbert together lifted her in.

But Mary had lain in her bed so long that the limited scene in front of her eyes had flattened itself in her sight like a painted scene in a picture, that same two-dimensional world one supposes the sea-anemone sees staying fixed to his rock; and even the changed perspectives effected by moving her just this foot or two were enough to make the familiar scene unreally three-dimensional suddenly, wholly ominous. . . . Once they began to wheel her moreover those new-found solids began to move, and all these restlessly-wheeling objects around her made her so giddy she longed to ask them to stop. She'd have asked them to put her back in her bed and to leave her there for good if she hadn't felt too ashamed; and worse was to come, for as Mary was wheeled from the room altogether doors hurtled towards her widening just in time to swallow her up (unable even to turn her head in its padded iron collar). Then she found herself suddenly out in the open air loosed on the outside world like a newborn babe from the womb, while everything kept on changing aspect and shifting—while statues and even trees walked across the distant scene, then totally vanished from sight. Firmly she told herself it was she who was moving while they stayed still; but even so this bodiless bodily motion beyond control of her will had made her so deathly afraid that at last she couldn't control her panic.

Obligingly Gilbert halted her chair, in one of those narrow paths between the small square tulip-beds with their edgings of box. Then at once the whirling kaleidoscope ceased, and the world grew sane and still as she sat in the unaccustomed sunshine, gazing straight ahead at the colours and shapes of the massed tulips in front of her. Soon she was gazing as

though she had never seen tulips before; and indeed, never
before in the whole of her life had tulips seemed real the way
these tulips were real. . . .

Polly was hovering near, and brought her an exquisite
parrot-tulip with frilly edges—wide open, its petals almost
ready to drop. She held it to Mary face-to-face so close that
the petals completely covered her mother's eyes. Thus the
sun shone in Mary's eyes through green veins threading
translucent scarlet; and now that so little of Mary's body was
'her' any longer it seemed as if even the trunk and legs she
had lost had never been Mary the way this tulip was Mary.

Moreover once she had thus far broken her old corporeal
bounds soon even these lawns and bushes—these gardens, as
far as the eye could see. . . . In short, it wasn't so many
months since 'every inch from the crown of Mary's head to
the tips of Mary's toes' had been Mary's limits, but now every
inch from the crown of Mary's head to the tips of Mary's
trees rejoiced at being alive.

Of course as summer wore on this sort of ecstatic vision was
doomed to fade into common day.

*

Meanwhile that summer of 1925 seemed likely to prove
Lepowski right: in Bavaria Hitler appeared content to be
marking time, while Gregor Strasser (joined now by his even
more radical brother Otto) already was scoring a marked
success in the North: there the Leftish yet patriotic Gospel-
according-to-Strasser was catching on fast, mainly among
the enthusiastic idealist young. Wherever he preached his
gospel he founded a Nazi cell; and soon there were quite
enough of a new breed of Northern Nazi who looked to Berlin
for their orders for even this pair of unflagging workers to
need more help.

Back in Bavaria, Gregor Strasser had had as his henchman
a youth called Heinrich Himmler: a faithful soul, and a
highly competent confidential clerk, but handicapped by a
fatally one-track mind. On Jews, for example: "Our Heinrich

looks for Jews underneath his bed every night before he dares get into it," Gregor remarked to his brother. Moreover some-one was needed able to wield a pen. Rosenberg's Munich *Beobachter* scarcely sold fifty copies among the capital's four million readers: these Northern Nazis needed their own Northern papers backing the radical Strasser line. . . . So Himmler was written off as someone with more ambition than brains, and instead they recruited his absolute opposite. This was a Rhineland working-class twenty-eight-year-old permanent adolescent adorned with an academic degree and almost too much imagination: the author of novels and verse-plays much too wild to get printed or staged (but ideas too far-fetched for fiction can yet be swallowed hook-line-and-sinker when offered as fact). Otto and Gauleiter Kaufmann saw him together, and both were impressed. The poor young man appeared club-footed, and almost a dwarf; but his brain-pan was big enough, and so were his large intelligent almost womanish eyes—while his dwarf's compensatory need to be loved and admired cried aloud.

With his beautiful speaking voice and his vitriolic pen, this young Dr. Josef Göbbels seemed worthy at least of a minor post in Kaufmann's office coupled with journalistic work for the Strassers.

Chapter 27

THIS summer of 1925 was indeed a notable summer: the Rhineland summer when Göbbels joined the Nazis, the Mellton summer when Mary had really begun to convalesce, the West Wales summer when Newton Llantony grew a new roof—and the unforgettable Coventry summer when Norah fell through the floor.

Saturday night was everyone's fried-supper night in Slaughterhouse Yard: for Saturday's food was cheap on the market stalls, where meat could be only ninepence a joint and for sixpence they gave you a whacking great cod. After this orgy the children were dosed with their weekly dose (alternately one week liquorice-powder with brimstone-and-treacle the next) to keep their blood pure. It was also bath-night. In every house the copper was lit to heat the water: the smaller children were bathed in twos and the larger in turns in a galvanised wash-tub in front of the kitchen fire, then chased up to bed for their parents to have a go. But something was changing in Norah this summer, something which seemed to require her to take her bath unobserved: so tonight she had carried the tub upstairs and set it beside her bed, while her brothers lugged up the buckets of water. Then Norah undressed, and sat in the wash-tub soaping herself like a lady in lonely glory.

Once she was out of the water however she'd finished with being a lady: she'd got the still more ambitious idea of practising being one of those naked statues which stand in the public parks. But these are always high on a plinth (to be out of the reach of rude little boys): so she climbed on top of the family chest-of-drawers and dried herself there in appropriate attitudes. All went well till somebody called her to hurry up: she jumped off the chest-of-drawers, and the floor was so rotten it gave way under her. Straight through the kitchen

221

ceiling she fell, and arrived on the kitchen floor in a cloud of dust on top of a pile of plaster. Norah was properly penitent (next time she went to Confession she'd have to confess her vanity). Everyone cleared up the mess, and her father mended the ceiling the following day; but it took him a week of scrounging to come by suitable bits of wood for mending the floor above. Till then, the hole in the floor must remain.

This was the end of anyone bathing upstairs of course, but not quite the end of the story. None of these houses had bedroom partitions upstairs, but in this one old cotton bed-spreads hanging between the beds divided it into 'rooms'. Norah's 'room' was one end of the line: then came her parents, and down at the further end came the boys—who each had a bed to himself, which was almost unknown in a Yard where most of the children slept happily hugger-mugger. Secretly Derek had stretched a string right along the floor and tied one end to his toe, while Norah tied hers to the other: so hot-line communication wasn't impossible.

Three nights after the floor had been finally mended Norah was roused by a tug so urgent it nearly pulled off her toe. Careful not to disturb the curtains she burrowed noiselessly under the bed where her parents slept, and surfaced at last between Derek and Charlie. Both their heads were under the bedclothes, and when she whispered "What is it?" Charlie hollowly answered: "Gh-ghosts!" Norah clutched at his hand and listened, rapidly saying her prayers: for something was making curious sounds—like something kept running across the floor. . . . But the moon was bright, and nothing was running across the floor. . . . Then came a terrible muffled yowl, and Norah jumped into bed on top of Charlie—then jumped out again and woke up her mother.

Still those invisible pattering feet. . . . It was Mum who guessed that this had to be something running *under* the floor, on top of the kitchen ceiling below. When Dad took up one of the boards he had laid only three days before, out leapt a cat and streaked through the window. She must have been trapped there for three days at least; but she couldn't be fatter and sleeker with all the mice she had found.

*

Norah's Irish-Catholic faith was simple, yet served her in all the changes and chances that Norah had met in this mortal life—so far. Mary's atheist-humanist faith was equally simple, but useless in Mary's present predicament. Mary believed in no 'God' she had vexed to get punished like this: no personified Destiny even by whom she could feel ill-used. There was no one to blame: it was just the luck of the draw which had rendered her nowadays only a desolate disconnected brain-pan—and one more akin to Friar Bacon's magical speaking Brazen Head than to any psalm-singing cherub. But 'Time HAS BEEN' said the Brazen Head, then fell to the ground of its own accord and broke. . . . Mary could easily die: even now it only meant giving up trying, and surely prolonged existence could serve no possible cosmic use. . . . Yet Mary elected to go on trying: against all reason, *something* inside her had won.

So the summer wore on, with sloping planks arranged wherever the house or garden had shallow steps: for by now she had fully recovered the use of her arms and could trundle her chair herself (so Nursemaid Gilbert was more-or-less out of a job). She refused to be helped: she had reached a prickly stage which resented special attentions suspecting pity—and pity was unforgivable. Mary indeed seemed bent by now on impressing the world with how little she differed from you and me, except that she went on wheels where we go on feet. Poor Gilbert durstn't even so much as pick up some book she had dropped, for Mary had special tongs (whose magnetic tips could even pick up a needle).

Augustine and Joan were constantly with her still. Joan was incredibly kind and good and Mary had come to love her; but Joan had her widowed Archdeacon to see to and even Augustine had got his dry-rot in Wales—as Mary kept on reminding them, often downright ungraciously. Both did

H*

their best to persuade her they came for their own sweet pleasure entirely, but Mary was hard to persuade.

Presently Jeremy came home on weekend leave. By common consent the pair of them teased her in front of him, telling him just how badly lately Mary behaved to all who loved her. But Mary was unrepentant, and gave them as good as she got: "Remember I've just been enduring a second childhood, so now you've got to put up with my second adolescence."

"Good God!" groaned Augustine, "As if your first one I didn't find trying enough!"

Then Mary's eyes grew suddenly very round, and out at last came the truth: "The thing is," she told them, "You're both getting much too dependent on *me*." Augustine gasped. "You two have got your own lives to live, and I will not be made the excuse for you not getting on with them!"

Chapter 28

BOTH the Strassers were Radicals: that was their reason for serving the Nazi Party at all. But if anyone tried to pin him down about 'Party Policy' Hitler would wriggle away like an eel: for only that way could the Nazi appeal cut clean across class and religious beliefs and indeed across tastes and beliefs of every kind, attracting both rich and poor. This maddened the radical policy-minded Strassers, and late that autumn they managed to focus the Party spotlight on policy—just for once.

The particular issue was whether the numerous former Royal Houses ought still to enjoy their former landed estates, the kind of divisive issue which Hitler would never have touched with a barge-pole if only the Strassers hadn't compelled him to come off the fence. For they summoned a Northern 'Leaders' Meeting'; and there, in a Hanover flat with tobacco-smoke almost hiding the dingy curtains and aspidistras, a motion demanding expropriation was just about to be carried when Feder, sent there by Hitler, rose to object: Herr Hitler (whom God preserve!) had dubbed expropriation a Jewish racket the Party must have no truck with.... Whereon a man called Rust banged his fist: "Then I move we chuck Herr Hitler out of the Party—the measly little bourgeois!"

Sensation and wild applause, so that Gregor himself had to intervene from the Chair pointing out that Hitler's expulsion was somewhat beyond the present meeting's competence: Hanover must content itself with the milder "Hitler can say what he likes but so can we: he's no infallible Pope!" Thereupon the original anti-Royalty motion was carried, and also a great deal more of the Strasser programme which Hitler would never conceivably stomach.

This was open rebellion, the Strasser tail announcing its firm determination to wag the dog; and yet the dog being wagged never even let out a yap. When Hitler failed to come down on revolt like a ton of bricks, "He knows he's beaten: it's only a matter of time before Strasser takes over the leadership. . . ." So crowed the Count. But Reinhold remained unconvinced: "I wonder what Hitler has up his sleeve? I bet you it's something which takes us all by surprise."

What Hitler had up his sleeve was a further meeting at Bamberg down in the South which turned down everything Hanover stood for; and ended with Hitler's affectionate arms round dear old Strasser's neck.

The 'dog which had failed to let out a yap' reminded Reinhold—a faithful student of Conan Doyle—of the 'dog which did nothing in the night-time' and thus provided Sherlock Holmes with his vital clue. "With the greatest respect, you don't understand the chap one bit! You thought that Hitler must either cave in or react like a man in a fight for his life; but instead he does nothing. . . . Didn't I warn you that Hitler sees five moves ahead of everyone else?"

"Holding his meeting where only Strasser himself and that little pip-squeak Göbbels were likely to come from the North was hardly outstanding cunning," Lepowski drily replied: "I'm only surprised that Strasser fell in the trap."

"My dear Watson," (the Count looked mildly surprised at this curious form of address) "You've missed the whole point: he saw this was never a real rebellion at all in the sense of a rival bid for the leadership, merely a clumsy attempt to make him adopt more Left-wing ideas."

"But. . . ."

"Strasser just hasn't the spunk. He's like Röhm, who resigned his command and vanished abroad instead of sending his thugs to take the man for a ride and be done with him. That's what all those Nazi 'leaders' are like: they'll fight each other like cats for the second place, but only Hitler wants to be first. I once knew a racehorse like that: it would run almost neck-and-neck with the winner but never would stick its nose out in front."

"That horse must have lost you a packet," Lepowski murmured.

"It would—if I hadn't backed it both ways. . . . But come back to Hitler. The policy-rumpus had no importance: what mattered was Gregor—that champion Fisher of Men whom Hitler himself had sent forth to fish—reporting nets now so heavy with fish that they threatened to break: it was high time to haul them in."

"Yet I'm told that at Bamberg they argued their rival policies out ding-dong and right round the clock before the Strasser Line was outvoted."

"Policies!" Reinhold exclaimed in disgust: "There lies Strasser's perennial weakness. To Hitler a policy's merely a means of gaining ascendancy over divers assortments of men, and wholly expendable once it's no longer of use. He was just as conscious as you are that Strasser was likely to make a better impression up here than himself, which is why he sent Strasser—the beauty of all this being that these were *Strasser's* Bolshy ideas being preached which he'd never endorsed himself, so once they had served their purpose recruiting hordes of the impecunious, Hitler was perfectly free to disown them before they started alarming the rich. No, the only future I see for Gregor is more of this same perpetual ploughing and sowing new fields for Hitler to reap, till the poor old work-horse has wholly exhausted his usefulness: then he'll be sent to the knacker's, like Ludendorff."

Count Lepowski paused for thought. "This must be much what those big brown intelligent eyes of that club-footed Judas perceived: for I'm told that he uttered no word in support of his master at Bamberg, and nowadays eats out of Hitler's hand."

"Göbbels knows which side his bread is buttered. He only speaks when he's sure of applause, and would rather cut out his tongue than defend the losing side."

Lepowski turned his face to the stove in silence, and spat.

*

By the truce patched up at Bamberg with Hitler's arms round Strasser's reluctant neck and the voluble Göbbels apparently stricken dumb, Strasser continued free to say what he liked provided it brought in votes but was forced to renounce all attempts to dictate the Party Line. In return, Hitler confirmed him as chief official voice in the North of the One Indivisible Nazi Party. In short the net hadn't broken, and Strasser's whole miraculous draught of fishes was safely landed—by Hitler.

Chapter 29

THAT autumn Mary insisted on sleeping upstairs once more like everyone else: so Gilbert must have a lift installed, and one she could work herself. It took the workmen ages putting it in: it was nearly winter before they had finally got it fixed. By this time her legs had wasted a lot, but in compensation her arms and hands grew even stronger than normal. Over her bed they had fixed a kind of trapeze with which she could swing her bulk on and off the bed unaided: before very long her arms and hands seemed strong as an ape's—till there came a day when the crushable Polly flinched from her mother's hug.

Those powerful hands propelled her chair much faster than anyone travelled on foot, so perforce they had to allow her to go about mostly alone. But her growing recklessness drove Nurse nearly out of her tiny wits. By December she found she could even force her chair up the ramp and into a horse-box. This was a feat which she kept to herself; and exactly one year from the day of her fall she had herself boxed to the Tottersdown Boxing Day Meet. There the Master loudly hailed a "Brave little woman—a plucked-un!"— though privately thinking (like most of the Field) that this skull-at-the-feast was in pretty poor taste; and the nervous horses had certainly thought so too when the ramp came down and her self-propelled chair bounced out on the Tottersdown gravel.

So another year drew to its end. Jeremy wrote to say that he couldn't get Christmas leave (he was something called 'Resident Clerk' at the Admiralty, something which saved him the rent of digs) but they'd give him the New Year instead. On New Year's Eve his father was taking a watch-night service, so Joan and Jeremy dined at Mellton to see the

229

last of this Year of Disaster with Mary, Augustine—and
Gilbert.

The first four did their best, but the fifth seemed determined to make it a gloomy affair. Jeremy told them his
Resident Clerkship required him to be on perpetual night-
call, ready to think up and issue appropriate orders—he and
the Duty Commander between them—if (say) the whole
Royal Navy capsized in the dark, or if mutineers dragged a
Commander-in-chief from his bed in pyjamas and hanged
him high from the yard-arm. . . .

Gilbert hinted that any such orders which Jeremy issued
would probably make things worse; and Jeremy proudly
agreed. He then went on to describe how even his china
chamber-pot carried Their Lordships' tinted foul-anchor
crest, which exactly denoted his status: for Admirals had
them of finest porcelain crested in gold, and so on right down
the Naval Stores pecking-order to 'Chamber-pots, Earthenware, Plain' (for ratings) and even 'Chamber-pots, Rubber,
Lunatics for the use of . . .'.

But Gilbert was still not amused. Gilbert indeed—with his
second honeymoon plainly gone the way of his first one—
remained a picture of gloom throughout, except for a notable
change of manner when talking to Joan. Mary seemed badly
on edge, wheeling away from the table on any excuse or
none; and when dinner was over her noiseless chair relent-
lessly circled her little drawing-room flock like a sheepdog
shepherding sheep. Moreover, whenever she (rarely) came to
rest she would talk about nothing but politics. Gilbert refused
to respond: like a drunkard reformed who shies at a bottle of
gin, he shied off the subject. Yet tactless Mary persisted. . . .

It seemed as if 1926 would never arrive, nor Wantage
bring in the punch.

"She wants him to go," said Joan, as Joan and Jeremy
bicycled home in the dark.

"To rejoin his fellow-Meistersingers of Westminster?—
Yes, you're probably right."

"Mary's a sensible girl. She knows what a hell in the end they'll be laying up for them both if he won't."

"What's more, you'd better look out!" the nephew bluntly informed his aunt: "Our saintly Gilbert is after you."

Then they pedalled in silence a bit, till Jeremy added: "Mary doesn't miss much . . .".

"Yes," said Joan a little off-handedly: "Didn't you notice how very much better old Wantage is looking since Mary saw that his thyroid was bigger and had it cut?"

Chapter 30

MARY was cautious: she never proposed out loud that Gilbert should go back to politics, merely kept talking about them and wanting the latest political inside news. But it wasn't long before she had him corresponding again with that eminent Liberal figure Sir John Simon; and two or three weeks after Easter, Mary invited the Great Man down. Busy though Simon was just then at the Bar, he accepted. Augustine was then back in Wales; and after dinner Sir John and the other two Liberal guests retired to the study with Gilbert.

The times were crucial indeed: for this was the April of 1926, and a General Strike in support of the miners was growing more and more likely. Before the War, coal had been one of Britain's principal exports and fortunes were made; but now the mines were ceasing to pay and the owners insisted on lower wages and longer hours of work. A General Strike had already been threatened last summer; but Baldwin had staved it off in the end by granting a nine-months' subsidy—ample time, he maintained, for the industry putting its own house in order; but now the nine months were running out with nothing whatever done, and Baldwin had flatly refused to renew the subsidy. Things looked ugly indeed. Nobody knew what a General Strike might bring, but most people feared the worst: for it hardly seemed possible Britain could go on escaping the virus of violent Revolution which since the War had swept the Continent— just as in 1918 the Continental infection of Spanish Flu had finally crossed the Channel. In Britain the Communist Party was small; but that seemed deliberate policy, aimed at establishing highly-trained cadres of subversives to work in secret and largely through stooges, inflaming the workers' relations with bosses wherever they got the chance. By now their leaders were mostly in prison, but nobody really knew how far the movement had got. . . .

Thus there was plenty of pessimist talk in Gilbert's study that night; but Gilbert found Simon himself "remarkably cool and clear-headed" (or so he told Mary afterwards, tucking her up in bed) "for times like these, when Emotion so easily gets the better of Judgement". For Simon had flatly refused to panic. Let others go white at the gills at the thought of a coming blood-bath: let Karl Marx turn in his Highgate grave and prick up his ears for the rumble of British tumbrils rolling at last—this former Attorney-General only seemed willing to talk tonight of his firmly-held view that General Strikes were illegal. Indeed it might well be his duty to rise in the House in order to point this out, for it seemed only fair to warn the poor fellows what risks they were running of civil actions against them for damages.

Gilbert asked him for chapter and verse: whereon Simon explained that a General Strike was bound to entail men downing their tools without having given whatever notice their contracts required. They surely must understand this would render them liable in the Courts if employers should choose to sue; but did the General Council inciting them realise they too risked in Law every private penny their purses contained? And further: interpreting strictly the Trades Disputes Act of 1906 not even a so-called 'sympathy' strike by a single uninvolved Union could properly claim protection for Union funds—still less could a General Strike: for that couldn't be reckoned a genuine Trades Dispute, since it wasn't aimed at any employer but openly aimed at extracting a mining subsidy out of the Public Purse over Parliament's head. Sir John had no intention of using a word so emotive in any public speech, but in private agreed that the only word for coercing the Crown by non-parliamentary means—in other words, by force whether armed or not—was Rebellion.

However, the busy Sir John kept putting off making his

speech; and when Baldwin's patient negotiations had finally failed, at midnight on Monday the Third of May the General Strike had begun.

Everyone rallied behind the honest and even Quixotic Baldwin, the man they believed to detest all crunches (indeed last July's derided appeaser) now brought face-to-face with things which have *had* to come to the crunch. Baldwin was stressing the Constitutional point that yielding to outside pressure like this must sound the death-knell of parliamentary rule; and even Thomas (the railwaymen's leader) had answered that once the Constitution was challenged "then God help Britain unless the Government won!"—and had stumbled out of the House of Commons in tears.

Baldwin had broadcast a simple man-to-man plea to the nation; and thousands were queuing all day to enlist in a Glorious Army of Amateur Blacklegs. . . . So how could our Cincinatus linger still at the plough? Could even a fairly broad hint from Mary be needed that Now was the Time for All Good Men to Come to the Aid of the Country? True, that 'awkward question' of whether the erring Liberal Party deserved his support any longer remained unresolved; but could this matter at times like the present when None was for the Party and All were for the State?

Yet Simon had still not spoken. Gilbert must strongly urge him to speak, with his legal proofs that this was a blow which a Faction unlawfully aimed at the Common Weal. . . .

Lloyd George—because he presumably thought they would win—was believed to be backing the strikers; and this must finally cost him all decent Liberal Party support, so with Asquith gone to the Lords if Simon played his cards right. . . . Indeed did Gilbert's conscience allow him to stay with the Liberal Party at all, then he might do worse than hitch his wagon to Simon.

Mary was urging him openly now; and yet when it came to the point Gilbert felt strangely loth to abandon his charge of the prickly Mary and go, for virtue as well as vice can turn to a habit surprisingly hard to break. However, at last (though not till the morning of Thursday May the Sixth) the Daimler set out for London with Gilbert inside it and all the cans of petrol the car could hold: for even to have himself driven to London by Trivett seemed safer than amateur engine-drivers.

As Gilbert was trundled to London he thought about Baldwin, become overnight a national father-figure whose fairness and honesty even the Labourites almost trusted. Baldwin (thought Gilbert) had certainly grown to his job. Nowadays few recalled their surprise when the King had chosen this unknown Baldwin instead of the Great Lord Curzon to follow the mortally-sick Bonar Law as head of His Majesty's Government. Even then the man had seemed in no hurry to try and impress himself on the public mind—except by quietly demonstrating the end in Affairs of State of all Lloyd-Georgian trickery.

Baldwin. . . . You couldn't deny him a certain magnanimous streak: when Churchill left the Liberals Baldwin had welcomed him, even appointing him Chancellor.

Chapter 31

THERE can't have been many British Prime Ministers quite so unknown to the Public as Baldwin when first he moved into Number Ten.

Barely a year ago—which was back in Jeremy's 'Postulant' days in the Order of Civil Servants—Augustine one morning had called at the Admiralty, bent on routing him out. Augustine belonged to the Travellers' (not that he used it much, but his family always had): the Club was in strolling distance, so now he invited Jeremy there to lunch. On their way in to eat, Jeremy nudged him: "Why—look who's here!"

At a nearby table, Augustine noticed only an unmistakable Welshman with half-closed humorous eyes and a beaky nose: a distinguished, but also a taking middle-aged face—and as shrewd as a basket of weasels. . . .

"Well?" said Jeremy afterwards over their coffee: "Tell me about your eminent fellow-Traveller." Augustine shook his head. "Don't you even know who he is?" Augustine said No. "But you'd guess?"

"Some South Wales mining valley. They're mostly brainy enough, but this one must have had just that little extra it takes to escape to London and land him a cushy job."

"You boob! That's only Tom Jones, a mere Eminence Grise: what I meant was the other bloke." So far as Augustine recalled, the man's vis-à-vis had been typical City: most probably head of some fossilised family firm. One seemed to remember a square slab of yellowish face with drooping eyes, a nobbly nose and a wide-stretched mouth like a frog's; but the creature had looked so solid and dull it was hard to imagine the link between this incongruous pair. . . . "That was Stanley Baldwin."

"A brandy?"

"No thanks, or I'll snore too loud in the office and wake the others." Jeremy looked at his watch.

As the friends descended the steps to Pall Mall, "Politics always gets only the second-raters," Augustine resumed: "But even so . . .".

"Don't be misled by his looks," said Jeremy: "Baldwin's a downy old bird—as he'd have to be, getting involved in putting the skids underneath Lloyd George as he did in '22."

"How was that?"

"Surely even you know that in '22 the Conservatives broke with Lloyd George's wartime Coalition, fought the Election on party lines and won? Behind the scenes, Baldwin was in it all up to the neck. . . . And yet," said Jeremy sounding puzzled, "Baldwin *appears* to be moved by ambition as little as you and me. It was purest accident plonked him in Number Ten; and I'm told he nearly refused."

"Accident?"

"Two of them: Bonar's cancer and Curzon's coronet.— *Three* of them rather, because his only Cabinet job had been Board of Trade till a few months before when McKenna turned down the Exchequer: he wouldn't have otherwise even been in the running." Jeremy paused at the top of Duke of York's Steps to indulge in a pinch of snuff. "I suppose you knew he was Kipling's cousin?"

"He does indeed seem accident-prone! It's a bit like a Kipling character though, to take on a thankless job just because there didn't seem anyone competent else."

"Kipling—whose most successful work of fiction of all is the British Raj, which everyone thinks is true. . . . So now you suggest he invented his Cousin Stanley as well?"

Augustine took hold of Jeremy's arm and gently swung it: "Come off it, you!"

"But I like your idea! It's pure Pirandello. . . ."

"No, off your 'fictional' British Raj when you know that the bloody thing's all too real."

"So Kipling has hoodwinked even you?"

"Damn it," Augustine suddenly blurted out: "It's time you and I grew up!"

Jeremy winced. "All right then, make me admit that a red rash covers indeed a third of the globe, and one-third of mankind is entitled to some sort of British passport. . . . But have a heart! You seem to forget my Branch is the one which works with the Naval Staff; and that even my Section is 'Ships', so I'm sick to death of my nose getting rubbed all day in Old Nanny Pax-Britannica." Jeremy rounded his delicate lips and emitted a raspberry.

"One thing I never realised quite till I went there," Augustine pursued undeterred, "is how, in spite of their money and size, the Americans don't even want to compete with ourselves in terms of international power. They don't see anything in it for them—any more than you and I see anything in it for us! But there's nobody really left in Europe either, so whether we like to admit it or not we are probably easily now the most powerful state in the world."

"And with half the shipping afloat," said Jeremy, "flying the Old Red Duster! The whole thing has got out of hand. Although there's no longer nowadays any aggressive 'Drang' about it, this ramshackle Empire Baldwin has shouldered just goes on growing—a banyan tree, blindly dangling aerial roots from the tips of its branches which turn into extra trunks wherever they touch the soil. Self-governing White Dominions—Protectorates—Colonies—India—and nowadays Mandates. . . ."

"A third of the globe," put in Augustine, "was even before we were born: if we don't look out, before we are middle-aged it could well be a half."

"And then," said a scornful Jeremy: "Everyone else being safely inside I suppose we shall see your dar-r-rling North American Rebels applying for re-admission?"

"Never!" Augustine said bluntly: "No more than whatever happened we'd ever join on as an extra United State."

"So you draw the line somewhere?"

"It just wouldn't work. It's like . . . like too close relations."

"You mean, we always annoy each other too much?"

"No. . . . Well yes, that too perhaps in a way. . . . What I really mean is they feel to us like our *sister*-nation."

"I see," said Jeremy: "Mary and you writ large—and marriage would count as a kind of international incest. . . ."

But now they had crossed the Mall to the corner door of Jeremy's workhouse and had to part: Augustine to Dorset again, and Jeremy back to dancing unwilling attendance on Old Nanny Pax-Britannica.

Jeremy fetched his tray from the wooden press where he'd locked it because the papers were 'Secret'—though only some mothbally long-term Contingency Plans which he had to bring up to date. This particular bundle of schemes was always the New Boy's task since they risked no immediate harm: they were merely concerned with the Navy's hypothetical role in some fancied future outbreak of 'Civil Unrest' at home—with landing-parties of naval technicians as well as help in maintaining public order. A scheme for destroyers ferrying Guinness's Dublin yeast to leavenless Liverpool bakers, and yet another for smuggled-in submarines used to furnish the London docks with electric power. . . . Fantasies maybe—and yet worked out in every detail, for this it appeared was the way that the Navy always worked: they planned in advance for everything, just in case.

*

All this had been barely a year ago, yet already those cobwebbed 'Contingency Plans' were in action: light cruisers policing the north-eastern docklands, the battleships *Barham* and *Ramillies* watching the Mersey in case things got out of hand—and the Pax Britannica now come *very* near home. At least to foreign observers the end seemed at hand of Imperial Britain, an ageing Goliath in clanging armour laid flat on his back by a heart attack: no need for even a well-aimed pebble.

Chapter 32

ALTHOUGH that Quixotic young Liberal Statesman had
not been seen in the House of Commons for eighteen
months, yet nobody took much notice of Gilbert's arrival
(which just went to show how wholly their minds were
absorbed by the present crisis). That Thursday night, moreover, John Simon was just beginning his strangely-belated
speech; and Gilbert was pleased to observe how deeply his
legal proofs impressed both sides of a House where both still
firmly believed in the Rule of Law. . . . Or perhaps (for this
was what Jeremy thought as he watched from the public
gallery) even the leftest of Labour Members had qualms
about brothers outside making history over their heads. . . .
And come to that, could a lawyer's like Simon's (he wondered)
be quite the eyes through which downy old—honest old—
Baldwin either would look on this giant trial of strength?

Appeasement never buys peace, but it can buy time to re-
arm: had Baldwin's derided 'appeasement' of last July been
simply playing for time? Last July, everyone's eyes had been
still on the raw deal offered the miners: the general public
needed time to forget about coal and adjust their one-track
minds to the Constitutional issue instead, and Baldwin
durstn't bring things to the crunch without the nation solid
behind him. Moreover the very appeasement they jeered at
had served to prove that Baldwin had done all he could for
peace, and that if things had finally come to the crunch then
the fault wasn't his. . . .

Clever old Baldwin! Appeasement had also served to lull
the appeased, who believed that Prime Ministers caving in
once go on caving in; thus the Union side had in fact been
totally unprepared for the crunch when it came. . . . And
indeed if a crunch had to come (it occurred to Jeremy), even
the downiest downy old bird could hardly have hoped for a
better crunch-time than now, with his plans all ready while
theirs so palpably weren't.

But wait: for this suggested that Baldwin might even have *meant* his peace negotiations to fail. . . . Well, hadn't Lloyd George as good as accused him of never allowing them once any genuine loophole although they had gone on expecting a truce to the very end—bamboozled by Baldwin's so evident efforts for peace?

Lloyd George was a crook himself, and wouldn't think twice about playing that kind of trick; but surely it beggared belief of the Baldwin one thought one knew. . . . So was his famous honesty fake—or at least expendable, once he'd convinced himself where the National Interest lay? Admittedly hardly a single 'honest' statesman before him had failed to succumb at least once in his life to this pinchbeck excuse—and it couldn't be merely another of Baldwin's 'accidents' causing the Strike to come when it did, this involved too much coincidence, too many strands in the build-up. . . .

Somehow he must have willed it. . . . Perhaps this was just another example of 'Jeremy's Law' of the righteous right hand blissfully unaware what his crooked subliminal left hand was up to: the downy old Baldwin Unconscious, his Machiavellian left hand leading them *all* by the nose including the Honest Stanley himself! Certainly bearing in mind 'Jeremy's Second Law' ('That it's almost unknown for a man to succeed in deceiving the rest of the world unless he's already deceiving himself'), this seemed the likelier explanation. Consider last Sunday night, that Eleventh Hour when Baldwin had gone to bed on the heels of his final ultimatum and slept the sleep of the just: a move which successfully rendered him incommunicado, frustrating all possible awkward attempts at a last-minute Union climb-down. . . .

But now the House was adjourning, so Jeremy had to carry his somewhat simplistic analyst's-couch type interpretation of Baldwin's complex mind back to his Whitehall bed: where even the coverlet bore that ubiquitous naval badge which never let him forget his job.

Chapter 33

THAT night as Baldwin stumbled upstairs in Number Ten he caught his toe in a carpet and nearly came a cropper.

The tycoon mask looked tired and sensitive, even a little helpless. So this was at last the Masses against the Rest—with those 'Masses', in England, outnumbered as well as outbrained! He need have no fears that the Strike could succeed: for even its Leaders were pulling their punches, scared stiff lest those Boys on the Left began making history over *their* heads. He thanked the God Above Who had chosen a time so auspicious for things to come to the crunch.

But crunches were means at the best, not ends: what victory had to lead to was lasting industrial peace, with the Unions back at their proper constitutional job and Parliament back at theirs. This called for patience and tolerance—endless finesse: yet provocative chaps like Churchill seemed all agog for excuses to call out the troops, and intent on rubbing fresh salt in the 'Enemy's' wounds. . . . It was hard to put up with Winston's concept of British working-men as the 'Enemy', Winston's ghoulish delight in a crunch for a crunch's sake. . . .

Though he got into bed and presently slept, only two hours later he woke. He had side-tracked Winston (the ablest lieutenant he'd got) into what seemed a harmless job just running a news-sheet, his *British Gazette*: yet even with Davidson censoring everything Winston wrote, was the job quite harmless enough? Parliament hardly seemed to think so! He hadn't sufficiently bargained for Winston's incredible taste for bombast, a total lack of the Common Touch which could lose us the people's support even now. . . .

Baldwin soon fell asleep again, being deadly tired; but it wasn't a very refreshing sleep. He dreamed he was balanced on top of a toy-cupboard filled with dolls; and one turned into a tiger.

Chapter 34

NEXT morning as Jeremy turned on his bath-tap he might have been scalded to death when nothing but steam jetted out. In a very few seconds steam filled the room, and he couldn't get near enough even to turn it off. No wonder the Office Keeper was begging the Board to send those Naval Stokers back to the Nore, for they'd whacked up his poor old boilers to something like thirty-five knots!

But other Naval Stokers (as Jeremy knew) were better employed, stoking the London powerhouse furnaces. Strikers had tried to counter this move by cutting the power supplies to the docks; but only to find there were submarines inside the docks already, able to generate ample electric power to keep the cold-storage working and even most of the cranes. . . . Oh yes, the Navy was really quite good at these 'brilliant naval improvisations' so carefully hammered-out years in advance!

Strange (thought Jeremy later, with half his mind on a bunch of routine signals from Simonstown) just how easy it seemed to put the national clock back—with even derelict windmills and watermills once more grinding local corn, their machinery mended a year ago.

To the public of course the General Strike had come as a bolt from the blue, but all Departments of State had their own Emergency Plans: all last year endless interdepartmental 'Supply and Transport' meetings had taken place, which Jeremy had to attend on Their Lordships' behalf. The Chairman remarked at one that half the population of Britain still lived within fifty miles of the sea, so shouldn't the moribund coastal trade be given a shot in the arm? Discreet Board of Trade enquiries to owners of laid-up craft had shown which needed the least repair, so now there were tiny

barnacled ketches and sailing-barges and brigs unloading
coal and food in forgotten silted-up harbours with grass-
grown quays—just as they'd done in Jeremy's childhood.
Home Office plans seemed bent on reviving an even remoter
past: they'd divided the country in ten independent autonomous regions, each one able if need-be to function alone
since each had its sovereign 'Commissioner' served by his
local high-powered experts—like back to the days of the
Heptarchy!

As for the Strike itself (he initialled, unread, some Office
Memorandum or other and shoved it into his out-tray)
response had been well-nigh total, with fewer blacklegs
remaining at work than the Planners had ever allowed for.
But far more amateur volunteers had enrolled than anyone
dared to hope, and these had taken control out of Government hands as completely as out of the strikers'. Oxford and
Cambridge were almost deserted: their young men were
grinding the guts out of lorries and buses and even loco-
motives, or working the skin off their backs unloading ships
in the docks. Private aircraft had offered themselves, racing-
car drivers and even galloping horsemen raring to act as
messenger-boys and carry important papers. London's
distributing-centre for milk was a mushroom miniature city
complete with telephones, water and light: he had seen it
grow overnight from the grass of Hyde Park, and by Tuesday's
dawn there'd been row upon row of lorries drawn up, all
placarded *Foodstuffs*. Below his window, Horseguards Parade
was become the largest car-park in Europe—a seething mass
of volunteer vehicles manned by skylarking amateur drivers.
Just as Augustine had said about Prohibition releasing the
frontiersman buttoned in every American business-suit, so
had the Strike resurrected the small boy dormant under each
clerkly bowler and boardroom top-hat; and now they were
playing at being engine-drivers, playing at being bobbies—
playing at all those wonderful he-man lives which they'd day-
dreamed about in Purley and Surbiton (just then the telephone rang, but the call was for somebody else). This was no

nation grimly enduring a crisis, but one unexpectedly let out
of school and enjoying a lovely romp—which just went to
show what a crass mistake it is to suppose that the grown-up
has any less need of play than the child! He probably needs
even more; and the fact that he mostly gets less is the likeliest
reason he's often so much more badly behaved.

'Skylarking': that was the secret of all this boundless good-
humour infecting even the strikers, who went in for plenty of
stone throwing, plenty of lovely breaking of glass—but with
almost nobody ever hurt. Busmen who emptied double-deck
buses before they gleefully overturned them just for the hell
of it: skylarking railwaymen greasing the rails, and laughing
their heads off to see trains skid to a halt. . . .

Then the telephone rang again; and the caller this time
was Augustine. 'Skylarking': this was the word which a
scornful Augustine used too, having driven straight up from
the mining valleys of Wales. He was nearly white-hot with
rage. What did these irresponsible skylarkers think they were
up to, forgetting the miners the whole thing was really about?
To people like these this was just a game, but the issue was
life-and-death to the miners.

Jeremy murmured the name of Baldwin, that downy old
bird; and something about defending the Constitution. . . .

"Bugger a Constitution which can't even give the miners a
living wage! And Baldwin deserves to be shot for distracting
everyone's minds from the crucial point."

"But have some sense: what good can even the miners get
in the end from just pouring subsidies down those big black
holes? And it's not really Baldwin's fault: MacDonald himself began the rot—*he* got the Frenchies out of the Ruhr, and
started the Germans digging again. Churchill has only
finished the job by putting the pound back on gold at the
pre-war rate and pricing British export coal right out of the
market."

"That's all politicians ever do is to make things worse!"

"From top to bottom the Industry needs re-thinking; but
that's the Industry's job, not Baldwin's. The Miners' Leaders

and Owners ought to be putting their heads together instead of fighting: I'd think those Miners' Leaders the stupidest men on earth if it wasn't for even stupider Owners."

This angered the partisan angry Augustine even more, for he'd just been driving one of those 'stupid' leaders from Wales to Eccleston Square and looked on the man as a hero. "What do *you* know of their leaders, stuck to your ivory office-stool?"

Indeed Augustine and Jeremy might have quarrelled in earnest had Jeremy not pretended the Head of his Branch had come in the room so he had to hang up.

Chapter 35

AUGUSTINE's gibe about Jeremy's ivory office-stool was not so wide of the mark: there were plenty of places where 'skylarking' wasn't a word you could use about either side. There were more than a million miners—as many men worked underground in the murky bowels of England as worked on the farms above them tending her smiling face: no other industry used one quarter as many men, and the miners' mood was to tighten their belts and fight to the death rather than see their wages cut. Or take a city like Coventry: here at least they could hardly 'forget the miners', with pits on their very doorstep.

Not that Coventry workers were much better off than the miners were: for in engineering a man might be out of work for two or three years on end, and the average worker was likely to find himself jobless for half of his working life. Now Germany couldn't pay her Reparations in gold and had started to pay them in kind: German castings were being used for building Coventry cars while Coventry moulders rotted away on the dole.

So far the Strike had been aimed at disrupting the nation's daily more than her industrial life: Amalgamated Engineering Union members hadn't been called out yet. Coventry engineering workers were under no obligation to join in this selfless strike in support of the miners, and thus it was no very easy decision their Union Meeting had come to on Wednesday night to walk out on Thursday morning without even waiting for orders from Eccleston Square. The way they saw it, so long as even a group of Unions fought alone defeat must follow defeat. 'United, we stand....' But the Coventry A.E.U. were weak. They were smarting still from a three-months' lock-out: membership since had dwindled, for members who'd drifted back to work on the bosses' terms couldn't pay their fines and had let their membership lapse. Moreover the unemployed man had little incentive to join, for to him the Union seemed so busy protecting members in jobs that it left the unemployed to the Commies.

Thus the General Strike found less than a third of Coventry workers Union Members at all. However the tool-room men were most of them ardent members, and these were key-workers without whom production was bound to come to a halt: it was only the Morris Works in Far Gosport Street (which employed no Union labour whatever) that managed to carry on; and in spite of the Union's numerical weakness the other car and bicycle factories all had to close—apart from apprentices doing the maintenance chores. The Transport Workers of course were out already, and somewhere like this no skylarking amateur driver would dare to show his face: so the city was left entirely without any buses or trams. For once, the streets were empty even of horse-drawn drays: so the children could play on the streets in safety—and made the most of their chance.

The leaders' orders were 'Keep your hands in your pockets and shut your mouths': which meant that for most there was nothing to do but stand about. Few of them bothered to go to Pool Meadow to hear their leaders orate: most of them much preferred the Market, where Albert Smith (that famous eccentric jester-philosopher) stood on his tub and kept them enthralled for hours. Albert had once been certified sane by the loony-bin doctor who let him out: if you heckled, he waved his 'Sane Certificate' in your face and demanded yours—which set the crowd in a roar. All the same, keeping your hands in your pockets and saying nowt was a weary business with work for once to be had for the asking: tension mounted, and rumours began to fly. There was only the *British Worker* to read, with the printers out; and the news it carried was sparse. We knew we were winning of course, but it seemed a long time to wait: why wasn't there something to *do*, apart from playing football and booing at blackleg trains?

Chapter 36

Having no buses to come to school by, half the Coventry teachers were kept at home: so even the Slaughterhouse children came out on strike. Picnics were better than sitting idle in teacherless schools, and day after day the Yard was emptied entirely of walkable children—except for Brian.

Then Norah had an idea. All previous efforts to tame the little savage had failed; but if he were somehow persuaded to come on a picnic with them, mightn't it do the trick?

None of the others much liked her idea, all dungy and bloody the way he was: his hair was clotted and matted—he stank, and the rags he stood up in could almost have stood up without him. But Norah had 'said', and her word was Law: so Tuesday morning early Norah had lain in wait for him just arriving. She wheedled and coaxed him, and finally wouldn't let him escape till he promised to come with them 'just this once'; but his promise was given under duress, so she kept him unobtrusively under guard till the party was ready to start.

It was then she caught sight of little Syl. Now that his mother must walk on foot to her pupils Nellie was out all day; and there was her chubby three-year-old, playing around alone by the tap. It seemed such a shame, so Syl must come too, even if somebody had to carry him part of the way.

The current craze was fishing for tiddlers, armed with jampots and home-made nets (the foot of an old lisle stocking sewn to a loop of wire with its ends stuck into a cane). The day had started warm; but May was early—too early, some of them thought, for anywhere further than Swanswell. Norah, however, insisted on Quinton Pool in spite of the longer trudge and the risk of possible rain: for with Brian to be converted this had to be a success, they must choose the best place they knew.

On their way down the Quinton Road they passed a brace of policemen. As loyal strikers they put out their tongues; but neither policeman appeared to notice, so once they were well beyond them they turned and jeered—then panicked, and started to run. . . . But how lovely it was to be out of the desolate crowded town in the blessed peace of the country! Arrived at the Pool at last, those without nets or patience for fishing pelted the moorhens—and might have kept at it all morning if only the moorhens had patience to wait and be hit instead of scuttling into the reeds. Then they started racing each other, the notion being to charge full-tilt downhill to the very edge of the water without slipping in (which sooner or later everyone did). After that, since their feet were already so wet that they couldn't get wetter, the boys rolled shorts to the groin and the girls tucked thin cotton frocks into thick serge all-the-year knickers and those whose clothes were simply cut down from their elders bundled them up as best they could: then boots and all they waded knee-deep in the duckweed, disturbing the fishers and trying to get to the kingcups. Meanwhile Norah fussed like a hen with its chick over Brian, determined to see he enjoyed his outing; but Brian had nothing to fish with and no desire to fish, nor could he abide getting wet, nor had the faintest liking for wild-flowers. . . . Thus, in the end, there was nothing to do but leave him alone to his own devices. She warned him about the bog, then watched him crawl through a hedge to talk to a lonely sheep—doubtless undressing it mentally.

Dinner time came. They looked for somewhere to sit not wholly infested with ants, then pulled off their squelching boots and stockings to 'dry' in the sun and pulled out their bread-and-jam. Everyone shared alike, so Brian didn't go hungry; but no one would sit very near him because how he smelled, in the sun—though a pair of Red Admiral butter-flies loved it, and wouldn't leave him alone.

After dinner most of the others went back to the water to get even wetter; but Norah sat on, in that place of jammy bits of paper and crumbs, downcast that her lovely idea for brightening Brian's life didn't seem to have worked. Presently three others joined her: Jean (who also was only twelve, though the length of her legs had won her a double portion of kingcups), Rita the Gormless—whose father was treating them better now, so pawning his Sunday suit had worked in the end; and Lily, the 'bad' one none of their mothers liked. Four girls the same age, and soon so engrossed with each other that presently even Norah forgot about Brian.

After a while they must have felt they needed some shade to sit in, or flowers to pick or something: for Brian saw them wandering off—still barefoot, and treading the tussocky turf like Agag for fear of prickles. So what should he do? If he joined those other ones down at the pool he might get splashed, or even pushed in; and anyway children were not much use when what his slaughterhouse day-dreaming needed was something four-footed and furry. . . . His sheep? As he crawled through the hedge to look, the quickset above him was suddenly all alive with wings; and poking his nose in the flowering weeds beyond he saw, two inches away from his streaming hay-feverish eyes, a head like a maniac horse's with disk-like eyes you couldn't tell what he was thinking and legs like enormous jointed derricks. . . .

That big green grasshopper's blank-looking eyes must have read the watery glint in his own: for it jumped one-tenth-of-a-second before he grabbed. Moreover his sheep was gone. There weren't even rabbits about: he nibbled some rabbit-droppings to taste how recent they were, though really he knew full well that at this time of day the rabbits would all be deep in their burrows. With restless hands in his pockets he tried to envisage a soft-eyed calf waiting its turn for the knife; but baseless imagination was not his strong point.

Then somehow it entered his head to follow those four big girls: not catching them up of course, just scouting stealthily after the sound of their voices.

Keeping well hidden himself, at last he sighted them

sitting among some gnarled old hawthorn bushes: a well-worn bower littered with cigarette-packets (and worse), but amply festooned with briars and brambles and old-man's-beard. Long-legged Jean had woven her kingcups into a coronet, Rita's head was wreathed in ivy and ragged-robin, Norah had stuck pink campion into her carroty hair and Lily wore cowslip earrings. They sat with their heads together and faces flushed: on the ground beside them were primrose bunches which nimble fingers unconsciously wove into chains, while the wicked Lily held forth in a furtive giggling voice and the other three listened entranced. . . .

He ought to have seen they were talking secrets, and made himself scarce at once—not mindlessly watched them from cover awhile, then crept out into the open and stood up shyly.

Chapter 37

As soon as they saw him the four girls screamed, they sprang to their feet and surrounded him calling him Peeping Tom and a spy. How much had he overheard? Lily said something about how he ought to be tore into bits by rights. . . . His knees felt ready to fold, for these girls were so awful big and look at them beefy great arms! But worst of all were them eyes, with a funny old look which had him wanting to run—though he couldn't of course, he knew he hadn't a hope. . . .

The next thing, Norah gave a high-pitched cackle of laughter and started dressing him top-to-toe in flowers. While all of them hung their primrose-chains round his neck, Norah set about properly decking him out as a Flower King: with a bluebell crown on his head, a half-made cowslip-ball as an orb to hold and an early ragwort stalk as a sceptre. Then four huge Flower Maidens joined their hands in a circle round him and started to dance. Trapped in the middle, he turned from one to the other with doubtful appeasing smiles: so afraid of their crimson excited faces and big blank grasshopper-eyes that he squeezed his orb and sceptre to pulp.

Suddenly Lily broke from the ring and snatched at the gaping front of his shorts so it hurt what her fingers tweaked. He started to grizzle; but Lily pushed him flat on his back, flung herself down on top and rolled on him. Norah dived to the rescue but. . . . Whew, that lascivious stench in the pitiless sun of terrified overheated boy and the blood of cowslips and bullocks mixed! The Devil himself must have brewed that stink: for instead of it letting her drag the incubus off him it rolled her on top of him too, and the little gold cross she wore round her neck cut his eye. Then all four rolled on the squashed little male in turns, squirming like dogs do rolling in something dead.

Even after they'd all got off him that awful Lily must put the lid on it, squatting down in the open and doing a country-one right where Brian could see.

As soon as he got enough breath back he started to cry, and wouldn't get up off the ground. It was starting to rain, and the other three girls all crept under bushes; but Brian just lay where he was, and Norah must stick to her guns (with that wicked old bog on the prowl for all lost little boys) till he promised to follow them back—he could lag behind them as far as he liked provided he kept them in sight.

That was luckily only a shower, though looking like more was to come with the sun already gone down in a stormy tumult of grey and gold as they started home. On the weary trek back to town there were punitive showers of hail, and the little ones started to cry: so they had to be carried, as well as the nets and jars and the branches and bunches of flowers for Mum. . . . Lucky Lily, whose baby brother and sense of sin seemed equally light! For Norah was burdened down by that awful load on her conscience as well as with fat little Syl on her back because he was nobody's brother. She needed both hands for his flowers, so Syl had to hold her tiddler-jar; but Syl was sleepy, and presently slopped it all down the back of her neck inside—the water and tiddlers too, so he had to be set down a minute and slapped and afterwards hugged and kissed (this made him wrinkle his nose, for now she was wet she smelled even more of Brian).

To speed their weariness Norah started them singing 'Three Blind Mice' in their innocent out-of-tune voices, while straining her ears all the time—wild horses couldn't have made her turn to look—for the sound of Brian dragging his feet a couple of hundred yards behind them, almost the only one neither carried nor carrier.

Darkness had fallen before they got home, and their mothers were wild; but the truants were quickly forgotten because of the wonderful news that the General Strike was

over—we'd won, and the Coventry Council of Action had
issued a handbill:

A MASS VICTORY MEETING WILL BE HELD TONIGHT
POOL MEADOW—6 p.m.
LONG LIVE THE BRITISH WORKING-
CLASS MOVEMENT!

(Meanwhile Norah's mother had taken one sniff and told her
daughter to thoroughly wash her hair; but nobody noticed
when Norah instead slipped out to Confession in case she
died in the night.)

After the meeting, jubilant strikers stayed up till dawn
preparing their victory celebrations; and when morning
came with the news that the Strike had really ended in
abject surrender by Organised Labour they couldn't believe
their ears. Some of the leaders hoped that the Strike could
be started again even now. They piled into somebody's car,
and went on a deputation to Eccleston Square; but all they
got was the dustiest dusty answer—and frankly, most of the
rank-and-file were only too glad to get back to work as soon
as the Boss would allow.

It was back to school for children as well as grown-ups; but
Norah found that in spite of her having had Absolution she
couldn't, today, do even the easiest sums.

She had lent her ears to impure talk, and her body to
impure desires: Absolution had washed her clean of her
carnal sin—for what that was worth, but Absolution couldn't
begin to undo the harm she had done to that poor little runt
she had set out to help! To the albatross henceforth hung
round her neck. . . . For she'd get no second chance: the Brian
who seemed unapproachable once would be even more
hopelessly unapproachable now. If her soul was indeed
washed clean that could be only its outside: inside it felt like a
sink.

She was feeling much as Augustine had felt that morning
he'd woken to see a reflected sunrise hanging outside his
Canadian window upside-down.

I*

BOOK THREE

Stille Nacht

Chapter 1

Two rattlesnakes fighting deny themselves the use of their fangs: they merely wrestle till one or the other admits defeat. The British appeared to have reached the ethical level of rattlesnakes, ending their General Strike like that with nobody shot or knifed or even kicked in the teeth—though this was the nearest thing to a civil war which Britain had known since heaven-knows-when. Jeremy thought all this had been Baldwin's predeterminate plan: 'Dr. Baldwin's National Vaccination' he called it, writing to Joan: 'A minimal dose of the Continental virus of Revolution aimed at conferring life-long immunity'.

Joan showed Jeremy's letter to Ludovic Corcos, who merely remarked: "Yes, they order things better east of the Rhine".

He left her to guess what he meant. But in Germany Nazis and Communists, Nazis and Social Democrats, Stahlhelm—these rivals could hardly meet on the streets without somebody getting killed. Fifty to eighty casual deaths each year was part of the normal process of winning votes; and if that was the norm which Franz's and Lothar's generation was used to, then England's bloodless General Strike (so far from being admired) could only portend a hopelessly lightweight nation that couldn't be serious even over its politics. Once Prime Minister Baldwin had let the fruits of victory slip through his fingers with nobody hanged or even thrown in the Tower, how could even the Anglophil Walther help wondering what had become of the sturdier England of Cromwell and Charles I?

But the English are famous for being incomprehensible. Father and son alike remembered that visiting English cousin of three years back, that 'Augustin'. Head and body

and legs had looked like a fellow-human yet nothing he said
or did made sense: his mind seemed unable to take in the
simplest basic human ideas, like trying to play a game of
draughts with your horse. . . .

*

One June morning at Tottersdown, Ludo was urging too
how very much nearer the knuckle it is to describe the
English as uncomprehending than merely incomprehensible
(Joan had come over to see the Manet his father had lately
bought: Augustine was there already, and now all three were
talking of other things in Ludovic's den upstairs). "You're
capable only of seeing the world through your own English
eyes, so all you see is a mirror reflecting your own English
faces and can't conceive that what makes Germans tick is
other than what makes you tick yourselves."

"We're hopelessly Anglomorphic?" suggested Augustine.

"Exactly. *You*'ve never known what it means to feel
cribbed and confined like Dr. Theophilus Wagner's psy-
chotic rats."

"What were they?"

"The Professor kept them close-caged in a garden shed,
where he found that their wild-state social system completely broke down and turned to a murderous struggle for
senseless dominance—each rat biting his neighbour's caro-
tid or peritoneum, and leaving the victim to die of internal
bleeding or sepsis."

"Rats are terribly human," sighed Joan.

"In that case, so are the Germans! This senseless aggression
of German against brother German was something unknown
in pre-War days. Then, wild-state Germans could wander all
over the world; but ever since 1918 the Germans have felt
themselves caged in by hostile keepers. This has produced
that same traumatic sense of confinement, an almost hysterical longing for 'Lebensraum' wrecking their once-exemplary
social cohesion."

"One thing Jeremy told me after his trip abroad was how

'political action' means opposite things today in English and German," said Joan.

"It does indeed! Here it means making a speech in the House; but there 'political action' lies in the streets, not in a Reichstag hamstrung by splinter-parties. The only German political party which counts is one with a 'Militant Arm'. The Nazi *Storm Troops*, the Tories' *Helmets of Steel*, the Socialist *Iron Front*—and the Communist *Red Front* guns for Socialists even more than for Stahlhelm or Nazis! All these private thuggery-armies excite themselves with uniforms, brass bands and flags—then out come their knives and knuckle-dusters and clubs." Ludo pulled out of his pocket some three or four inches of iron pipe: "Have you ever seen one of these?"

"No," said Augustine. "What is it?"

"They're called 'Stahlruten', and now become regular Storm Troop issue. The weapon is little enough to lie hid in the fist, but swing it and out fly small iron balls on the end of springs which can crack the solidest skulls. They're far more lethal than old-fashioned bicycle-chains." He swung it, and shattered a vase he had never liked.

"What beats me," said Joan as she picked up the bits, "is how the Weimar Republic still holds together at all. Yet Reichstag elections take place, and Members go through the motions of passing laws and making or breaking governments."

"Only because of the Regular Army," said Ludo. "The Army stands aloof in the background, like Gallio caring for none of these things yet always ready to put in its oar if an actual Putsch is threatened—it happened to Hitler in 1923 when he tried it on. Moreover, their Head of State and Supreme Commander-in-Chief is now their old War-Lord, Field-Marshal Hindenburg. That makes the Army's allegiance doubly secure. . . ."

"But does it?" broke in Augustine: "You never quite know with Germans—how they'll react, I mean. Jeremy once heard a Junker colonel he met in Vienna denounce the old man as a traitor for breaking his oath to the Kaiser—*he* wanted your Field-Marshal President hanged!"

Ludovic glanced at the clock. "Talking about 'old men', my Papa's away: why don't you both stop to lunch?" He turned towards Joan: "Do stop: I'm off on a trip to Morocco, and shan't see you or Augustine again for a while—unless he would like to come too?"

Chapter 2

AFTER lunching with Ludo, Joan and Augustine crossed the Abbey grounds on their way to the Rectory gate in silence, a yard apart and avoiding each other's eyes—like children suddenly taken shy and increasingly dreading speech till the silence grows more impossible still to break. Relations between these two were come to their point of no return, and both of them knew it: both felt highly charged with emotion, and knew that at any moment an accidental touch or a single word could alter the course of their lives. . . . At the prospect Joan felt panicky, torn in two. In earlier days she'd have married him like a shot had he asked her then, but as time went by and he didn't, in self-defence she had grown more critical. Now she was pulled one way by the man she had loved at sight, the other by dreary jingles about young men who come to the age of twenty-six without a career of any kind (for surely the beauty of private means is your freedom of choice what work you do, not having no aim in life and doing no work at all?). Now that he seemed at last to have fallen in love with her too, she was finding it hard to break down these very defences she'd raised herself. . . . Able young men who drift through life without ever showing the faintest desire to leave their mark. . . .

Perversely, it wasn't till Joan had already begun to show signs of disillusioned withdrawal that slow-coach Augustine had even begun to find her desirable. Now he most certainly did: he was well aware that his feelings towards this friend of his had lately been changing fast, and might soon be beyond control if they weren't already so. But Augustine also was feeling torn in two this afternoon; and that had been Ludo's doing, for Ludo's harping on Germans all morning had conjured up Mitzi's ghost. . . . However much he might long for Joan, how could he ever marry her knowing he'd never love anyone quite like Mitzi again if he lived to a hundred? No wonder Augustine was torn two ways, for imagine Joan in a Newton whose mistress he once had expected Mitzi to be: with the ghost of Mitzi blindly feeling its way room-by-room to wherever they were—creeping between them in bed. . . . Yet the thought of renouncing Joan was a terrible thing to face; and in fact (he asked himself) decently could he, still? Or had he gone so far that Joan by now had the right to expect him to speak? If only he'd time to think all this out. . . . With his eye he measured the distance ahead: to the Rectory gate was some three hundred yards, if their silence could last that far.

When they got to the gate at last Joan seemed to expect him to follow her in, but dumbly he shook his head. '*You never know when you're lucky*' the gate he was holding open seemed to creak: which made him look at its well-worn paint in surprise, for when had he heard those words before? Then he had a sudden inspiration: "You heard what Ludo said—about Morocco, I mean". He paused, with averted face. "I'm going back to the house to see if he'll really take me too."

In spite of a heart which fell like a lump of lead Joan breathed at least a tiny sigh of relief: she felt pretty sure of him now, and a few weeks' absence should help her to make up her mind. "Yes, I think that's the best thing to do" she told him at last, and even managed to launch a tentative smile at the back of his head.

Of course she knew nothing about that intrusive ghost, or that speaking (ambiguous) gate.

Their boat would leave Southampton early tomorrow morning: Augustine must bundle his things in a sheet and take empty cases to pack when they got on board. . . . He could buy his ticket on board. . . . Ludo had sounded delighted; and when he got back to the Chase Augustine found Gilbert delighted too. Augustine had given him no explanation but none was needed—it stood out a mile: 'Against all the betting' thought jubilant Gilbert 'Joan must have turned him down, and he's off to Morocco to lick his wounds.' Joan had always been much too good for Augustine: thank God she had found that out in time! Then a further thought: after this, the girl was bound to feel a bit lonely. . . . Glad of a sympathetic friend. . . . Open to new impressions. . . . They'd have to do all they could to keep her amused: it was only decent to do so, the proper thing. . . .

For a while his day-dreaming rambled on in this pleasant vein, only marred by the fleeting thought 'But Mary had set her heart on the match. She'll take this badly.' Then came the Bentley's sonorous voice in farewell as Augustine departed, a bundle of boots and clothes in the dicky.

*

When Gilbert expounded to Mary the cause (as he thought) of Augustine's headlong departure she certainly took it badly. Fond as she had been of Joan, she couldn't forgive her for treating Augustine like that: the girl was a conscienceless vamp, and comforting lonesome damsels was out—right out, so far as all Wadamys were concerned (to Gilbert's heartfelt regret, but not entirely to Mary's who read rather more of his mind than Gilbert supposed).

Thus Mary was left with neither Augustine nor Joan at a time when she sorely needed friends: for a large abdominal swelling had lately developed which secretly made her afraid she was starting a growth. So she was; but her uterine 'growth' turned out to be nothing more than another baby. This was as great a surprise to Mary herself as the doctor: she couldn't think how, and Gilbert's answers were all a bit incoherent—implying indeed that a Statesman mustn't be badgered about little personal things in such crucial times, when Baldwin's Mining Industry Bill was before the House re-introducing the 8-hour day.

It must have happened while Mary slept, and the doctor guessed that a 'nurse' who had got in the way of interpreting night-duty quite so widely could hardly be proud of his near-necrophilous practices. . . .

Something however which Gilbert was even less likely to want to admit was his succubus-fantasies, turning the quite impersonal body beneath him to Joan's not Mary at all—so that if by Gilbert's off-hand behaviour you'd think the baby was barely his, in a sense what it really wasn't was Mary's....

Meanwhile, however, the patient was four months gone: since this was already too late for abortion her doctor advised an operation at once, it was risky to let things run on when normal childbirth was anyhow out of the question. But specialist Second Opinion admitted when pressed that pregnancies quite as abnormal as this one had, on occasion, been brought to successful terminations with skilful obstetric help—that is, if Mary was willing to take the serious risk involved if the baby turned out a large one.

She told them at once that she was. . . . But that silly old Gilbert! Mary was tickled to death he could want her still—but why not have done it openly?

Chapter 3

WHEN the English in 1684 abandoned Tangier to the much more powerful Moors, on leaving they blew up the breakwater. No one had mended it since, although the place was now in international hands and ruled like a tiny stagnant separate state 'on the Sultan's behalf' by a concert of European Powers including the English once more. But P. & O. liners made Gib. their port of call, and only the Rotterdam-Lloyd ones called at Tangier—that is, they did so unless there were easterly gales: for a ship that size had to anchor at least a mile from the shore. So the ship that Augustine and Ludo had sailed in was Dutch, with outlandish ideas about serving food; and it made Augustine feel very broad-minded indeed to accept his meat-course before the fish, and to eat cheese only at breakfast.

Among the passengers bound for Java and points even further east were a number of German businessmen, looking remarkably prosperous. Money indeed was said to be running again in that country's veins; and Germany's new prosperity puzzled Augustine, only used like the rest of the world to a Weimar Republic perennially down-and-out. Exercising himself on deck with his friend (the Bay of Biscay was calm—for the Bay of Biscay), Augustine enquired about it and found that—according to Ludo—this economic miracle came from a more than paradoxical source.

"My father says it derives directly from Germany's obligation to pay those unpayable Reparations."

"I don't doubt your father's word, but I hope he explained to you how."

"It's Euclid's Reductio ad Absurdum, applied to the Keynsian proposition that vast debts between States can never be paid. Germany has no gold, it's all in Paris already:

she's got no foreign exchange, and those debts are far too large to be paid in goods without ruining every creditor's own economy. Only one possible way remains: the 'absurd' one of borrowing money abroad with which to pay."

As a sudden squall blew up they sheltered behind a boat, watching the wind blow the tops off the tiny waves.

"That seems an ideal solution," Augustine mused, "since that way nothing passes but paper and ink. But who's going to lend the money?"

"British as well as American bankers are only too willing to lend—at a price. But the interest rates they charge are exceedingly high, and it's this of course which has proved so advantageous to Germany."

"Blessed if I see how it can!"

"When you lend to a State, the charges are paid out of taxes?" Augustine nodded. "And taxes can only be paid out of Gross National Product? Only when that goes up can the tax collector's takings rise and the lenders be paid?" Augustine nodded again. "So once you lend the German Government large sums of money at very high rates, in the creditors' interests German Industry has to be given a pretty spectacular shot in the arm; and that has meant further loans from abroad, with private investors tumbling over each other to lend since there's nowhere else that their money could earn so much."

Augustine gazed at his friend wide-eyed: "You mean, for the Reparations bill to be paid more money has to go into the country as 'loans' than could ever come out again now or hereafter?"

"Far more. My father thinks just about twice as much."

"To draw one bucket of water you prime the pump with a couple of buckets. . . ."

"Exactly. Because the priming process is bound to spill over in projects not even remotely connected with German industrial output. Look at Herr Bürgomeister Konrad Adenauer, playing Cologne's new Kubla Khan and financing his stately pleasure-domes with hundreds of millions of borrowed marks that once were dollars and pounds! He is clearing a 'Green Belt' right round the city, and building a new kind of super-motor-road out to Bonn—something he calls an 'Autobahn', copied from Mussolini's Autostradas. It's all very fine, and gives work to the unemployed—but it doesn't even remotely help to rebuild bombarded Belgium and France."

"Wow!" said Augustine (by now the squall had passed, and they once more paced the glistening deck): "High finance seems almost as crazy as politics."

"All the time and all over the place that sort of thing happens. Take Kammstadt, a small Bavarian middle-class market-town and a County Seat where some co-religionist friends of mine are unlucky enough to live."

"I know the place," Augustine put in. He frowned: "There's a convent there . . ." and his voice tailed off.

"Then you know that her citizens mostly are self-employed: dealers, professional men like lawyers and doctors, skilled artisans and other small tradesmen—not forgetting the publicans. . . ."

"All I've done was to change trains there."

"The town has almost no industry to promote apart from a small municipal brewery: placid Kammstadt enjoys a notable absence of toiling masses, apart from the railwaymen at the Junction's engine-sheds and its own municipal workers. Nevertheless she too must launch her own municipal loan, if only to keep in the swim: so her City Fathers have planned to replace the derelict rat-ridden wartime army camp outside the town by a new municipal race-track and playing fields, at the cost of God-knows-how-many borrowed marks!"

*

So large a municipal project of course had entailed additional City Hall staff; and this had given Lothar his chance. The gaunt old Geheimrat, his father, was dead. Lothar was

now twenty-one, had muffed all his early exams and was tired
of studying Law, so was glad of even a minor Local Government job when young Baron Franz persuaded his father
to pull the appropriate strings and got him engaged as a
clerk.

Chapter 4

THE weather was luckily fine enough to anchor in Tangier Bay, where Augustine got his first distant glimpse of this westernmost (more-or-less the Meridian of Greenwich) outpost of Islam. Away to the right, on two-hundred-foot cliffs, he could see the crumbling walls and minarets of the Kasbah: below lay the scrambled Arab Medina, and outside the walls of the town to the left stood a few new blatantly European blocks which he tried to ignore. At that moment from one of the minarets a muezzin was calling the Faithful to prayer; and his wailing voice, heard over a mile or so of intervening water, sounded as eerie as wolves in Canadian forests.

Then sweating oarsmen rowed them ashore in a kind of wherry to land on a wooden pier (before that pier had been built they'd have had to be carried shoulder-high through the final surf). They landed in Babel—or Bedlam—or both, with bare-legged hooded porters and touts and hucksters fighting each other and yelling like mad in Arabic, Spanish, or even a lousy word or two of incomprehensible English to get their custom. But Ludovic sorted everything out. Their luggage was hoisted on skeletal donkeys; and soon they were forcing their way through the fancy-dress crowds which thronged the steep and narrow (and only more-or-less cobbled) streets.

As they threaded a maze of alleys all smelling in turn of donkeys and incense and leather and urine and spices Augustine felt strangely elated, as if this was 'home' at last! But Ludo told him to wait: Tangier was a mongrel city, with nearly a third of its population impoverished Europeans (assuming Gibraltar's 'Rock-Scorpions' counted as such). During the days of Morocco's independence the Sultan had very sensibly kept all Foreign Embassies here in a kind of quarantine-station, instead of allowing them near his Sacred Person: thus even today, when most of the diplomats-proper

271

had moved to Rabat, the place was still a hive of Legations
down-graded to overgrown Consulates each with its army of
hangers-on. To these you must add some hundreds of down-
at-heel Spaniards, unable to earn a living at home and doing
no better here or escaped from the Spanish convict-
settlements down the coast; and indeed men of all nations
fled to Tangier to be out of the reach of the Arm of the Law
(much as you may think Augustine had fled from the Arms
of Love). Contrabandistas, drug-addicts, perverts—and
simpler folk who had merely been rather unlucky with
knives in their simple way, or with other men's money. . . .
"No, if you think you like this place you should wait till
you've been to Meknes and Fez, and Marrakesh: the real
Morocco is very different."

That night as he lay on his curtained big brass bed in the
grandiose house on the Marshan where yet more cousins of
Ludo's lived, Augustine mused on how strange it was he
should feel a place 'home' which he'd never even visited till
today! If Meknes and Fez—and Marrakesh—were even
better. . . .

Tomorrow he'd better start learning Arabic.

After a day or two Ludo inducted his friend in the arts of
pig-sticking, out at Sharf el Akab within sound of the roaring
Atlantic: and there Augustine first met 'The Glaoui'.

The Glaoui was here on a visit, and also out pig-sticking
with the British. He looked superb in his flowing Moorish
robes with his hooded saturnine face, riding an Arab stallion,
in yellow Moorish slippers and eighteen-inch golden spurs—
and couching his spear at a level for men-sticking rather
than pig, for a lifetime's technical habits (he told Augustine)
were too strong to break.

Augustine questioned Ludo about him while riding home.
Of the former 'Three Great Caids of the South', the Goundafa
and M'tougga stars were now in final eclipse and the Glaoua
star was nearing its zenith (so Ludo said). On the late
Madani el Glaoui's death this warrior-brother, T'hami—

already the Pasha of Marrakesh—had become 'The Glaoui' as well, the Premier Lord of the Atlas: a combination which made him the most powerful Moor in Morocco not even barring the Sultan. As Pasha down in the plains, perforce he favoured the conquering French; and the French favoured him, since they looked to his Atlas realm as their southern bulwark; but all the same (added Ludo) they sensibly poked no noses in mountain passes where captured Frenchmen—or so the story went—were buggered to death.

Ludo's own family ties with the House of Glaoua went back to a certain Ischoua Corcos who'd helped to finance the elder Glaoui's ousting of Sultan Abd-el-Aziz in favour of Mulay Hafid. Ludo's father still kept many a gold-tipped finger in Glaoui's financial pies, and Ludo himself—though the one was a Jew and the other a Moslem—had long been as close a friend of T'hami el Glaoui as men like that could allow themselves friends. Thus Ludo had much to tell Augustine about that spectacular, fabulous figure beneath whose fleecy immaculate robes was a sinewy body scarred head-to-foot. A horrible trench in the flesh ran the length of his back where in youth defenders had poured boiling lead on him scaling a fortress wall—he had had to lie in a bath of oil for a month. Few people knew that a knife-thrust had severed a nerve in his cheek, because by a Herculean effort he managed to hold his face straight in public in case you should think he had suffered a stroke. . . .

In boyhood his sport had been potting a pigeon's egg balanced between the ankles of one of his father's slaves with a flintlock: a dangerous sport indeed for a worthless younger son, should he lame for life some favourite slave! Today he shot partridge with ball at the gallop. . . . Then Ludo went on to say that the Glaoui had to keep in with the French but privately seemed to prefer the English. But sometimes he showed this in somewhat equivocal ways: as once when he'd asked a highly distinguished English friend to bring home one of his brides, instead of sending the more conventional *physical* eunuch. . . .

Indeed the Glaoui showed rather a pretty wit in this devious sort of way. At Marrakesh, when trying a case, he would publicly lay all the bribes he'd received on the table —the envelopes still unopened. He gave some away to indigent widows—unopened still; but when in private he opened the ones which remained, if they didn't come up to scratch he either appealed against himself and retried the case—or that litigant just disappeared.

Chapter 5

THE war which had lately overflowed from the Riff—the mountainous 'Spanish Zone' which lay to the east of Tangier—was over at last, and Tangier no longer cut off from the rest of Morocco except by ship.

For six years Abd el Krim (though outnumbered a hundred to one) had vanquished and massacred Spanish armies, repeatedly driving the Spaniards into the sea. For the last two years he had taken on France as well, and only last summer was threatening Fez itself. Unencumbered by wounded (the Red Cross flatly refused to allow him medical aid), and with troops who could march and fight on a handful of dates, his forces could fight two battles in twenty-four hours a good forty miles apart. But they weren't without Western technical skills: having captured a field-gun from the French they took it to pieces, manhandled the pieces across the trackless mountains, re-assembled the parts in a cave and used it to bombard Tetouan. . . . It had taken the utmost might of Spain and France combined to defeat him, and only last month had the famous Mohammed ben Abd el Krim el-Khatabi been finally forced to surrender to Marshal Pétain's 160,000 men. But now the overland routes were open again: Augustine and Ludo could travel towards the south whenever they liked.

Joan had reckoned Augustine's probable absence in terms of weeks. When weeks turned into months, and when autumn even had come without him returning, Jeremy started suspecting his friend must be having a whale of a time among Djinns and Afreets, Sultans and brigands, gazelle and wild boar: for surely simple heartache could never have kept him away so long!

After a whole month in Fez Augustine and Ludo had reached the coast at Rabat, where (or rather, across the river in Salli) they got themselves stoned and spat-on by blue-eyed and red-bearded Moslems (descended from Christian slaves, and thus all-the-more fanatical). Then down the coast past dreary commercial Casablanca to Mazagan; and on to Saffi, where beautiful bronze Portuguese cannon with handles moulded like dolphins and knobs like bunches of grapes still lay about on the Keshla ramparts just where—centuries back—the Portuguese gunners had left them. There they turned inland again, towards Marrakesh; and saw for the first time—floating as if detached above the heat-haze—distant snow-covered peaks: the tempting, forbidden Atlas Mountains. . . .

This turned their thoughts again to the Glaoui, whose hold on that mountainous south was nowadays said to be pretty complete—apart from his infamous nephew Hammou, whose torture-chambers and vast arsenal-fortress of Telouet were defended by cannon forged (for the Franco-Prussian War) by Krupp; and one or two lesser ruffians no doubt, whose eyries lay too far from the caravan routes for the Glaoui to bother about them. . . .

Thus Mary was once more nearing her time, with Augustine on this occasion even further removed in Epoch than Space—in the Calendar Year 1345. That was by Muslim computation of course; but he might just as well have been back in Christendom's Middle Ages, in mountains where Berber chieftains living in fortified castles snapped their fingers at Sultans and even Protecting Powers. Like Christendom's mediaeval barons, each one ruled as far as the arm of his wrath could be made to reach till somebody stronger did him in.

It was wholly by Glaoui's personal favour and quite unknown to the French—who'd have done their damnedest to stop it—that late in October Augustine and Ludo had found themselves three days' journey already into those xeno-

phobe Atlas Mountains. Tonight they were lodged in a
Berber castle. . . . But this was a castle (it happened) whose
brigandish owner was counted among those 'lesser ruffians'
with little love or respect for the Glaoui—though that was
a fact they had found out rather too late.

Indeed there seemed good reason to doubt if tomorrow
morning would find them alive.

Chapter 6

A WEEK ago, in Marrakesh, Ludo had played his cards well when they called at the Pasha's vast and desolate palace. Sipping his scented coffee, Ludo had hinted (no more) at their crazy impossible pipe-dream of crossing the mountains from Asni towards Taroudant "had the French been less insanely jealous of British intruders". This nettled the Glaoui: the Atlas was his domain, and permission had nothing to do with the French. . . . Without more ado he had given his blessing; then turned to one of his Berber body-guard, Ali, and told him in Shleuh (the Berber tongue) to guide this Jew and this Christian, and guard them—and not to come back without them. . . . Whereupon Ali—knowing full well what that warning meant from the merciless Glaoui —had sat up the whole night sharpening knives.

They had ridden on horseback as far as Asni: from there the grooms must take the beasts back, for horses were useless on mountain tracks. With the plains and their acres of olives and palms left behind, Augustine had felt like a boy escaping from school and inclined to behave like one: hoping 'to stretch his legs' (among mountains anything up to 14,000 feet high), he had even pleaded for making the journey on foot. But this was a country where only the scum-of-the-earth went on foot, and Ludo had had to insist on hiring three mules to ride—with three little slave-boys thrown in—as the minimum style required when personal friends of the Glaoui took to the road. So the two of them covered their 'Christian' clothes in Berber cloaks and the cavalcade had set off, with the taciturn Ali riding in front and the three boys joking along in the dust behind letting out occasional ear-splitting yells to encourage the beasts.

They sat side-saddle without any saddles—just panniers

flung over each animal's back, incessantly drumming its near-side ribs with their heels since the moment the drumming faltered the sluggish animal stopped. At first it made even the seaman Augustine giddy to find himself riding like this on the outside brink of a four-foot track cut across the face of a cliff, and looking sheer down between his own drumming heels to a green-edged thread of quicksilver hundreds of feet below: then meeting a convoy of baggage-camels, and having to lie out flat on his animal's back—with the animal somehow walking with bended knees like a slinking cat—while a camel's side-bales of merchandise swayed just an inch or two over his nose.

When rivers had to be crossed there weren't any bridges: they had to be forded, towing the three boys behind through the ice-cold water gripping the tails of the mules in their teeth. At night they would come to some mud-built village, where Ali would summon the Sheikh and the magic of Glaoui's name would secure them lodging of sorts: a carpet to sleep on, mint-tea and rock-like bread—and possibly hard-boiled eggs. For three days, indeed, all had gone well: three magical days. . . . But then on the fourth—and late in the afternoon at that—they had come to a spreading valley where Ali had seemed uncertain which track to take (so uncertain that Ludo suspected they'd taken a wrong one already to find themselves there at all). There was no one about to ask; but on cresting a rise they had sighted this castle, and sanguinely hoped for rather higher-class entertainment here than villagers could afford.

The bare earth was crimson; the snow-capped mountains were crimson and even the river was tinged with red. The castle itself was crimson, with splashes of white high up round the few outside windows—like eyes. . . . As they neared it, hundreds of sharp-sighted pigeons flew out and wheeled in the crimsoning evening sky. The final approach to the castle was cut single-file through a thicket of otherwise quite impassable thorn, a thicket which barely left room to skirt three sides of the fortress and get to the fourth where alone

K

was there any gate—and even then they were still single-file,
on the narrow bank of a raging pinkish river. The gate moreover was masked by a short curtain-wall which would leave
attackers no room for wielding a battering-ram, and no hope
of covering-fire from across the torrent. . . . "Whoever
planned this castle's defences," Augustine remarked, "certainly knew his job!"

But where had they got to? "Who owns this castle?" Ludo
had asked their 'guide' more than once; but Ali seemed not
to hear. The gates were closed; but now a wizened face had
looked out through a wicket, so Ludo made Ali ask him in
Shleuh. . . .

When he learned at last where he was even Ali blenched,
and pulled his hood over his face. He whispered to Ludo that
Allah had brought them to country where claiming the
Glaoui's friendship merited instant death. "Mashallah,"
said Ali. . . . But 'Allah's Will' be damned, and hastily Ludo
conferred with Augustine.

The sun was already setting, and nobody spends the night
in the open but footpads and cut-throats. . . . Anyway,
turning back once they'd been seen would be fatal. . . . Bluff
seemed their only hope: two English travellers (thanks be to
heaven at least they weren't French!) who pleaded the law of
Koranic hospitality, naming themselves 'deeaf Allah'—
'guests sent him by God'.

Hoping against all hope that no one would recognise Ali as
one of the Glaoui's men, Ludo boldly beat on the gate with
his fist while Augustine felt like some wretched MacDonald,
back in the days of Glencoe, beating by night on the gates of
the Master of Stair. Then the wicket was opened again, to
reveal this time an almost gigantic elderly negro: a man
of majestic presence, dressed in a black-and-white striped
jillaba and wearing a silver-sheathed koumiyah nearly as big
as a scimitar. Ali was hiding his face in his hood and appeared
struck dumb, so it fell to Ludo himself to say the piece which
ought to have come from his man: "Tell your master that

two very high-ranking Englishmen—intimate friends of the English King—have been sent by Allah to stand at his gate and await a hospitality rightly famous among the Faithful."

The man looked doubtful (perhaps he didn't know very much Arabic). Anyway, back he went for orders; and dusk was already falling before at last he heaved wide open the groaning gates and they found themselves in a pitch-black vaulted darkness filled with the roar of rushing water. . . . For here was the final attacker's hazard, and only a narrow booby-trap bridge crossed a sluice which ran like a mill-race. Guiding hands, however, were laid on their arms; they crossed a courtyard where tribesmen were camped, and climbed the outside stair of a corner-tower.

This small upper room was completely empty. Across the four corners were cedar-beams polished with age providing racks for their cloaks, but otherwise—nothing. A bare polished plaster floor like old ivory faintly reflected the reds of the richly-painted cedarwood ceiling; bare polished-ivory walls reflected the dying hues of the sunset. The windows were small and unglazed, with beautiful wrought-iron grilles looking up at the pink of snow-covered peaks or down at the darkening vegetation around those mountains' feet. The very air seemed the colour of blood.

Augustine had never seen any room quite so lovely—or quite so ominous, chilling and comfortless.

Chapter 7

I n England, on that same October Saturday afternoon Joan had been visiting Jeremy's rooms in Ebury Street (he had lately ceased to be Resident Clerk), and had asked for news of Augustine. But Jeremy shook his head: "Nothing for two or three months. They were then in Fez, but thinking of moving south to Marrakesh as soon as the weather got cooler."

'Still no signs of him coming home?' was what her eyes asked; but Jeremy merely shrugged. 'It's those Djinns and Afreets,' he thought (Augustine's own letter from Fez had indeed likened Morocco to living inside the Arabian Nights).

Four long months had done nothing to ease the ache. In a way that was nowadays automatic whenever she felt the need of an antidote, Joan began to rehearse in her head her private list of Augustine's faults: his lack of ambition of any kind, and even of any consistent aim in life. At last she complained out loud: "In a few more years he'll be thirty!" and added "he'd money enough to embark on any career he liked."

Jeremy snorted. "I suppose what you mean is the Diplomatic, or governing bug-ridden tropical colonies! Surely it's one of the sourest fruits of our prevalent Classical Education, this antique 'liturgical' notion about the duties which go with ample private means." He paused. "Or—since wealthy poets and painters don't need to debase their gift by having to make it pay—what a pity Augustine can't even paint for nuts. . . . But perhaps you think all the same he should have a try?" Joan winced at the irony in his voice, and he wagged an accusing finger: "I almost believe you'd go for some absolute moron, provided he played the part at least of a conscientious squire—ready to open bazaars at the drop of a hat, or to plant

282

a spinney when times were bad! Men ready to sit on the
Bench, and the County Council. . . . D'you want Augustine
to settle at Newton and live like that?"

"You're not being very helpful."

"Perhaps. . . . Because I bet I can read what you've really
got in your tiny mind: Augustine's curious craze for his
miners, you think, should have led to an active role in the
Labour Party—like Mosley, or Strachey's son."

Joan was startled into confessing that some such idea
might indeed have entered her head. . . .

"Then you couldn't have read him wronger!—Look, my
girl. . . ." He paused, to think how best to put it. "Can't you
hoist in that Augustine's miners are no mere impersonal
aggregate Cause, they're a 'Twm', and a 'Dai'?—Because
people can't be added together like 'things', which is where
the root of the whole Political Fallacy lies." He was cocking a
doubtful eye at Joan to see how much he was getting across,
having learned by now that to most of mankind it is far from
axiomatic—this sacred particularity of the 'self', as something wholly outside the domain of number.

"Then why not use his money to help them in other ways?"

Jeremy stared at Joan in astonishment: "Now it's the
miners you're utterly failing to understand."

"Constructive ways, of course—like those Quaker work-
shops."

"Can't you see how any experienced miner must hate those
Quakers' benevolent guts—expecting the salt of the earth to
waste time cobbling shoes or knocking up tables and chairs,
instead of their proper job?"

But misery made Joan stubborn: "All right then, over to
you! What *does* Augustine intend to do with his life?"

"Perhaps it's a rarer achievement than you imagine,
Augustine's knack of having things happen to him without
ever needing to lift a finger to make them happen," said
Jeremy softly.

Joan's snort was an infinitesimal snort, but suddenly
Jeremy's patience snapped: "Very well! But if he must have a

'career', please remember how being rich has narrowed his field of choice."

"Has 'narrowed' it?"

"Yes. For all manual work—and that's nine-tenths of the field—is strictly reserved for the poor."

Joan gasped. "But why on earth, with his brains and his education. . . ."

"Why on earth not—or have you forgotten how blissful he was on that rum-running schooner? If that sort of thing is his natural bent his brains needn't get in his way—his highly-intelligent miners are proof of that. Although I admit that his lack of even the most elementary manual education might. . . ." Suddenly Jeremy sprang to his feet and started striding up and down: "Have you ever thought that instead of just hero-worshipping miners he could have been one himself, if instead of his horrible Public School he had gone underground as a fifteen-year-old? And that takes us back to the days when the Rhondda was still Eldorado, the Saturday pubs as full as the Sunday chapels. . . . It just isn't fair on a man, this blight of the silver spoon in his mouth!"

Perhaps this paradoxical gospel of manual work would have mystified Joan even more had her glance not fallen on Jeremy's paralysed arm—when the sudden insight caused her a twinge of pity.

Later, "I've never been underground even to look," said Jeremy sadly, over their tea. "Say what it's like."

"Do you want to be told how they carry their food in strong tin boxes, because there are more rats than men down those human ratholes? And take down quarts of tea to make up for the sweat they lose? And their ironclad boots, fit to stand up to kicking against sharp rock eight hours on end in the dark?"

"That much I've seen; but say what it's really like right inside a mine."

"Augustine has only taken me once, myself—and then not the kind you go down in a lift, but merely a 'level' with ferns

round its mouth." She paused. "I found myself gasping for
breath like a fish the moment I got inside: the air had been
breathed so often there wasn't much left except vaporised
sweat, and even my lamp burned dim. All its glimmer
showed was drips like tropical rain from the roof, and the
shine on the rails I must balance along because the roadway
was knee-deep in water. Then, fifty yards in . . ." (her voice
took on nightmarish tones) "a strong smell of iodine. Stone,
and splintered timber—and yards of sodden discarded
bandage got snarled round my ankles, I didn't know what it
was in the dark."

"A fall of the roof, and someone'd got caught?" Joan
nodded, speechless. "Well, carry on."

"I can't. That's as far as they'd let me go—thank God, for
already I felt the whole weight of mountain on top of me,
squeezing out pebbles and ooze from between the props."

"Have a try," he wheedled. "From things you've been
told."

Joan took a deep breath, and put down her muffin half-
eaten. "You may have to crawl, with only a couple of feet of
headroom, to get to the coal-face at all; and lie there for
hours on end, in water, listening all the time to the pump in
case it chokes and you haven't got time to escape. Meanwhile you're patiently undercutting the seam till the
Atlantean weight on top of it forces bits down. Then these
must somehow be shovelled back up the roadway to where a
tram can get near enough in to load—still crawling, of
course. . . ."

"So now don't you pity the poor little rich boy, who
mayn't get his knees and his back rubbed raw by the floor and
the roof like this for night after night—and with grit ground
into the meat wherever the skin is gone?" cried Jeremy,
watching her wince. "Remember, he's only a half-grown
fifteen. . . ."

"That's enough from you!" said Joan in an ominous voice.

"But I mean it you booby, you must see that! And when he
gets back to his lodgings—through streets where grimy sheep

from the uplands scavenge the dustbins like alley-cats—who might he find there but *you*? You, still not out of your teens and down on your two knees scrubbing the doorstep, showing a great deal of leg. . . . He's 'blacker than Midnight's arsehole' (to quote the Classics), and dripping black puddles all over your lovely work—but you're used to that. . . . Then you move indoors, where a wooden tub stands in front of a kitchen fire with the breakfast bacon frying; and there stands your Dad, sponging his naked lodger's bleeding back —with Augustine bashfully trying to hide his newly-fledged private parts from you, you shameless hussy, standing there blankly wondering when the wind will change and stop blowing coal-dust over your washing-line. . . ."

Joan bent her head to examine the teapot: "It needs more water," she said.

"But those of course were the palmy days." He paused, and cocked his ear to sounds from the street below. "Whereas now. . . . Just listen to that." Both of them crossed to the window to look. "They must have walked the whole way from Wales, like their fathers the drovers before them."

Across the street an Unemployed Miners' Choir sang in the autumn drizzle, as wholly absorbed in their singing as if on the stage of the Albert Hall. Joan thought they looked as if none of the bowler-hatted ninnies scurrying past them was even worth their pity. . . .

"Now you see what Augustine has missed," said Jeremy's deadpan voice.

Suddenly Joan clutched his arm: "But there *is* Augustine!"

"Where?" With her heart in her mouth she was pointing directly below at a threadbare figure, its back towards them, shaking an upturned cap for pennies under embarrassed averted Londoner's faces—that unmistakable six-foot frame. . . . "The lunatic!" Jeremy gasped: "That's carrying things too far!"

He darted downstairs to the street, and was just about to seize hold of Augustine's sleeve when 'Augustine' turned—to reveal a different face altogether. Though much of the same

age and height, Augustine's 'Doppelgänger' had lost one eye
and his blue-black nose had been crushed back into his face;
his clothes hung loose on his bones. When Jeremy fumbled
out a coin, he was thanked in an almost inaudible windless
voice from lungs it would take a stonemason's chisel to cut.

Chapter 8

MEANWHILE slaves had brought carpets to spread on the floor and mountainous cushions to loll on, followed by other slaves bearing candles enormous as any in Catholic churches; and somebody closed the shutters to keep out the chill. Then had come slaves with glowing earthenware braziers poised on their heads, and incense thrown on the white-hot charcoal filled the room with blue aromatic smoke. The jittery Ali must have been badly in need of warmth, for he squatted on top of one of these braziers tucking it under his skirts as a personal central-heating system, and groaned with pleasure as tiny smoke-wisps of incense came curling out at his neck.

As they sat cross-legged on the floor, Augustine and Ludo took pains to appear without a care in the world; but on learning their dreaded host was away from home, hearts leapt. . . . Though he hadn't gone far (they were told), and a runner already had set out to find him—whereon their hearts fell again, and further still too when they heard the Khalifa's orders were soon expected if not the Khalifa himself.

After a time, however, their supper began to arrive: so every right hand that must dip in the dish was washed in water scented with orange-blossom, and then came the ceremonial breaking of bread (for bread must never be cut). Long-legged radishes helped to inspire those grateful belches good manners required as dish followed dish: cous-cous with quails in it sprinkled with cinnamon, roast chicken basted with honey and garnished with walnuts, a highly-spiced stew—and a lamb roasted whole, so tender its flesh came away in pinches (there being no knives or forks). But Ali, his hood still hiding his face, ate almost nothing right down to the final 'gazelles' feet' honey-and-almond pastries.

288

There must have been fully a dozen courses before more washing of hands was followed by mint-tea served in ornate little gilded glasses. . . . What ages it seemed before the servants had all withdrawn, and at last they were left alone! It was close on midnight—and no one had told them whether their absent host the Khalifa had sent his instructions or not.

Ali was smoking pipe after pipe of comforting kif; but he seemed to draw little comfort from it, and told them that crossing the open yard he had recognised someone. . . . Suppose this someone had recognised him, and had spread the tale that these 'guests' were spies of the Glaoui? Augustine looked at the door; but the door hadn't even a bolt—or at any rate none on the inside, if somebody came in the night. Suppose someone did, was he really about to have his throat cut? Ali was surely the one to know, and Ali certainly seemed to think they would. . . . If so, it's silly enough getting killed for a 'Cause'; but what a consummate fool he would feel if he got himself killed in so pointless a fashion as this! Really at twenty-six he ought to have had more sense. . . . Playing at being a he-man, that's all this crack-pot excursion was: playing at being Walter Harris—or even at being Lawrence!

Augustine thought of the god-like glamour of T. E. Lawrence's presence at Oxford, its stunning effect on some-body really young: how it made one remember his lightest word, as when he'd refused Augustine's sherry since "wine might spoil my palate for water" (for weeks after that Augustine had noticed the flavour of every glass of water he drank, self-consciously savoured the peaty bouquet of mountain streams). He recalled one sacred evening spent in Lawrence's All Souls rooms, with even Jeremy fallen respect-fully silent while Lawrence explained how he'd cut the rail-way precisely enough to hamstring the Turks but never enough to render them desperate. Lawrence had told them the *Art* of war was to win it while getting not only as few of your own men killed as you could but as few of the enemy too. . . . No, Lawrence was not the conventional he-man but one of the subtlest minds Augustine had ever met: a mind

like an onion—skin after skin to peel off without ever finding
the final Lawrence within.

It would take a bit more than a Berber cloak and a spice
of danger to turn an Augustine into a Lawrence; and this
was something he should have got wise to ages ago.

When the time came to put out the candles Ali stationed
their three little slave-boys to sleep on the stairs outside, their
Negroid faces invisible in the dark once their eyes and their
lips were closed: he hoped they would squeak loud enough to
give the alarm if any intruder trod on them. Then he laid
himself down right across the door with his hand on the
drawn knife under his cheek—a copybook 'Faithful Guard'.
But both these precautions were more dramatic than useful,
Augustine remarked to Ludo: for even had their party been
armed to the teeth—and Ali's collection of razor-sharp
knives were the only weapons among them, at least they'd
had that much sense—nothing they did could prevent the
Khalifa from having them killed in the end if he'd made up
his mind to kill them; and Ludo agreed.

Walter Harris never went armed. . . . He had once told
Ludo if trouble arose and you had a revolver the best thing to
do was to throw it over their heads and start them fighting
each other to get it. . . .

It tickled Augustine to find himself more fatalistic than Ali
the Muslim; and since his staying awake could serve no
possible end, he settled himself in his cushions and soon fell
fast asleep.

*

Throughout what might well prove his last night on earth,
Augustine slept like a log. The person who got little sleep that
night was Joan, in her Suffolk Street hotel—and this wasn't
simply her lumpy bed. The nonsense Jeremy talked and that
strange apparition outside had re-opened the wound, and
revealed—in the light of these wretched four months—that
living without Augustine was life with its radiance gone and

its very reason. Wanting him otherwise than he was—that was useless.

She'd have to swallow her pride and summon him home: which was probably all he was waiting for, in his chivalrous way, a point she ought to have thought of before. . . .

That poor dead Henry (she thought), whose only existence today was when his resemblance stared at her ghostlily out of Augustine's beloved face! But she and Augustine were made for each other. . . .

Just for one somnolent moment she dreamed of two blazing suns revolving entirely around and merging into each other; but 'Two into one can't be done!' said a sonorous voice; and that piece of profoundest wisdom woke her to wonder what changes she'd make at Newton, and where she would put her grandmother's chest-of-drawers. That awful Billiard-room needed a lot more light; but orange curtains and cream-coloured paint work wonders. . . .

So where was her pen? In a minute she'd get out of bed to look, but the room was cold and the light-switch was by the door. She hadn't Augustine's address in Morocco, but Ludo's father was certain to know—and on second thoughts, it might be better to cable than write.

Chapter 9

Augustine woke next morning teased by the thought there was something vital he had to remember but couldn't; and several agonised seconds had passed before he recalled that he might have woken up dead. But now he was being offered the standard 'hareerah' breakfast soup: fresh bread, with shavings of butter kept crisp by snow rushed down from the peaks, and a bowl of delicious honey. . . .

Ludo and he avoided each other's eyes, both trying to kid themselves they had never been taken in by Ali's ridiculous fears last night. They sent a message of blessing and thanks to their still-invisible host, distributed ample largesse and were feeling as pleased as Punch as they joined their mules at the gate.

A-guest-is-a-guest-is-a-guest, even when personal contact has been avoided with care lest any magical 'baraka' pass and the host be obligated. But once the party had gone through the gate they were guests no longer: before they had even mounted, peremptory orders came out to go back by the way they had come; and the messenger secretly tipped them the wink to make all the haste they could to Marrakesh. Solely because they weren't French the Khalifa might give them a few hours' start before sending out tribesmen to hunt them down—and he rather fancied himself as a cat-and-mouse man. . . .

A slow cavalcade of mules, pursued by galloping tribesmen. . . . Crossing the courtyard Augustine had seen their horses, tied by their feet to pegs in the ground. "All the same, we mustn't appear to hurry," said Ludo.

"Why not?"

"For one thing, we're not supposed to know. For another, as soon as those three boys twig something's up they'll contrive to decamp with the mules."

"That's true. . . ."

But Augustine's wits were working fast; and once out of sight of the castle walls he pretended hilarious spirits, proposing a mule-race by way of amusement. He promised a prize for whichever boy's mule was the fastest: the boys were delighted, and off they all went at the gallop—the boys leaping over the rocks and thorn-bushes yelling their heads off, and each one prodding his mule from behind with a sharp-pointed stick whenever he got within reach. It was hard to believe how those two-miles-an-hour mules could fly once they took it into their heads! Ali's mule easily won, for Augustine nearly fell off with laughing as Ludo behind him came bouncing over the scree like John Gilpin.

No question of course of stopping to rest or eat all day: like camels, they had to live on their (last night's) humps; and they kept the boys going by jokes and mockery laced with bribes. The mules seemed to know they were facing home, and by sunset they'd covered ground enough for more than a normal day-and-a-half. They were even beginning to hope they might now be beyond the Khalifa's reach, till outside the village they hoped to sleep in a villager warned them his Sheikh had orders to apprehend them on sight. The man had no idea where these orders came from: it could be the French, or it could be someone whose mercies might prove less tender; but simply to spite his own Sheikh (that uncircumcised son of a strumpet who'd stolen his calf) he proposed to hide them himself, if they waited outside till dusk.

So they waited till dusk, then spent a hilarious night in a windowless mud-walled stable half-full of dung and lit by a single candle: the three grown men and the mules and the slave boys all hugger-mugger, and playing infantile jokes on each other—except for Ali, who didn't seem given to jokes. The boys were enchanted, and begged them to buy them when they got back: all three—they swore—wouldn't come to more than the price of a goat (and a spell in Gibraltar gaol, under British Law).

Soon after midnight they heard a staccato drumming outside, and a voice crying "Where are those dogs of Christians?
Death to the Infidels!" Augustine peeped through a crack in
the door: a single Negro with frothing lips was waving an
awesome axe in one hand and wildly rat-tatting his drum
with the other.

Humourless always, Ali darted across to the door with his
knife; but Augustine forestalled him. In this sort of situation
it sharpens the English Explorer's wits no end not having a
gun, and Augustine remembered a prep-school performance
of his which always had little boys in stitches: so out he went
now, and presented himself to this one-man Holy War in the
role of a monkey catching fleas.

The dumbfounded fanatic's curses began to give way to
giggles; and finally, helpless with laughter, he flung his axe in
the bushes and came in to join the party.

The next night they slept in the little French inn at Asni.

"The net result has been merely return to Marrakesh a
trifle sooner than planned," said Augustine.

"With sobering thoughts that the wily Khalifa may never
have sent out a posse at all: he may even have prompted the
'friendly warning' simply to make quite sure he was rid of
us."

Galling—but all-too-possibly true, thought Augustine. A
sobering thought indeed, that perhaps from start to finish
there'd never been any danger at all. . . . But how could they
ever know? Kaleidoscopic Morocco was like that: once the
passing moment had shaken the bits you never would know.

"We'd better not call on the Glaoui and face his questions,
for old Ali's sake," said Augustine. "For Ali really did make a
pretty good balls of it all: why didn't the lunatic tell the
Glaoui straight off this part of the mountains was country he
didn't know, and shift the job on to someone who did?"

Ludo shrugged his shoulders. "He wouldn't dare question
the Glaoui's orders. And anyhow everything lies in the hands
of Allah, so why should he worry?"

Chapter 10

THEY were back in Marrakesh. Ludo had gone for their mail, while Augustine was sipping a Bock in a hotel garden where tourists were boasting about the bargains they'd bought in the Souks. Augustine wondered what they'd have thought of the 'bargain' he hadn't bought: three half-starved human boys for the price of a goat—three pairs of reproachful eyes he had left behind him at Asni, looking like dogs whose master was inexplicably starting out for a walk without them.

But buying one even in order to set him free was a penal offence for a Briton—and rightly (Augustine thought), for 'freedom' would merely mean that nobody any longer had any obligation to feed him: like setting superfluous kittens 'free' on the London streets.

In so lovely a garden as this those tourists' appearance was truly an eyesore, their voices an earsore; and Bock was conducive to meditation. Augustine ordered a second glass. He then began to study himself in the light of their Atlas escapade, and with growing amazement at what he found: for whether their danger had ever been real or not he had certainly thought it was at the time—and in that case, what on earth could have made him behave almost like some-body out of the *Boys' Own Paper* the way he had? Calmly composing himself for sleep, with only a fifty-fifty chance of ever seeing the morning light: confronting unarmed that fanatic who threatened to chop them up with his axe? He hadn't been 'brave', because that means conquering fear and he'd acted throughout with a total absence of genuine panicky fear: whereas in the past that Long Island landing for instance had frightened him out of his wits, and so had the Bearcat chase. . . .

It was all so incredibly out of character! Could he be really changing his nature like that with advancing years—or was it just something perhaps in the very air of Morocco, and quite automatic when thrown among people who rate life cheap to devalue your own? Like in hospital: back in 1918, finding himself in a whole ward dying of Spanish Flu, death had seemed the natural thing and not worth fussing about. . . .

Augustine lifted his puzzled gaze to a branch overhead, where a subfusc mottled chameleon's bulbous eyes (they had only a tiny hole in the middle to see through) focused a fly. Creatures believed to keep changing colour to match their surroundings—though all this one did was to dart out an eight-inch tongue and whip in the fly. . . . So perhaps his own curious lack of fear had been merely a human chameleon's unconscious 'doing-in-Rome-as-Rome-does' deep-psychological automatic reaction? But that was a pretty alarming thought: if the leopard can't change its spots but a civilised rational humanist atheist quite so easily can, he had better watch out in case this applied right across the board in surroundings where man-made law was totally disregarded but no one would dream of disobeying the least of the Laws of God!

As a psychological force outclassing the Will and Reason—outclassing Ethical Absolutes, Sex, and Self-preservation alike—his new 'Automatic Chameleonism' Law could account for a lot in human behaviour. Placed in general heretic-burning surroundings, for instance, that was how decent intelligent men could have acquiesced and even approved (St. Paul joining in when Stephen was stoned). One day he must try the idea out on Jeremy. . . .

Just then Ludo arrived with a bundle of mail, sat down and clapped imperious hands for a drink: "I'm a wreck—that bloody British P.O. here is quite as slow as the French!"

On the top of Augustine's batch were a couple of telegrams. One was from Mary: she'd had her baby all right —this time a six-pound boy, her 'infant Gilbert' at last. . . .

But then Augustine read Joan's; and his heart gave a curious sideways leap, neither properly up nor down. He read it through twice; but all he said was, "It looks like I've got to get home at once."

Ludo showed no surprise. "From here the quickest is probably hiring a car to Casablanca or Mazagan, and catching a boat from there."

"Then that's what I'd better do, I suppose."

"I'll try and find out about sailings" said Ludo, and vanished inside the hotel.

Augustine read through the cable a third time, wondering still at how little elation he seemed to feel. As soon as he *saw* Joan, of course, it would probably boil up again. . . . But meanwhile, incontinent thoughts kept creeping back to their late expedition.

For decades the whole Souss Valley and Taroudant had been closed to all Europeans: suppose they'd got through? And Ludo and he would have certainly tried it again, if he'd stayed. Maybe they would join a caravan through the mountains dressed as Moors—with himself a pretence deaf-mute: or maybe they'd try to work their way round by the coast. . . . Then a recollection flashed through his mind of the 'Mulay Abdullah' Quarter of Fez: of a coal-black Senegal sentry on guard at an ominous Gustave-Doré hole in a vast blank moonlit wall (the only way in), after which a gigantic groaning water-wheel had to be passed in the dark. Like the groans of ten thousand unfortunate clients with Clap it had sounded, and quite enough to put anyone off before getting through to the girls and the bright lights at all. . . . But now it seemed to him more like the groans of ten thousand happily-married men—trapped by that same simple thought of four bare legs in a bed—who had had to abandon for ever all hopes of one day entering Taroudant on a mule. . . .

Still, Augustine had got to go home; but he knew his chameleon-mind would have to go in for some drastic chromatic changes before it was once more fit for drab old

Europe—and marriage. So surely the thing to do was to
concentrate all his thoughts on Morocco's beastlier side, and
forget all the glamour: how no one could count the people
the Glaoui alone must have killed to get where he was, how
Caids grew rich by torturing people to make them hand over
the title-deeds of their farms: how Ali had said their Khalifa
—even while he and Ludo were feasting upstairs—had
starving prisoners chained in his dungons who'd been there
for thirty years. . . . It was no good pretending he didn't know
what went on, like some ignorant tourist—of course he
knew!

He knew that horrible tale of the little Fez Jew, dressed in
his first European suit, who had failed to take off his natty
suede shoes while passing a mosque; and crossing the market
afterwards stall-holders flipped pats of butter at him or
splashed him with oil—but not merely to spoil his clothes as
he thought, for on reaching the far side someone had taken a
torch and set him alight. . . . At least there was this much to
say for Europe: not even those nasty Jew-baiting German
screw-balls that Ludo's so het-up about would ever do something like that!

Men maimed. . . . Yet that cheerful couple of crippled
beggars (one with his hands and feet cut off, the other his
eyes put out) had regarded their ancient sentence not only as
fair since they'd both been thieves, but the obvious common-
sensical one since now they could thieve no more: "After a
mere spell in gaol like under the French today we'd have just
gone back to our former lives". They had tried to make him
admit European penal ways were the crude unintelligent
ones!

To him it had come as a breath of fresh air that—unlike
most conquered 'colonial' peoples—the Moors felt no faintest
inferiority complex towards Europeans: for Unbelievers
could barely be thought of as equals, much less superiors.
Once, the Moors had overrun Europe and now it was
Europe's turn; but come the next swing of the pendulum
Moors would be back in Spain and France. . . .

One couldn't help liking a country moreover with no class-distinctions, which commonly used the same word— one meaning 'friend'—for *master* and *servant* both: whereas in Dorset imagine a caller at Mellton asking Wantage if Wantage's 'friend' was at home!

But, trapped by that simple thought of four bare legs in a bed. . . .

"Mazagan's first: a tramp-steamer bound for Liverpool sailing tomorrow night," said Ludo thrusting a sailing-list under Augustine's nose.

Augustine's neck went a brick-red colour not wholly the fault of the sun. "Sorry. . . . Perhaps. . . . Well, I don't think I need be in quite so much hurry as *that*," he mumbled.

"Next week would do?"

Augustine mumbled again even more indistinctly, but seemed to imply that he mightn't be going at all after second thoughts. They could hardly expect him to leave Morocco again so soon, now he'd got there at last. . . .

Once again Ludo showed no surprise; but 'Poor fish, Morocco has got you truly and properly hooked!' was what Ludo thought.

Chapter 11

I N Dorset all had gone well at the birth, with only a vaguely
disgusting unease which Mary couldn't even locate while
her third—and as it were posthumous—baby was winkled
into the world without any help from herself.

The boy had been born on October the 29th. November
was hardly the month for large marquees on the lawn, so
thank God (thought Gilbert) for Paxton's Disciple! That
glass-roofed acre was eighty yards long and sixty yards wide:
the 'ballroom' could easily hold such an omnium-gatherum
Christening Party as this one, with drugget to save the
parquet from hobnailed boots and carpets spread on the
part reserved for the gentry.

After the sun—if any—went down, all seventy gauntleted
forearms clutching electric bulbs must blaze into light even
if some of them needed rewiring first. The only serious
problem was heat. . . . In places the chimney-pipes of those
cast-iron stoves were rusted through, which inclined them
to smoke. But surely so many hundreds of guests could
generate quite enough natural animal heat of their own
without any stoves at all? And Mrs. Winter had six suits of
Wadamy livery laid up in mothballs since the War, so foot-
men to wear them would have to be hired from an agency. . . .

As for the date, that would have to depend on the Bishop's
other engagements: so Gilbert wrote to find out (what a
pity that Mellton Church wasn't larger!).

Meanwhile the names for the boy must be settled. As heir
to the Mellton Acres and other even more lucrative sources
of income, it stood to reason his first name had to be 'Gilbert'.
But Gilbert père was magnanimous: one name at least
should commemorate kin on the mother's side. Mary's
father turned out to have been another 'Augustine', so

he wouldn't do. . . . Great-uncle Arthur, or Great-Uncle William? But Gilbert didn't much like either name: "Didn't you have a young cousin killed in the War who, if he'd lived? . . ."

So 'Henry' it had to be, on the Penry-Herberts' behalf: with a lot more besides, traditional Wadamy names from the family tree which Gilbert already had up his sleeve.

Choosing the godfathers called for even more thought. They had to be fairly young and be future prime-ministers: spotting the right ones taxed even Gilbert's powers of fore-sight, and almost called for a crystal ball. But the god-mother. . . . Surely, surely, the obvious claimant was Joan—if only Gilbert had dared to propose her?

*

One raw and windless November morning poised on the very brink of frost, ecclesiastical duties had called the Arch-deacon to Salisbury. Joan had some shopping to do, so had driven him in.

Once her shopping was done she had slipped inside the cathedral. There her mind had divided. The purely habitual half—triggered off as it always was as soon as she got inside by the perfect triple cube of that wonderful nave—began for the fiftieth time to speculate what the cathedral looked like before those Georgian vandals got loose on it tearing down mediaeval chantries, smashing the ancient stained-glass windows simply to get at the lead, and dumping cartloads of priceless glass in the City Ditch. That aesthetically insensitive eighteenth-century Age of the Georges had much to answer for to posterity. . . . Such reflections however were quite automatic, and meanwhile the upper half of her mind got busy on what she had really come for: choosing a quiet spot in which to study again Augustine's evasively-worded cable. For nearly a week she had carried it everywhere in her bag, but she still couldn't quite make out what he meant to do except that he might not be coming home 'just yet'.

She finally slipped to her knees: for God at any rate ought to know what Augustine's intentions really were, even supposing he barely knew them himself!

Fully five minutes had passed before she began to be vexed by a feeling she wasn't alone after all. She raised her eyes; and there stood a young man silently watching her. Somebody, surely, she didn't know from Adam. . . . Or was that face perhaps vaguely familiar after all, and merely someone she couldn't quite place? When she rose from her knees he stepped forward and bowed, and spoke of that fateful Boxing Day Meet nearly two years ago. For this was Anthony Fairfax, Augustine's American friend—and as for meeting Miss Dibden again by chance like this, he couldn't be more delighted!

But what had brought him to England? In order to talk more freely they moved outside to the porch. The young American said he had come back mainly to pay his respects to a distant kinsman, head of the Fairfax line and only American citizen ever to have his right to an ancient peerage confirmed by the House of Lords. But of course he had hoped to meet up with Augustine as well. He had written before he sailed, but had got no reply: was Augustine abroad?

Joan remarked in an off-hand way she believed he had gone to Morocco or some such outlandish place where the letter was probably lost. Anthony then went on to explain he had come down here intending to call at Mellton and ask for news of his friend, but couldn't until he knew if that poor unfortunate Mrs. Wadamy still was alive. . . .

Just then Joan saw her brother crossing the withered grass of the Close: a black and almost emblematic appearance under those silent limes and elms, their bare boughs hoary-bearded with rime and mist. Mr. Fairfax was introduced, and insisted on walking them both to Milford Street to lunch at the ancient inn where he lodged. There, quite a passable claret was found; and over their chops he charmed the Archdeacon so much that the latter invited him over to dine.

And of course this meant he must stay the night if he hadn't a
car, for branch-line trains didn't run very late. . . .

Mr. Fairfax accepted with thanks, if it wasn't too great an
imposition.

Their talk then turned to the tombs which that infamous
Georgian architect Wyatt had so disastrously rearranged: a
subject on which the Archdeacon felt strongly. Mr. Fairfax
duly deplored their present higgledy-piggledy too (he had
ancestors buried here on his mother's side). As for Wyatt's
wanton destruction of Beauchamp and Hungerford Chantries and even the Bell-tower, Archdeacon Dibden possessed
some rare old prints he would like Mr. Fairfax to see this
evening. . . . And bless me, why not stay for three or four
nights if their guest could spare the time?

Mr. Fairfax politely demurred at first; but his new friend
assured him that Rectory life was deadly dull for an Archdeacon's sister, he had to be out so much: she saw so few new
faces these days it would be an enormous kindness to Joan as
well as himself.

As for trains. . . . Since he hadn't a car he had better come
back with them now, if he didn't object to an hour's drive in
a rather ancient and battered Morris-Cowley.

Chapter 12

I T must have been four or five weeks later that Ludo had ridden out from Marrakesh one day with Augustine, to lunch with a friend of his father's—'lunch' being a meal that had started early and lasted nearly five hours. Their host the Shareef was hardly the shape for climbing stairs, so there weren't any stairs in his castle but only the gentlest of ramps which took perhaps fifty yards to rise to the floor above; and even then he moved so slowly he almost appeared to be standing still (not that his guests felt anxious to move much faster than he did, after that meal). All the same, they had to ascend to the top of the walls from which to admire the miles of olives he owned, and on which his ample income depended as well as on holiness.

Therefore before going home they were sent to inspect his olive presses. These looked ancient and crude contraptions of boards weighed down by stones; and yet they produced from superlative hand-picked, hand-peeled, hand-pipped fruit the most delectable 'virgin' oil. This wonderful oil was famous throughout the country, and far too rare and fine to be sold: the Shareef made his money by afterwards shipping the pulp to Marseilles to be squeezed again in hydraulic presses, then pulverised in hot water and anything oily skimmed off the top like the fat off soup—or be doctored with carbon disulphide and God-knows-what—to produce the 'Huile de Provence' of commerce.

Augustine's mind was still brimming over with olive-oil and even dreaming of buying some olive-groves of his own when at last they got back to Marrakesh and Fernet Branca, which wasn't till after sundown.

There Augustine found a letter from Anthony Fairfax, dated from Garland's Hotel in Suffolk Street: a place that the Cloth frequented—a place not so much a home-from-home as a Close-from-Close. This was the sort of London hotel Archdeacons were likely to recommend: which might have provided a clue, had Augustine known the place. . . . And a clue was needed, for this was an unexpected letter indeed—challenging him to a duel but giving no hint of the reason. It merely asked him to choose his weapons and name his seconds.

Augustine tossed it across to Ludo: had poor old Anthony gone off his head? Ludo was tired and overfed and feeling silly: "You'd better choose rubber balloons, and name the Archbishops Ebor and Cantuar as your seconds". He tossed the letter back. "What has he got against you?"

"God knows: we haven't seen each other since Mary's fall."

"You're right: he must be nuts. But does anyone really fight duels nowadays, apart from French politicians who shut their eyes and shoot at the sky?"

"Oh yes, in the Southern States they apparently do. This would be Anthony's third. The first was when someone accused him of giving his ball a push at the County Croquet Tournament. . . . I can't remember about the second."

"You'd better just tear it up."

But Augustine was rather more worried than Ludo guessed, for on no account did he mean to lose his friend if that could by any means be avoided. It certainly wouldn't do to send an even faintly facetious reply: misunderstandings can be cleared up and even some unintentional slight be forgiven in time, but poking fun on the sacred subject of duelling—never, not by an Anthony Culpepper Fairfax of South Carolina! No: even though he might have his tongue in his cheek he must pen a carefully-worded and dignified answer instead, declaring he had not the faintest idea how he might have offended and taking his stand on the point that he could not, in honour, accept the challenge without being told this in black-and-white. 'Fairfax' could hardly expect 'Penry-Herbert' to stand and be shot through the head without even knowing what crime he was dying for.

*

Posts from Morocco were slow, since each Great Power maintained its own; and perhaps the postman who carried the bag to the coast had run out of kif on the way, for the ration His Majesty's Postmaster-General issued them was— to say the least of it—niggardly.... Anyway, Penry-Herbert's reply only landed on Fairfax's breakfast tray on Christmas morning.

Anthony read it with growing disillusion. Since Penry-Herbert's pretence not to know the issue was arrant nonsense, he must also know very well his demand to have it expressed in writing was one that could not be met (for the name of the lady concerned, and even the fact that a lady's name *was* involved must never be breathed in Affairs of Honour). What saddened him most was to think he had ever called 'friend' a man who could make such flimsy excuses to get out of fighting.

Anthony even thought of pursuing him out to Morocco in order to slap his face and thereby compel him to fight—but why should he bother? The long and the short of it was that Penry-Herbert was yellow: which put him beyond the pale, leaving Anthony free henceforth to pay court to Joan with an easy conscience.

*   *   *

It only remains to record that the next time Augustine went to Dorset he wouldn't find any hardly-used Patient Griselda awaiting him. Long before that Mrs. Fairfax was gone: all Tottersdown Rectory had to show was an elderly housekeeper, someone (alas for the poor Archdeacon!) who ruled her master's goings-out and his comings-in with a rod of iron.

Chapter 13

IT was lucky for Joan that Anthony wasn't a gambling type, and that land-speculation hadn't hit South Carolina. In England, spring had seen the collapse of the General Strike; and across the Atlantic, this autumn saw the collapse of the Florida Land Boom. That was America's first warning bell, which almost nobody heard (America's final bell wouldn't ring for another three years, when the Stockmarket bubble burst as the Florida bubble had burst—but that was a tocsin you had to be deaf-as-a-post not to hear re-echoing round the whole capitalist world).

The Florida boom had been based on selling the Garden of Eden strip by strip to the exiled Children of Adam; but even the previous year it had passed the stage where people bought Florida land at all. Now they only bought options to buy it they never meant to take up—only to sell on and on at a profit. So when a hurricane finally jogged the Boomster's elbow by laying the paradise-city of Coral Gables flat, the whole pack of cards collapsed; and many Exclusive Residential Lots (which might in actual fact be pestilent sections of mangrove swamp and fit habitation only for crocodiles) found themselves back in their old original owners' rueful hands.

But these Florida speculators hadn't by any means only been proper professional Real Estate men: they included every get-rich-quick Tom, Dick and Harry, throughout the land. By now these were hopelessly hooked on making more and easier money than what they could earn as drugstore clerks and garage mechanics, and so when Florida failed them they turned their fledgeling attention to Wall Street. There they quickly developed the same sort of fatal dealing in options and buying on minimal margins, till prices of Stocks soon soared far beyond any possible values in terms of a Corporation's profits or earnings—just like Florida land, but soon on a far vaster scale as professionals also began to climb on the golden band-wagon.

During this Stockmarket Boom you made money so fast just 'playing the market' that loans to Germany lost their former allure. Thus Germany's former imports of easy money suddenly dried at the source, which spelled an untimely end to Germany's brief prosperity. Grandiose schemes (such as Kammstadt's new municipal race-track and playing-fields) were perforce abandoned half finished, and workers again laid off. Thus while the rest of the world still enjoyed the Great American Stockmarket Boom—so that even Britain would prosper so much at the height of the Boom as to see her workless drop to the one-million mark—depression and mass unemployment hit Germany once again; and that spoonful of honey they'd lately enjoyed only made it taste even more bitter.

This played straight into Hitler's hands. But it might play even more into Strasser's: so Hitler that autumn appointed Göbbels as Gauleiter in Berlin: chiefly to keep an eye on those former Messiahs of his, the radical Strasser brothers. In short, he had to be ready at all times to contradict the official 'Voice in the North of the One Indivisible Nazi Party'.

Lothar was lucky: he somehow contrived to hold on to his City Hall job, and meanwhile was secretly working heart-and-soul for the Cause.

When he moved to Kammstadt that summer he'd happened to find himself a room in the house where little Ernst Krebelmann's school-teacher, Lehrer Faber, already lodged on the floor above. At first they had known each other only as fellow-lodgers, bowing stiffly without a word whenever they met on the stairs. But one day Lothar had happened to open his door just as the Lehrer passed on the tiny landing outside, those two square yards of shining parquet floor with their rubber-plant and their smell of furniture-polish; and Lothar would never forget that momentous sight, for the day

had been hot enough for the Lehrer to carry his jacket over
his arm which allowed a glimpse of the swastika badge that
was normally hidden behind his lapel.

This had given the young man courage to speak. As yet he
himself had never officially joined the Party: indeed the only
signed-up Party Member in Kammstadt then at all was the
lonely Lehrer, who had to keep mighty quiet about it if only
because of his job; but the latter had welcomed Lothar with
with open arms as a veteran of the Putsch. He took him up
to his attic room with its piles of books and aroma of stale
cigars (the underpaid Lehrer smoked one each Sunday, and
had to live on its smell for the rest of the week).

After some brotherly talk the Lehrer had looked for some-
thing to lend him to read. Luckner's *See-Teufel*, or Junger's
In Stahlgewittern perhaps? But Lothar had read them both.
Or something by Heer, or Naso, or Brehm, or Geissler?
Finally Lothar had carried away both volumes of Houston
Chamberlain's *Grundlagen*, once he had learned that before
he died last winter the septuagenarian sage had said of Hitler
that 'here was a man to be followed blindfold'.

Lehrer Faber and Lothar were pioneers: there was still a
long row to hoe, but during the next three years the Nazis
began to gain a tiny footing even in ultra-conservative
Kammstadt. There the only 'Marxists' one had to fear were
the highly respectable Social-Democrat councillors ruling
the City Hall (for Kammstadt's working class was a trifle
larger than Ludo supposed), the only Jews were Ludo's
friends whose father was tied by the leg to the private bank
he owned. Most of their first recruits had joined them simply
because they liked and respected the Lehrer—anything *he*
could belong to must be all right. These formed the as-it-were
intellectual wing of the local Nazi cell, still meeting in secret
and mostly discussing philosophy half through the night.
But Lothar himself deserved the credit for bringing in a much
more forceful recruit: one Ludwig Kettner, a bankrupt
builders' merchant nagged by a tireless energy.

No one could ever call Kettner an intellectual! During the War he had won an Iron Cross for valour, losing an eye at Verdun. After the War was over, starting from scratch as a scrap-merchant mainly dealing in surplus government stores, he had seized the chance of the building boom to launch out on building materials proper. Kettner had seemed to be one of Kammstadt's coming men when suddenly everyone ceased to build. Lothar had dealt with the man at the City Hall during his prosperous days: he had liked him then, and now he was on the rocks Lothar had been one of the few to befriend him still.

By temperament more of the condottiere type, Kettner soon tired of endless midnight discussions. He wanted action. ... It shows how behind the times little Kammstadt was, that is wasn't till 1928 that Kettner had even begun recruiting an embryo S.A. squad among Kammstadt's 'veteran' organisations.

Chapter 14

'AMERICA'S final bell. . . .'

That tocsin tolled on October the 29th, 1929: the climactic day of the Great American Stockmarket Crash was the day little Gillie Wadamy reached the momentous age of three (though he wasn't allowed any cake because of a stomach-upset).

Wall Street prices had started to fall a fortnight before, shaking out early the smallest fry—such as Anne-Marie Woodcock's numerous Beaux (for Ree was now seventeen, and a budding beauty "with plenty of Beaux to her string and Boy does she string 'em!" was how Russell put it). But now "all her Beaux come undone", all their chickenfeed winnings were gone; and by close of play on Tuesday the 29th, her father was broke as well.

Bramber had thrown up his job to give his whole time to the Market, and only a fortnight before had been worth (on paper) a cool quarter-million dollars. Misled by occasional ups in the midst of the downs even after the selling began he had gone on buying, hoping to make this a half. So now he was back behind even his starting-point; for now their precious New Blandford farm would have to be sold and the proceeds go to his brokers. All-Hallow-e'en was a properly haunted affair for the Woodcocks this year, with hardly a cent in the house or a steak in the ice-box.

Bramber could hardly expect his job back—not in a city chockful of these Bramber Woodcocks. Earl (you remember the ocarina-player?) and Baba and even Junior were still in school: the only possible bread-winner seemed to be Ree, who could surely get some sort of personality-job even in times like these. . . . But the prospect held little attraction for Anne-Marie: instead she wrote to the grandmother down in Lafayette (La.) whose name she bore, sold her furs for the fare and left for the Deepest South by rail alone in a day-car.

She promised—and meant it—to send them what help she could, if and when she could. But Grandmother Voisin had never approved of the Woodcock match, and her generosity seemed to depend on the prior claims of sundry young painters and sculptors from New Orleans. All the same, Ree expressed no intention of coming home: the young painters and sculptors were plenty fun, the countryside pleasant down there round Acadian Lafayette on Vermilion Bayou, the weather quite warm enough without any furs. . . .

So that was that: Junior and Earl would have to do news-paper rounds before school, and their mother must take in piece-work for garment makers.

The height of the Crash saw perfectly sound securities finding no bidder at any price; but roughly-speaking overall prices dwindled no more than an average third from their previous peaks, and merely fell back to a rational level. This was cold comfort however to dealers in 'margins'; and victims like Bramber regarded this third not as fairy gold (which had never existed except in accountants' brains) but as genuine wealth being swallowed down by an opening earth like it swallowed those men in the Bible.

He perked up a little when President Hoover pronounced the economy rock-bottom sound even so, and immune to whatever 'healthy' and 'realistic' adjustments took place in Stock Exchange ratings. But Russell was less optimistic. He stressed the economy's new and now almost total dependence on Hire Purchase systems in retail trade: for that too (said Russ) was dependence on fairy gold. Germany's fighting the War on the never-never had landed her later in terrible woes, so how (asked Russ) could America hope to escape them when doing the same thing in times of peace? Countless insolvent investors must fail to meet their instalments on goods they had 'bought', so that half-used automobiles and washing-machines would be dumped back on dealers who thought they'd got rid of them. New production would have to slow down—and men be laid off; and with highly-paid

wage-earners losing their jobs a second wave of instalments
must fail to be met, more goods be returned, more men be
laid off. . . .

Bramber was quick to point out it was pretty good nerve
for a sassy young Jeremiah to contradict the accredited seers.
But the factory chimneys did cease to smoke; and (as Russell
was brash enough to remark) things had advanced quite a
bit in the business world since the bad old days when the
overriding charge on a bankrupt plantation was feeding its
slaves till sold. Slaves couldn't simply be fired and left to fend
for themselves, as nowadays free labour could be—and was.

*

If Peace is indivisible, so is Prosperity: slow economic
paralysis gripped not only the U.S.A. in 1929 but the whole
of the trading world. Germany's industries lost with their
export markets the foreign exchange they needed to service
their foreign loans, plunging the country's unstable finances
even more deeply into the soup.

Hitherto, merely a million Germans had been without
jobs; but Hitler was able to rub his hands as the figures
mounted by leaps and bounds. By the autumn of 1930, in
less than a year they had topped the three-million mark—
three million hungry and desperate men, on a wholly in-
adequate dole for the first few months and afterwards Parish
Relief. . . . He had merely to bide his time. By giving Strasser
his head with the poor and the workless, while still refusing
to rubber-stamp Strasser's Bolshy ideas himself, he ensured
the panicky middle-classes would vote for *his* protection
against those selfsame menacing hordes who voted for
Strasser—securing the Party a double harvest of votes. And
indeed when polling-day came the Nazis netted more than
a hundred seats in place of their previous measly gadfly
dozen: the Nazis were right on the map at last—and
Lepowski was eating his hat. . . .

"He has only to bide his time," said Reinhold the Hitler-
watcher. "A couple of years may well see unemployment

double again—and likewise those hundred-odd Nazi seats.
There are times when sudden and violent action is needed to
change the course of events, times to simply sit still and be
carried along by the tide—and Hitler always knows which.
Those constant complaints of his 'indecision' are simply a
failure to grasp that *what* you do often matters so very much
less than *when*."

Chapter 15

HOMELESS unemployed men were housed in makeshift barracks: mostly in Great War left-overs, derelict army camps like the one still only half-dismantled when Kammstadt's Playing-Fields Scheme was shelved. Its menacing presence, a bare half-mile from the city walls and crammed with soup-kitchen scarecrows from miles around (for it served three neighbouring counties), scared the pants off Kammstadt's respectable burghers.

And yet the Depression had scarcely touched Kammstadt itself at all. The City had less than two hundred unemployed of its own on the books at a City Hall with Flemish gables and outdoor frescoes of lords and ladies; and most of these paupers were well out of sight in a suburb down by the railway-tracks where nobody went on his Sunday walk. Merchants might do a shade less business, banks be chary of overdrafts, shoemakers find themselves using more sole-leather now for repairs than uppers-leather for new, cabinet-makers have time for occasional glasses of beer: that sort of thing—but that sort of thing was all. And yet there was fear in the air: fear of the outside world, fear of what 'they' were doing 'out there'. They discussed it whenever Kammstadters met in their clubs—in their Shooting Clubs, their Veterans' Clubs, their Singing or Gardeners' Clubs, their Patriotic Clubs (there were almost more clubs in Kammstadt than Kammstadters). What 'they' were up to 'out there' was the topic at every Stammtisch; and nobody knew the answer, that was the trouble.

Meanwhile the Nazi Cell in Kammstadt was growing: they hadn't yet reached double figures, but made up in energy what they still lacked in numbers. The principal hurdle they had to face was the common talk of Storm Troop excesses elsewhere: for they themselves behaved well enough,

315

apart from occasional quarrels with 'Marxist' Reichsbanner men only used hitherto to getting their eyes blacked by Communists. Meanwhile they laid on 'mammoth' public meetings in halls small enough to make them look crowded— meetings which everyone heard of, even if very few went. They staged patriotic plays, and concerts: they sang patriotic songs, and on Public Holidays Kettner paraded and marched (rather stage-army marches perhaps, importing the same Storm Troopers to march who had yesterday marched in one neighbouring town and were due to march in another to-morrow). Kettner was now the Deputy Storm Troop Leader for Kammstadt County; and likely to rise even higher the more the County Leader himself succumbed to the bottle.

Patriotism was a keynote stirring answering chords in every Kammstadter breast. Herr Krebelmann's clients were most of them ultra-conservative 'Blacks' who despised the hooligan Nazis, and Krebelmann counted as 'Black' him-self; but even so he could not fail to observe that these Lothars (and Fritzes and Heinzes) were young and starry-eyed, a phalanx of youth dedicated to sweeping away the Augean mess which the old men had made. For if no one else knew what 'they' were up to 'out there' these Nazis were certain they knew, and were ready to pay their pennies and lay down their lives to stop it. . . .

Still, when Ernst decided to join the Hitler Youth he deemed it wiser to keep this dark from his father as long as he could.

Ernst was an overgrown, rather flabby thirteen in that winter of 1929: too young to join by the rules, but Ernst was his father's son and in Kammstadt the 'Deutsches Jungfolk' —the proper organisation for kids—still didn't exist. So they sent him to be enrolled at Party Headquarters (a roll-top desk in the back of a saddler's shop, where his first Heil Hitler salute brought down a whole shelf of neat's-foot oil). He hadn't the foggiest notion of politics: all he desired was the heady coagulation of boy with boy which his grammar school failed to provide: the worthwhile boy-scout games, and the summer camping—but most of all, that 'belonging' feeling.

Weekly meetings were held in a country inn. No one except the Gefolgschaftführer—a humourless eighteen-year-old—wore uniform: all that the other boys wore 'on duty' were badges and swastika armbands. Ernst was so much the youngest he tended at first to be somewhat despised by these working-class fifteen- to eighteen-year-olds; and his first night began with a lecture on street-fighting tactics where Ernst was utterly out of his depth (except for the little boys' job of standing on roof-tops and dropping flowerpots). After the lecture, however, a sing-song began, and Ernst's accordion-playing won him a bit more respect.

Almost everything done indoors with the other boys that winter was fun; but the long formation-marches through snow and slush had even the hardiest beefing—in spite of their Leader telling them all how lucky they were to be out in the open where 'men' belonged, instead of crouching over a stove like pot-bellied bourgeois. Then came the summer months, with nothing to beef about excepting the heat of the sun; and as soon as electioneering began for the autumn elections the group had plenty to do delivering hand-bills, shaking collecting-boxes, and secretly daubing slogans and swastika signs on walls. This last was what proved Ernst's undoing, for Father caught him paint-pot in hand and had the whole story out of him. Father's reaction at first seemed mild, merely deploring the waste of time which he ought to give to his homework; but then, as if as an afterthought, Father added he'd flog the skin off his back unless he re-signed (it wasn't till two years later that Father himself saw the light, and encouraged him to rejoin).

Meanwhile his elders were busy electioneering too. Nazis and Stahlhelm and Reichsbanner marched and counter-marched on each others' routes, each Laocoon-band wreathed in its boa-constricting brass and attempting to deafen the rival band with its thundering drums and its stertorous trombone work. Noses were bloodied and eyes

were blacked, beer-mugs were broken, scandalous broad-
sheets appeared and libel-actions were filed, 'mammoth'
meetings became a daily occurrence—meetings where nobody heckled twice, for Kettner's men saw to that. The Nazi
climax came with a mammoth meeting indeed, for which
they had taken the Circus Hall where the human odour of
sweating crowds mixed well with the lingering angry and
terrorised smell of performing beasts; and the principal
speaker was billed as a leading Nazi Reichstag Deputy—
Hermann Göring.

Lothar was torn in two whether or not to be there. In
his adolescence, the brave young Hermann Göring—that
'Nonpareil among Birdmen'—had been his hero: he longed
to see him again and perhaps even shake his hand, yet he
feared to be disillusioned.

Göring had reappeared in Berlin three years ago, but less
of the dashing birdman now than the canny commercial gent
grown sybaritishly paunchy, dealing in aircraft equipment
and spares on behalf of a Swedish firm. Hitler at first would
have nothing to do with him. Party Funds, however, were
short at the time; and Göring had plutocratic and aristocratic
and even royal contacts which Hitler hankered after—if only
to counterbalance Strasser's pull with the Plebs; and once
he'd a foot in the door Göring would not be denied—for he
hadn't become a travelling salesman for nothing.

A Reichstag Deputy's income and perquisites suited his
fading-film-star's tastes much better than chancy commis-
sions on parachute sales. He had even paraded the scars he
got in the Munich Putsch to blackmail his way to a place
high up in the Nazi candidates-list.

Chapter 16

THE elections of 1928 had seen Göring take his seat as one of those 'Gadfly Twelve'. But return to a niche in the Nazi inner circle would not be so easy to bring about: by now it was jealously closed, and Göring could hardly expect to see a Göbbels (so newly installed himself) willingly making room for a newcomer.

Even after those 1930 elections were finished and Hitler decided to change the S.A. Command, Göring—although in earlier days the Storm Troops had been his creation—was never even considered. Instead a letter went off to South America, summoning home his former supplanter Röhm; and home Röhm forgivingly came to be reinstated, notwithstanding that five years ago Hitler had flung him out on his ear. Thus Röhm at a single stroke was back at Hitler's right hand, making secret high-level contacts on Hitler's behalf in Berlin and soon to be back in command of his faithful S.A. But Göring would have to wait quite a while for the smallest chance himself of returning to Hitler's personal favour.

For one thing, Göring's Reichstag duties kept him more or less tied to the City; but Hitler himself was spending as little time as he could in Berlin, where he knew that nobody liked him much: it was better to keep out of sight—and anyway, Hitler adored the Bavarian Alps. For a while he passed whole seasons in various mountain inns, biding his time (as aforesaid) and writing the second part of *Mein Kampf*. But at length he acquired a modest mountain retreat of his own above Berchtesgaden; and then the obvious thing had been to send for the Raubals to housekeep for him, that indigent sister and niece of Adolf's whom Putzi had taken such pains to run to earth in Vienna.

Geli was twenty years old when her mother came to take charge of her uncle's house; and she certainly had not lost her good looks. So there the Führer spent many contented and even blissful months, enjoying his sister's homely Austrian cooking and doing his best to thaw those frost-bitten loins of his in his niece's intimate heat.

Incest (or quasi-incest at least) seems perhaps the obvious theoretical answer in cases of psychological blockage which stem from an overweening solipsism, like Hitler's. This sexy young niece was blood of his blood, so could perhaps in his solipsist mind be envisaged as merely a female organ budding on 'him'—as forming with him a single hermaphrodite 'Hitler', a two-sexed entity able to couple within itself like the garden snail. . . . At least that sounds all right in theory: practice however had proved less simple, and Geli had found that she had to do curious things for her uncle. She once told a friend "You'd never believe the things which this monster makes me do"; but whatever they were, in time he became so hooked on these deft little things she did that he came to look on his growing addiction as 'love'—and even the outside world was soon to mistake it for love, when he started behaving towards her in public like any romantical juvenile moonstruck lover who worships his virginal lady afar. Yet surely (thought those in the know) this moping and mooning contrasted oddly with all those salacious *billets-doux* he kept sending her, letters adorned with pornographic drawings—depicting her own private parts, and patently drawn from the life!

These keepsakes of course had little attraction for Geli. Often she carelessly left them lying about; but Father Stempfle, or maybe Party-Treasurer Schwarz (for this happened more than once), had found them such very expensive things to retrieve from blackmailing hands that in future they had to be taken from her as soon as she got them, and locked in a Brown House safe where the artist could brood on them—Hitler flatly refusing to hear of his Valentines being destroyed.

So things had gone on for a year or two, with Hitler making most God-awful rows if Geli so much as winked at another man—let alone if she jumped in an alien bed for somewhat robuster forms of fun. But in 1931 she dropped a bombshell: she begged to go back to Vienna. "For singing lessons" was what she said; but rightly or wrongly her mother believed she had lately been got with child by an Austrian Jew from Linz, that she funked the row-to-end-all-rows this revelation must mean and was hoping to meet the man in Vienna and marry him there. . . . Be that as it may, her uncle by now could not possibly do without her and flatly refused to let her leave him on any excuse.

Whereupon he lost her for good. One September morning, she locked herself in her room at her uncle's imposing Prinz Regentplatz apartment in Munich, and shot herself dead with her uncle's pistol.

So ended the sole 'romance' in Adolf Hitler's life. Or so the hermaphrodite snail was sundered, the cynic might say, the addict cut off from his dope; but even so, it is tempting to call the withdrawal-symptoms 'natural human grief'—as one would with some lesser man who was able to love—when the news of her suicide sent him nearly out of his mind. Schreck drove him back to Munich at breakneck speed; and the Führer seemed so distraught that the faithful Strasser feared he might do himself a mischief and never once left his side, nor closed an eye, for a couple of days and nights.

But one thing Strasser refused to do for his stricken friend: he refused to be party to trying to kid the world that— whatever the coroner said or the papers printed—this death had been accidental. Then Göring at last saw his chance! He too had rushed to his Führer's side, and in breaking voice assured him that he at least was convinced this was all a tragic mischance, all came of playing with guns. . . . Where- upon Hitler turned from the obstinate Strasser to weep upon Göring's neck: "This shows which one of you two is my real friend!" he sobbed.

Perhaps this is just what the incident did do; but still it

ensured that Göring was back in the Führer's personal favour, and Strasser had one more black mark against his name.

Moreover Reinhold's forecast was right: next summer's elections saw Hermann Göring installed—as leading the largest single group—in the Reichstag President's Palace: a national figure at last as well as a leading Party one.

*

Three weeks after Geli's death in September 1931, Hitler and Hindenburg met for the very first time; and withdrawal-symptoms were still so acute that the President more-or-less wrote Hitler off as a serious factor henceforth in German politics.

Seeing him as he was then, the old man would find it hard to believe that fifteen months later he'd find himself sending for Hitler to make him Chancellor—even with highly-experienced politicians (ex-Chancellor Papen and Co.) in his cabinet holding his hand and pledged to see he behaved.

In December 1932 came Chancellor General Schleicher's bid to secure a working majority of the Left, with Socialist help, by detaching Strasser and sixty Nazi deputies with him. But Strasser refused to play: if anyone joined the Cabinet that must be Hitler himself—which Göring and Göbbels strongly opposed.

The fracas was such that the Party seemed to be splitting. All Hitler did to heal the breach was a suicide-threat; and all Strasser got for his loyalty to his Chief was a tongue-lashing row with Hitler. Thereupon Strasser resigned—not to switch his allegiance to Schleicher, but simply to disappear into private life rather than tear the Party in half.

Thus Hitler was once more safely on top. Then Papen the arch-intriguer got busy intriguing with Hitler, with Schröder the banker. . . . With Göring. . . . With Oskar the President's son, and Meissner the President's chief official adviser. . . .

And Hitler himself got busy on Oskar with certain private promises and/or threats, until the web was woven so tight that Hindenburg saw no other way out.

On Sunday the thirtieth day of January 1933, the Hitler-Papen-Hugenberg-Blomberg Cabinet duly came into being. That 'Coalition' Cabinet only contained three Nazis—but three were to prove quite enough, with the aid of Göring and Reichstag Fires and Enabling Acts and everything else which followed.

The nest with only *one* cuckoo-chick in it soon sees all the legitimate nestlings tumbled out.

Chapter 17

In England, the post-War 'Geddes Axe' had rendered promotion slow for a civil servant who joined in the twenties: allowing for normal retirements and people above him moving up higher, Jeremy knew he'd be lucky to get his first rise in status to 'Principal' roughly in 1938 (as if some Army subaltern had to wait thirteen years for his second pip). Thereafter promotion—if any—depended on merit; and meanwhile, to give him a proper grounding, they moved him about from branch to branch. He had started in 'M': from there he was sent to the Registry, filing papers and learning who properly dealt with what: then to 'C.E.', handling internal questions of organisation and cutting down everyone else's staff; and then to Finance, another unpopular branch whose principal job was apparently finding out what Little Tommy is doing and telling him not to. . . . But 1934 found him back in 'M', a branch on almost affectionate terms with the Naval Staff: which led to a curious, quite unofficial assignment for Jeremy.

Two years ago the 'Ten Year Rule' (the directive year after year handed down from On High that there wouldn't be war for another decade) had been rescinded, and nothing put in its place. But navies must plan ten years ahead at least the fleets they are likely to need. For even when Parliament voted the money, before any warship began to be built its requisite speed and endurance and armament had to be argued out by the Naval Staff (with the First Sea Lord knocking their heads together, if argument lasted too long): then sketches and models must be submitted and argued further about and decided upon before the detailed designing could even begin—and a battleship's working drawings took two or three years to prepare, after which she was five to seven years in the building. . . .

January last year had seen the Nazis coming to power: so what of the future? Foreign Office reports and forecasts were many and various—far too various, contradictory even; and Diplomats anyway only come in contact with high-ups (which means with *successful* liars or else they wouldn't have got where they are); and nations in any case change their high-ups rather more often than changing their minds. Germany's dangerous new batch of high-ups could only last as long as Germany wished them to last—they might be out on their ears again in six months. . . . So some bright lad in Naval Intelligence thought it a possibly useful idea for the Naval Planners to have their own unofficial private assessment anent the 'basic mood' of the German man-in-the-street.

Journalists help, but all have their axes to grind. This junior Commander was rather in awe of Jeremy's brains, and Jeremy knew the language. . . . If Jeremy chose—mind you, entirely off his own bat—to go take a look-see and put it on paper. . . . Well, he could rest assured that (naming no names) his screed would be read.

Jeremy planned his leave to start in the first week of June. Travel by train wouldn't do: so having no car himself he suggested Augustine coming. Augustine hated the place too much and refused; but asked him at least to lunch, to meet a girl just back from Berlin.

They lunched in Soho: a party of four, for Polly came too (she was now sixteen).

As for the girl herself. . . . According to Mary, Augustine had got a new girl but she wasn't at all his class and Mary was not very happy about it: so *this* couldn't be the one, for this was a 'Lady Jane—Something', he couldn't quite catch the rest of her name. No, this was probably merely some friend of Polly's. . . . Indeed it soon transpired that Polly and Janey had known each other as children and met again at their Finishing School in Geneva. This also accounted for Polly's presence: for Janey had grown up a shy and excessively diffident girl, deferring to Polly in everything—even the food she chose—though Polly was two years younger. At just eighteen she seemed to be finding the burden of adult life already too much. . . . 'If they don't look out' thought Jeremy 'sooner or later she'll swallow a bottle of aspirin.'

Janey indeed had hardly spoken at first; but when she did speak at last it all came out with a rush. Yes, she had been to Berlin and had stood for hours outside the Chancellor's Residence hoping that Hitler would come to the window, till somebody told her he hadn't got back from Munich yet. Still, she had kicked off her shoes and stood in her stockings. . . .

"Why?" asked Jeremy.

"This was the pavement his feet had trod," said Janey reprovingly.

Next day Janey had stood there again—and the next, till at last she had had her reward. As the Führer's car drove slowly past his eyes had sought out hers in the crowd for a long penetrating look which had pierced to the depths of her soul: she had felt transported.

"I don't quite get it," said Jeremy: "What makes you feel like that about him? You aren't a German yourself."

Helplessly Janey turned an imploring look on Polly. "You can't be in Germany twenty minutes without," said Polly abruptly: "You'll see for yourself."

"Your 'Chameleon Law' again!" said Jeremy *sotto voce*.

"You ought to see Polly's room," said Augustine accusingly: "Portraits of Hitler all over the walls."

But Polly was quite unabashed. "One photo is signed!" she exclaimed in triumph.

A pause: then Jeremy asked: "Do you mean to go there again?"

Janey glanced quickly at Polly, and Polly at Janey. "Promise you won't tell Mother?" They promised. "We thought, on our way back to Mme. Leblanc's next term, we might give the Dragon the slip and arrive in Munich quite by mistake. . . . You know—wrong part of the train or something."

"We want to see some of the Holy Places."

"The street where the Martyrs died."
"The inn where Hitler was born."

After they'd seen the two girls into their taxi, *"Christ!"* said Augustine (who seldom swore).

"Exactly," said Jeremy, adding: "I wonder they don't come out with miraculous Stigmata—swastika marks on their hands and feet."

*

Jeremy next thought of Ludo. Ludo had cars to choose from; and Jeremy wanted to see how the Nazis behaved to a visiting foreign Jew, if Ludo was willing to face the music.

Luckily, Ludo was willing. His father had business interests there, and Ludo was anxious to wind them up.

Then Joan and Anthony turned up out of the blue to visit the old Archdeacon, so Ludo and Jeremy carried them off as well. It was quite a party that finally set off through France in Ludo's voluptuous Rolls.

Chapter 18

THEY got their first sight of the Nazi flag in the Saar. The Saar had been under Geneva control for the profit of France ever since the War. In six months time they could choose to return to the Reich or belong to France or remain more-or-less as they were; but the swastika banners festooning the village streets left little doubt which way the voting would go.

"They won't be half as well off," said Jeremy.

"That, they know; but it won't affect the issue," said Ludo. "Germans are not 'Economic Man', in the which-side-your-bread-is-buttered sense: nor are they a 'nation'—or not in the sense you mongrel British are one. They're more like a wandering horde who have settled down here and there in Europe almost by chance: their ties are still not so much with any particular patch of soil (or State) as tribal 'kinship' ties. Rosenberg's right that far. . . ."

"A bit like you Jews," interrupted Joan.

"Except that the German Tribes have focused their kinship ties in a single, godlike Paramount Chief."

"But you do too—except that you keep *your* Führer up in the sky, which is very much safer for all of us."

Jeremy nudged his aunt, glancing at Ludo in some alarm.

"Where do we eat?" asked the practical Anthony: "Some of these Gasthauses look pretty good to me."

It was hard to believe these smiling meadows and woods housed one of the major coalfields of Europe, Jeremy mused, when you thought of the needless degradation and ugliness Coal had inflicted on Wales. For 'wandering tribes' the Germans were pleasingly tidy people. . . . But then a Poilu lifted a pole which barred the road: a German policeman saluted with outstretched arm, looked at their passports and

328

smilingly waved them on into Germany proper. He hadn't batted an eyelid at Ludo's name or at Ludo's nose.

They crossed the Rhine on a bridge of boats where the anxious Rolls seemed to walk like an overweight cat on a slender twig, and passed through peaceful country where pine forests skirted the fields. Peasants were carting their hay in ox-drawn wagons, or spraying their fruit; and the gentle breezes of June barely ruffled the growing wheat. Young men stripped to the waist and burned a mahogany-brown were laying pipes. There weren't many cars on the dusty road, or even lorries: only occasional motor-cycles ridden two-or-three-up, and a single trio of holiday cyclists sweating over their pedals—including a fat white woman in shorts. There wasn't much sign of political ferment here—only an overweening friendliness, everyone making these foreigners welcome and going out of their way to be helpful; and a pleasant but all-pervading scent of anti-sunburn cream.

True, in the village streets there were Nazi flags and bunting inscribed with slogans: GERMANS—A NATION OF AIRMEN (without one single aeroplane in the sky), or YOUNG MEN! VOLUNTEER FOR THE LABOUR SERVICE; but no one seemed ever to lift his eyes to look at them.

Stuttgart was Ludo's first port of call. There he disappeared for a while; and after they'd toured the partly burnt-out castle the rest of them sat in the Railway Hotel, watching an S.A. Parade in front of the brand-new station. The Troopers drilled with a Guards-like precision, but looked rather jolly young men with peeling cream-daubed noses and hardly the sort to go beating-up Germany's Ludos. . . . They presently drove away in lorries, singing their heads off.

Jeremy talked in the bar to a young man wearing a Nazi badge, and smelling of sunburn-cream like everyone else. Why all this soldierly drilling and marching by two or three million men still called civilians? The French were bound to think it a threat. . . .

The young man smiled, turning such candid and almost

affectionate eyes on this total stranger that Jeremy felt embarrassed. "It's just that they don't understand us, poor dears. . . . Yet it's perfectly simple: why do you English play football? Because you enjoy it—and nobody looks on a match between Chelsea and 'Spurs as threatening civil war! We long to make friends with the French: hasn't Hitler said so again and again? No German wants a new war: our fathers have told us too much about the last one. . . ." But then his brow clouded. "No, but the French might start one. . . . They've evil men at the top; and when they do overrun us what have these 'two or three million men' got to fight with?—This!" (and he brandished a table-fork). "That's why we want the whole world disarmed like ourselves."

The man was transparently truthful and honest. 'It isn't me he is trying to kid so much as himself; and I wonder why?' thought Jeremy.

Just then two Hitler Youths came round, shaking collecting-boxes 'For Aircraft'; and everyone put in a coin in exchange for an aircraft badge, like a charity flag-day. "That's only for building *civil* aircraft of course" said their Nazi friend; but he added "The French could blast us out of the skies!"—a mental connection more likely than logical, Jeremy thought. He remembered the red-and-white model bomb in the square outside with a slit for similar contributions. A placard on it had read: A SINGLE FOLK   A SINGLE DANGER   A SINGLE DEFENCE.

But then came an awkward moment, when Joan unthinkingly lit a cigarette: whereupon a somewhat pimply creature in S.S. uniform smugly remarked to the world at large: "No *German* woman of decent breeding smokes." Hurriedly Joan stubbed out her fag. But a bystander loosed on the man the cutting edge of a whiplash tongue: "No German *man* of decent breeding insults his country's guests" —and a lot more besides, in which other bystanders joined till the S.S. man scuttled away with his tail between his legs amid claps and guffaws.

"He knows no better," their friend said to Joan: "He's only an ignorant pig of a Prussian. There's far too many of these down here lately, riding the bandwagon."

Meanwhile the loudspeaker-set on the bar was blaring forth panegyrics extolling Hitler's historic first meeting with Mussolini at Venice, from which the Führer had just returned.

Chapter 19

No one at Stuttgart knew how unlikely it was that this meeting would ever take place at all.

When first it was mooted, Hitler had been most unwilling. He spoke no language but German, knew nothing of foreign life and wished to know less: once his Austrian-immigrant roots had struck in the Reich he could see no reason for further crossing of frontiers except as an armed invader. For him and the Duce to meet, however, Mahomed must go to the Mountain; and Hitler found the whole idea of 'abroad' so repugnant he kept on putting it off.

But that wasn't all: for Hitler had troubles enough at home, this June. He was reaping the harvest of having come to power by legal (if not entirely legitimate) means: whereas from earliest days the cauliflower ears of Röhm's thick-headed S.A. had rung with the summons to violent revolution, and these were a couple of million men whose forte was none of your hair-splitting logic—licentious and arrogant bullies who weren't to be balked of their revolution merely because he had come to power without one.

Once Hindenburg died and Hitler was Head of State. . . . But to let them kick over the traces just now could be fatal, it meant provoking too many opponents at once—the Army, the whole establishment, even the President. The one man they all adored and followed was Röhm: only Röhm could jolly them out of it, everything therefore turned on persuading Röhm to keep his men on the leash at least for the few weeks ailing President Hindenburg had to live. . . . But a marathon tête-à-tête had failed to make Röhm understand his point of view—oh why was Röhm such a fool?

At first he had thought he could bargain with Röhm by taking into his Cabinet radical Strasser to counterpoise right-wing Göring; but Strasser refused to serve not only with Göbbels his personal Judas but Göring too, he preferred to remain in private life. And time was short, for Hitler had promised to meet the whole S.A. High Command on the last day of June at Wiessee (where Röhm was at present on sick-leave) and answer their case. . . . In such abysses of indecision a couple of days in Venice seemed suddenly less of a hateful chore than a welcome respite: so finally Hitler went.

The only remaining hope of persuading Röhm to hold in his men for these vital few weeks till the Head of State died and Hitler stepped into his shoes seemed to be Göbbels's silver tongue. Two fellow-radicals—Göbbels too had lately been blowing his top against the Establishment. . . . Therefore, the last thing before he left, Hitler had authorised secret talks between them. These talks took place in a private room at a Munich tavern; and secrecy suited the faithful Göbbels fine, since that way Hitler need never know that instead of dissuading Röhm he was egging him on. For to Göbbels this seemed the obvious course because, should the Radical cause succeed, he would thus be well in with the winning side: while if it was doomed, then Röhm's broad shoulders alone would take the rap and Göbbels himself would be free, as soon as he saw which way the cat intended to jump, to jump just ahead of the cat. . . .

But now the cat was away in Venice; and Göbbels and Röhm not the only Nazi mice at play. On the opposite side, Göring and Himmler were playing a deadlier game. Göring had always hated Röhm for filching his storm-troops from him. 'Hatred' perhaps was too warm and human a feeling ever to motivate Himmler; but that made his enmity, rooted in cold self-interest, none the less implacable. Röhm's S.A. were blocking the path of his own S.S.: it was not Röhm alone who stood in his way, but these couple of million men.

If a rock is too large to be rolled aside then it has to be blasted: only the total destruction of Röhm and his whole monolithic S.A. could satisfy Himmler, and Göring was only too ready to help. Between them, they held the means: Minister-President Göring's control of Prussia, Reichstag-President Göring's Establishment friends, General Göring's Army contacts, Reichsführer Himmler's S.S., Head-of-the-Gestapo Himmler's Secret Police—this five-fold couple between them could furnish the gelignite even for such a vast demolition as this one. . . . Ah, but only the Führer could fire the charge; and how could they make the Great Non-decider do anything quite so drastic?

The only answer was Fear: once convince him that Röhm had designs on his life he would strike so fast that you wouldn't see him for dust. So the two of them put their heads together, concocting a 'Röhm-Strasser Plot' to expose to Hitler—a Left-wing conspiracy aimed at his murder. It hardly mattered to Göring and Himmler that Röhm was no more likely than anyone else at Court to raise a finger against the Führer's person because (like themselves) he was fighting strictly for *second* place. . . . It would hardly have mattered, that is, if it weren't for Hitler's uncanny knowledge of men.

*

Meanwhile Hitler paced the unyielding marble floor of the Royal Suite at Venice's Grand Hotel, profoundly wishing he'd never come. He pondered all he'd been forced to endure in the way of humiliation and boredom—*in primis*, the public insult of having to watch someone else spellbinding a crowd. . . . As he stepped from his plane in those wretched civvies von Neurath had made him wear he'd been met by a Duce out-Göringing Göring in splendour of uniform. Cheering crowds lined the roads—but cheering their Duce: for them the dim little Charlie Chaplin in pork-pie hat and shabby old trench-coat had only shone in their Duce's reflected glory.

Yesterday's lunch at the Villa Pisani. . . . What joker had chosen that peeling malarial mausoleum for yesterday's top-level tête-à-tête? For there they'd been eaten alive by giant mosquitoes—two hectoring titans bobbing to scratch an ankle with one hand and slapping their necks with the other (he'd got his own back all right, by wittily pointing out to his hosts that this was the insects' very first taste of a white man's blood)! But if yesterday's choice of the Villa Pisani had been sheer folly, today's had surely been prompted by malice—the Duce's crazy proposal to hold their talks in a boat on the open lagoon. That knowing smirk on the Duce's face when the Führer flatly refused. . . . Some spy must have told him the Führer's fine-strung nerves couldn't bear bobbing about in boats with all that water below him.

Moreover, he hadn't escaped even here from the problem of Röhm and his Brownshirts: the Duce had had the infernal nerve to read him a lecture on cutting them down to size! The man had been got at, of course: though the hands were the Duce's the voice was the unmistakable voice of Papen and Göring—there seemed no end to the way those puny swine underrated their Führer's intelligence. . . .

Hitler flew home next day; and headlines in every paper that Jeremy found in Stuttgart lauded the visit's 'historic success'.

Chapter 20

O N their way to Ulm the English party met with such welcoming loving-kindness at every wayside stop (as well as that all-pervading odour of sunburn-cream) that Jeremy found himself sorely puzzled why: for surely this couldn't be normal—it isn't in human nature to love the whole human race. Suppose it some day went in reverse. . . . When a barmaid even ran from an inn to give Joan a rose, while three of her customers left their beer to dispute the honour of changing a wheel, he decided the symptoms were downright pathological, marking a very queer kind indeed of euphoric state these people must all be in.

But they presently made a detour. A turning-off to the left was sign-posted ARBEITDIENST. "It must lead to one of their Labour Camps," said Ludo.

"They don't have women: I wonder whether they'd let me in?" said Joan.

"We can only try." Then they overtook a bunch of glistening torsos shouldering shovels who told them to go right ahead and ask for the Camp Commandant; and one of them jumped on the running-board to show them the way.

When they got to the huts the Camp Commandant (he was rather a scoutmaster type) raised no objection to Joan, and seemed only too happy to have them talk to his lads. "It's their rest-time now." A hint of the showman crept into his voice: "Reveille is half-past-five and they work six hours a day. We feed them and clothe them and pay them twenty-five pfennigs. They're all volunteers—except that the students have made their own rule that no one can sit his degree till he's done six months like this on the Labour Front. They come from all walks of life, for we've utterly finished with Class in the Nazi State—and Gott sei Dank!"

"How many camps like this have you got?"

"Twelve hundred. That's nearly a quarter-million of lads all told, kept busy draining marshes and making roads instead of propping up lamp-posts. They're all of them young and unmarried, and taking them out of the labour-market has helped a lot with providing jobs at regular wages for older, family men. In the eighteen months since we came to power unemployment has halved—six million workless has dropped to three."

"I wish we had something like this in England!" said Joan, her mind on all those desolate dole queues: "I simply can't think why we don't. It seems such a simple solution."

But meanwhile Jeremy did a rapid sum in his head. "All the same, that can't be only because of your twelve hundred camps: the Industrialists must have helped. What about heavy industry in the Ruhr—about Krupp for instance?"

"They are splendid: they all do their bit. Krupp alone has provided three thousand new jobs in the last few weeks: he's an ardent Nazi now."

Krupp, the Armament King. . . . 'And all making safety-razor blades, I suppose!' thought Jeremy, rather surprised at getting such vital information quite so easily (spying seemed money for jam!).

"Ask the Commandant if he's ever met Hitler in person," said Joan, whose German was somewhat shaky.

The Commandant turned towards her: "Yes, I indeed have talked with my Führer face-to-face," he answered slowly in English, then lapsed again into German: "For only five minutes; and yet he is so transparent I feel I have known him the whole of my life."

"Then tell us about him," said Joan.

"I shall tell you exactly about him. He's. . . . Well, to begin with he's what a Christian would call a 'saint'—there's no other word for the manifest supernatural power working through him; and yet he's as simple and unassuming to meet as you and me. And gentle: all children love him at sight. But he has one fault: so pure and honest himself, he's a little gullible—easily hoodwinked by self-seeking rascals

hanging on to his coat-tails. But then he's a man so loyal to
all his friends that he won't hear a word against one of them
—more's the pity, in certain cases. . . ." He sighed. "But now
you must talk to my lads."

He shouted a word of command and they all came tumbling out of their bunks, their tins of sunburn-cream in their
hands. What struck Jeremy most about them—apart from
their blooming health—was how almost everything made
them laugh, as if something irrepressibly joyous was bubbling up inside them: more like schoolboys than men in
their early twenties. Even their 'Heil Hitlers' sounded like
somebody passing on a wonderful piece of news; and
Jeremy commented on it.

"That's just what it is!" said the Commandant: "What
Hitler has done for us all is to wake us out of the nightmare
we've lived in for sixteen years. He has started us Germans
hoping again, when we'd almost forgotten how to hope."

With a glance to make sure that Ludo was out of earshot,
"For _you_—but I don't see very much hope for your Jews,"
said Jeremy bluntly: "Why do you hate them so?"

For the fiftieth part of a second a curious flicker had
crossed the Commandant's clear blue eyes. "Lads—Go back
to your bunks!" he cried, and the audience vanished. Then
he went on: "We don't _hate_ the Jews, not as individual
persons: you mustn't think that. All we ask is justice. In
England you've never known what it means to live under a
Jewish hegemony: one per cent of the population with more
than fifty per cent of all the important jobs—you can't call
that fair! But once they're reduced to the one per cent of
important posts they deserve. . . ."

"All the same you set about combing them out pretty
brutally," Jeremy ventured: "Your Storm Troops beating
them up and looting their shops."

"Ah, that was the early days—enthusiastic Youth kicking
over the traces. It's been put a stop to now." Then he laid
a hand on Jeremy's shoulder: "However your English,
French and American Jews don't help us to love ours

much by boycotting German goods, and trying to cripple Germany's export trade: you should tell them they're doing their brethren here a very bad turn indeed."

But even one per cent of the creamy jobs. . . . 'I don't believe a word of it,' Jeremy thought: 'And this time, neither does he.'

On the way to Augsburg Anthony sat so silent that Jeremy asked him what was wrong. "Why can't we have an American Hitler?" Anthony burst out at last: "We sure do need him." He paused. "But I reckon there aren't two born in a thousand years."

*

Augsburg they found a blazing sunset of red with its Nazi flags, which vied with the natural sunset behind its steepling gables: banners hung out to welcome some World War Veterans' group. But the party seemed to be over, with veterans filing out of the Rathaus and wandering off in twos and threes. Jeremy couldn't see very much 'hope' in the eyes of these middle-aged men who had fought one war already; and beer seemed only to make them sadder.

In Munich, Jeremy went by himself to look at the famous 'Brown House', the Nazi headquarters. Some buildings next door had just been torn down, and whatever was being done to the site was securely hidden by ten-foot palings; but Jeremy found a knot-hole to peep through. 'There's some-body *here* who doesn't set very much store by the Ten Year Rule,' he thought: for those massive concrete domes could be nothing else than underground air-raid shelters.

After Munich, Ludo still had business to do in Leipzig, and then Berlin. But June was running out, and so was Jeremy's leave: so he left the others at Nuremberg, travelling west by train. As he sat in his second-class carriage he pondered what kind of report to write. He had seen enough of the public mood to know that the Nazis had certainly

come to stay; but what else could he put? Talk about
'pathological friendliness' wouldn't make very much sense
to the D.N.I.! Increased production at Krupp's would be
more his line. . . .

Just then, through the open window, he heard a distant
burst of firing. 'Ah, Saturday rifle-practice' he thought: 'I
must put that in.' But he wasn't quite right. What he really
had heard, that peaceful last day of June, was the sound of a
firing-squad in some lonely place; and it wasn't the only one.

Chapter 21

HITLER had got back from Venice to find that the crisis had not been dispelled simply by shutting his eyes to it. S.A. brawlers showed scant respect for anyone, even the sacrosanct Army. Then Göring had met him with ominous whispers of Party plots for a left-wing Putsch; and Himmler had dropped particular hints about Röhm and Strasser, promising more revelations to come as soon as his men reported. Berlin, moreover, was full of rumours that Hitler was slipping; and Count Lepowski was not alone in believing that Strasser would soon be Chancellor, Röhm at Defence and the S.A. absorbed in (or rather, absorbing) the Army.

But outside the Party, Conservative piper-players were claiming to call the tune. The day after Hitler's return Vice-Chancellor Papen's Marburg speech—an oration so well and carefully written that no one believed he'd composed it himself—had called for an end to S.A. excesses so openly Göbbels forbade the papers to mention it, let alone print it. Thereupon Papen had dared to complain of the ban to Hitler himself as insulting his next-to-the-Chancellor status, declaring the President backed every word he had said and threatening resignation. . . . This at least was too much to be stomached. Pygmy Papen's place was to wait to be sacked, not to talk of resigning; and Hitler decided to fly to Neudeck forthwith and have things out with this senile meddling President.

Hindenburg flatly refused to discuss things with him however. Hitler was met at the door by an icy General Blomberg deputed to act as Hindenburg's mouthpiece and carrying Hindenburg's ultimatum: if Hitler couldn't or wouldn't curb the S.A. and ensure public order instanter the Civil Government would be suspended, Martial Law be declared and all authority placed in the Army's hands.

Hitler was hardly tempted to linger on Hindenburg's doormat: he hadn't even been offered a chair. He flew straight back to Berlin, where Göring and Himmler got busy at once with the 'new revelations' they'd promised. Röhm and Strasser meant murder (they said); and had fixed on Saturday next for their coup, the day of his June-the-thirtieth meeting at Wiessee. As soon as Hitler had left for Wiessee, Karl Ernst's Troopers would seize Berlin; and if Hitler ventured his head in the Wiessee hornets-nest he would never get out alive, his only hope lay in striking first.

Inwardly Hitler rejected this cock-and-bull story as totally out of character. Röhm he knew through and through. Debauched and brutal and mulish his old friend might be, but that was a far cry from wanting to bypass a murdered Führer and stand at the apex himself: for he lacked the exceptional urge for *absolute* power, not having the brains (and he knew it) to cope with the endless problems which absolute power entails. And Strasser too was another congenital runner-in-second-place. . . . Ideally, now that the days of street-fighting were over Hitler himself could do very well without Röhm just as already he did without Strasser—except that without Röhm the Storm Troops would break into open revolt, which would spell the end. The boiling Storm Troops themselves were still the genuine danger.

But gelding the whole S.A. apparatus *as well as* stripping Röhm of all power. . . . How very much simpler the answer would be if only that farcical tale of a plot were true!

It is easy enough to 'strike first' when the other party has no intention of striking. . . . Had this been Ramsay MacDonald, or Baldwin, one might have supposed this merely a crooked subliminal left-hand groping towards that first ray of light at the end of the tunnel; but Hitler was morally ambidextrous, with no such distinction between unconscious self-seeking and what he was consciously up to. He *knew* that the plot was a fabrication invented by Göring and Himmler, and perfectly understood why; but what he *believed* was entirely controlled by his will. If the White Queen 'believed two impossible things before breakfast', so could he too if he wanted to.

Meanwhile the S.A. grew more and more outrageously out-of-hand and four days after the Neudeck Ultimatum the President showed he had meant what he said: the Army were stood to their arms, waiting in threatening silence. But Hitler would keep his options wide open as long as he could, of course. Only five days were left, so the whole planned anti-plot operation would have to be put in provisional motion—S.S. and Police be alerted and told their roles, and Gauleiter Wagner in Munich be briefed since his was to be the opening gambit; but this must be done on Göring's and Himmler's sole authority. Hitler's own being still uninvolved *his* options would still be open, and only theirs compromised.

So Hitler still stalled; and on Thursday—with only forty-eight hours to go—he blandly announced his immediate departure for Essen, and watched their faces. The trio (for Göbbels had joined them as probably being the winning side, though still prepared for a hedging bet or he wouldn't be Göbbels) were near despair. 'Terboven's wedding', and 'trouble at Krupp's over one of Röhm's henchmen'. . . . The Führer's excuses for going were both so flimsy they feared some diabolical trick if they let him out of their sight. Yet *someone* must stay in Berlin at the helm—with somebody else 'to lend him a hand', since none of these three conspirators wholly trusted the others. . . . Finally, Göbbels got his way. Let Himmler and him remain in Berlin while Göring attended the wedding and then returned post-haste: thereupon Göbbels would fly to wherever Hitler was spending tomorrow night, with some juicy 'news' from the horse's mouth—something to finally tip the scales. . . .

This Göbbels' plan ensured that he alone would be close to the Führer's side on D-Day Eve when the cat *must* jump, and could switch if he had to switch. Moreover, Göbbels didn't trust Göring and Himmler not to do him in too once the Purge began (if it did begin): only under the Führer's personal wing could he really count himself safe.

M

Chapter 22

So Hitler departed to Essen; and after the wedding, to Krupp's. The reception he'd lately met with at Neudeck was fresh in his mind; and Bertha and Gustav Krupp were potentates hardly less awe-inspiring to visit than Hindenburg.

Hardly a parallel elsewhere exists for the time-honoured exterritorial status of Krupp's in the German Reich. Like the Vatican City in Rome, Essen itself was a capital city controlling its own international empire. The 'Krupp Konzern' was the largest in Europe. Its steel had built the great American railroads, its cannon had armed (as well as the Germans themselves, and the Russians) the second-class world from China to Chile, the Boers to Siam. It was Alfred Krupp—not Bismarck, nor Moltke nor even the men of the Prussian Army—who vanquished the French at Sedan, thus founding the Second Reich: his son Fritz Krupp who had started building the Kaiser a navy simply to use up some surplus steel; and Gustav Krupp who had battered Liège and Verdun. Moreover, if Krupp guns founded the Second Reich, Krupp gold had gone a very long way towards founding the Third.

Today the Romanovs, Hapsburgs and Hohenzollerns, Wittelsbachs—most other Royal Houses in Europe had fallen; but not the Krupps.

In the Villa Hügel (the Dynasty's palace at Essen) the reigning Krupp had been used to receiving those former Crowned Heads as equals: even the German All-Highest himself, for Krupp was not only a richer man than his Kaiser but also a much more Absolute Monarch with no Constitution whatever to irk him: in Essen his slightest word had the force of Law for his forty-thousand 'Kruppianer', whose lives he ordered in every detail from birth to death. Democracy everywhere seemed on the march; but not in the Krupp

Konzern, no Union Labour was ever employed in the Works nor a stranger allowed inside the Works. . . . Yet three weeks ago the unheard-of had happened: the Head of Röhm's Political Staff had presented himself at the gates— had forced his way in—had ordered the men to down-tools and harangued them, preaching the Revolution to come!

Whatever other reasons Hitler might have for visiting Krupp there certainly *had* been 'some trouble with one of Röhm's henchmen which needed ironing-out'.

Ever since Anton Krupp made guns for the Thirty Years War the whole Konzern had been owned and controlled by one single man, descending from father to son. But in 1902 the scandal which dogged his pederastic orgies in Capri had driven Fritz Krupp to killing himself without leaving a son to succeed. So his daughter Bertha was now the Reigning Queen: for she was the Krupp of the Blood, while Gustav 'Krupp' (though confirmed in his right to the name by the Kaiser's own decree) was a mere Prince Consort—and Hitler's impending visit found husband and wife at logger-heads. Bertha flatly refused to invite this upstart Chancellor-Führer to tea, or even allow him inside her house. He deserved no better reception at Essen than Neudeck: if Gustav proposed to hob-nob with trash, he must see the man at his down-town office—and so at the down-town office it had to be, with the minimum fanfare possible.

There, at the splendid doors of the marble entrance-hall, not Bertha herself but her dark and shy and far from attractive daughter scarcely lifted her gaze from the Führer's glittering boots to hand him a bouquet (the face she didn't see was wreathed in smiles, but the eyes were a couple of bloodshot pebbles). Somebody tried to raise a 'Heil', and the ominous couple of tons of chandelier over his head tinkled a note or two; but that was all. He slipped on the polished marble as Gustav carried him off to his private office; and there the 'ironing-out' began, behind closed doors.

Although his reception had not been quite so insulting as at Neudeck the message was much the same. The time had come when Hitler could keep his options open no longer: tonight, when Göbbels arrived, he must finally make up his mind whether to 'put his head in the Wiessee hornets-nest' tomorrow—or what. . . . And still he hadn't a clue, if he didn't fall in with Göring's and Himmler's plans. Was his Daemon deserting him?

Chapter 23

FROM Cologne that afternoon black truckloads of S.S. guards had thundered along the new Autobahn under a blazing sun to Bonn, then out to Bad Godesberg. There they pulled up in the grounds of the monumental Dreesen Hotel.

The youngest among them and latest recruit was Ernst the Krebelmann boy, whose father had vetoed his joining Gruppenführer Kettner's S.A. since 'a much better class of people' joined the S.S. and his father could get him accepted. Looking in at the dining-room's big French windows, he caught one glimpse of waiters shifting the heavy furniture round as if preparing the room for a conference. Nazi big-wigs were meeting here, said the grapevine: so that's who we had to guard! But what were Party Big-wigs doing so far from Berlin, which was where the trouble was brewing?

Nobody really knew what the 'trouble' was, and rumour and counter-rumour fell over each other: yet most seemed agreed that the threatened danger came from the Right—from Papen, Hugenberg, Schleicher, the Army. Everyone knew that the Old Bull of Neudeck was gaga—in short, that Papen had President Hindenberg under his thumb, while Hindenburg in his turn had control of the Army; and ten days ago, at Marburg, Vice-Chancellor Papen had made a speech so disloyal towards the Führer the papers had not been allowed to publish it. Now the Commander-in-Chief had cancelled all Army leave: troops had been concentrated on Berlin, and their camp in the Tiergarten bristled with guns. . . .

"There's a rumour the Berlin S.A. will be alerted: they've just had a tip that the Army are plotting to kidnap the Führer! General Schleicher is back. . . ."

"So that's why the Führer has left Berlin again almost as soon as he got there!"

347

" 'Alerted'? But who'll give the order?"

"Their Gruppenführer of course."

"But he can't do. He's not even in Berlin: he's just got married, and off abroad tomorrow night on his honeymoon. Who was it told you? And isn't the whole S.A. being sent on its usual annual furlough tomorrow morning? It doesn't make sense."

"Their furlough was really fixed last April: I bet it gets cancelled."

"But Röhm's neuritis is worse. He's on sick-leave at Wiessee: who'll take command when the ruddy balloon goes up?"

"Isn't von Krausser in charge?"

"All this S.A. furlough business is stupid," somebody grumbled: "I know they're an awful lot of scallywags—still, they're a couple of million men and the Army'd think twice about taking on even a semi-armed force that was ten times their size."

"It's crazy, it's leaving the Führer a sitting duck for the Army!"

"But *we* have been mobilised, meaning the Führer prefers to rely upon *us*" said Ernst the youngest one, puffing his S.S. chest.

"S I L E N C E, there in the ranks!"

Everyone clicked his heels to attention; but "Where *is* the Führer?" Ernst whispered, not moving his lips.

"He's not far off: he went to Terboven's wedding at Essen today," Hans (his friend) whispered back with the same ventriloquial technique. "My brother. . . ."

'Essen for weddings!' thought Ernst: 'At times like these! I bet you he really went to see Krupp. . . .'

But now the sentries were being posted. Ernst and Hans together were stationed outside on a terrace lined with bay-trees and oleanders in tubs in front of those dining-room windows, and "Good!" said Hans, "We'll be able to see who comes."

"Nobody so far," said Ernst, glancing sideways but keeping his face to the front in case they were watched: for the next pair of sentries included a swart young fellow—Schellenberg—known to be Heydrich's pet. . . .

The next half hour was spent *tramp, tramp*, fifty yards up the terrace and fifty yards back; and though a black S.S. tunic and breeches and jack-boots look fine on a springy young man, Ernst found them hardly the ideal wear for a hot afternoon in the steamy Rhine-valley air. Below them, the winding Rhine with its strings of barges: beyond that again were vine-clad mountainous hills—the Siebengebirge, capped by thunder-clouds white in the sun. A heat-haze was rising from Bonn, showing only the top of its tall Minster tower; and all the shade to be had was by marching as near as you could to the hotel building itself.

"Whew!" said Ernst: "It's close!"

"Thunder about," said Hans. Then he added: "I wonder if anyone's come yet?"

"Take a peep next time we pass."

A minute later, "Gosh" said Hans: "He *has*—it's the Führer himself!"

"*No!*"

Forgetting discretion, the two young men turned their heads till they nearly twisted them off their shoulders. But then they had to stop their patrolling entirely to goggle, for windows alas are made to look out of not into—the plate-glass reflected the brilliant blue sky, the mountains, the thunder-clouds, even their own silly faces but barely revealed those dark living figures inside, as faint and as insubstantial as ghosts. Yet the Führer was certainly there, striding the length of the room and biting the nail of his little finger. At Hitler's elbow was Göbbels, and . . . Was that or wasn't it Göring, away at the back there with all those others?

"Göring was with him at Essen," said Hans: "After, they said he'd gone back to Berlin. . . . But yes, there's Friedrich my brother!" he added excitedly.

"Where?"

"There, with his fellow-adjutant Brückner."

So that was Friedrich: a granite-faced man not a bit like Hans, and taller even than Brückner—taller than anyone else in the room. Jealously, Ernst supposed he'd been picked for his muscles rather than brains. . . . Friedrich he knew was fifteen years older than Hans and only a half-brother really, and Hans hardly ever saw him; but still, any relative quite so close to the Führer gave Hans an almost visible aura in everyone's, eyes—even Ernst's.

But then a movement among the reflections betrayed to the pair they'd been joined by a third. They turned—and stiffened, like small boys caught at the jam: for the worst had happened, and this was that bumsucking. . . . Still, the dangerous newcomer said not a word and goggled as much as the best of them.

All at once (and as if they'd been tantalised quite enough), a cloud passed over the sun and those brilliant reflections suddenly dimmed and faded, the shadowy figures behind the glass turned solid and clear. Yes, there indeed was Dr. Göbbels: his lambent eyes never left the Führer—they'd almost the look of a ferret's eyes watching which way the rabbit would bolt. . . . His lips were moving, he seemed to be urging something; but not a word could be heard through the thick plate-glass—not even a sound.

"It's like at an old silent movie," said Hans.

"Yes," said the new arrival: "Only there aren't any sub-titles telling us what's going on."

Meanwhile it grew even darker. A flash, and a rumble of thunder—and then came the rain. It fell like a cloud-burst. The three young men turned their backs to the glass, and flattened themselves against it for shelter as best they could. The thunder crashed, forked lightning weirdly lit the Wag-nerian scene as the rain-lashed tree-tops bent to a sudden wind.

Cold water was slowly trickling down his back inside his clothes when something made Ernst turn his head; and there—behind his shoulder, and only an inch or two from his own—on the other side of the pane was the Führer's face looking out.

The gaze of a man half-conscious: vague, shifty, glassy, settling nowhere and seeing nothing.

Chapter 24

AT last the storm had rumbled away. Somewhere behind the hotel the sun was setting, but heavy curtains were drawn at once as soon as the lights came on indoors: there was nothing more to be seen.

The interloper was gone, and the two friends briskly tramped the terrace hoping at least to keep warm if they couldn't get dry. Then it was growing dark, with pin-point lights twinkling out all over the valley—and still the meeting went on.

One by one the few remaining tugs on the river lit up, preparing to dock for the night. A reddish glow above Bonn was lighting the undersides of the lowering clouds as the storm retreated; and after a while there were stars.

It must have been after midnight before they were called to the trucks, but you couldn't see your watch. Ernst climbed aboard his truck just as the first of those big black Mercedes cars with official numbers began to move off; and then they were roaring after them through the trees and the sleeping countryside, taking the road to the Eifel hills.

On the little Hangelar airfield an aircraft was waiting ready and warming up, its propeller turning slowly. Standing on guard on the grass, Ernst saw Hitler again as he went on board with Göbbels still at his elbow.

The plane climbed into the starry sky, while they watched its red and green twinkling lights to see where it meant to head. Ernst glanced away at the Plough and the Pole Star to get his bearings: Berlin must be over there. . . . But no, the plane was steering a steady course towards the south-east. That was where Frankfurt lay, and Stuttgart—and further still, Munich. . . . Yes, Munich it must be: for Röhm (as everyone knew) was resting and taking a course of treatment near there, on the shores of the Tegernsee. Tireless, tomorrow morning the Führer intended consulting his old friend Röhm on whatever that meeting had been about. . . .

"Did you see Friedrich again?" asked Hans: "I did: he went up the gangway just behind Dr. Göbbels."

Soon they were once more back in their crowded trucks and bound for their beds in Cologne at last, the string of vehicles coasting downhill and backfiring like guns—Ernst sneezed at the stinking exhaust of the one in front. Nobody sang now, nobody spoke: the others already seemed half asleep as they stood squashed tight and swaying together at every bend in the road like trees in the wind. To them this had been just another routine assignment—and boring at that: for none of these others had seen what the two friends had seen. . . .

Cologne was near: for now they were racing along the empty Autobahn through the 'Green Belt' trees on the very last lap to the old, grim, ex-army barracks the S.S. had taken over. Arrived there at last, Ernst changed his clothes and got into something dry: for he felt quite sure he wouldn't be able to sleep. Something entirely momentous had been decided that night, right under his eyes; but what? For of only one thing did Ernst feel certain—that this was a night that would live in history. All that dumb-show behind the glass had been history in the making. . . . He drowsed a moment—and found himself walking past rows of enormous museum cases, each with some famous Crisis of History being enacted inside it on public show there (for fifty pfennigs) behind the glass.

He nodded himself awake. The heat and the smell of his room-mates drove him across to the window for air. Behind him his room-mates snored, and one of them talked in his sleep. The window faced north, looking over a city lit only by street lamps (for all the little houses were dark). Then a cock crew. . . . Those black-paper crenellations silhouetted against the paling sky would turn into factories soon, and houses: for dawn was coming and somewhere a baby had started crying. The air was cool enough now, but that smoky orange glow in the east portended the heat of this coming last day of June. . . .

'Stille Nacht, Heilige Nacht' hummed Ernst. The short summer night was passing, the night when nowadays all good Germans could sleep in safety under the spread of their Führer's unsleeping, protecting wings. He yawned. Protected from Marxists, and Jews. . . . And the French. . . . 'From ghosties and ghoulies' (as we would say), 'and everything else which goes bump in the night.'

He rocked on his feet; and almost before he fell on his bed he had fallen asleep.

Chapter 25

Ernst had been right: Hitler was bound for Munich, to keep his appointment with Röhm—though a little ahead of time.

Three weeks ago, when Röhm's neuritis became so acute that he had to take sick-leave, the S.A. Chief had rented some downstairs rooms in a quiet and unpretentious mountain inn on the shores of the Tegernsee. Not in a lonely place, for Wiessee's sulphur and iodine springs were famous for cures: the village consisted almost entirely of clinics and sanatoria. Here, in the Pension Hanslbaur, Röhm had transported himself just about as far as he could from that feverish city of rumour and intrigue, Berlin, while remaining in easy reach of Munich for secret talks with Göbbels. Apart from Count Spreti, his permanent boy-friend, he only took with him a couple of adjutants, leaving his staff-guards in Munich.

Röhm's doctor had ordered a sedative course of injections, and drove out from Munich each time one was needed to give it himself. Tonight the final injection was due; and the doctor had got to the inn just in time for dinner, so he and his patient had quietly dined together first (a Gruppenführer called Bergmann making a third). After dinner the three of them sat around playing cards till eleven o'clock, when the doctor suggested his patient was better in bed if he hoped to be fighting-fit for tomorrow's meeting. Röhm nodded, and rose to go. He hadn't abandoned the policy struggle, and (as his doctor knew) tomorrow's meeting was crucial: the Adolf who never seemed able to make up his mind alone had got to be helped. Tomorrow he had to be faced by the whole S.A. Top Brass presenting their

355

case in unison: either these two million S.A. men must become a recognised Army Reserve (in other words, be allowed to engulf the tiny Professional Army and open the way for a leftward swing in policy), or. . . . Or if Hitler wouldn't agree, Röhm said he had made up his mind to resign and return to Bolivia, leaving Our Adolph to cope with those turbulent fellows himself. He would soon find out these men had none of those ancient and deeply-ingrained emotional ties to his person which handicapped Röhm; and indeed he (Röhm) was heartily sick of keeping a couple of million men on the leash whose claims he believed in, simply to make things smoother for Adolf!

Tomorrow Adolf would certainly turn on all his charm; and the thought gave Röhm a sinking feeling. . . . But this time his mind was made up to resist. After all he'd resigned once before, and if need be could do it again: South America had its charms. . . .

So Röhm retired to his ground-floor room and obediently went to bed. The doctor pricked him, and left him to sleep it off.

The doctor was just on the point of returning to Munich when Bergmann suggested it being so late why not stop the night? Some unexpected tourists had come from Berlin, so the inn was full; but the room the two adjutants shared upstairs had a third bed in it the doctor was welcome to doss down on. . . . He accepted; and then—since neither man wanted to turn in yet—the pair of them sat around chewing the rag in the lounge.

At half-past-twelve the first invitee for tomorrow's meeting arrived. This was the S.A. High-up from Breslau: a man who still looked the part of one of Rossbach's gallant toughs of old Freikorps times—which is just what he was, with his whipcord muscles and winning girlish face and girlish behaviour and (girlish) murderous record. This Edmund Heines wanted to talk to his sleeping chief at once; but the doctor was firm, the drug must be left to work undisturbed. So

Heines grumbled a bit, then swallowed a yawn and wandered along the passage to room No. 9. He would see the Chief in the morning. . . .

When the doctor finally went to bed himself it was gone one o'clock, and both the young adjutants sound asleep.

Chapter 26

DURING the two-hour flight Hans's fortunate brother—the granite-faced Friedrich—had snatched what sleep he could in the air as the only rest he was likely to get; and the early midsummer dawn was already tinting the spires of Munich with rosy light as their plane touched down.

The Führer himself had put through a call before leaving Godesberg. This, Friedrich knew, was to trigger certain provisional orders to Gauleiter Wagner in Munich—whatever those orders might be; and now he was soon to find out what they were, for instead of heading for Wiessee at once the cars drove first to Wagner's Ministry. Friedrich indeed had a fair idea; but he got it confirmed as the party climbed the ill-lit, deserted and echoing stairs on their way to the Minister's private room: for there on the stairs he caught sight of somebody staggering blindly from wall to wall who screamed with fear at the sound of approaching feet.

Then this apparition—his head all covered in blood and his face bashed in—turned and upbraided the Führer. Faithful old S.A. comrades invited by Wagner had all sat drinking together till dawn (it appeared from his ravings), expecting the Führer's arrival: then Wagner himself had given a sign whereon half the party had set on their neighbours with bottles and pistol-butts. It was senseless cold-blooded murder, this slaughter of faithful S.A. Old Comrades: if this had indeed been done on the Führer's orders the Führer was mad. . . .

Friedrich had drawn his gun; but Göbbels laid a restraining hand on his arm, for the Führer was stammering out excuses! He seemed completely taken aback by this Banquo's Ghost, and assured him there'd been some ghastly mistake—that he wouldn't have anyone hurting one hair of dear Banquo's head: "You'd better go straight to the doctor."

There'd been some ghastly mistake indeed, thought Friedrich—so simple a killing bungled to start with! The superstitious Führer must think it an omen. . . . Then Friedrich felt the hand on his forearm tremble, and glanced at a Göbbels whose face was a mottled grey: 'Aha!' thought Friedrich, 'You've guessed like me, that the Führer may still change sides and disown the whole operation—and then where will *you* be, my friend?'

But now from the top of the stairs came a happy babel of slurred Bavarian voices: a group of 'Old Guard' all looking as pleased as Punch, like terriers after a rat-hunt. The Führer perked up at once when he saw them, and went round slapping their backs.

"We're sorry one bastard escaped, Herr Hitler—but still, we'll soon pick him up!"

"Don't worry about him, boys! I need you for bigger game."

Dug-outs, most of them were, from Hitler's own street-corner past. . . . Friedrich already had recognised Esser the scandalous, scandal-mongering journalist: Emil Maurice, the man who had trained for him all his earliest strong-arm squads before the S.A. (as such) existed; and Weber, the 'Party Hercules'—nowadays run to Gargantuan fat. Weber had served as chucker-out in a pub before leading his 'Oberlanders' in Hitler's abortive Munich Putsch of eleven years back. . . . "You've shown you're a strong man still under all this lard!" said the Führer, jovially jolting him in the ribs till the man-mountain burped. "And you too, Esser: all those mistresses haven't drained you entirely of spunk!"

Then they all passed into Wagner's room, while Friedrich was left outside in the passage on guard and the door was firmly closed. Friedrich couldn't hear much through three inches of wood, except for the muffled voice of a frenzied

N

Führer cursing somebody's dastardly treason (só some of the party in there must still be alive, whatever Banquo supposed). Then the door was flung open again and there was Göbbels, whinnying over his shoulder: "Remember that's just the hors-d'oeuvre—and we'd better get cracking before the news of it gets to the Chief of Staff!"

Inside the half-open door an unseen Führer was counting out loud, and murmuring names: "Du Moulin . . Schneid-huber . . . Schmidt. . . ." (who had just arrived). But at Göbbels's words he seemed to wake with a start, and came hurrying out. As he passed through the door, 'I wonder how Adolf is feeling about it now?' Friedrich asked himself: 'He *looks* like peeing his breeks. . . .'

But then the two adjutants had to sweep up the killer-team with them, and all pile back in the bullet-proof cars.

Chapter 27

A T Wiessee, at half-past-six, the doctor was roused by a
terrible rumpus and hullabaloo downstairs, with a
shouting and hammering fit to wake the dead. He found
both adjutants gone, and one of those Berlin 'tourists' each
side of his pillow: the pair were plain-clothes Gestapo men
from Berlin of course, and they put him under arrest.

Even before Hitler's party had got there Dietrich's men
had arrived in Army Transport, together with some of the
staff from the Concentration Camp at Dachau. Together
their forces surrounded the inn. As soon as Hitler appeared,
a 'tourist' had crept downstairs and quietly slipped back
the bolts: then Friedrich dragged Count Spreti out of his
bed in Room No. 5—the whole room smelling of sweaty
pyjamas and hair-oil—while Brückner and Emil Maurice
burst into room No. 9, where Heines was sharing his bed
with his chauffeur. Though Heines was famously quick on
the draw his callers were quicker, and clubbed him over the
head; but the hammering heard was Hitler himself. He was
using the butt of his fetish—his old rhinoceros-whip—to
beat on the locked door of Room No. 7.

"Who's there?" asked a slurred sleepy voice.

"Me, Hitler! Open the door!"

"You're early. I didn't expect you till noon."

When the door opened, Hitler began to upbraid the
swaying pyjamaed figure still heavy with poppied sleep. But
Röhm made an effort to clear the clouds from his brain, and
Hitler's incredible accusations of treachery got through at
last. So he started answering back.

"Bind him!" said Hitler.

Roused by the shindy, the landlord appeared in his nightshirt wondering who'd let these rackety strangers in. Then
he caught sight of Röhm his illustrious guest, and 'Heil

Hitlered' with lifted arm; but his guest made no move to
salute him back—which of course he couldn't, in handcuffs.
"Na, ja—Grüss Gott!" said Röhm bitterly. Friedrich then
escorted Röhm outside and bundled him into a car, while
Hitler took hold of the trembling publican by the arm and
apologised for the disturbance. . . .

'So far, so good!' thought Friedrich, who saw how the
Führer almost danced with relief.

As for the doctor's protestations that all the effects of his
treatment were being undone. . . . This wasn't England,
where even an ailing murderer couldn't be hanged if the
doctors considered it bad for his health; and somebody soon
shut him up.

To avoid any possible ambuscade the hunting-pack
rounded the lake, rejoining the Munich road by a different
route. There, as they sped back again towards Munich the
number of prisoners snowballed. Röhm's orders (issued in
Hitler's name) had summoned the S.A. leaders for ten
o'clock; but Heines was not the only high-ranking leader
who hoped for an early word with the Chief before the
meeting began. They were stopped in their cars one by one,
and the men drawn up by the road in a single line for Hitler
to take this strange parade of his ancient comrades-in-arms
—the World War heroes, the Freikorps fighters, the men
who had marched in his Munich Putsch.

One was a certain Ludin, a former Army Lieutenant
cashiered and gaoled four years ago for preaching the Nazi
creed in the Officers' Mess. Unlike his fellow-accused he had
borne no grudge against a Führer who'd stood in the witness-
box and there (for Reasons of State) had disowned him, but
stuck to his Nazi guns: since when he had risen fast and far
in the Storm Troops. Ludin had hoped for so much from
this Wiessee meeting: so often before the Führer's presence
had served to resolve some seemingly insurmountable
impasse. . . . But what had gone wrong? They hadn't expected the Führer himself to arrive till noon—and now,

how seedy he looked! His face was puffed, yet haggard: he hadn't shaved, his eyes were bloodshot and dull, he was wearing a leather coat in the heat of the morning sun and he hadn't a hat. His forelock was plastered against his forehead with sweat, and beads of it shone on his little moustache. . . .

Meanwhile the Führer was passing in silence from man to man, pausing to give each face a look which seemed to use each pair of eyes as open peep-holes into the brain behind; and each man suddenly grew afraid. He spoke only once, when "Ludin" he said in a far-away voice before moving on. Whereupon Brückner gestured bewildered Ludin back to his car, and Ludin was free to drive away wherever he liked. . . . But the rest were swept into the bag; and they presently found themselves standing in ranks in the dust of Stadelheim prison yard, for most of the vacant cells had already been filled with the battered remains of Wagner's midnight drinking-party. But Röhm had privileged treatment: for him a cell inside the gaol had been held in reserve.

Röhm was no stranger to Stadelheim gaol: it was where he'd been lodged long ago when the Munich Putsch failed. These were familiar walls that recalled the past and those 'ancient emotional ties' which bound him to Hitler's person, their friendship through thick and thin. Only a few months ago 'Your Adolf' had sent him a letter expressing his thanks to Fate 'for giving me men such as you, my dear Ernst Röhm, as my friends. . . .' And indeed, since 1919 when he'd spotted the latent political gifts in this scrubby lance-corporal lately discharged from the Army, and given the man his chance. . . .

But a loaded revolver was laid on the table. "A German Officer knows what he has to do," said the gaoler; and locked Röhm in.

*

Wearing 'S.A. Standartenführer' badges of rank at Kettner's behest, Lothar had travelled from Kammstadt to Munich by train. All incoming trains were met by parties of S.S. men to escort any S.A. leaders aboard them to waiting cars; but these were all of them 'Gruppenführer' at least (more or less, 'Generals'). Lothar, because of his lowlier rank, seemed likely to get left out. . . .

"Excuse me," he said.

"Who are you?" The S.S. Officer looked at him rather strangely, he thought.

"Gruppenführer Kettner. . . . That is, he's broken his leg and he sent me to represent him."

"So you're bound for Wiessee too? All right—jump in if you like!" said the man, with a Cheshire-cat grin. So Lothar jumped in. But it wasn't Wiessee their drivers took them to—only Stadelheim Prison. There the astounded men found themselves under arrest. They were drawn up in ranks with those others; and waited, strictly forbidden to speak.

A sudden stentorian shout rang out from inside the prison: "What's that bloody thing for? No, I won't do Adolf the kindness: he'll have to do his own dirty work if he wants me dead!"

The ghost of a groan swept the men outside in the yard like a small puff of wind. After that, once more silence. They stood there and waited, surrounded by hundreds of armed S.S. men. For Hitler had gone to the Brown House; and nothing more could be done till Hitler himself arrived.

Chapter 28

THE Brown House was cordened off by Police and Regular Soldiers. Rudolf Hess had flown direct from Berlin and had taken charge: any S.A. man who liked might enter, but after five in the morning none might go out.

Hitler had urgent instructions for Hess: for a flash of inspiration had shown the elated Führer that Röhm and his S.A. leaders need not be the end of this happy event by a long chalk! A lot of old scores remained to be settled, and this was an opportunity not to be missed: liquidations discreetly carried out now would hardly be noticed in all the excitement. . . .

Gustav von Kahr for example, who'd dared to out-double-cross Hitler himself back in 1923, thus postponing his rise to power for many a weary year. . . . Kahr was now in his seventies, living in strict retirement; but Kahr couldn't dodge his eventual punishment—not if he lived to be ninety! So Hess took out his notebook, and noted down 'Kahr'.

There were others who had to be silenced simply for knowing too much: such as Father Stempfle (he knew far too much about Hitler's affair with Geli). So Hess noted down 'Stempfle'—without in the least knowing why. There were others as well, including a certain Bavarian Colonel from back in Hitler's own Army days who knew. . . . Hess also remembered that Colonel, and wrote down his name (Hess too had served with Liszts).

"Oh, and then there is Schmidt."

Hess wrote down 'Schmidt'. But still, which 'Schmidt? He didn't quite like to ask. . . . But then he remembered how strongly the Führer felt about music: he must mean Willi Schmidt, the musical critic.

Once Hess had written in 'Willi' that seemed to be all, down here in the South—unless Rudi had names of his own to add? But Hess shook his head, replaced the elastic with care and thrust the notebook back in his pocket. Had Göbbels got names to add? But Göbbels too shook his head: those Bratwurst-Glöckle waiters who'd witnessed his meetings with Röhm, these certainly had to be silenced—but this was a matter he'd rather attend to himself.

Hitler was feeling a little light-headed from lack of sleep. He summoned all company present, and started to read them a lecture denouncing the moral evil of homosexual vices; but had to cut it short, for he seemed to be losing his voice. As he thought of the business still to be done at Stadelheim Prison his lips felt dry, and he licked them.

*

Sepp Dietrich, commander of Hitler's own 'Leibstandarte' (his personal guards), was given the job.

The sultry afternoon sun was still high overhead when Dietrich stepped out on the Stadelheim prison yard with an S.S. officer at his elbow. Except for Röhm, the men in the cells had all been brought down and stood with the rest in the dust. There Dietrich saw all the familiar faces: Peter von Heydebreck, gaunt and one-armed—the hero of Annaberg: Hayn (under whose command, as Lothar remembered, his dear brother Wolff had fought long ago on the shores of the Baltic): Fritz Ritter von Krausser, Röhm's deputy during his sick-leave and wearing his decorations for gallantry: August Schneidhuber, battered and bloody and barely able to stand: the young Count Spreti, no longer so debonair. . . .

Röhm himself could be seen had Dietrich but raised his eyes to that second-floor window; but this he didn't do, for his mission was not with Röhm. Instead he scanned each well-known face till he came on a face which he didn't know, and silently pointed at Lothar. His S.S. aide called the man out, and Lothar sprang forward saluting.

"Who are you?"

"Gruppenführer Kettner. . . ."

"You're not Kettner! Where is he?"

"He's broken his leg, and he sent me. . . ."

"I said, where is he?"

"In bed."

"*Where*, dumb-bell?"

"At home, in Kammstadt."

"Kettner: make a note of it," Dietrich remarked aside to his aide: "Tell Hess where he is."

The officer made his note, then enquired: "But this young man? Should he. . . ." Sepp Dietrich however was moving on, and Lothar returned to the ranks.

'If only the Führer would come as they say he will,' thought Lothar, 'and clear all this up!' For there must be some inexplicable misunderstanding—but *no* misunderstanding could baffle for long the Führer's all-seeing eyes. . . .

All day they had stood in the sun and not been allowed one drop of water to drink: Lothar picked up a pebble to suck but he couldn't, it burned his tongue. 'When the Führer comes he will let us all drink, and then set us free.'

Lothar glanced at the westering sun: for a moment it darkened into the Führer's face, then blazed once more as a ball of fire. Yes, the Führer was more than mortal: the Führer was Fate incarnate, the power that predetermines all human lives. Therefore for some mysterious cause which it wasn't for Man to try to fathom he must have willed even this misunderstanding, since nothing could happen he had not willed. But the light of his coming presence must just as surely dissolve it again by a further act of his will, for he loved his children. . . .

Lothar had hoped for so much from that Wiessee meeting, but most of all for the chance of seeing the Führer face-to-face—even as once before he had seen him (years ago, during the Putsch) in that upper room at the Bürgerbräukeller with Göring and Ludendorff. . . . Then the strange coincidence struck him that here was a Lothar once again dressed up in borrowed plumes! Then he'd been

N*

accidentally wearing a General's overcoat: now, this Stand-artenführer's uniform equally didn't belong to him. . . .

Dietrich had backed to the end of the yard, and a sudden movement among the guards caught Lothar's eye—ah, this must presage the Führer's arrival at last! But then he looked up and saw Röhm, who had gripped the bars of his window and shook them with all his might. For that was the moment when Dietrich gave the signal, the firing-squads raised their sub-machine guns and started mowing them down; and Lothar at least was to die with a look of intense surprise on his face.

Chapter 29

LATE that same afternoon the Führer (and Göbbels, who stuck to his side like a leech) flew back to Berlin, leaving Hess in Munich to tidy things up—as per instructions.

Berlin had seen Göring and Himmler work to a somewhat wider brief, freely adjusting the 'Plot' to fit desirable victims. Not that their hands were entirely free. . . . To take those three ex-Chancellors first, in common prudence Brüning should have been shot—but in common prudence Brüning had smelled his danger and taken himself abroad. Vice-Chancellor Papen also had got to survive (alas!), since Papen was Hindenburg's pet and the Old Bull's approval was needed to cover the whole affair: von Papen's arrest indeed had been partly to guard against accidents. Still, he had to be given a fright: so two of his closest advisers were shot, his offices seized and ransacked. . . . Having been shot as it were by proxy, Franz von Papen would certainly take the hint: there'd be no more dangerous Marburg speeches from him!

But the third was ex-Chancellor Schleicher; and here no obstacles stood in the way. Soon after breakfast a friend had been chatting with Schleicher over the phone, and heard him turn to someone behind him saying: "Yes, I am General von Schleicher. . .". The friend then heard three shots ring out in the General's house before the phone went dead.

Gregor Strasser was lunching with his wife and children at home when the Gestapo took him away, without saying why or where. . . . And so on—and so on. Karl Ernst, the Berlin S.A. Leader, didn't get far on his honeymoon: bridegroom and bride were both arrested at Bremen, about to embark for Maderia. From there he had to be carted back alive to

Berlin, for the 'Plot' scenario said he'd been caught in the act of trying to seize the city on Röhm's behalf. . . .

Even Putzi Hanfstängl's name had somehow got on to somebody's list, but Putzi was luckier: Putzi was hitting it up with his old college chums at Harvard while all this was going on. So Putzi survived—which nobody minded much, he was nowadays hardly worth powder and shot so far as political influence went. Yet plenty of others worth even less were unluckier. 'Luck' where these private enmities were concerned was mostly a matter of bargaining—rather like blackballs at London Clubs: 'If my friend So-and-so stays on your list, then your friend What's-his-name goes on mine—either neither, or both!'

Rumour of course was sizzling all through a frantic city where nobody knew whose turn would be next: 'Röhm has committed suicide!' 'So has Strasser!' 'Schleicher . . .'. The Foreign Press was avid for cast-iron news, and unwilling to wait. That Saturday afternoon, since Göbbels was not yet back from Munich (and Putzi, whose job was the Foreign Press, was abroad), Göring in person called for the correspondents, outlined his 'Röhm-Strasser Plot' and gave them a potted lecture on S.A. corruption. "And Schleicher?" somebody asked, as Göring was turning to go.

"Schleicher too had been plotting against the State with a Foreign Power: he was foolish enough to resist arrest, and lost his life in the mêlée."

So that was that. . . . But word had arrived that Hitler was shortly expected back, so Göring hadn't got time to answer any more questions and left them—stunned.

*

Göring and Himmler were both on the tarmac to meet their master at Tempelhof Airfield. But Hitler's plane was delayed; and before it a tiny Junkers landed from Bremen. Out of it stepped Karl Ernst. . . . That made the onlookers rub their eyes: Karl Ernst was arriving late for his own execution—announced three hours ago! This the prisoner didn't know, of course: he took his arrest as some sort of nonsense of Göring's which Röhm and Hitler between them would soon iron out. . . . Indeed he died convinced that this was the Rightist coup he'd foreseen—an Army coup, which Göring had joined (which is just what it was, in a way); and shouted 'Heil Hitler!' straight in the teeth of the firing-squad.

So what had Ernst really been guilty of (no one believed the official line)? Had Göring, people wondered, wanted him silenced for knowing the truth of the Reichstag Fire?

'Heil Hitler!' At last the Chancellor's plane was announced, and came in to land.

If Hitler had looked a bit under the weather in Munich, he now looked a great deal worse with his puffy and pallid features lit up by an almost Wagnerian blood-red sunset. To save his voice he greeted the group in silence, shaking their hands; and the only sound as the sun went down was the Guard of Honour clicking their heels.

Then Hitler started towards his car with Göring and Himmler, Göbbels limping behind with a terrible haunted face; and once out of earshot of lesser fry, Himmler pulled out his own list of names—most of them ticked already—a lengthy list, and thoroughly dog-eared by now. Hitler took it and ran his finger down it, asking them questions with Göring and Himmler each side excitedly whispering one in each ear. *What about Papen, first?* Göring smiled: he had tricked the tricky Vice-Chancellor nicely, luring him round to his private apartments while Himmler was seizing his office. . . . The fool had tried to pull the 'Vice-Chancellor' over him, claiming command in the Chancellor's absence— wanting to phone the President—wanting the Army called out! But Göring had soon put a stopper on that tommy-rot. . . . *So where was he now?* Papen was shut in his home surrounded by armed S.S., cut off from the world—unharmed, but equally harmless. Meanwhile Heydrich was having his office files gone through with a tooth-comb, looking for something juicy enough to hold over his head. . . .

Hitler nodded approval. *And Schleicher?* Ah, the intriguing Field-grey Eminence now lay dead as a doornail, and so did his wife. Hitler nodded approval again. *And Strasser?* Now Himmler chipped in: his former patron was lodged under lock and key in Prinz Albrechtstrasse Gaol, awaiting. . . .

What! Strasser was still alive? From fifty yards off folk saw the Führer jerk back his head in a paroxysm of rage: though only Göring and Himmler himself knew why.

*

Strasser had first been lodged in the crowded gaol with a group of others, then moved to a cell alone. Late that night, while Hitler was getting at last some well-earned sleep, his erstwhile Fisher of Men saw a gun-barrel poked through the grille in the door. He moved, and the first shot missed: so he dashed to a corner the gun couldn't reach. But then the door opened, and Heydrich and Eicke themselves came in to finish the job.

A lowlier gaoler followed with bucket and mop to clean up the mess, for Strasser had bled like a pig. But he wasn't allowed: the blood must remain, a useful exhibit for showing the world what 'GESTAPO' henceforth meant.

Chapter 30

Sunday dawned. As yet the public at large knew little of any 'Röhm-Strasser Plot', nor how narrow the margin by which the Führer's heroic action (and Göring's) had saved the State; and Göbbels grew restless. Soon the whole propaganda machine must be thrown into gear, justifying the Purge by blackening Röhm and polishing Hitler's (and Göring's) haloes to shine like the noonday sun; and instinct urged him to go on the air at once. But Himmler's Gestapo begged for the black-out of news to go on for a bit since the killing programme had got behind schedule (some unmethodical victims who failed to be found where they ought to have been still had to be hunted down).

At noon the Führer at last got dressed and appeared. In the eyes of his Court he had played his essential part: he should now sit back and relax, leaving them to play theirs without any overwrought Führer under their feet; but that wasn't to be. He was nervous and over-excited, as if working up to one of his dangerous *crises-de-nerfs*.

As Friedrich and Brückner knew, yesterday's strong-arm stuff is only a tithe of a proper adjutant's job: the rest is more like a kind of running psychiatry, reading and soothing the master-mind. So Brückner got busy arranging a Chancery Garden Party with tea, and ladies, and plenty of sweet sticky cakes; but this couldn't come off till the afternoon, so the problem of how to avoid any Führer-explosion meanwhile devolved upon Friedrich.

Granite-faced Friedrich was not such a fool as his fine physique had made Ernst suppose, but even he found it hard to divine the cause of his Master's near-hysterical state. Given the Führer's solipsist Weltanschauung (whereby the rest of the universe human and otherwise equally ranked as inanimate 'things'), yesterday's slaughter of awkward old

friends should have roused in him no more compunction
than bulldozing buildings which stood in the way of development schemes; and yet he seemed strangely obsessed by
his yesterday's doings, retelling them over and over again.
In somebody lesser—some mere Macbeth—you'd have
thought it was Conscience; but Conscience was right out of
character. . . .

Something, however, had to be done about it at once; and
Friedrich had often found it surprisingly easy to switch this
solipsist mind from that artist's material we distinguish as
'men' to some other and rather less sentient form of clay. So
he phoned the Führer's young architect: "Speer—for God's
sake hurry and bring us round anything new you have in the
way of models or drawings".

At first the treatment seemed to succeed: Speer's eleva-
tions and plans for an eighty-feet-high flight of steps, flanked
by vast megalithic abutments and topped by a long colonnade, seemed to have a remarkably calming effect. But all
of a sudden the Führer straightened his back, exclaiming:
"Approved: start building at once". And then he was off
again, pouring the story of yesterday's deeds into this new
pair of ears—as if yesterday's coup was a *chef-d'œuvre* in
human relations surpassing anything Speer could devise in
stone.

He began with his dawn arrival at Wagner's Ministry:
"There stood a group of the traitors, Speer, not even disarmed . . .". (Not a word about Banquo's Ghost on the
stairs, noted Friedrich, nor corpses laid out on the Minister's
floor.) "These men had plotted my murder—yet none of
them dared raise a finger against me. I walked towards
them unarmed and alone, and tore off their epaulets." Next
he described his descent on Wiessee, "with no means of
knowing if Röhm had machine-guns trained on me through
the windows. Everything rested on me, as alone and unarmed I rushed the swine before they could fire a shot."
Then he suddenly stopped, and turned his embarrassing
clear blue glare on their blank uncomprehending faces.

What Friedrich read in those eyes was despair at their
incomprehension: could none of these fools hoist in.....
Then Friedrich at last understood: 'Hoist in' that *he* might
have been killed! For after all nothing on earth can equate
with a solipsist losing his life, since that is the End of the
World itself: so this was simply the after-effect of an
eschatological class of fright unknown to mere mortals!

More than ten years had passed (reflected Friedrich)
since Hitler had faced those unexpected Residenzstrasse
bullets in Munich; and those had given the man his bellyful,
judging by 'Adolf Légalité' since! The solipsist's role is to
sit up aloft like a Caesar signalling life or death with a thumb,
not plunge in the bloody arena himself.

Just before luncheon, disturbing news reached Himmler:
the 'suicide' Röhm was still alive. Well, if Röhm still refused
to do the decent thing he would have to be helped; and
Eicke was just the man, so he telephoned Eicke.... So long
as Röhm lived the Führer might still revoke and use Röhm
against them!

At luncheon itself the Führer was still on the subject of
Wiessee; but now he dwelt on the nauseous orgies that
bourgeois respectable inn had been forced to witness half
Friday night (and even Friedrich was taken aback by his
master's inventive powers). "Those brawny transvestite
dancers, those naked boys we saw kept locked in a scented
room till needed to satisfy Röhm's unnatural lusts": he
made it all sound like the late Fritz Krupp's notorious orgies
in Capri, rather than poor old Röhm's rather shame-faced
Consenting Adults—and anyway, why all this fuss? Half
of the old Imperial High Command had been perverts (or
pseudo-perverts) as part of their cult of manliness, like the
Spartans. Early this century General Count von Hasler—
the man who demanded 'a mountain of corpses', etc. on
which to build a temple to German Kultur: it was dancing
before his Kaiser in pink ballet-shirt and a wreath of roses
that made him drop dead of a heart-attack....

Now Brückner chipped in, with shocking accounts of Röhm's Standartenstrasse Berlin headquarters: the opulent tapestries, crystal mirrors and thick pile carpets reminding one more of a millionaire's whorehouse than Army barracks. Menus the searchers had found of Lucullan banquets on frog-legs, shark-fins, nightingale-tongues and the finest vintage champagnes: the kinky cabaret-programmes. . . .

"There" cried Hitler "you have these ascetics who found my revolution too tame for their tastes, and were plotting to kill me and plunge our country in blood in the name of Social Equality!"

Hitler was still in full spate when Brückner's welcome summons arrived to tea, and Society ladies, and sweet sticky cakes.

*

Tea, and chit-chat, and wonderful summer hats. . . .

That garden-party was still in full swing in Berlin when Eicke reached Stadelheim gaol, fresh from the killing of Strasser and anxious to score a double in twenty-four hours. Michael Lippert, also from Dachau, was with him.

They found Röhm stripped to the waist, for the heat in his cell was intense; and his barrel-like body glistened with sweat. "Protocol calls for distinguished heads to fall to distinguished headsmen," said Eicke by way of explaining his mission. Röhm gave him a look of contempt such as even Eicke would never forget, then stood to attention while Eicke and Lippert riddled his body with lead.

Chapter 31

A T the back of the Schloss in which Walther and Adèle lived, where high unscalable cliffs overhung the stripling Danube, the room which had once been Mitzi's was now her mother's boudoir. Directly beneath its windows projected an inaccessible ledge, where the rock was crowned by a stretch of ruinous rampart which Walther declared was original Roman. Once she took over the room, Adèle had steep wooden stairs built down from the window to reach it: then she had baskets of soil and afterwards vines and plants carried through the house, to make it her private garden—a miniature Eden grown in an eyrie. Enough of the ancient walls remained for protection from wind and to stop you falling over the edge; and for shade she had them re-roof a roofless watch-tower, turning it into a summerhouse.

That had been ten years ago; and for all these years an Adèle decked in yellow gardening-gloves had tended her plants like gems. But alas, she had made her lovely private garden too lovely and now it was private no longer. This Sunday morning—as often, in summer—the whole Kessen Clan was gathered in 'Grossmutter's Garden' for breakfast, trampling her rock-plants and even bringing their dogs. The whole of the Clan, because though nowadays Franz and his family lived on their own on the floor above his parents this was a Sunday, and Walther adored his grandchildren.

Tables were there already; but everything else must be carried down outside stairs that were narrow and steep as a fire-escape. Franz's little Leo could manage alone, by crawling down backwards on hands and knees; but Ännchen had got to be carried, and so had the wriggling dachshunds. Then came the coffee-urn with its antique spirit-stove (for Walther insisted always on coffee at boiling-point): the basins of hard-boiled eggs, the ham, the numerous kinds of

377

sausage, the crocks of butter straight from the icehouse, the long loaves of bread, the china and knives and forks, the sugar, the jugs of cream—and of course the Baron's own Dundee Marmalade. Meanwhile, as Lies trapesed up and down those ladder-like steps with her loads like a giant spider climbing its thread, Leo and Ännchen stood at the bottom and peered unashamedly up her skirts. For those puppy-fat knees which had once caught Augustine's eyes were now at least three times their former girth; they were thicker than Leo's waist.

Franz was there at the breakfast: still lean and athletic, except for a small round paunch as if he were newly enceinte (his wife was a wonderful cook). Trudl was just twenty-one, and engagingly plump: Irma was two years younger, and almost gaunt. Trudl's betrothed (this young Hungarian diplomat seemed to be always on leave) kept trying to hold his sweetheart's hand, confirming Irma's belief *she* never wanted a husband. Soon the twins came in from an early-morning ride, for both were passionate horsemen: two handsome young adolescents in pipe-clayed breeches with hair bleached almost as white as that by the sun, and their skins tanned almost as black as their boots. The only family absentee was Uncle Otto, away at Kammstadt on business: the only outsider present was Father Petrus the Parish Priest, who had just been saying Mass in the family chapel.

Adèle turned her back on the hubbub to gaze out into the azure sky, then down at the sunlit patchwork plain below where oblongs of yellow and green cultivation filled every space between the dark blue patches of forest. The nearer distance was dotted with rows of tiny new pinhead haycocks, and lines of round green beads that were fruit-trees planted in rows; and moving specks of brilliant colour like miniature ladybirds—groups of women crossing the fields on their way from Church. Where the landscape began to merge into haze, on a distant broken chalk-line of road a creeping cloud of dust like a silkworm's cocoon was too far off to reveal the truck which it must contain. . . .

Then Walther called her name; and she turned to face the
invasion, smiling politely.

Walther himself seemed in wonderful form, alternately
wolfing slices of sausage himself and throwing bits to a pair of
adoring dogs, while discussing the breathtaking news from
Munich with Franz: for the Kessens were nothing if not well
informed. So Röhm had committed suicide! Frankly, a jolly
good riddance. . . . There wasn't much to be said for the
upstart Hitler, but even less for the blackguardly Röhm!
He had tried to stage a revolt with his rag-tag-and-bobtail
'army' (as everyone always knew he would); and then when
it failed he had taken the easy way out. . . . Those Storm
Troops of Röhm's were almost as bad as Eisner's 'Guards'
in the old Red Terror days: "D'you remember—but no, of
course you wouldn't you're much too young—the day when
a posse of Eisner's rapscallions attempted to seize the Castle?"

"I wasn't a child at the time," said Franz in a patient
voice, "but a boy of sixteen, and away at cadet-school.
You're mixing me up with the twins, who were babies then."

"Quite . . ." Walther turned to the Twins: "The rascals
had somehow got through the gates, but a cowman soon
chased them out with a pitchfork."

The twins looked suitably blank: they had heard the
story so often before, and anyhow hated to be reminded how
young they were.

"The fact is," said Franz, laying down his fork, "that this
latest master-stroke is additional proof that you all underrated the Führer right from the start. 'Crude', you called
him. His burning love for his country you couldn't deny; but
what you failed to observe was the streak of political genius
governing every move from his earliest days. I remember
having to point out, years ago, to my learned friend Dr.
Reinhold Steuckel, how cleverly Hitler employed the ancient
maxim Divide and Rule to retain the Nazi leadership even
in prison: 'burning his empty shoes himself rather than
letting anyone step in them', that was the phrase I used."

Walther was nettled. "Thank God the fellow has done

what any self-respecting Chancellor had to do, and brought
the S.A. to heel! I admit that it took some guts, but I fail to
see anything 'clever' about it: these men were his rivals
within the Party, but vis-à-vis everyone else they were
Hitler's staunchest supporters. Destroying their power has
weakened no one so much as Hitler himself. . . ." There
came a small interruption as Franz was called away to the
phone, but Walther went on to the world at large: "In
short, he has bound himself hand-and-foot and delivered
himself to the Army: we've got the little man just where we
want him, now!"

He looked round the family circle in triumph; but no one
gainsaid him—if anyone heard him indeed, for the twins
were thinking of horses, Janos was tickling Trudl's ear with a
flower. . . . And women, of course, hold no political views.
"Darlings, put Fritzl down!" said Adèle, as Leo and
Ännchen each attempted to lift one end of connecting
dachshund: "Come back and finish your milk."

"But Granny, he *wants* to look over the wall!" said Leo.

"Who was the call from?" asked Irma when Franz returned.

"Nothing. . . . No one I knew: only some old Army friend
of Uncle Otto's who hasn't seen him for years and wanted to
know where he was."

"You told him?" asked Father Petrus quickly.

"Of course. But I said he'd be back to lunch."

Chapter 32

"MY coffee is cold!" complained Walther. So Irma set the urn on the flame to re-heat, and without remonstrance emptied her father's still-steaming coffee-cup over the wall.

"Do fishes like coffee?" asked Leo; but nobody seemed to know.

"I was just explaining," said Walther to Franz, "that we've now got Chancellor Hitler properly under our thumb. You mark my words: henceforth he'll be merely a figurehead, serving those Great Conservative National Forces on which he now completely depends."

"Frankly, Papa," Franz answered coldly, "you seem to forget that the man is a patriot through-and-through. He and the Army are natural allies because their aims are the same—the resurrection of Germany: therefore the question of 'figureheads' doesn't arise. After all, Hitler has done already something that mountebank Papen alone could never have done: he has scourged the moneychangers and time-serving politicians out of our Augean Stables. And now that he's ridded himself as well of all Leftist and otherwise unreliable elements inside his Movement, then everything wholesome and sound in the land will be proud to rally behind your derided 'figurehead'!"

Walther was losing his temper: "You really expect any man of breeding . . .".

But now Father Petrus had got to go: he had Parish duties. . . .

*

So Father Petrus tucked up his cassock and chugged away on his little two-stroke.

He had to visit the Forester's house (where the Forester's

aged mother was said to be *in extremis*), so left by the dusty Kammstadt road and presently entered the forest. The sun was already high in the sky, the smell of pines and the forest shade a refreshing change; and so was the forest silence, for Father Petrus had had about all he could take of von Kessen politics.

So far, he seemed to have managed to hold his tongue. But the Church had her own (and a pretty efficient) grapevine: the Priester knew a lot more than anyone up at the Schloss about what had been going on. As yet the Nazis had only admitted a few dozen deaths, but he knew it must run into hundreds; and not by any means all of them S.A. thugs, nor even Men of the Left. There was Erich Klausener killed, the leader of Catholic Action; and Adalbert Probst, the Leader of Catholic Youth; and also that other prominent Catholic Herbert von Bose, who some said had written von Papen's Marburg speech. Adding these three gratuitous deaths to von Papen's abject humiliation, things hardly boded well for the Church.

Others said Protestant Edgar Jung had written the speech —and they'd killed Jung too! And von Kahr, that harmless old has-been: someone had telephoned only this morning to say he'd been dragged from his bed in his nightshirt and taken to Dachau, where no one knew what had become of him. Poor harmless Willi Schmidt had been playing his 'cello last night to keep the children quiet till supper was ready, when he too was dragged away—Heaven alone knows why. . . . And all on the Führer's orders! So this was the kind of Patriot 'everything wholesome and sound in the land' should be proud to rally behind!

And yet (Father Petrus thought, as he turned down the ride which led to the Forester's house) these Kessens were fundamentally decent people; and somehow, that made it worse. . . . Not that he or anyone else could suppose this a massacre only of innocents: prayers for those on whom lay the heaviest guilt must expressly include the dead. Heines and Ernst and their kind were bloodstained rascals. . . .

That made him think of Chicago, where once he had worked in a German Catholic Mission: a city where rival gangsters murdered each other with nobody minding much unless there were innocent bystanders shot by accident. Civilised Germany wasn't Chicago, however; and ours no common outlaws—no mere O'Bannions, Torrios, Gennas or Druccis! Killers and killed alike had been men deemed worthy of holding the highest offices in the State; and *this* Al Capone was Germany's Federal Chancellor, sitting in Bismarck's seat!

Order, disorder. . . . Here in the twilit forest all was meticulous order: pine-needles clean as a drawing-room carpet, straight lines of tree trunks at regular intervals stretching for miles. . . . He hardly dared glance to the side as he rode, or he might fall off: for the twinkling changes of geometrical vista exerted mesmeric effects on the passing eye.

Then he reached the deer-fence surrounding the forest nursery, looming ramparts of metal and wire like that awful Dachau camp. Inside it, delicate tree-children stood to attention in rows as stiff as their forest elders: no one a hand's-breadth taller than anyone else in his row, and no one a hair's-breadth out of line. There were tree-babies too, in long rectangular seed-beds capped with gleaming aseptic pebbles: seedling conifers only an inch or two high, and not ready yet for their first transplanting. . . . But now the Forester's distant watchdog had heard the sound of his sputtering engine's approach and had started to wake the echoes, till every tree trunk around him barked like a separate dog with the same identical voice.

The Forester's little daughter was freckled, and loved Father Petrus dearly. Almost before he had stopped his engine the child had climbed on his handlebars, tenderly wiping the sweat from his face with her tiny wisp of a handkerchief, trying to rub off his worried frown: for Father Petrus need worry no longer, she told him, since Granny was better.

Indeed when he climbed to the frowsty room where she should have been dying he found the old lady throned fully-dressed in a high-back chair, with a glass of schnapps in her hand.

*

After this wholly abortive Appointment with Death, Father Petrus set off for home. The schnapps he'd been plied with sang in his head, and his tiny two-stroke kept up a merry *chug-chug*: his stomach began to think about lunch. So he rode along slowly, keeping a careful look-out for Pinewood Boletus—a summer fungus to which he was equally partial roasted with onions, or flavoured with fragments of ham and broiled in olive-oil seasoned with herbs, or frittered—or even with sugar and lemon-juice, ending the meal. . . .

But then he was brought up short by the sight of an ancient Adler, parked off the high road right at the forest's edge. He knew it at once for Colonel von Kessen's car; and why was it standing there empty? The Colonel might have gone mushrooming too: yet he couldn't be far off—not with that leg! Then he saw new wheel-marks churned in the dust which that Adler had never made—marks which looked more like a truck; and at once he forgot about lunch.

With a sinking heart he caught sight of a boot sticking out of a straggly bush too small to conceal a body. He left his machine and touched it; and found himself holding a loose artificial leg. There was blood, and the straps had been cut. On that he began to search in earnest; and found the body at last in a clump of bilberries, battered and half-undressed —stained with bilberry juice and sprinkled with pine-needles.

That's why he'd heard no shot: Otto's own leg had been used to beat him to death.

Chapter 33

A DAY or two later von Kahr's body was found in a swamp near the Dachau Camp, apparently pick-axed to death. Father Stempfle was found in a wood, with a broken neck as well as shot through the heart. On the other hand, Frau Willi Schmidt—the widow of Munich's most eminent music critic—was sent not only her husband's coffin but with it a handsome apology for the mistake, and even a modest present of money. She wanted to send back the money; but Himmler himself came on the phone and 'advised' her to take it with no more fuss.

In short, Father Petrus had much on his mind the day when he came to Carmel to break the news of Colonel von Kessen's death to Colonel von Kessen's niece.

The Prioress sent for Sister Mary of Bartimaeus, then had the Father sit at the Parlour grille and unburden himself of all he knew from beginning to end. Mitzi was deeply moved, and the tears trickled down her face. The Prioress watched her in silence, then took her hand and promised a Mass for the rest of her uncle's soul. But the blind nun shook her head: "You mustn't misunderstand me, Mother: I'm only crying because of my ignorance. No one had told me such wickedness could exist."

"Man cannot live without God...." The Prioress hesitated a moment, and then went on: "But even the heathen know that. Surely the Good News Jesus of Nazareth brought was rather that God cannot do without Man, not even the men who would drive the nails. Himmler and Himmler's men are also His children." She paused again; and then added, the ghost of a smile in her voice: "Though as to His purposes for them—as for ourselves, we can know no more about that than a tea-cup knows about tea."

*

But once Great Silence began not even Mitzi's long de-
tachment from home could save her from feeling bereaved.
She seemed to be living in two different places at once, two
different times. So many years had passed since she'd heard
it, and yet Uncle Otto's voice sounded just as fresh in her
ears tonight as that desolate morning his leg creaked into
her room and he'd sat with her reading from Thomas-à-
Kempis aloud:

> Shut your door, and call to you Jesus your beloved:
> Stay with Him in your cell.

'Yes,' she had grumbled inside herself at the time: 'But
suppose you call Him and Jesus won't come?' For this had
been over ten years ago: she'd been little more than a
child—and a juggins at that, in her fond belief she already
knew God like the back of her hand.

Midnight.
Alone again in her cell, and this time in bed, she heard the
distant hoot of an owl. The midsummer midnight air came
through her open window and brought with it many a
peaceable midnight sound, cooling her cell with all those
particular garden scents one only can smell at night. Breathing this heavenly air from outside it was hard to believe there
could be such evil abroad in the land. She thought of St.
Peter's words:

> Brethren, be sober, be watchful: your adversary the devil
> as a roaring lion walketh about, seeking whom he may
> devour: whom withstand, steadfast in your faith.

She was moved by a strong presentiment worse was to come;
that these last few days were just the beginning of wickedness.
That presentiment turned her thoughts towards Franz,
and their hopes of a shining country reborn from the chaos
after the War. What would Franz? . . . But then she recalled
her brother was now a staid married man of thirty or more.
He had long ceased writing her letters. No doubt he was
changed.

But then another presentiment filled her mind, that a time would come when she had to meet and withstand that roaring lion herself. For Carmel was 'in' the world where he walked about seeking to tear such children of God as Himmler limb from limb: that much she knew, though admitting it still was something she didn't quite understand and glad to recall her Reverend Mother's words about tea-cups having no need to understand tea.

She tried to compose herself for sleep. But the chimes of the distant Minister clock had prefaced the sonorous single stroke of One and still she was lying awake, oppressed by the thought of Satan loose in the country she'd grown up to love. She was wakeful still, with the same presentiment strong within her and praying for steadfastness in her faith whenever her time of testing should come and however it came, when she grew aware of an overwhelming advent of God; and a God this time so stark she could barely endure His Company.

Carmel had neither a rag nor remnant of solitude left to pull over her, not in *this* immanent presence of God! The wall beside her was stone: when she thrust Him away with her hand He wouldn't be thrust. When she pulled the blanket over her head it was Him she pulled up and hid under—and shut Him in with her. Naked to God no apron could hide her: each word of her mouth, each thought of her mind, each lifting of a finger—God knew its meaning even if she didn't. God was an Eye; and the Eye never slept and the Eye was inside her. God was an Ear which never slept, and the Ear was inside; and the Eye never blinked nor the Ear mis-heard.

No man can see his own soul clearly and live: he must hood his eyes which look inwards as if against a dazzling by light when the light is too much—though this is a dazzling by darkness, his soul is too dark to bear looking at. Yet God can look: as the eagle can stare at the brightness of the sun, so God stared at even the blackness within without blinking;

and under the burning eye of that burning relentless Love she was molten metal that heaved in a crucible under its scum—this girl Augustine had thought must prove so easy to teach his simple, unshakable, childlike faith that God doesn't exist.

HISTORICAL NOTE

"The Historical characters and events are as accurately historical as I can make them. . . . In no case have I falsified the record once I could worry it out."

This undertaking prefaced *The Fox in the Attic*, and I am reasonably confident that my narrative there of Hitler's 1923 Munich Putsch was accurate at every point. But the Nazis destroyed all official records bearing on the Blood-Purge of 1934: thus surviving contemporary sources tend to be the work of known liars on both sides, so that disproof of one version cannot be taken as establishing any other. This reduces 'belief' at certain points in the narrative of the Night of the Long Knives to a matter of choice.

Hanfstängl credits Röhm's doctor with an eye-witness account of Röhm's last night before his arrest. The knowledgeable will notice that I treat this account as authentic, and likewise von Salomon's description of Ludin's arrest and release. He will also see that I tend to credit Otto Strasser's story of Banquo's Ghost on the stairs, a story historians tend to ignore with the rest of Strasser's hearsay about the Purge—but after all Strasser names his 'Banquo' as Ernst Udet, who lived till 1941 and could therefore easily have given Strasser the lie; and the story seems to me strange enough to be true. It fits.

R. H.

THE HUMAN PREDICAMENT

Twelve chapters from the unfinished final volume

Chapter 1

Coventry in the Year 1934: Number 17 Court off Godsell Street, better known as Slaughterhouse Yard. . . . Pitch-darkness, warm and smelling of jam-packed sleeping bodies: the only glimmer a small square of window, a dim blob wavering vaguely outside it and clumsily bumping against the glass. . . .

The two "boys" (now in their twenties) stir at the sound of the knocker-up's long unwieldy wand but lapse back again into slumber, having no jobs to get up for. Only a single candle-end bursts into light, turning the flimsy curtains screening one bed into a giant Chinese lantern; and that is their sister's—Norah's.

Dad is still snoring; but Mum has long lain awake, and now raises herself on an elbow to watch the gigantic leaping shadows thrown by the girl inside there dressing herself in bed: for this is the very last time, now even Norah has got herself the sack.

Six years ago, turned fourteen, Norah's school sewing-prize had won her a Mender's job at the Mill; and what mother wouldn't rejoice at her girl being picked for a Mender instead of just one of those foul-mouthed Weavers, yelling their voices hoarse against that awful racket of looms? For Menders (with microscopic if not downright myopic eyes, and sensitive fingers) tend to the toffee-nosed sort mums prefer as their daughters' companions, respecting themselves and others. And look at the place where they work, a sort of quiet greenhouse right up in the roof of the Mill! Rats teem in the filth of the weaving-sheds, but would never venture up here where everything's clean and the Menders' lights are so bright. . . .

A spanking job; and the girl could have stopped in it all

her life if only she needn't go throwing her weight about!
Mum sighed. This former boss-kid of Slaughterhouse
Yard, used to running everyone's lives before she even left
school. . . . Granted, her passion for seeing that weaker-
minded girls than herself didn't get put-upon was the best
thing about Our Norah—but now it seemed to have turned
out the worst thing too, for what Foremistress twice her age
would for ever stand being bossed about? It was only
because her work was so good that the Manager let her
finish the week. . . . She'd had plenty of warnings—and
now, this actual sacking: a black mark against her name, as
well as six years of skill and experience gone down the drain
(and with them, thirty to forty shillings a week).

Mum had been chewing this bitter cud half the night; but
Norah herself was almost dressed before coming awake
enough to remember that this was her very last day at the
Mill: the end of a long drawn out coming-to-womanhood
spent just day-dreaming over a Mending Desk. The end,
too, of all the friendships made in the course of those six
lotus-eating years: she would miss the girls badly, not only
the cash.

Perhaps if the work itself had made any calls on her
brains Norah might have kept out of trouble. But hands
and eyes had soon learned to do the job on their own; hands
had whisked the fluff off material reaching them rough from
the loom, then felt for burls too tiny to see which they
marked with chalk and afterwards teased out those minute
knots with delicate tweezers, spotting threads in the pat-
tern machine-looms had missed, had guided her needle
replacing them, even down the whole length of some close-
woven roll of showerproof gaberdine. *This* could hardly
suffice to keep a girl's brains out of mischief: not even such
simple mischief as hiding mice in the Foremistresses'
boots. . . .

But now Norah must hurry: already two pairs of high
heels (Jean's and Rita's: she knew every footstep in

Slaughterhouse Yard) had clattered past below on the cobbles; and least of all on her Last Day must she be late!

She blew out her candles and bolted downstairs; and at first the diurnal routine took over almost as though there were nothing so special about today. But hurrying helter-skelter up Godsell Street something suddenly rose in her gorge like a cold lump of sick: the thought of that empty *tomorrow*.

"Book oop, me gel," Norah scolded herself out loud: "Tain't End o' the Weld!"

All the same, even if this was not the End of the World new jobs wouldn't fall in her mouth: she must put on her thinking-cap. . . . What was it that someone had said to her two or three weeks ago, about some rich cripple who wished to learn tapestry-work (that amateur hand-loom stuff which the clumsiest Mender could do with her eyes shut)? That must have been Young Syl's mum, who had a sister working for nobs in a big house somewhere down south. . . .

At the time Norah hadn't thought twice about it—who would? But now—well, now she had better find out.

It would mean leaving home, of course; and surely the whole wide world held no nest so snug as her natal Slaughterhouse Yard (with its mice and black-beetles and overcrowding, its single communal tap and its single row of latrines all together down the far end). Moreover it meant getting mixed up with the Rich, an alien breed she despised. All the same, a sacking against her name left her little hope of a Coventry job (and there wasn't another Coventry mill, come to that). But need her banishment be for ever? Surely her lady would soon tire of tapestry work or die; and boasting this teaching experience, might she not then come back and aspire to a Coventry Art School post?

She was still turning over the pros and cons when she got to the Mill. There those . . . those silly young coots had all clubbed together to buy her a bottle of scent as a farewell gift.

Syl's Mum (that superior widow who went out to teach rich shopkeepers' kids by the hour, and only the oldest Yardsters dared to call Nellie) had both the rooms now, facing the sheds where the beasts were killed, where once the "Balloon-woman" used to live in the downstairs one till her dropsy carried her off. Nellie kept the house spotless. Eleven-year-old Sylvanus was only allowed inside in his stockinged feet; and the bicycle Nellie used for visiting pupils on was wiped every time, and lived on its special washable mat.

Norah looked in that night, while the pale bespectacled boy was doing his homework and Nellie was washing up tea; but the latter couldn't say if the post would be vacant still, she would have to write to her sister and ask. So Norah gave her three-ha'pence to pay for the stamp.

*

By Tuesday the answer had come: it was Yes, and that Norah was wanted at once on trial.

The place was in far-away Dorset, which set Norah worrying how to raise cash for the fare. But Syl's Mum said not to worry: her sister wrote they'd be fetching her there by car, so could she be ready ten-o'clock Thursday morning round at the King's Head hotel?

That was better perhaps than some snooty chauffeur poking his nose in her Yard: all the same it confirmed her worst fears about Nobs. The King's Head on Broadgate was Coventry's grandest hotel; and if that was where even their chauffeurs were sent to kip for the night, how was her sort of girl to stomach the like-on-the-Pictures extravagant kind of life that such swank-pots lead? Sooner or later for certain she'd blow her top and end up out on her ear. But Nellie (the Mellton Housekeeper's sister) was able to re-assure her that life at Mellton wasn't a bit like those flash millionaires on the Pictures. . . .

"It isn't all squandering and carousing?"

"No. And poor Mrs Wadamy's ever so nice: you won't be able to help yourself liking her."

Chapter 2

There was no time for Mum to cut her out something
new to make up, so Norah simply pressed her one
decent frock and gave her hair a good curl—reminding
herself that she wasn't the sort to go scaredy-cat over
anyone, not even chauffeurs who stopped at King's Head
Hotels. Then, the night before, they all went round to the
Fish-and-Chips shop for a farewell feast.

That King's Head Hotel "on Broadgate" was not
strictly-speaking on Broadgate at all: it had three ways in,
but none was on Broadgate. The first, the original entrance, was right round the corner on Smithford Street.
There in centuries past you rode in under a gated arch, and
found yourself in the typical narrow central yard of the
modest provincial inn which this used to be. But the cutting
of Hertford Street as a way to the railway-station had made
this a corner site, creating a new façade for a new front
entrance; and new upper storeys, which did indeed have a
view up Broadgate.

As for the old inn yard, they had roofed it over with glass
like a shopping-arcade: one almost expected pile carpets
and potted palms. . . .

The third way in was down a modest cul-de-sac, mostly
frequented by dogs in search of a quiet lamp-post. It turned
off beside the Empire (the Picture Theatre where Norah
had learned all she knew of the ways of the rich); and it led
to the hotel garage direct. It would never have entered
Norah's head to storm the hotel itself and enquire at the
desk: so on Thursday morning this was the way she took
(giving the Empire's familiar gallery-entrance a loving
farewell pat as she passed).

But arrived at the garage like this, she somehow had to
divine which car. Most likely a Rolls, she thought. There

were four; and she wished she understood number-plate codes to discover if one of them came from Dorset. Or was it that Daimler? The rest were names which hardly suggested their owners were genuine slap-up gentry, unless. . . . But of course, what a goose she was! These Wadamy moneybags surely would own a whole fleet of cars and never send one of the grand ones meant for themselves. . . .

So which was the Wadamy chauffeur? That looked an easier question to solve since only two were in sight. One of them (all spit-and-polish, dressed in brown and green livery) stood by the doorway smoking a last cigarette. With his short but carefully-waved grey hair and his rice-powdered jowl he looked like a matinée idol going to seed. She hoped it wouldn't be him; but still, "Mister," she asked: "You frum th'Wadamys?"

"No, Young Woman!" he boomed in the voice of a pantomime Earl: "We are Sir Frederic Thomas, if you wish to know." And he turned on his heel.

"Keep y'r 'air on, old cock!" she muttered. "Moost be tootherun."

This was a rather pimply young man with his chauffeur's tunic off: in shirt-sleeves, orange braces, dark blue breeches and long rubber boots he was hosing some foreign car in the yard outside. But it wasn't him either: "Wadamy, Sweet'eart? No, never 'eard on 'em"—adding under his breath: "Sodomy'? Coo what a monniker!" Then he laid down his hose and advanced towards her with all sorts of cheeky remarks on the tip of his tongue. But the steely look in her eye was enough; crestfallen, he started to whistle a popular tune instead and shambled back to his work.

By now it was past ten-o'clock, and Norah was starting to panic. . . .

The only other person in sight was an unimpressive figure in grey flannel bags and an old tweed jacket with leather patches: a weather-worn man in his thirties, leaning against a large old-fashioned open two-seater and wholly absorbed in a map. Still, he might at least know where she

ought to enquire: so she walked across. But even when she
was standing right over the man he never looked up from
his map.

"Hi," she said, "You! Wakey-wakey!"

He jumped. "O-oh. . . . Are you the young lady I've come
here to meet? Forgive me: I'd told the girl in the office to let
me know.—Coffee before we start?"

Dumbfounded, to answer both questions at once she
nodded first and afterwards shook her head.

Just then a hotel porter arrived with a large leather case
which he strapped to the luggage-rack at the back. Whereupon the Mystery Man said "Allow me," took Norah's
small cardboard case from her hands (it was glaringly tied
up with string where a catch had burst) and carefully
stowed it away in the dicky.

"Now: are you sure you've got all you want? If so we'd
better be moving."

He handed her into the passenger-seat, tucked her well
up in a Shetland rug, cranked the engine—and Lo! Before
she had fully recovered her wits they were off, with a roar,
amplified in that cavernous place, which recalled the
cathedral organ.

Chapter 3

The car might be ancient but ate up the miles: the scruffy driver looked scarcely a regular chauffeur but certainly knew how to drive! They had shot through Warwick before he remarked: "Did Nellie tell you how my sister got crippled?"

(His *sister?* Crikey. . . .) "No, Sir."

"A toss out hunting, ten years ago. She broke her neck."

"But—that kills yer!" Norah blurted out in surprise.

"They saved her life. But it left her paralysed."

"Cruelty, not to let her die!" thought Norah —They would, one of us. . . . "How she pass the time?"

"She still has the use of her hands: which is where you come in."

Norah thought for a moment. "Kids?"

"The eldest is just sixteen. She's abroad in school—But frankly," (he spoke with a note of deep concern in his voice) "Polly's more a source of worry now than a help."

"Boys, is it?"

"*Eh?*" He seemed rather taken aback: "No. It's her craze for Hitler." (Hitler? Surely that name rang some sort of bell—but never mind now. . . .) "She's twice done a bunk from school in Geneva simply to hear him speak."

Without losing speed he swerved to avoid a wandering horse and cart with the carter asleep, throwing Norah from side to side in her ample seat. When that was over,

"G'roother kids?" she asked.

"Two. A girl of ten and a boy nearly eight who is backward a bit: slight brain-damage when he was born, though not too bad—mental age, six." He drove at a dizzying speed, but Norah was more elated than frightened. 'Most of the day she reads; but it tires her eyes. Or listens to Wireless Talks; but they're often boring. She

398

doesn't care much about music—like me: so gramophones aren't any use. Hence my idea that she ought to learn something new she could do with those hands of hers. It was Mrs Winter suggested tapestry-work, and offered to ask her sister to find us a teacher: it *had* to be somebody young who wouldn't get on my sister's nerves, as one of those usual middle-aged Homespun Emmas would. Mary isn't a fool; and she finds that jabbering hospital-nurse we have to keep in the house quite trial enough!' He gave Norah a sideways appraising glance: "I can't tell you how grateful we are to you, saying you'd have a go."

"Think I'll do?"

"Nellie's certain you will. She told me so only last night."

Norah stiffened: "*Last night?*"

"Why yes: I came round, hoping to find you and meet your mother. No one was in, so I went to see Nellie instead."

Cheeky blighter, poking his nose in her Yard on the sly while they were all round at the Fish-and-Chips! "Well, what did you. . . ." Norah corrected herself: "What did she tell you?"

"Plenty—from when you were still just a kid but ran the whole place and had all of them eating out of your hand. But it all boils down to she thinks you're a girl in a thousand. You're bound to be very much missed. And" (he was wondering how best to put it) "you're bound to miss them very much—the whole box-of-tricks, I'm afraid." He glanced at her quickly again: "Frankly, I wonder what makes you willing to leave."

"So do I wonder!" thought Norah, pondering what lay ahead in that outside world which she knew so little about.

An awkward silence set in. She was prickly still about what he must think of her home, whereas he—though of course he had noticed the sudden abrasive note in her voice but couldn't guess why, having seen too much of how out-of-work Welsh miners lived to find anything odd in any Coventry yard—had let his mind wander off onto other things. What a curious city this Coventry was, he mused. In spite of its noble cathedral, that fairy-tale medieval centre was not a bit like the centre of other cathedral cities, but mostly the derelict relics of ancient trades (and medieval "yards", like the one where this young woman lived): then in contrast, those miles of enormous up-to-date factories hemming it in! A continuous manufacturing town ever since the Middle Ages, and still one today. . . . Moreover the worst of the slump must be over, he thought: shift-working was starting again, to judge by the distant roar of machines all night and the glow in the sky. . . .

But soon the awkwardness seemed to fade of itself, and they found themselves simply enjoying together the autumn sun: the rush of the wind, and the way that these High Cotswold roads allowed his old Bentley—built to his order while still at Oxford—to show its paces.

In forty-three minutes they'd covered the forty-five miles from Warwick to Cirencester ("We won't go through beastly Swindon: I made that mistake coming up"); and stopped for an early corned-beef and pickles lunch at a pub on the Warminster-Shaftesbury road.

The nearer they got to Mellton, however, the less call there seemed for speed. He wanted "to show her the country", and presently turned up a sunken lane (incredibly steep, with the Bentley just fitting between its banks) to somewhere on top of the downs which he called "the chase". It was wonderful, seen through the single turreted gate in its miles of lofty wall: there were streaks of red and yellow already in wilder woods than Norah had ever seen. "What picnics!" Norah thought, even though the deer he'd promised her failed to appear.

Then headlong down to the flint-built village of Mellton. There he stopped the car by the church: "Let's leave the car here, and walk—no, don't bother about your case, Young Trivett will drive it round." He paused, and grimaced: "Thank heaven that after his second stroke Old Trivett retired at last, and passed the job on to his son!"

Crossing the park together on foot she found herself almost forgetting how unlike he was to anyone else she knew; and that in spite of his B.B.C. accent, and some of the words he used which made you keep on your toes all the time to make out what he meant. Then they passed through a gate, and entered a twilit tunnel of ancient yews. Here two children suddenly dropped from a branch overhead, shrieking and jumping all over the man like puppies. "*They* seem ter like 'im," she thought as the pair of them clambered up, one on his shoulders and one on his back.

"Susan and Gillie," he told her: "And there goes my sister!"

Norah gasped with surprise as something crossed a distant lawn at speed with the pop-pop-pop of a two-stroke engine, then vanished behind some trees: for surely cripples were kept indoors wrapped up in rugs, not left running wild in the garden like jumping-crackers on Guy Fawkes night!

"She didn't see us; but never mind, you'll meet her tomorrow."

Decanting the children he led her into the house and down lots of passages: "Now let's find Mrs Winter."

At last they found that majestic person—a monument in black silk. He attempted an introduction: "Ah Mrs Winter, this is Miss. . . . Gosh, do you know I'm afraid I've forgotten your name?"

"How like a man!" said the queenly presence, already lit up by a welcoming smile: "Anyway—here you are my dear, safe and sound! We all thought he might have killed you, driving the pace he does." She took Norah's arm in a motherly way: "Well, come to my room for a nice cup of tea: you'll be glad of it after your journey. And tell me all the news," she went on, leading Norah away: "How's my Nellie? And dear little Syl?"

Chapter 4

Next morning when Norah woke to a tap-tap-tap on her window she couldn't believe at first she was really in bed at all: for the sun shone straight in her eyes! No window she'd known in the past looked out on anything better than somebody's wall; you had to go right outside for even a glimpse of the sky.

Yet indoors and even in bed she most certainly was, as she found when she wriggled her toes; and this tapping against the glass was not that old knocker-up any more but just an inquisitive bird. From her bed she could see the gardens, just waking up too; and the misty trees of the park. Beyond that again rose the high bald downs, with hanging woods on their sides. . . .

Norah heaved a luxurious sigh, surprised at beginning to feel that in time she might even come to *like* living somewhere like this. "Seein' the sky through yer winder's what done it," the slum-child decided.

Then, after breakfast with Mrs Winter and somebody called Mr Wantage who seemed to know Coventry well (he'd been born just outside at Binlay, he said), she had to be taken to see the loom. This was the queerest contraption, designed for not using your feet, and had had to be specially made. As she studied its workings, "You won't find teaching the Mistress too easy, you know," Mrs Winter warned her: "She's got back the use of her hands, fair enough—and they're strong as a blacksmith's, but clumsier than she thinks."

Norah mused for a moment. "What she *can't* do, how she take bein' 'elped?"

"Ah, that needs a bit of doing. . . . "

Upstairs in her room, she made her bed under Mrs Winter's watchful (but tactful) eye. While talking of something else Mrs Winter still managed to teach her the front from the back and the head from the tail of a sheet, and how to fold in "hospital corners". Norah took it all in good-as-gold because Mrs Winter was kind and because there was manifest sense in it—*if* you'd got time. It was just as they finished the bed that they heard a high-pitched hysterical hubbub which rose from the garden below; and Norah crossed to the window to look.

The morning was bright for the time of year but colder: hoar-frost lay on a lawn where two Red Indians—fully tricked out with small bows-and-arrows and feathered head-dresses—chased an unfortunate Paleface she recognised as yesterday's driver; that "Mr Augustine" (everyone here called him this, and she couldn't remember the rest of his name). They pursued with blood-curdling yells as he leapt over bushes and flower-beds, vainly crying for mercy. Then one of them shot an arrow: it went pretty wide, but the archer shouted "You're dead!"—and at once the obedient Paleface died, falling flat on his face on the frosty grass.

The whooping Red Indians fell on him, savagely tugging his hair and almost tearing it out as they fought for his scalp. "Mother of God!" murmured Norah, vaguely shocked at the violent scene although she didn't exactly know why.

Mrs Winter forbore to refer to the children as "highly strung" (which is what their governess would have). All she said was: "That's how our Mr Augustine is."

This "Mr Augustine": an uncle only, yet somehow he seemed like the only man in the family, Norah thought: not once had anyone mentioned the children's Dad. "This *Mrs* Wadamy: is there a *Mr*?" she asked on the way downstairs.

"Yes."

That was that! Norah thought she sensed a warning it wasn't her place to ask too many questions. But presently Mrs Winter went on: "The Master can't get home very often these days, not since the time of the General Strike when he went back to Parliament. Now, he's a Minister."

Mary herself had made of the General Strike a crisis-excuse to insist on Gilbert's return to the Parliamentary stage, rather than letting his life be wasted dancing attendance on someone as good as dead. There he had soldiered on in the Liberal ranks till Labour's disastrous second tenure of office had led to the stirring events of 1931: to Financial Crisis, an all-party National Government formed, new elections called.

In those crucial days, with the Liberal Party split wide-open again (and this time, for good), he had simply followed his conscience. Gilbert had long distrusted Lloyd George (who was it said Lloyd George had been "born with a silver tongue in his cheek"?); and Herbert Samuel only "led" under L.G.'s orders, while L.G. was ill. Moreover Gilbert suspected dear Herbert himself of failing to understand that the country's paramount need today was for National Unity, not any outworn King Charles's Head (or in other words, that Samuel's stubbornness over Free Trade must soon force him out of the "National" Cabinet). Clearly then Conscience called him to throw in his lot with his old friend Simon among the faction leaders, and fight that autumn election of 1931 on the Simonite "Liberal-National" ticket. . . .

This meant that the Tory opponent to whom he'd so nearly lost his seat in the Liberal shambles of 1924 had been forced to stand down; and not only had Gilbert romped home on the "National" landslide but found himself given (at last, after all these frustrating back-bencher years) a small ministerial post.

*

Norah was not someone easily scared; but this Friday morning when first she saw Mrs Wadamy close she was scared like you feel when you walk in a graveyard at night.

That corpse-like body, on top of which was a head never moving except for the lips and eyes; and too like a head popping up at you out of a grave for comfort—like somebody starting to resurrect but got stuck. . . . It shows how badly she wanted to look away that she glued her eyes to Mrs Wadamy's face and stared.

Mary guessed that this rudely staring girl was in fact ill-at-ease and why. Had it been anyone else she'd have inwardly laid back her ears, for she hated reminders that her way of life was not quite the normal one; but now resentment was drowned in pity: "How lost the poor creature must feel, plonked down in somewhere so strange and faced with an apparition like me!"

"I hope you'll be happy here," said the apparition.

"Yes Ma'am. . . . And the same to you!" Norah burbled on, too addled to know what to say (and it's hard to know what you *can* say when talking to only a face). But Mrs Wadamy stretched out her hand, and took hold of hers in what felt like a friendly prize-fighter's grip.

"Parliament 'usband's a right pig!" thought Norah, "Leaving 'er all on 'er own like this!"

Chapter 5

E ven when Parliament goes in recess the Whitehall
Departments don't. Moreover when Cabinet Minis-
ters leave their desks (summoned to Chequers or Number
Ten, or to shoot with a Duke, or merely to sort things out
with difficult wives or go on the razzle), this doubles a
Junior Minister's work; for you can't let your Civil Servants
go taking decisions which ought to be left to their
Masters—or not if you're conscientious, like Gilbert.

Twice he'd been moved, and though neither move really
carried promotion one day promotion *must* come: one day
he would indeed walk in the Corridors of Power, like Simon
himself (whose thirty-five Liberal-National followers' seats
had earned him the Foreign Office). A dog's life, meanwhile? —Perhaps; but a heady, responsible one. Even now
he chaired committees where everyone called him "Minister", found himself rising to speak in the House armed with
a departmental brief instead of spouting whale-like out of
his head; and it's strange what a sense of power it gives you
when somebody else has composed the words you speak
and written the Minutes you sign. Gilbert was now forty-
one, but felt at least ten years younger: Office had done for
him all the advertisements tell you their Pep Pills will do
(but don't).

Most of his women friends these days were political
wives or Society hostesses. None of his London acquain-
tances however had half the beauty and charm of long-ago
Joan, that young half-sister of Archdeacon Dibden who'd
been such a friend to them both when Mary was first
brought home. He hadn't seen her for years; and the news
of Joan's unexpected return to Dorset brought Gilbert
hurrying back to Mellton the first time in months. He
travelled that same Friday night: for he'd heard she was

only in England for two or three days, collecting some books which her brother wanted in France. . . .

Six weeks ago, Archdeacon Dibden (father of Jeremy, one of Augustine's oldest friends) had been getting ready to die. He had passed Man's allotted span. Each Tottersdown Monachorum winter bronchitis had laid him low, and each winter the bouts got worse. This year he had only been properly well at the height of summer; and now already the wheezing and hubble-bubble were starting again in his chest. When the cold weather came he would have to take to his bed, with a pile of folio volumes under the mattress to raise the upper part of his trunk: then must follow the doctor's new-fangled injections of manganese *and* his housekeeper's (old-fangled) steam-kettle filling his room with steam. How he hated the smell of her Friar's Balsam! He hardly could hope to live to enjoy the smells of another Spring; not unless. . . .

Kind Lord Tottersdown (bless him!) had tried to persuade him to go to the South of France, and had offered to foot the bill. A Jew, a man of a different faith with no obligation whatever towards his Cloth: it seemed ungenerous to refuse. But frankly, was it worth while? Whether he died or not, his *useful* life would be over: he'd have to resign as Archdeacon, and even his Cure of Souls.

A bronchitic's death is seldom an easy one: unless his heart suddenly fails he slowly drowns in the fluids flooding his lungs. But if that was God's Will, surely a priest would be better employed preparing to meet his Maker than running away from Death. . . . And imagine his isolation, cooped up in a Pension—say, in some suburb of Nice—if he went there alone! "If only dear Joan had been keeping house for me still—or even had married Jeremy's friend Augustine, as once we hoped!" But no, Joan had married that nice Southern boy and gone to live in the States. . . .

Such had been the state of play those six weeks ago, when a letter had come from Joan in South Carolina heavily edged in black. Anthony Fairfax's foible of building his own automobiles himself by hand had come to a sorry end: the latest one had exploded, killing him dead. The widow was coming home, "for she felt sore need of a brother's comfort. . . ." His poor bereaved Joan! This intimation that God still had a use for him here on Earth tipped the scales: if a warm winter climate would help, the Archdeacon made up his mind not to die after all. . . .

*

This same news of Joan's reappearance which galvanised Gilbert had greatly disturbed Augustine: fond as he'd been of her once, he had hoped he need never see her again. He felt that resentment we all tend to feel towards somebody once very close we suspect we have treated badly, and therefore had hoped to forget. Surely at least she'd have the good sense to steer clear of Mellton while he was there? But Gilbert so took it for granted his wife and everyone else were as anxious as he was to see Joan again that he broached it almost while crossing his doorstep: "Ask her to dinner tomorrow: we can't put it off because the Archdeacon has started abroad already and Joan is to join him almost at once."

Gilbert was greatly astonished to find his wife most unkeen to ask the girl to the house. "Not after the way she treated Augustine," she said; for they both believed it was *she* who had turned *him* down.

"But surely a girl has the right to refuse a man?"

"Not after leading him on the way Joan did."

"But all that was seven or eight years ago: it's Ancient History now. Or do you insist on a blood-feud, with Dibdens and Wadamys shooting each other on sight? What about Jeremy: isn't he still very much your brother's friend instead of them drawing beads on each other?—Not that *I* care of course," he went on, "it's just that asking her seemed the civil thing. . . . And I seem to remember you used to be rather fond of her once, yourself."

Mary sighed. He was so transparent. . . . But jealousy wasn't a trait in herself to encourage—not someone in her condition: she'd better give in. "Very well then, ask her tomorrow night if that's what you want."

Gilbert was tempted to take out a car and deliver the invitation by word of mouth; but that might be going too far, so he wrote a note on Mary's behalf and sent it over by hand. Joan was perfectly well aware of Augustine's presence but saw no reason in this for avoiding Mellton, since this was the very "comfort" the widow had crossed the wide Atlantic to find. So the answer Young Trivett brought back was "Yes".

Augustine might almost have fled to his home in Wales then-and-there, were it not for Norah. Having only just brought her here he ought at least to hang on till he saw how she settled in, and how this tapestry-work experiment shaped. . . . Already there'd been one row in the Servants' Hall over someone so plainly out of the bottom drawer taking her meals in the "Room"—where she had to be waited on, eating with Mrs Winter and Wantage. Mrs Winter was solving this one by finding her village lodgings; but that left her even more to her own resources if he himself wasn't there to see she got a fair deal. She was more-or-less under his wing, and he'd just have to face meeting Joan again this once. . . .

He had his reward when he heard that Jeremy—now taking a rare weekend from Whitehall to visit this aunt only four years older than he was himself—would be coming too. For Augustine loathed going to London, and saw his friend so seldom now that Jeremy worked in the Admiralty.

Chapter 6

When Jeremy joined the Civil Service in 1924, post-war contraction had led to terrible overcrowding upstairs: his first promotion was bound to be slow, a minimum thirteen years—a third of his whole career before setting foot on even the second rung. If he weren't to die of boredom before the reigning upper echelons came to retiring age and the rat-race really began, Jeremy had to opt for whichever Department of State seemed the most entertaining one for a junior marking time to explore.

Here the Admiralty seemed unique. A living organism rather than man-made organisation: an organism moreover (as Jeremy told Augustine once) which resembled such Siphonophores as the jellyfish commonly called a Portuguese Man-of-War, where what appeared to the layman's eye a single creature consisted in fact of independent medusas and polyps clubbing together and each developing into different useful organs (say an inflatable float, or a sting or a stomach or swimming-bell). For this symbiotic conglomerate too was largely composed of departments with independent histories ("Naval Stores" dated back at least to 1514) which had only coalesced in the last hundred years. Some still offered their own complete civilian careers, with no transmigration of even non-technical staff: some were staffed in whole or in part by Naval Officers serving short-time shore appointments. Each had its own Magna Carta, its "Board Instructions"—for here again this jellyfish was unique, in that supreme authority lay with Their Lordship's Board and not with a Minister (vested in it by Royal Prerogative, not by Parliament: Patents of Board Appointment had to be signed by the Monarch himself). In a Constitutional sense this Board was a single "person"—the Lord High

410

Admiral put In Commission: in token of which not even the
First Lord himself might fly the Foul Anchor flag unless
he'd a fellow-commissioner with him. Thus, if a First Lord
ever determined to overrule the others he'd have to do it not
as "First Lord" at all, but wearing his Cabinet hat and so
representing the Crown—as the King overruling his Lord
High Admiral . . .

No one will feel much surprise that this was the place
where Jeremy's lively enquiring mind should elect to serve:
for the Secretary's Department, to which he'd belong, had
a finger in every other department's pie—including links
with the latest accretion of all, the Naval Staff (which didn't
exist until 1911). What may surprise the reader more is
how well on the whole he found this strange polymorphic
conglomerate seemed to work—but so, after all, does the
Portuguese Man-of-War. . . . This jellyfish seemed well
adapted to meet the incredibly diverse fields of work and
skills involved in building, arming, maintaining, recruiting
and fighting the largest navy on Earth. Up above, each
Superintending Lord had his own allotted sphere where he
ruled supreme in the name of the Board as a whole: down
below, each man seemed to know his own particular job
and did it. The Secretariat's Function, apart from financial
control, was chiefly providing articulate lines of communication between that Below and Above as well as links with
the rest of Whitehall.

Jeremy'd been on the job ten eyars before that September Saturday night when Joan and he came to dine at
Mellton. He rather enjoyed the work, on the whole. He had
learned early two important lessons. A Civil Servant must
often choose between getting something done and getting
the credit for it: he can't have both. Again, that officials
don't understand officialese: you can put the most outrageous proposals across the high-ups cocooned in
officialese which would raise the roof if proposed in
plain English. "Joan and Jeremy, Gilbert and me and
Augustine", thought Mary; "that's one girl short. You

can't ask somebody in at a moment's notice, it's much too rude: Miss Penrose must dine, for a sixth." Miss Penrose normally supped in her room, but a governess fits into any old fold—at a pinch.

So Miss Penrose had taken her place at dinner on Gilbert's left: though only her other neighbour (the charming young Mr Jeremy Dibden—how sad about that paralysed arm!) seemed to talk to her much, Mr Wadamy being too taken up with his Guest of Honour.

That Guest of Honour had greatly surprised her old friends by the Southern drawl she'd acquired, till Mary reminded them all how Augustine himself had been teased for his Yankee twang after just a few months—whereas Joan had been there seven years: "After all that time you've a right to your South Carolina accent." Gilbert warmly assented: he found it delightful.

"Honey, you-all's bein' jest too dandy to poor little me!" said Joan in self-parody, raising a general laugh.

Champagne hinted at celebration: yet not even Gilbert had dared make this a white-tie affair. To lend it sartorial sparkle he had to make do with a new-fangled hybrid fashion launched by the Prince of Wales: he was wearing a double-breasted white waistcoat under his dinner-jacket. In contrast, Augustine—as if to ignore the presence of Joan altogether and just en famille in his sister's house—was revolting against starched linen and wearing a soft silk shirt with his dinner-jacket and black bow-tie. Only Jeremy's evening clothes were strictly correct, and as soon as the men were left to their port he took up cudgels: no wonder Hitler thought England had gone to the dogs when gentlemen showed no respect for the Laws which their Fathers had graven forever on granite! Augustine's sloppy soft shirt was as sorry a sign in its way as the Oxford Union's refusal to fight for King and Country. He even criticised Gilbert's waistcoat. . . . Oh yes, he knew it had Royal Assent; but so gross a misuse of Perogative surely raised doubts of the Prince's future fitness to reign . . .

Augustine felt ill-at-ease: Gilbert was born to be teased, and this pair always fought; but Jeremy seemed tensed-up, and personal rudeness like this wasn't up to his usual form.

Not only did Gilbert look pained, he remarked in an acid voice that no Minister of the Crown could allow attacks on the Heir to the Throne at his own dinner-table; now it was Jeremy's turn to look wounded: "As one of the Crown's most loyal, obedient servants. . . . Well, here's to the Prince—God bless him!"

He downed his port at a single gulp, and eyed the decanter; but Gilbert showed no sign of passing it on.

Chapter 7

Augustine felt still more uneasy when Jeremy started
again: "But Gilbert, old cock!" (you could hear the
inverted commas), "You've side-stepped my point. This
Disarmament blah in high places, this Leave-it-all-to-the-
League tommy-rot. . . . You and I may know that the
British Lion is just taking forty winks; but in German eyes it
looks like death and decay. They think us Anglo-Saxons a
moribund branch of the ancient Germanic tree which calls
for the forester's axe. When we do wake up it may be too
late, with the Führer driving in state down a bombed
Whitehall.—Heil Hitler!" He greatly embarrassed them
both by grotesque attempts with the other hand to support
his polio-stricken right arm erect in a Nazi salute: "You're
better fitted to practise this pantomime gesture than me,
old boy—and we'll both of us find ourselves having to learn
it in earnest unless your Cabinet pals do something pretty-
damn-quick!"

"All Germans are cracky," Augustine put in, "But aren't
they disarmed? They're hardly so cracked as to try to
conquer the whole British Empire with just their bare
hands."

Gilbert smiled a superior smile: "Yes, you seem to
envisage a sudden German attack—next week, as it were;
but with what?" He glanced at his watch (he was longing to
join the ladies, but couldn't quite yet): "As a junior Civil
Servant," he went on in cutting tones, "You claim to be
better informed than my 'Cabinet pals' as you call them?"

"They've had the information all right! But it runs off
their backs, because you politicians can only believe what
you feel in your bones that the bulk of electors already
believe—which is what, after all, it pays to believe: that's
what has got them their lovely jobs. Their beliefs are a

414

matter of choice and scarcely ever affected by facts."

"But. . . . "

"Just a moment, please: I haven't dealt with your other point. I said nothing about 'next week'—that's absurd. But in two or three years. . . . "

"You did say, 'pretty damn quick'," interrupted Augustine.

"Because this Year of Grace is our very last chance to hang on to our lead: they're re-arming fast. We suspect that they're secretly laying down battle-cruisers of 26,000 tons, far above the Treaty limits. U-boats they aren't allowed at all; but we know that the frames and the parts are already in storage at Kiel, all they need is assembling. They've tripled their naval personnel. . . . Of course *we* are laying down warships too, but we're hampered at every turn. Most British armour-plate firms closed down in the Twenties, we have to import it from Czechoslovakia! Half our gun-sights and submarine periscopes have to be ordered from *German* optical firms."

"You and your naval friends!" said Gilbert with withering scorn: "All you can think of is ships. Today our foremost line of defence is a modern Air Force, soon to be reinforced with another forty-one squadrons."

"'Soon'? In another five years, with luck! And the Germans are building far faster than us: their Air Force already's two-thirds the size of our own and will equal our own in another few months. In a year from now they'll have fifty-per-cent more machines than ourselves and almost catch up with the French."

"Nonsense! Where did you get those incredible figures?" said Gilbert, startled in spite of himself.

"Never mind where: they're reliable."

"Bosh!" said Gilbert: "They haven't an Air Force at all: only civil planes, and a number of engineless gliders for sport. . . . "

"Or for landing troops!—Now, here's one other thing which I hope may convince you: Hitler has gained great kudos by halving his Unemployed; but how? By sending them all to the Ruhr! Krupp the Armament King is taking on thousands of extra hands, as I found out myself last June. And I.G.Farben, who make synthetic petrol from coal: they've motionless acres of turbulent Danube ice, which a thaw must one day release. . . . "

Yet surely Jeremy couldn't be right—not *another* war! "I must think all this out, and talk to him quite by himself some time."

Then all three of them, civilly smiling, entered a room from which a discreet Miss Penrose had disappeared. A room where a dazzling Southern Belle sat impatiently waiting, alone with a chair-borne mummy.

"He hasn't altered one bit!" thought Joan with a desperate pang in her heart as Augustine walked in.

Chapter 8

Two days later Augustine departed briefly for Wales, leaving Mary and Norah together engrossed with coloured chalks working out weaving designs.

On his way he paid a short call on old friends in the anthracite valleys; and what a relief that Welsh miner's kitchen was after Mellton with Gilbert in it! From there he carried on west through Carmarthen, St Clears and Red Roses by roads increasingly narrow and winding the nearer they got to the Pembrokeshire coast; and finally down a mere muddy track—once the back way, but now the only way in. Then the Bentley rolled under a noble Regency arch, stampeding a score of cross-bred Rhode Island Reds as it came to rest in a vast Piranesi-like stable yard.

The birds flapped over the bonnet, squawking. The ten-year-old feeding them droped his bucket and dashed to an open window hollering "Mam!" then dashed back again to heave with the whole of his ten-year-old strength at the groaning Gothic-cathedral doors of the coach-house—grinning all over his freckled face as he caught the apple Augustine threw. . . .

Augustine was home at last.

The latent anchorite in him still loved this ancient enormous house where a lone and servant-abhorring Augustine could live—as he still supposed he would always prefer to live—more like a single pea in a big bass drum than the wealthy squire which he was.

Ever since his great-uncles died, Newton Llantony had slept an enchanted Mabinogion-sleep. Most of its hundred rooms were shut up, with its gardens climbing unchecked till they darkened the first-floor windows: its drawing-rooms shrouded in dust-sheets, mirrors veiled against lightning, lustres and chandeliers guarded from spiders and dust in brown holland bags. The baize of its billiard table was still scattered with camphor under the covers to keep away moth, although it had not heard the crack of cannoning ivory balls for some twenty or thirty years—not since the uncles had grown too old for such strenuous exercise.

Furniture, family pictures, the knick-knacks of centuries: nothing was consciously changed from the closing days of that previous reign, except that those two old emblems themselves were under the sod instead of enthroned each side of a blazing billiard-room fire. Even that monstrous photokit portrait in oils of Henry, the cousin who should have come into the place but had perished at Ypres instead, still hung where it always had hung: while Augustine's own pictures (his late Van Gogh, his Cézanne and his little Renoir) still hung—as they had hung ever since crossing the Channel—in Mary's boudoir at Mellton Chase.

Blissfully coming back from a day spent shooting snipe on the Marsh to a vast and totally empty house, there to cook for himself on the gunroom stove and climb by night to the small attic room where he'd slept as a visiting child. . . . That's what Augustine liked. But, alas, how closely Dilapidation and Dry-rot tread on the heels of Neglect! Caretakers seem an intrusion which even hermits may have to endure. . . .

It was Wantage who'd thought of Lily—and Jimmy the knife-boy, sacked for getting this little scullery-maid with child. Hence now that invisible "Mam" with her panicky chickens, the helpful small boy and indeed the rest of a fast-growing family tucked away in a distant wing.

*

Next morning Augustine went out "to shoot"—or, at any rate, carried a gun. But whether he did this simply from habit or vaguely meant to excuse him for spending a rainy September day in the open is hard to say. He wasn't on serious shooting bent, for he took no dog; and moreover in oilskins and waterproof Cording's boots he went by way of the upland fields and woods, not down on his wildfowling sea-marsh at all.

The thing is, Augustine had come home expressly to think; but not just now about Jeremy's revelations over the port, those must wait for some other time. His unexpected meeting with Joan had revived the past: it had given this bachelor (now in his thirty-fifth year) plenty to think about, crouched down under a favourite ash-tree in sight of the Bristol Channel and feeling the rain-drops plop on the yielding tweed of his deerstalker hat.

Joan was incredibly beautiful still; and attractive, although of course more—mature. . . .

"As for your Hermit-of-Newton ploy" (this sour voice, of course, was the ingrained Defensive Principle in him), "that woman knows how to get what she wants! She'd have soon had the dust-sheets off and the spare-rooms painted; and even yourself fitted out with a proper Purpose in Life."

Oh yes, the Defensive Principle in him was heartily thankful he'd sheered off in time, those years ago when he'd fled to Tangier, as he squatted here trying to focus his eyes on the distant sea—its far horizon dissolved in rain. Glimpsed through curtains of rain he could see the dull reddish-brown of the sails of a couple of trawlers, probably French: they were using their engines of course, the sails were simply to stop them rolling. . . .

However, this wasn't his only interior voice. That marriage had once been a damn-near thing, and now it was plain that in spite of the passing years Joan still felt the tug. It was equally plain that seeing her only a few times more he could all-too-easily find himself feeling it too. . . .

"Then for God's sake give her as wide a berth as you can!" warned Augustine's Defensive Principle.

Quite, but. . . . That is, provided you're sure that you want to remain a bachelor all your life like your uncles, and end up a childless old fuddy-duddy?

"She didn't give Anthony any children, and then you'd be properly caught!"

Could it be that he wanted a child or two of his own without really wanting a wife at all?

All this mental to-ing and fro-ing had taken a couple of hours. The rain kept on and the wind was rising: it must be blowing up for a gale for the gulls to be flying so far inland, for this wasn't like Spring when they mob the potato-planters for worms. . . .

Very well, then! Agreed, the undoubtedly sensible thing was to steer clear of Dorset till Joan was safely in France. But that too raised problems. She'd seemed so surprisingly vague after all about her departure-date: how would Mary get on without him once Gilbert was back in town, if Joan hung around for weeks?

Of course, she had Norah now. . . . But stopping away from Mellton meant leaving Norah to cope all alone; and was this entirely fair yet on someone he'd landed in strange surroundings and totally unfamiliar ways—to be robbed of her only interpreter so-to-speak, the only one with an inkling of working-class life? Mrs Winter couldn't take her too openly under her wing, not after that row over Norah's meals in the "Room". Suppose this tapestry-loom idea with Mary flopped, or if anything else went badly wrong? She'd be out on a limb. . . .

Perplexed, he took off his hat to scratch his head: where-upon the tree he was sitting under seized the chance of giving itself a shake and decanting a cupful of rainwater down his neck.

Yes: it was plain that the nub of the problem was Norah. He *had* to go back to Mellton because he must *not* risk letting Norah down.

"A girl in a thousand!" Her gamine appearance and pitiful cardboard case in that hotel garage. Driving beside him across the Cotswolds wrapped in his rug. . . .

Corned-beef and pickles shared in a pub. . . . Then up Goggledown Lane, and her widening eyes when he showed her the Chase. . . .

*

By now, the partridge had left the stubble and all gone early to roost. Augustine rose to his feet: it was futile sitting here in the rain—and certainly doing his gun no good.

"A girl in a thousand," Nellie had called her. But what did she really think about Mellton—and Mary—and him? He sighed. An enigma: the Welsh aren't worried too much about class, but in England what pariahs gentry are! There you can never get properly inside the mind of somebody born lower down in the social scale, you only imagine you can.

"Will you *never* learn to know when you're lucky at last?" the tree he'd been sitting under remarked.

Augustine jumped: when and where in his life had he heard that oracular voice before? He even turned to look back, though he knew it was only a tree.

Chapter 9

Yet in spite of that Talking Tree, Augustine had been back at Mellton for fully a week before he found out that he'd fallen in love with Norah.

Alas! For how could she even consider a man like him? He knew that to Slaughterhouse Yard a gentleman isn't a "boy": he is something not fully human, and certainly not to be thought of in marriage. Something much on a par with what Germans think about Jews or Americans, negroes. A dire taboo, with roots as deep in the past of the English Prole as couch-grass in English gardens. . . .

Augustine was spending the morning alone in the leathery smell of the Mellton library, pulling books out of the shelves and pushing them back unread (often upsidedown), while he told himself that Cophetua Syndromes are find in fairy-stories but every beggar-maid knows them for hell in actual life. Even today, in 1934, there was still this Pyramus-Thisbe wall. Marriage could never turn Norah into a lady, quite, nor Augustine gain acceptance as genuine working-class—as he would most willingly try to do had that been a possible answer, rather than *her* lose caste and be looked at askance by all her Coventry friends.

On the wall hung a steel engraving, the portly Sir Peter Wadamy KCB, Vice-Admiral of the Red. "The lower orders, if comely," said Admiral Wadamy's roguish eye, "are there to be tupped. But however besotted you are let that be the end: as 'My Lady' they're neither flesh, fish nor fowl." From the picture, Augustine's gaze wandered back to the shelves of books. . . . If only he'd stuck to his writing, for poets counted as mules who had opted out of their species already! Like painters and actors, nobody knows where they really belong—whereas he and Norah both knew all too well exactly where they belonged.

If Norah *had* been able to love him then nothing could keep them apart—not hell nor high water! But Norah's falling in love with him simply was not on the cards—like her falling in love with a horse.

His love was hopeless; and therefore something he had to take by the throat and choke before it hurt anyone else. Norah must never guess it because it would shock her so frightfully, killing all dawning liking for Mary as well as himself. But it shouldn't be too hard to hide, as the last thing Norah would ever expect. . . .

Or even pretend he was pining for Joan?—But no, that kind of dissembling belongs in Restoration Comedy not in real life; and with deliberation he dropped Dibdin's *London Theatre* smack on the library floor.

What grimly ironical words that tree had used, "Will you never learn to know when you're lucky?"!

*

"Nellie's right, nobody couldn't help liking her!" So Norah thought, crossing the park from the village that same afternoon. For you can't go on pitying someone who flatly refuses to pity herself; and once she had learned to treat Mrs Wadamy not as a freak or disaster but just like anyone else, Norah had found her top-hole.

But *he* was right too: she hadn't enough to do. In the house, with Mrs Winter and all those servants, the Mistress was more like a guest. Her kids? She loved them O.K., but Miss Penrose gave them their lessons and took them walks, Nanny Halloran saw to their clothes and their meals and put them to bed (her chair couldn't anyhow climb to the second floor): they were daffy about their uncle. Not much room there for a loving Mum! About all she sees of them seems to be. . . . Yes, there they were, climbing a tree with their uncle—and there she was too, watching behind a bush. As always, watching it all from a distance: the ground too rough for her chair to get anywhere near.

As for him, he's barmy about those brats: funny he never got married. . . .

But then a bough broke, depositing Susan and Gillie both on the turf: and Norah broke into a run. As she reached them, "Don't tell Nanny!" she heard him plead: "I'm in trouble enough with her already, as well as you're late for bed."

"We will, though!" wailed a furious Susan: "You know it was all your fault!"

"We will, we will!" echoed Gillie: "You *told* it to break!"

"Little b's!" said Norah, smacking both bottoms left and right.

They were so appalled that they stopped their crying at once, and eyed her. "You dare. . . . " ventured Susan at last, uncertainly.

Norah's eyes flashed. "Want me t'do't again?—Tell y'runcle Sorry."

Susan held out as long as she could: then "Sorry," she muttered almost inaudibly.

Norah turned to Augustine, unconsciously switching her voice to as near as she could "B.B.C.": "That's my Good Deed for the day!" she said to him cheerfully. Then she turned back to the children, all sunshine and holding out both her hands. Like mesmerised rabbits they took them, and started back to the house each side of her still holding hands. This left Augustine to bring up the rear alone, until Norah made room for him in between her and Susan— insisting he held hands too. . . .

"Needs looking after, poor lamb!" thought Norah, firmly gripping a hand gone limp and slippy as if agog to escape: "Even if only to make him wear proper clothes, not look like a tramp. What would Mum have thought, if she'd seen him come in the Yard dressed like that?"

As they neared the bushes where Mrs Wadamy watched, she was noiselessly wheeling her chair out of sight by hand: she didn't wish to be seen, so they all looked the other way.

"Lucky me, landing this job!" was what Norah was thinking now: "If you call it a job when it don't seem one—except getting paid."

She liked to be able to send money home; but how far off Coventry was already, the Yard and the Mending-room at the Mill and all that! She raised her eyes to the bare Dorset downs, and remembered those picnics outside the town where she used to take all the kids. . . . Perhaps at heart she was really a country girl all along?

Meanwhile: "I can hide it from Norah herself all right," thought Augustine: "Mary I'm not so sure about. . . . "

"What do we call you?" asked Susan peaceably.

"Norah."

"Norah. . . . I like that name," said Gillie, and started swinging her arm.

Chapter 10

Two letters on Mary's tray next morning bore Swiss stamps and were postmarked "Genève". She opened first the one from Mme Leblanc: Polly shall travel home as soon as adequate escort can be arranged and shall *not* return next term.

Mary was hardly surprised: poor Mme Leblanc had put up with a lot, but this was the final straw. For Polly's skill as a mimic was famous, and Sylvia Davenant (Janey's aunt) had told her already about some fake Lady Sylvia telephoning the school to ask if Janey and Polly might take a steamer-ride down the lake to spend the weekend at Vevey. It had only been after the two girls failed to return on time—and their passports were missing, and nothing was known at Vevey of them or of Lady Sylvia either—that Mme Leblanc discovered the hoax.

Polly's own letter was long and excited and seventh-heavenly incoherent: it had to be read at least twice to extract any facts at all, piece them together in narrative order and try to imagine the rest. But the long and the short of the matter was this. The truants, indulging their strange obsession with Hitler, had made their way to Munich and then on to Berchtesgaden. There they fell in with a German cousin of Janey's at school nearby. This young Countess Sophie was given to mountain walks, and told them she'd sighted the Führer more than once enjoying a glass of milk outside the Hochlenzer mountain inn (his favourite port-of-call on the Scharitzkehl). But that wasn't all: for this very morning, on one of the forest paths which traversed the Obersalzberg itself, she had suddenly met his cortège face-to-face: the Führer striding ahead with his dog, and a dozen or so dim figures who followed discreetly behind.

Sophie had tried to shrink out of sight but the Führer's Alsation had flushed her, knocking her over and pinning her down till the Führer called it to heel. A gigantic adjutant lifted the tousled schoolgirl onto her feet: the Führer's own hand picked pine-needles out of her yellow hair and then—as further amends for her fright—he told her to go back to school, choose a couple of friends and bring them up to his mountain retreat this afternoon for tea.

The aristocratic Sophie affected to treat the whole affair as a bit of a bore. She was ready enough to agree when Polly insisted—while Janey nearly sank into the ground—that Polly and Janey themselves were the girls she must take. . . .

Mary read on with increasing dismay, and tried to imagine the scene when the same gigantic adjutant came to collect the three girls: drove them for twenty minutes or so up a narrow road all pot-holes and hairpin bends, and finally set them down near a small wooden chalet with wide, overhanging eaves. A typical middle-class weekend cottage, "built" (Sophie said) "by some Hamburg businessmen, Hitler rented it first and afterwards bought it outright." A few yards further along the road, on the opposite side, was an inn—which was lucky, for Haus Wachenfeld itself was too small for even one overnight guest.

Mary had to imagine an Alpine meadow which soared up to peaks aglow in the clear autumnal air for herself, since neither Polly nor Janey were there to admire the view! It must have been cold at that height moreover, and all three girls would be glad to be brought inside to the warmth. There (from Polly's description), apart from some cushions embroidered with swastikas, all the sitting-room furniture too was in typical German holiday-cottage taste: fake antiques in the farmhouse style, a self-consciously plain wooden bench round a "rustic" fireplace, dimity curtains, a chirping canary-cage and a rubber-plant. . . . But then the

Führer himself had appeared, wearing leather shorts and a jacket of Cambridge blue—and instantly Polly had ceased to see anything else but him. *Any* background blurred by the dazzling light of his presence was rendered invisible. . . .

Had this Sophie been doubtful how Hitler might take her choice of two foreign girls as her fellow guests? Perhaps; but as soon as he learned that Polly and Janey were not only English but well-connected, he beamed. So! Janey's papa was an Earl, with a seat in the House of Lords; and Polly's papa was in the Government? Taking each girl by both her hands he jigged her a step or two: you must tell your papas how glad he had been to welcome their beautiful daughters, for friendship with England had always been the dearest wish of his heart—and here were its two lovely harbingers!

Henceforth Polly's letter claimed to be quoting him word for word, as he told them that England's so-called alliance with France was a crass denial of History, brittle and artificial. England and France were historic enemies— always had been and always would be—whereas our two great Germanic nations, the allies of Waterloo. . . . With England ruling the oceans, her Island Home's security guaranteed by a friendly Germany back at her rightful post as a great Continental Power, we two could thumb our noses at all the World! "To you I reveal my inner thoughts: when you get back home you must tell your papas. . . ."

But then tea came, and a car drew up with three young women to whom they had to be introduced. Two were "my excellent secretaries". The third (a Fräulein Eva Braun) was left unexplained. . . .

Mary laid down the letter. The whole thing seemed such a typical schoolgirl's dream that she almost wondered if Polly had made it up.

*

Alas, all too soon the girls had found themselves shepherded out through the door. They climbed back into the Führer's car just as another Mercedes drew up: a man with a somewhat preoccupied look got out, and passed them into the house. As their car drove off they heard the Führer's voice once again: no longer (it seemed) the genial tones of five minutes ago, but an ear-splitting noise. . . .

"Some poor devil is getting it hot," remarked Sophie.

Nobody spoke for a time; but just before reaching Berchtesgaden, "Those wonderful deep blue eyes!" sighed Janey.

"Blue?" cried Sophie, amazed: "They're not blue at all."

"Then what colour are they?" asked Polly, surprised that she couldn't remember.

"The colour of codfishes' eyes on the fishmonger's slab," declared Sophie. "And as for his voice, it sounds as if Goebbels had stuffed a microphone up his nose." Polly and Janey looked at the blasphemous creature in horror. "I know what's wrong with those eyes! They haven't had proper sleep for weeks—and no wonder, after those June-the-thirtieth murders!"

Relations were thus somewhat strained by the time that the two English girls ran into the railway station to catch the slow train to Munich.

Relations might have been even more strained had they known what Sophie did, once the Führer's Mercedes had driven her back to her school and news of the tea-party spread: had they known that she took off the shoes which had trodden the Führer's carpet and sold them as sacred relics—and then, since she found the market so good, went straight downtown and sold all her other six pairs as well with identical affidavits.

Chapter 11

B ut it hadn't been any "poor devil getting it hot" which the girls had overheard as they left. Hitler had merely been thinking aloud to a favoured friend: confiding his innermost thoughts to this latest arrival at Haus Wachenfeld, this small pink man with the turned-up nose.

Some successful businessman, you would probably guess: taking note of his well-cut clothes and of small, grey-green eyes, the shrewdness of which seemed at odds with a flabby and almost expressionless face. His name was Paganuzzi; but Herr Paganuzzi was German in spite of his name or Hitler would never have packed him off to the Saar with the delicate task he had come to report on—if able to get a word in edgeways.

A couple of hours later his audience was over. A dark-red ball of sun was setting behind the pine-clad peaks and a sickle of new moon hung in a luminous greenish sky as Paganuzzi started his walk across to the "Zum Türken" inn, reflecting how often his interviews with the Führer had ended like this—with Hitler apparently blissfully unaware that he'd changed his mind and adopted the very course he'd rejected at first!

*

Versailles had ceded the coal of the Saar to France; and for fifteen years the Saar had remained cut off from the Reich, a tiny paternalistic state ruled by a League of Nations Commission. Not subject to German Law nor to Germany's economic troubles (its currency being the franc had escaped the Great Inflation which ruined the Weimar Republic), the Saar had achieved the only luxurious living-standards for miners of any coalfield in Europe—night-clubs, and evening dress! But now the Saarlanders' time had come to decide, by secret ballot, whether they wished to return to the Reich, and place themselves under the aegis of Hitler open-eyed. . . .

This was the situation which Paganuzzi was sent to appraise. Nobody doubted which way the voting would go: indeed most observers expected a 90% majority opting for Hitler's Reich—if it ever came to the vote. But what Paganuzzi feared was the risk of the Nazi "Deutsche Front" fatally overplaying its hand and provoking riots: for once the situation got out of control the League's instructions to Knox (the British diplomat serving as Chief Commissioner) told him to call on the French for troops to restore public order; and that might well mean postponing the Referendum—even if nothing worse!.

So Hitler had to be warned after all, there was nothing to lose by "telling the Deutsche Front to soft-pedal a bit till the quarry was safe in the bag". . . . But how had this been received?

Hitler had simply pooh-poohed his fears. The Foreign Office in London were far too cagey to let Knox call in the French, thus setting a match to the powder-barrel—and even supposing he did, the French themselves would refuse. Though possessing the finest army in Europe those cowards in Paris would pass the buck to the League, and propose some International Force manned only from neutral states. The Deutsche Front were to be encouraged, not curbed: they must feel the final victory due to their own efforts alone. . . .

The louder the Führer declaimed, the louder had sung the canaries. Paganuzzi was perched on that hard wooden bench, he recalled; and as Hitler strode back and forth had been forced to keep turning his head to and fro like somebody watching a tennis-match. But at this point Hitler had turned and faced him: "Remember that this is the decadent France of 1934, not the France of 1914!" And let Paganuzzi make no mistake: the degenerate Jewish democracy

masquerading today as Imperial Britain had no more
spunk left in it than France or the U.S.A. They knew how
defenceless their island was in these days of the bomber and
the submarine. . . .

Reminiscently Paganuzzi massaged his Wimbledon
Neck as he strolled in the twilight now, recalling how Hitler
had started his back-and-forth pacing again while dubbing
the British Empire a tree-load of over-ripe pears which
would drop at the first breath of wind: "If *I* don't gather
them, Russia will. Even left to itself it could hardly survive
to the second half of the Century."

Here Paganuzzi had tried to demur that the end of the
British Empire was hardly to German advantage: a far-
flung empire like hers was a source of weakness rather than
strength. Today Britain knew she had neither the wealth
nor the men to police half the world and fight in Europe as
well; but once their Eastern Empire was gone they'd stop
worrying over the Japanese, and be that much more of a
factor in Europe to reckon with. . . .

"There speaks an ignorant fool!" the Führer had
shouted, thumping that bench so hard that it tingled poor
Paganuzzi's bottom—and even the loudest canary had
faltered a trill or two. "Nations which cease being able and
willing to hold down others by force soon forget how to
govern themselves. With her whole raison-d'être in World
History gone, a putrescent Great Britain will soon disappear off the map as even a minor power."

"Perhaps . . . in some twenty or thirty years. But now"
(waving his pocket-diary) "isn't this still the Year 1934—
or is my little book here mistaken?"

"You *jest*?"

"Far from it, Mein Führer! I merely point out that what
we have to deal with today is the Britain of 1943, still (if she
chooses to act) the greatest Power on Earth; and that what
we possess today is no more than the fledgeling Wehrmacht
of 1934."

"Exactly! Re-armament's now reached a point where it

can't any longer be hidden: the next stages need the Versailles Powers' agreement. That's why there has to be no provocation just now, no shred of excuse for British or French interference by force until I am ready to meet it with force. To gain the agreement I need I am ready to sign any treaty—to guarantee frontiers, make non-aggression pacts and alliances, *anything* leaving me free to go on re-arming at will!" Once again he had halted, addressing his hearer direct: "Why refuse, merely because some day some solemn promise may have to be broken?" He put his arm round Paganuzzi's neck and playfully pinched his ear: "*Why not* commit perjury six times a day—eh, little man?"

Then he took hold of both Paganuzzi's shoulders and stared in his eyes till they—tactfully—dropped: "My friend, it is only to you I confide my innermost thoughts. They are not for the rank-and-file of the Party, nor even their leaders. But *you*, as a Business Man, have to understand this: I, Adolf Hitler, can claim no right to a private conscience which interferes with the greatness of Germany! That is the moral burden I lay on myself. . . . "

A tear had stood in his eye, and he even choked back a sob as he paused for a solemn moment—then stole a quick glance at the cuckoo-clock and barked, "Go back to Saarbrucken! Tell those hot-headed zealots . . . what was the phrase I used? Ah, yes: tell them they have to 'soft-pedal a bit till the quarry is safe in the bag'. Knox must have no excuse to call in the French—do you understand?"

He then turned away, the interview at an end, just as somebody brought in a big black cloth to silence at least the birds for the night. . . .

*

The scents of the forest are always strongest at dusk; and the first few stars were appearing as Paganuzzi paused to drink in the oncoming night while reflecting again on the scene he had just rehearsed in his head.

"Those belittling overtones in the way that I spun this

yarn to myself: were they wholly fair, or was my own amour-propre playing tricks with my memory?" Herr Paganuzzi frowned: God knows that the hardest of tasks for the clever man is paying due homage to genius.

"Genius?" Perhaps; but those innermost thoughts of the Führer were hardly impressive. Everyone knows that treaties are seldom kept much longer than keeping them pays; but why attempt to erect dishonesty into a principle? Surely because he assumes that all businessmen are dishonest—and I am a businessman: so that this was bound to find welcoming ears when poured into mine. . . .

Perhaps it's the same with all Hitler's innermost thoughts: they are always whatever that man imagines his hearers are thinking themselves, so that hearing the Führer confide in you comes to no more than seeing yourself distorted in Hitler's unflattering mirror: in fact, you see nothing of Hitler's own mind at all.

If indeed any such thing exists! For that makes the whole nature of Hitler's "greatness" merely a preternatural empathy, turning him into a caricature of yourself whoever you are—and even, however many you are: an incarnate caricature of the whole German Nation. "And that" (as Euclid would say) "is absurd." Or at least confusing, because it implies that the more you believe in Hitler's this-sort-of-greatness the less you believe in Hitler's intrinsic existence—and, damn it, we know he exists!

For one has to admit his mysterious gravitational pull. —Like you moon up there, the amazing tides which that force personalised as his "will" can raise among men are proof-positive Hitler exists. . . .

But now Paganuzzi had reached his inn and demanded a bath.

Chapter 12

Ten days later Polly arrived at Victoria Station.

Warned by Mme Leblanc, the "adequate escort" she'd had to wait for (an Indian Civilian's leathery widow) had taken charge of Polly's passport and tickets as well as her own: had bribed the ticket-inspector to lock their compartment door, and had never allowed her slippery prisoner out of her sight for a moment except when Polly wanted to wash her hands—and even then she had waited outside till Polly emerged. Only while crossing the Channel was any respite allowed, since Polly was hardly likely to want to swim.

Yet Polly had shown not the slightest signs of any wish to escape. As if in a daze she had taken it all with an icy politeness, a passive non-resistance as if she couldn't care less: she had sat in her corner seat all the time, reading Zane Grey—except in the restaurant car, where she ate like a wolf.

In London they spent the night at Brown's Hotel. Gilbert was due at a crucial conference somewhere and hadn't got time, so Augustine it was who came to collect his niece. In Brown's Hotel she didn't look much like a schoolgirl—and even less like a penitent: dressed in the height of expensive good taste, her slender and graceful figure looked almost grown-up. It was only her starry-eyed little face which still had a childish look as she greeted without any vestige of warmth the uncle she used to adore.

Handing her over, the escort almost seemed to expect a signed receipt for the package safely delivered; and Augustine indeed had to meet a whacking bill for expenses (a bill which left the leathery widow sufficient margin to pay for a visit to Harvey Nichols before retiring to Kew).

It was roughly a decade since once before Augustine had

435

driven alone with Polly from London to Dorset. Staines and Basingstoke, Stockbridge, Salisbury, out at last on the beautiful Dorset downs. . . . His Bentley's purring organ-like roar. . . . All these were much the same; but instead of that much-loved carolling woollen ball that had bounced around on the seat beside him, all he had now was an alien lackadaisical nymph who answered him only in grunts. She read Zane Grey all the time, never once looking out at the places they passed.

Just before getting to Mellton he stopped the car to read her the Riot Act: "Look here, Polly," he said, "Pull yourself together! Me you can treat how you like, but you can't go meeting your mother like this. Snap out of it!" Polly lifted her eyes for a moment only, and then returned to Zane Grey. Firmly he took the book out of her hands: "I intend stopping here till you've had a good cry. You'll feel better after it."

"Then we stop here all night," said Polly: "I haven't the slightest desire to cry." She surveyed the familiar Dorset lane with distaste: "I'm glad to be home again. . . . I suppose. Give me back my book."

She was still reading Zane Grey (though without taking in one word) when they reached the front door—but then, how would Peter or James or John have responded, if only a short while after witnessing Christ's Transfiguration, someone had tried to make him "snap out of it"?

Mary was less upset than Augustine by Polly's zombie behaviour: at Polly's age she had felt for a Latin Mistress almost exactly what Polly felt for the Führer of Germany. Hitlers or Latin Mistresses, what's the odds? If a rose-is-a-rose-is-a-rose a pash-is-a-pash-is-a-pash. . . . So without one word about Polly's escapade and expulsion she kissed her daughter goodnight and sent her up to her room.

When Polly was gone, "I suppose she's now lighting candles in front of her Hitler Ikonastasis," grumbled Augustine bitterly. "Mary, I'm not so sure we were right after all to shield the child from all contact with Christianity.

Even a God young girls are encouraged to dwell on the torturing of and imagine they eat seems somehow healthier."

Mary smiled to herself: "Poor Augustine is jealous-as-
hell of Hitler," she thought. "No idol takes kindly to being
supplanted."

Augustine chuckled. "The sheep to be eating the Shep-
herd for once! It's a bit of a change of role. . . . "

Because of his Christian upbringing, saying this kind of
thing still made him feel a bit like a naughty small boy
scrawling rude words on a wall.

*

But when Polly got to her room she had barely glanced at
her Hitler ikons: the photographs looked so insipid and
posed compared with the Real Thing.

Instead she leaned from her window and gazed at the
moon in a halo of luminous haze which extinguished the
nearer stars. It was brilliant, and verging on full. She stared
at those shadows across it which look like a face, but which
Gusting (for this had been back in the days when she still
called him that) had told her were mountains and plains.
Mountains, and "seas without any water in them" he'd
said. He told her about the telescope he himself had made
as a boy, and how clearly it showed ring-craters of dead
volcanoes: night after night he had mapped them, picked
out by the "dawn" on the moving line which divided the lit
from the darkened part of the orb. He had taught her some
of their names ("Copernicus with its rays" was once she
remembered suddenly). Also that rift, like a knife-cut many
miles deep and hundreds of miles in length: "the Valley of
. . . something" (was it "the Alps"?).

Of course she'd believed all he said. But then as now,
looking up at that shining disc with the naked eye, it was
hard to believe there was nothing mystic about it. Merely
another world like our own—yet not like our own, because
it had neither water nor air. No life, just a desert hotter than
any Sahara by day and colder than any Greenland by night.

No *life* on it. . . . That meant no possible Polly up there—in which case, what was it for? Was it there just to shine on this one particular night when she chanced to look out of the window—to flood this one particular Dorset garden with silver, exciting her dog to howl and the frogs to croak and keeping the screech-owls awake?

No . . . for as Polly had gazed at the moon she was moved by a deeper thought: the moon's skyline had nothing to do with her! That moon had been there forever, the same and unchanging, whatever might happen on Earth. Since before the Evolution of Man. . . . Since even before she was born!

That gave rise to a further stupendous thought: it would shine there the same even when Polly was dead. Even when she was no more (that unthinkable kind of time) the moon would be there just the same. . . .

The light was so bright that her eyes were beginning to water. She wiped it away with her hand because now she felt sure she could read in that very light the answers to all those ultimate questions she'd tried to read in the face of Hitler. The answers which no philosopher—not since the Dawn of Time—has been able to put into words, she could read them all now in the face of the moon: what the Universe meant, and why Polly existed. . . . Even if (like other sages) she couldn't yet quite put the Answers she brimmed with in words, that could wait till tomorrow: already tonight she was greater and wiser than anyone else in the World!

—All the same, once in her pyjamas, she went to the secret place where she kept that worn three-legged old teddy bear which she counted on still to keep away bogies; and fell asleep with it tightly clutched to her breast. Next morning, when Susan and Gillie crept in to jump on her stomach and wake her that way, the bear was still there. But, alas, no longer the Key to the Universe: somehow that seemed to have taken wings in the night.